DEAD
DOWNWIND

A SIM GREENE MYSTERY

ROB AVERY

Jack Tar Publishing
Provo, Utah

Published by
Jack Tar Publishing LLC
86 N. University Ave., Suite 300
Provo, Utah 84601, U.S.A.

Dead Downwind / Rob Avery – 1st ed.
www.robavery.com
ISBN 978-1-945809-15-6
Library of Congress Control Number: 2022913897

To my Dad who faced every challenge with courage.

"A sailor is an artist whose medium is the wind." — *Webb Chiles.*

1

WE keep a picnic table on the dock behind the dive shop. A six-sided umbrella plastered with Coca-Cola logos sticks up out of the middle shielding it from the seasonally hot Caribbean sun. And the sun was definitely in season that day in mid-July. Ninety degrees, humid, and windless. The locals call it "hurricane weather."

Three thousand miles away, a low pressure wave marches off the west coast of Africa into the warm Atlantic. Moist ocean air rises into that wave and the earth's rotation swirls it into a counterclockwise tempest. Somebody at NOAA will call it a tropical depression. Days pass and the depression eases into the central Atlantic where it works itself into a tropical storm. By the time it reaches the Caribbean, it's a full-fledged hurricane worthy of a name and a number that tells you how tough it is.

But the big hurricanes almost never hit the British Virgin Islands. The vast majority pass either to the south and into the Gulf of Mexico or north to attack the Bahamas or the east coast of the United States. Rarely do they get close enough to cause anything worse than a half-day's power outage. Locals might sometimes openly hope for a blow to get close enough to bring some wind and rain; a pleasant break in the monotony of summer. That casual attitude changed for good when a category five hurricane aimed itself directly at us.

My first summer in the BVI had been a quiet one with few paying tourists and not enough salvage work to keep Al and me busy. We regularly listened to NOAA's weather predictions and noticed rising concern over a hurricane named Irma. On September

4th, Al and I took our two boats south. Al, his wife, and *In Depth II* made it to Guadeloupe in a little over eight hours. The same trip took me a day and a half aboard *Figaro*.

Irma was followed by Jose, Katia, and Lee. Jose turned to pass north of Barbuda aiming for New England, Katia hit the western Caribbean and Mexico, and Lee made a sharp right turn in the mid-Atlantic heading north to peter out somewhere between Newfoundland and the Azores.

About the time we started thinking it was safe to return, Maria showed up and aimed herself straight at us in Guadeloupe. We sailed farther south and holed up in St. Lucia. Maria destroyed nearly every building on Dominica, put the hurt on St. Croix, and then cut a deadly swath across Puerto Rico.

It was a bad year for the Caribbean.

When we returned to Tortola, I saw a spectacle of destruction I could have never imagined. The green canopy of trees that had covered the island was gone, replaced with a vision of post-nuclear war bare earth and debris. Tall coconut palms—known to survive hurricanes by shedding leaves and bending with the wind—had snapped their trunks four or five feet above the ground. Eighty percent of the island's buildings were destroyed. A 42-foot catamaran—fourteen tons of fiberglass and stainless steel—had been picked up by the wind like a child's toy and wedged into the ceiling ten feet above one of my favorite beach bars. Our harbor-side warehouse and all our gear had disappeared.

But Al and I had a couple of things going for us. We'd acquired a stash of "rainy-day" funds during some previous adventures. And the hurricane created a lot of salvage work for divers. Hundreds of millions of dollars' worth of boats, most of them insured, needed to be either re-floated and repaired or removed and scrapped. We rebuilt our ratty old warehouse into a world-class dive shop.

The shop was still located between the fuel dock and that forgotten section of the harbor where derelict commercial vessels rust and sink their keels into the harbor mud. But our business doesn't rely on walk-in customers. Our commercial accounts have our cell numbers; they never come to the shop. And our retail customers are all tourists staying at various resorts that dot the islands. We prep the gear and snacks at the warehouse and then pick them up in our boat to go diving. We don't need to be in a posh area.

So we stayed in the harbor's low-rent district. Still, we had state-of-the-art equipment, good air conditioning, and a brand spanking new picnic table with a Coca-Cola umbrella on the dock where a guy could relax at the end of the day watching the sun set across the harbor with a cool drink in his hand.

We almost never have visitors.

We had a visitor that day, though. Constable Millet sat on the bench under the Coca-Cola umbrella and watched the three of us back *In Depth II* up to our dock and tie her off. I hadn't seen him in nearly a month. He looked like he wanted to arrest somebody.

Al jumped off the boat with the passenger manifest and the day's receipts. He mumbled something under his breath about island police and jogged past the Constable to the office. Running a dive tour business isn't all just air compressors and swim fins anymore. Fortunately, Al was good at handling the books.

Eryn and I carted the empty SCUBA tanks and other gear off the stern while Millet watched. I asked Eryn to wash off the regulators, buoyancy vests, and other dive gear with fresh water and hang them to dry. She ran to the job with her characteristic enthusiasm and I walked over to speak with the good Constable.

I led him into my office, tossed my L.A. Dodgers bill cap onto the top of my filing cabinet, and sat down in my old steel and Naugahyde desk chair, the only piece of our furniture to survive Irma. He sat across from me and crossed his excessively long legs. I don't run into a lot of guys taller than me and I'd always wondered if, at six-five, he'd have made a decent point guard. Being British, he'd probably been steered toward cricket. He was way too skinny for rugby.

"What can I do for you, Constable?" I asked.

He sat there with a stony face and I wondered what obscure island law we had unknowingly violated. I thought of Julian, the young fellow who hung around the shop and helped occasionally, and wondered if he'd gotten into some trouble. Julian had that tendency, a quality he shared with Al.

"I'd like to have a beer if I may," he said.

"You're off duty?"

He nodded and I reached into the small refrigerator under my desk, pulled out two Caribs, and plucked the caps off the bottles with the church key that hung from the wall. I handed him one and he drained half the bottle in one go.

"Who's the young lady?" he asked.

"Eryn? She's from the States. She decided to take a year off and intern as a dive instructor before starting law school. Bright young woman."

"Very pretty," he said. "A bit young for you, wouldn't you say?"

He forced a smile.

"She's too young for anyone," I said. "Sweet and innocent. Goes to church on Sundays over at the Bin-Cal building. Doesn't even drink."

I hoisted and drank some of my beer in celebration of that last comment and wondered what this interview was all about. A Detective Constable of the Royal Virgin Islands Police Force doesn't usually show up at our dive shop—off duty or not—requesting cold beer and information about our employees. This was, in fact, a first.

"Do you consider me to be an okay bloke, Mr. Greene?" he asked.

"You're an honest cop," I said. "You work hard at your job and you're not sloppy in your procedure. You're okay in my book."

He nodded.

"And I've told you at least fifty times to call me 'Sim,'" I added.

He smiled.

"Are we friends, then, Sim?"

"We're drinking beer in my office. Of course we're friends."

He forced another smile and emptied the bottle. I grabbed a replacement from the little fridge, opened it, and handed it to him.

"You did an excellent job figuring out who killed that Brownell fellow," he said.

"Thanks."

It hadn't been an easy case and Constable Millet hadn't exactly encouraged my involvement at the time. He thought Al had murdered the guy and I had to turn over quite a few rocks to find the real killer and get my best friend out of jail. But it had worked out all right, for most of the parties involved.

"I was more than a little miffed that you shot the murderer," he said.

"He didn't leave me much choice."

He waved his hand as if my killing the fellow was merely the stuff of small talk among friends.

"You seem to have a gift," he said. "Weighing issues and probabilities. Drawing connections between seemingly unrelated facts. Finding things that cannot otherwise be found."

I took a drink from my bottle and tried to draw a few connections between the unrelated subjects our conversation had covered in the last ten minutes. I didn't see any.

"Right now my gift is failing me. Can you just tell me why you're here?"

He put his half-empty bottle on my desk and placed his hands on the arms of his chair. He looked straight into my eyes. There were new lines in his face that spoke of nights without sleep and days filled with worry.

"Our daughter has been missing for almost three weeks."

2

"DOROTHEA?" I asked.

He nodded.

"We had words one night," he said. "Gina and I were concerned about her activities of late and the friends she kept. She wasn't in her room the next morning and some of her things were gone. We thought she might have run off to stay with a girlfriend for a day or two but it's been almost three weeks now and we can't locate her."

"She's seventeen?"

"Eighteen last February," said Millet. "She just graduated from St George's Secondary School and she's been accepted to King's College London with a considerable scholarship. She's a bright girl with a marvelous mind and, until recently, quite responsible."

"Any friends she could be staying with?"

"We've asked every one of her close friends and they all say they haven't seen her. But I am sure she's still here on the island."

He picked up the bottle and drained it.

"She won't answer her phone?" I asked.

"After a few days, we tried calling her. She wouldn't answer. Last night we checked our phone bill and realized she hasn't used her phone once since leaving the house."

"No activity at all?"

"Not even a text message. And only a few of those before she left. I asked the phone company to ping it but they say the phone is off. They can't locate it."

"Is she posting on social media?"

"Not a thing," he said.

He leaned forward with his elbows on his knees and stared at the floor.

"My wife and I want you to find her. We'll gladly pay you."

I had a good idea what a Detective Constable with the Royal Virgin Islands Police Force was paid and I didn't imagine there was a huge surplus in their bank account to hire a private detective.

"You're one of the head cops in this country," I said. "And it's a small country. None of your patrolmen or other detectives can find her?"

He fidgeted.

"Much as I would like to, I cannot use the full resources of the RVIP to locate my runaway child. Frankly, my position may actually hinder my ability to find her as those with actual knowledge may be reluctant to contact me."

That made sense. Normal sources of information could dry up if they detected a personal interest at stake. Bad news could cause problems for an informant. And the disappearance of a child was frequently bad news.

"And you think the folks who might know will talk to me?" I said.

"You may be less threatening." He paused a moment. "Or more."

Was there ever a man more misunderstood?

"Do you have a picture?" I asked.

He reached into his back pocket and pulled out an old brown leather billfold. He fished out a wallet-size photo and handed it to me.

"It's nearly a year old," he said.

The picture featured two laughing teenage girls sitting on a lawn in a back yard playing with a black and white puppy. The picture hit me in the gut. It was a casual photo taken at a happy time but it reminded me of two younger sisters I'd once had.

"Dorothea is on the left. She does her hair differently now. Long and straight."

"I'll find her for you," I said. "But I won't allow you to pay me."

Millet protested.

"You can't pay me, Constable. I'm not licensed. And I don't want to piss off the local cops."

Millet smiled wanly.

"You will be discreet, though?" he said. "Your last investigation caused a bit of a stir."

"I'll keep it out of the papers this time," I said. "But I'll need a list of her close friends."

"I've already spoken with them," said Millet. "They are absolutely no help at all."

"Humor me. I've got to start somewhere."

3

HE left and I walked out to the shop to help Eryn finish cleaning and storing the dive gear. Al stood near the compressor in the corner filling empty SCUBA tanks. Even in his late-fifties, he could swing a pair of forty-pound tanks with ease.

"What's that guy want?" he asked.

"That *guy* could be the next head of the RVIP," I said. "It'd be a great idea for us to stay on his good side."

"That rat bastard stuck me in his jail for a week."

"He's apologized over and over for that. He's even had you up to his house for dinner."

Al grumbled.

"And you know what? Given the facts he had, I'd have put you in that jail myself."

Al mumbled a tired profanity and continued with his task like a gentle Grizzly bear. If there were such a thing.

Eryn rinsed the salt water off the last of the gear and hung the regulators and swim fins on the drying rack. She was a fine-looking, leggy young redhead who always wore modest shorts and a baggy T-shirt over her one-piece swimsuit. Pure innocence.

"Tired of this job, yet?" I asked.

"Oh, no, Mr. Greene. It's wonderful. That last group of divers was so nice. One of the ladies gave me this lovely bracelet as a tip."

She held up her wrist, now circled with multi-colored octagonal glass beads. It was either worthless Chinese junk or expensive Italian jewelry. Judging from what I'd seen of those divers, I suspected it was the latter. And it was pretty.

"I'm glad you're having a good time. I don't suppose law school will be quite so much fun."

"Probably not," she said. "I'm so happy Ms. Tanner was able to persuade you into taking me on for the year."

I didn't tell her that Marie Tanner had the singular ability to talk me into almost anything.

"I'm glad it's working out for you," I said.

We finished cleaning up the gear and putting it away. Eryn rode off into town on her little scooter. Al hopped into his blue Isuzu.

"Where are you headed?" I asked.

"Meeting Liv at the Virgin Queen. Want to join us for some ribs?"

I'd known Al a long time. He'd been a devout bachelor until the previous year and the marriage had shocked everyone who knew him. I still hadn't gotten used to the concept. But it worked for him and Liv was a wonderful woman to take him.

"I'll pass. You two have a great time."

He roared off in the little car and I went back to my desk to finish up some paperwork.

Constable Millet returned a few minutes later and walked into my office carrying a slim manila folder. It held a more recent picture of Dorothea, a sheet summarizing the usual stats—height, weight, hair and eye color, distinguishing marks, etc.—and a list of her five closest friends with home addresses and phone numbers. Millet had reacquired his British sense of conversational self-restraint and he left almost immediately.

The picture in the folder showed a pretty brunette in a blue top and faded jeans with sunglasses perched on the top of her head. She smiled at the camera with an air of untarnished innocence. A little voice deep inside told me that, if I found her, she wouldn't be coming home in the same condition.

Her best friend was a girl named Marisha. She lived less than a half-mile from the shop but three hundred feet up the hill overlooking the harbor. It seemed like the logical place to start. Had it been cooler, I would have walked. I drove up there in my truck.

She lived in one of the older homes on the hill. It stood on the mountain in a hollow, flat spot between two ridges. The cinder block walls and the palms near the house had survived Irma's wrath but the new red metal roof revealed where Irma had found a weakness. I parked on a flat grass-covered area in front of the house and knocked on the door. A black woman in her late forties answered.

"My name is Sim Greene," I said. "I'm trying to locate Dorothea Millet for her parents. Is Marisha home?"

"Yessir," she said. "You come on in and have a seat, Mr. Greene."

She pointed me toward the living room and walked down a hallway while calling her daughter. The home was modest but clean, the living room bright and airy. A slight bit of ocean breeze blew through sheer blue-tinged draperies. Watercolor paintings hung on the walls and a large glass-covered bookcase stood at one end of the room. I walked over to read the titles and recognized my two favorite Steinbeck novels, several Austen titles, and *The Adventures of Huckleberry Finn*. I sat on a brown couch and waited.

Marisha was a pretty island girl about five feet tall with dark ebony skin, a round face, half-frame horn-rimmed glasses, and an infectious smile. She walked in and sat across from me. I introduced myself.

"I told Dottie's dad that I don't have any idea where she is," she said. "I still don't."

"Well, she isn't here, is she?"

Marisha shook her head.

"Why not?" I asked.

She looked confused and thought for a minute.

"I don't know what you mean, Mr. Greene."

"You are her best friend and she's run away from home but she's not here," I said. "Why not?"

"Well, we were best friends. But not anymore. She got all weird and it got so's I couldn't stand to hang around with her."

"How long had you been friends?"

"Since sixth grade, I guess."

"And that friendship changed?" I asked.

"Yeah, it did. Almost overnight. She just got really weird."

"In what way?"

She shrugged.

"When did you see Dorothea last?"

"A couple of weeks ago, I guess. Just after graduation."

"What happened then?"

She thought for a minute.

"Like I said, she got weird. She never seemed to have time for the rest of us. Always talking with some guy."

"Who?"

"I don't know. But all she wanted to do was be on the phone with this guy. She texted him constantly. It got to be annoying so we just stopped asking her to hang out with us."

"Did any of her other friends stay in touch with her?"

"No," she said. "At least, I don't think so. She turned most of us off. She just got too weird, you know?"

"I don't know," I said. "That's why I'm asking."

She fidgeted in her seat as if the chair were suddenly less comfortable.

"You keep saying she 'got weird' but you're talking around it. What do you mean by weird?"

Marisha thought for a minute.

"She started talking about old Greek myths and stuff. This guy filled her head with that garbage and it got to be the only thing she'd talk about."

"Did she tell you anything about this guy? His name? Where he's from?"

"No. I'm sorry."

"Did she have a boyfriend?"

"Lyron Samuel," she said. "He's the smart boy in our school."

"There's only one?"

"He's the only one going to college in the States on a full-ride scholarship."

I checked the list Millet had given me. Lyron's name wasn't on it.

"Could they still be seeing each other?"

"No."

"How do you know?"

She smiled broadly.

"Because Lyron is seeing me."

4

SHE didn't have any more information that seemed remotely useful but she did tell me where Lyron lived and where he worked. I thanked her for her time and walked back out to my truck.

Lyron worked at one of the little shops in Road Town that sells stereos, cell phones, and other consumer electronics. Marisha had told me he worked every weekday until six and it seemed like a good idea to catch him as he was leaving.

I walked into the shop and a tall young man with a broad smile approached me immediately. An embossed name tag on his shirt pocket read "Lyron."

"How can I help you, sir?"

"My name is Sim Greene and I'd like to ask you a few questions about Dorothea Millet."

He looked confused for a moment and I pointed at his name tag.

"You are Lyron Samuel, aren't you? You used to date her, right?"

"Yes, sir," he said. "Can I talk to you after I get off work, sir? I don't want to get my boss mad at me."

"Sure. When do you get off work?"

Some people have eyes that can talk you out of your life savings and some have eyes that only betray their guilt. Lyron's weren't firmly in either camp but I saw a flicker of the latter. Not enough to worry me but enough to make me take notice.

"We close in ten minutes," he said. "I can talk to you then."

I pointed across the street.

"I'll be sitting on that bench under those trees," I said. "See you in ten minutes."

He nodded and smiled and I walked out the front door. I waited five minutes and doubled back around to where I could see the shop's rear door. A few minutes later, the door opened and Lyron walked out toward a small yellow Suzuki automobile. I beat him to it. He froze when he saw me.

"Did you forget about the conversation we were going to have?"

His face fell.

"No, sir."

"You were trying to duck me," I said. "Why?"

"I don't want any trouble with the Constable, sir."

"Why do you think you might be in trouble with the Constable?"

"Last year he told me he didn't want me seeing his daughter anymore. I did anyway."

"When did you see her last?"

"A little over three weeks ago, I guess. That's when we broke up," he said.

"Why'd you break up?"

He undid one of the buttons near the collar of his shirt. It was a lot hotter outside than it had been in the air-conditioned electronics shop.

"She changed," he said.

"In what way?"

"She got interested in religion."

"Another couple unequally yoked?" I said.

He shot me a strange look.

"Never mind," I said. "Which religion?"

"Not one I'd ever heard of," he said. "It had something to do with Mediterranean history and some ancient queen. It got to be the only thing she'd talk about. And it was the strangest stuff I ever heard. She wanted me to get interested in it. I finally told her I wasn't and I never heard from her again."

"Were the two of you having sex?" I asked.

"I'm not going to answer that, sir."

"That actually *is* an answer, Lyron."

"It had nothing to do with sex," he said. "I just didn't want anything to do with some strange religion."

I thought for a minute.

"Do you think there could have been another boy in the picture?"

His eyes widened a bit.

"I never met him."

"How'd you find out about him?"

"She got a new phone as a graduation present. She showed it to me and I checked her message history. Dozens of texts with some other guy."

"That made you angry," I said. It wasn't a question.

"Yes."

"Did you hit her?"

"No. Absolutely not. Sure, I was angry, but I never hit no woman."

"What kind of phone was it?"

"It was a new model. We sell it over there at the shop but almost nobody buys it. Hella expensive."

"You say she got it at graduation?"

"A few weeks earlier. Her folks gave it to her for an early graduation present."

"Her parents haven't seen her for three weeks," I said. "Do you have any idea where she's staying?"

"I don't think she's even on the island. None of our friends have seen her. I think she left to meet this new guy."

He wasn't being entirely straight-arrow with me. I attributed that to his fear of Constable Millet, a fear not unreasonable given the circumstances.

I thanked him, got into my truck, and drove down Waterfront Drive to Sea Cow Bay and *Figaro*.

Figaro is a tired, old, thirty-nine-foot sailboat. And my home. I first saw her while investigating a suspicious death—back when I did that sort of thing for the U.S. Navy—at the National Defense

Reserve in the upper reaches of the San Francisco Bay. The forlorn-looking boat sat at a dock in Vallejo with a large red "For Sale By Owner" sign tied to her lower shrouds. The owner hadn't moved her in years and a thick green carpet of leafy algae blanketed her waterline. But her sails were in good shape, her engine didn't have a lot of hours on it, and her hull and rigging were sound.

The asking price was north of what I considered fair but the seller came down quickly and I became a proud boat owner. An enduro of tightening, adjusting, cleaning, greasing, and scraping followed. Once she was shipshape, I sailed her out the Golden Gate, into the blue Pacific, and south to Oxnard. When things in California turned sour, I sailed her south to Panama and then east to the BVI.

She'd been my home for nearly ten years.

I'd kept *Figaro* tied to our dock while we rebuilt the dive shop. It had been a hectic winter season and having her close by had been convenient. When the weather warmed and business cooled off, I moved her to a spot behind the reef at Sea Cow Bay. It's a quiet anchorage with a constant sea breeze and free wireless internet hosted by a nearby marina.

I climbed into my dinghy, started the outboard, and motored to *Figaro's* stern. The sun set behind Mt. Sage as I unlocked my boat's cabin and stepped down the companionway. I opened up the ports and hatches to get a little fresh air flowing through the boat, pulled up a classic rock playlist on the stereo, and thought of a young island girl running away from home in pursuit of religion. It didn't seem like the smartest idea in the world but, compared to the truly dumb things a lot of teenagers do at that age, it seemed relatively benign. So why was the little voice in the back of my head, usually a faint whisper, speaking up so loudly?

One of my favorite tunes cued up and Mick Jagger sang about walking a young girl to a train station with a suitcase in his hand. It was a slow cover of an old Robert Johnson song but the Stones' live version was excellent. Robert would have approved.

I pulled some cold lobster salad and a Carib out of the fridge and took both up to the cockpit. Gentle swells lapped at the hull as I ate my dinner in the last dying rays of sunlight. I was on my own comfortable boat in the warm Caribbean eating lobster and listening to Mick Taylor play a marvelous slide guitar blues solo. Could a man ask for more?

5

"I don't think she's on the island," I said. "I don't even think she's in the BVI."

"What makes you say that?" asked Constable Millet.

We sat in his office at the police station. It was spartan, at best. It held a scratched white steel desk that probably weighed two hundred pounds, a worn metal office chair behind the desk, and two small wooden chairs in front of it. I barely fit into one of the wooden chairs and the office seemed to strain at holding us both. An air conditioner off in the distance wheezed and creaked, struggling against the July heat.

Dorothea's other friends had been less helpful than Marisha and Lyron. Interviews with other sources—people I knew wouldn't talk to the Constable—were equally unproductive.

"Did you buy her a new phone before graduation?"

"No."

It was the answer I expected.

"Nobody has seen her," I said. "And Tortola is too small for hiding. Is her passport missing?"

"She doesn't have a passport and she can't leave the country without one. She's still here somewhere."

"She's eighteen. She could have applied for one without asking you."

A scowl crossed his face. He pulled a directory out of the top drawer of his desk, thumbed through it, and picked up the phone. In a few minutes, the Civil Registry and Passport Office confirmed that Dorothea Millet had, indeed, applied for a passport five weeks earlier and received it ten days later.

He thumbed through the directory again and called Customs and Immigration. After some feverish hunting by a junior officer, the proper records were located. Millet glowered and requested copies. He hung up the phone and left to go wait by the fax machine. I sat there and listened to a fly buzz against the office's small window in a futile search for freedom.

Millet returned a few minutes later and handed me a copy of the main page of Dorothea's passport and a record of her paying the departure fee at the West End ferry dock.

"I think now would be the proper time for you to call me a fool, Sim."

"Worried father? Yes. Fool? Never."

I took the copies Millet gave me, hopped in my truck, and drove the ten miles of Waterfront Drive to Tortola's West End.

Three ferry boat operations provide scheduled service out of West End. They sail to Cruz Bay, St. John, and to Charlotte Amalie and Red Hook on St. Thomas. All three ports are in the U.S. Virgin Islands. Only one service operated a boat that left within an hour of the time Dorothea had paid her departure fee. That boat went directly to Charlotte Amalie. I bought a round-trip ticket and hopped aboard.

The water was flat as slate and the ferry made good time. I walked around the boat and showed Dorothea's picture to the crew but none of them recognized her. When we got to Charlotte Amalie, I cleared through U.S. Immigration and Customs and walked across the parking lot to the line of taxis waiting to take fares to the airport. I hit pay dirt with the fourth driver I interviewed.

"Well, sir, I do believe that girl looks a bit familiar," he said. "But my memory fades."

I pulled a twenty out of my wallet.

"That do refresh a man's memory, sir," he said. "Pretty girl. She came right off that ferry in a big hurry to get to the airport. Only had two small bags, they did."

"They?" I asked. "She had somebody with her?"

"Yessir, a young man. Early thirties, I'd guess. Maybe a little younger."

I handed him the bill.

"Can you describe him?" I asked.

"Tall fellow. A little shorter than you, maybe. Skinnier, too. A white man with dark skin. Not really a tan, just a dark complexion. Black hair; a little too black, maybe. I remember thinkin' he must've dyed it some. He had a couple days' growth on his beard, too. And real thick eyebrows."

"You've got a good memory," I said. "Once properly prodded."

He smiled, folded the twenty, and put it in his pocket.

"Would you happen to know which airline they took?"

"I believe they walked toward the Delta counter, sir." He cracked a wide grin. "If memory do serve correctly."

I thanked him and returned to the ferry.

By the time I got back to West End and cleared through Customs, I'd decided that the Millets were going to have to accept the hard and unpleasant fact that their adult daughter had left the island with a new boyfriend. Telling the Constable wasn't going to be easy but I saw no way out of it.

I drove to the RVIP station and walked down the hall into Millet's office. He looked like he'd eaten something that didn't agree with him.

"You're not going to like it but Dorothea took the ferry to Charlotte Amalie and a taxi to the airport. She boarded a Delta flight with a man and flew off somewhere to have an adventure away from the folks and the island and all her old buddies."

He picked up a sheet of paper off his desk and handed it to me.

"Read this," he said.

I looked down at the paper. It was a printout of an email from Dorothea to her father.

Dad – I'm sorry I ran away but I met this wonderful guy and Luke invited me to vacation with him at his home in Colorado. I know it was all sudden and everything but don't worry about me. I'll be back in a couple of months. Give my love to Mom and Fran.

-- Dorothea.

"There's your answer," I said. "Like I said, she's off on a big adventure."

Constable Millet looked up at me with hollow eyes.

"She didn't write that," he said. "She has never called me 'Dad' once in her life. She calls me 'Poppy.' And she has never referred to her younger sister as anything but 'Sissy.'"

I felt that twinge in the pit of my stomach; the one that signals bad things ahead.

"Finally," said Millet, "she ends all of her emails with the word 'Cheers.' I could show you dozens of them to prove my point."

I couldn't think of anything useful to say so I kept my mouth shut.

"Somebody else wrote that," he said. "Somebody who's trying to cover something up."

"Can you get access to her email account?" I asked. "We might be able to figure out who she's with."

"Dorothea uses a free email account with one of those giant internet firms based in the States. Getting information from them is like trying to pick up spilled mercury."

"Do you have any connections with U.S. authorities who can get them?"

"I have an acquaintance in the FBI," he said. "But I doubt I will get much interagency cooperation on a personal case like this. The casual observer will draw the same conclusions you did. And every observer over there will be decidedly casual."

He looked at the email printout and shook his head.

"The BVI is home to less than thirty thousand souls," he said.

"Our entire country amounts to a small town in your Midwest."

I could see where the conversation was going and watched my plans for the next few days change before my eyes.

"Let me see what I can do," I said. "I'll need roundtrip airfare to the United States."

"Where to?"

"I'll let you know in the morning."

I told him what I needed and he promised to have it in my hands within the hour.

The drive back to the shop lasted only five minutes but a few ideas popped into mind before I pulled into the parking lot. I found Al in the back repairing some gear.

"I may be gone a couple of days," I said. "Can you and Eryn get along without me?"

"No sweat. We've got a group of four advanced divers scheduled to dive the *Chickuzen* tomorrow morning and another group of six diving the *Rhone* the day after. It's a bit of work but we can handle them without you. Where are you goin'?"

"To the States, I guess, to find Dorothea Millet."

Al gave me a puzzled look.

"What?" I said.

"Nothing."

"Out with it."

"You're running off to track down somebody's runaway kid? That's not like you."

"Life is full of little surprises."

I went to my office and opened the filing cabinet. It took me a while to find the unmarked file of miscellaneous contact information I keep. Millet's assistant showed up a few minutes later with the documents I'd asked for. I sat down to review it.

The folder held copies of the passport photo pages of the people who had checked out through the West End Customs office the same day Dorothea had. It took me only a few minutes to find a guy meeting the taxi driver's description. But the address on his passport said he was from Allentown, Pennsylvania, not Colorado. And his name wasn't Luke.

6

I picked up the phone and called a guy I hadn't spoken to in over a year. I expected the call to jump directly to voicemail but, oddly, he answered on the first ring.

"Speak," he said.

"Frank?" I said. "This is Sim Greene."

"Sim Greene? Well there's a blast from the past. What are you up to these days?"

"Are you asking professionally?" I asked. "Should I be worried?"

"No to both questions. You're not on any of our bad-boy lists. Not anymore, anyway. Not since your little—how should we say it—Caribbean accomplishment."

"I don't know what you're talking about, Frank."

"Sure," he said. "Of course not. So, what are you up to?"

"Still enjoying the blue Caribbean."

"That's what we understand."

I let that one pass.

"I'm guessing you guys in Homeland Security keep a database of all the folks that fly into and out of the States these days."

"Really?" he said. "What makes you think that?"

"Sarcasm is the language of the devil, Frank."

"Whatever."

"I'm wondering if you could track a couple of passport numbers for me. Two people took a Delta flight from the U.S. Virgin Islands a few weeks ago. I need to find out where they went."

"Absolutely. I was just sitting here in my office collecting my government paycheck and thinking how bored I was tracking terrorists and catching smugglers and keeping my bosses happy. They'd be tickled to death knowing I spend my time acting as an on-the-spot resource for ex-pats who want access to government information."

"Did you forget what I said about sarcasm?"

"No."

I told him about Dorothea and the Millet family and some slick guy talking a much younger girl into flying away with him. I told him about the fake email sent to her parents.

"You think you can help?"

"I think so," he said. "I got a daughter of my own. She's almost sixteen."

"I'll owe you, Frank."

"That's what I live for these days. A beach bum owing me favors."

I gave him the passport information along with my cell number. He promised to call me back.

I shuffled a few papers on my desk, put all the information I had on Dorothea and her little trip into a big manila envelope, and checked the Caribbean hurricane report on the internet. A new tropical wave with some disorganized thunderstorms lay about fourteen hundred miles to the east. The general consensus of opinion was that it would be a tropical depression by the end of the day and a tropical storm the next. As the fourth such storm this season, NOAA would name this one Dina. If it picked up more warm moist air on its way west, they'd call Dina a hurricane.

Even if it became a hurricane, it was days away. Still, I thought, better safe than sorry. I called my friend at the Ft. Burt Marina and asked if she had a slip for *Figaro* in her little hurricane hole of an anchorage. She did.

I grabbed my papers, drove to Ft. Burt, and left my pickup in the parking lot. The air was hot and muggy; the coconut palms lining the marina driveway still and listless. I walked into the office and bought a Coke from the vending machine they had set to the perfect temperature; just cold enough to form perfect little ice crystals when I popped the top. One of life's little pleasures. I walked back out to Waterfront Drive, hitched a ride to Sea Cow Bay, and dinghied over to *Figaro*. My phone rang as I unlocked the companionway and stepped below. It was Marie.

"I was just thinking about you," she said. "It was a nice thought."

Her voice had a special timbre to it, a warm sensuousness that almost compelled me to try crawling through the phone so I could wrap my arms around her.

"So, uh, what are you wearing?" I asked.

"Stop that!"

"Okay, different tack. When are you coming down to visit? It's been over two months and *Figaro* is telling me she's lonely."

"I'd love to be with you on your lovely little boat but I'm presenting my draft to the dissertation committee in two weeks and I still have loads of work to do. Maybe I can come down after that."

"Hearing your voice makes me want to fly up there right now."

"That would be nice."

She said it in a way that made me want to grow wings.

"Do you still have that silly little beard?" she asked.

"Beards are a pain in this heat. So I shaved it off. Come and see."

She laughed.

"I might be coming up to Allentown tomorrow. Is there any chance I could see you?"

"Allentown?" she said. "That's only a couple hours away. What brings you up here?"

I told her about Constable Millet's daughter.

"She met him over the internet? That is so dangerous. How well does she know this guy?"

"I have no idea," I said. "But her parents are worried."

"If you find her in Allentown, please bring her to Stamford. Maybe I can talk some sense into her—you know, woman to woman—and encourage her to go back home."

"I'll try."

We talked of her dissertation and the committee and of her plans to fly down and spend the first two weeks of August with me before returning to finish her doctoral program. It bugged me that her desire to teach kept her up north for so much of the year. I quietly hoped the Caribbean's hold on me annoyed her just as much. But I couldn't see myself living ashore and I had no right to expect her to give up her lifestyle for mine. I should be grateful to get as much of Marie as I did.

She said she had more work to do on her presentation so we told each other how much we missed each other, promised to see each other as soon as possible, and hung up. I put my phone on *Figaro's* chart table and looked around. The cabin was suddenly emptier than usual.

The best solution for melancholy is physical exercise. With a half-hour of sunlight left in the day, I put on my trunks, dove over the side, and swam toward the innermost part of Sea Cow Bay five hundred yards away. The water was flat and shallow and warm and it felt good to let the long muscles in my back unwind and pull me toward the shore.

The sun sank behind Mt. Sage as I crawled onto Figaro's swim step. I went below and dug around in the icebox to see what might pass for dinner. I found nothing compelling so I made pancakes and orange butter. It wasn't the most balanced meal but I am a bachelor who lives alone on a boat. Nobody was watching.

Frank called back as I was drying the dishes.

"Your lovebirds flew to Savannah, Georgia, by way of Atlanta," he said.

"No problems getting into the country?"

"They weren't exactly on our terrorist hold list."

"What can you tell me about the guy?" I asked.

"Clint McCord; thirty-two years old; currently residing in Serenity, Georgia."

"His passport says he's from Allentown, Pennsylvania."

"Some people don't bother to update their passport when they move. Our info says he lives in Georgia."

"Serenity, Georgia? Where's that?" I asked.

"What am I, your travel agent? I'm reading this off a computer screen. Get a map and look it up."

"Sorry, Frank."

He gave me McCord's street address.

"There's one more thing," he said. "It probably doesn't mean anything but another guy, a fellow named Mitch Danforth, was on the same Delta flights from St. Thomas through Atlanta to Savannah. He wasn't in the BVI but flew in from St. Croix. He's also from Serenity. Could be a coincidence."

He was an experienced law enforcement officer working for Homeland Security. I had been a Master-at-Arms during my twenty years in the U.S. Navy. Neither of us believed in coincidence.

"Know anything about either of these guys?"

"No. I figured I'd leave some work for you to do."

I thanked him for the information and hung up.

I opened my laptop, logged on to the internet, and sent Marie an email telling her I was going to Georgia instead of Pennsylvania and that I probably wouldn't see her until August. A phone call would have been quicker but much harder.

I found a map of Georgia on the internet and saw that Serenity was a lot closer to Jacksonville, Florida, than Savannah. But a flight to Jacksonville, with multiple plane changes and layovers, would take much longer than the flight to Savannah and the drive south. I bought tickets on the same flights Dorothea and her boyfriend had taken.

7

THERE was a little extra wind the next morning. Just enough to confirm my decision to take *Figaro* to Ft. Burt. I weighed anchor, raised the main, and trimmed the sails for a beam reach. It was only a couple of miles up the coast and I could have motored there but I dislike the sound of a diesel engine, the fuel is too expensive for my Scottish blood, and I love to sail.

Figaro seemed to enjoy it, too. She climbed the short swells eagerly, the water hissing by her transom. She made nearly seven knots through the water and every creak and moan in her lines and rigging begged me to take her on another long trip to another island, another country, another adventure. Instead, I furled the jib, dropped the main, and poked our way under power into a slip at the Ft. Burt Marina.

My friend Dale walked out onto one of the docks as I approached. He was a big, happy guy who always wore a thick gold chain around his neck. A giant "D" hung from the chain with the letters "A," "L," and "E" imprinted on the upright part of the big "D." He was Dale and he was proud of it. The dock swayed and groaned as he walked out to take my lines.

"You gonna be here long, mon?"

"Only a day or two. Taking a short trip to the States."

"You bring Dale back somethin' fine, okay mon?"

I grabbed my duffel and walked toward my truck.

"What could you possibly need that you haven't already got?" I asked. "This island already has the best rum."

"I could use a new shirt, mon. You find me something nice in de States, yeah?"

The drive to West End was short, the ferry to St. Thomas smooth, and the taxi ride to the airport quick and inexpensive. Four hours after takeoff we touched down in Georgia, the Peach State, the last of the original thirteen colonies, and a high point in Ray Charles' musical legacy. After a tolerable layover, I was soon on my way to Savannah. It was a short trip, one of those flights where the jet barely reaches cruising altitude before it starts its descent.

We approached Savannah/Hilton Head International over a large expanse of South Carolina swampland. The plane slowed on its final approach and streaks of condensed moisture formed over the wings as humid Georgian air thinned and cooled while rushing over the jet's airfoil. We landed as if on greased rails and the passengers erupted in applause, a testament to the pilot's skill.

The rental agency issued me a new silver Nissan, a car so ubiquitous and nondescript that it passes by almost unnoticed. I saw two dozen clones before leaving the airport. The car's navigation system set me on a course southwest along Interstate 95 past miles of tall green trees that completely obscured any views to the west or east. An hour later, the trees gave way to glimpses of water. Bridges led over rivers to small islands with shorter and scruffier trees.

Dozens of billboards advertised the usual fare: fast food, legal services, soft drinks, and payday loans. It being an election year, plenty of smiling, trustworthy, fourteen-foot-tall faces gazed down upon the highway and promised more than the other guy. Religious billboards peppered the landscape, too. Some were welcoming; some predicted doom. Each promised more than the other guy.

About forty miles south of Savannah, I noticed something different: a smiling couple advertising "A Way to Happiness" and listing a highway exit number near Serenity. There was no phone number or the usual marketing "call-to-action." Odd.

Night fell and the billboards' lights sparked to life. Two more billboards with smiling couples appeared as I drove south. The last included the word "Sidoni" as if it were meant to mean something to me. It didn't.

The Nissan's nav system led me off the highway and onto Riverside Drive, a two-lane road serving as Serenity's main thoroughfare. Serenity stadium—home of the minor league Seagulls and large enough to hold a few thousand fans—stood sentinel at the north edge of town. Half the lights illuminated the stadium and only four cars occupied the parking lot. The last of the cleaning crew picking up empty peanut bags and sweeping the aisles after a late afternoon game.

A hundred yards past the stadium stood a complex of city buildings: Serenity City Hall, a public library, police station, and courthouse. These four buildings were relatively new, probably less than three or four years old.

I continued down the town's main street past a small used car lot, a fabric store, an antiques shop with an old wagon parked in front, an independent gas station, and a few old, but well-kept, brick homes. Everything was clean and tidy. No graffiti, no trash. Through the trees I caught glimpses of a rising gibbous moon reflecting off a wide river east of the road.

Farther down and on the east side of the street stood a magnificent brick building. It appeared to be an old county courthouse planted on a bump of ground at a bend in the river. The car's navigation display indicated that this was Clint McCord's address. A sign outside the building identified it as *Sidoni*. It didn't look at all like a residence and appeared to be closed.

Even in the reduced light of sunset, the building was impressive: Victorian design built of red brick with white stone accents and Ionian columns. A white, domed tower topped the large central structure of the main part of the building. It was three stories tall but the second floor windows stretched all the way to the top implying a high ceiling for the second story. That second story had probably housed the original courtroom. Two wings of red brick, each two stories tall, flanked the center structure. Tall narrow arched windows topped with white keystones filled each wing.

South of *Sidoni* stood a small block of four older brick homes. A temporary sign in front of the block featured an artist's rendition of a modern steel and glass two-story building. The caption read "Future Home of the Sidoni Multi-Media Center."

Directly across the main street stood a block of upscale commerce: a trendy sandwich place, a coffee shop named "Fully Woke," and a small restaurant advertising locally-sourced, wood-fired pizza. The old center of town had turned upscale.

Commerce dominated the next few blocks. A supermarket and a chain restaurant shared a parking lot. Farther south was an entire block of older retail shops: a nail salon, the Jean Scene, a real estate brokerage, Roy's Ice Cream, a menswear shop, and Marv's Toys. A fishing tackle shop advertised "licenses, bait, and worms." I wondered if there was a separate use for worms in this town other than as bait.

I continued south.

A block of fine old homes with well-kept yards lined the street on both sides followed by professional offices and a branch of a large national bank. A furniture store, an older three-story office building, and a small pharmacy stood across the street from the bank.

At the southern end of town stood a red brick building covered in old fence boards. Two orange neon signs in the windows flanking the door declared that the "BBQ" was "OPEN." A few other lit signs, provided by well-established American breweries, filled the other windows. A collection of older pickup trucks and aged American sedans sat in the cracked asphalt parking lot indicating this was the locals' choice for food and drink. I parked and went in.

Through a cut-out in the wall behind the counter, I saw a very large black guy moving around the kitchen assembling plates of food. A good sign. You can't trust a skinny cook. A middle-aged lady with streaks of grey accenting her brown hair stood behind an orange Formica bar and talked to a couple of men in their forties. She moved and spoke with confidence. A half-dozen couples sat at tables and booths. All of the men wore bill caps.

"My name's Becca," said the lady behind the bar. "Sit anywhere you like."

I sat at the bar two stools down from the men she'd been talking to and examined the menu on the chalkboard nailed to the wall. Becca walked over and put a glass of cold water on the orange surface in front of me.

"What'll y'all have?"

"I'm torn between the beef ribs and the pulled pork."

"That's a no-brainer. Our pulled pork is a hundred times better than any ol' ribs."

I looked at the list of brews offered and struggled in deciding between Sweet Georgia Brown, Terrapin, and Jailhouse Mugshot IPA. The little voice inside suggested something lighter. I've learned to listen to the little voice.

"I'll have a half-pound of the pork, side of coleslaw, and a Coke," I said.

"You want inside meat or outside meat?"

"Inside," I said. "Light on the sauce, please."

She gave a look of approval and nodded as if I'd passed some sort of test. She walked back to the kitchen to place my order.

I looked around at the patrons. Townspeople with clean fingernails and decent haircuts. Nobody under forty. Several over sixty. Clean clothes. Nothing flashy. Most of them were quiet. Becca returned with my Coke.

"I'm just driving through," I said. "But I couldn't help but notice that beautiful old courthouse you have downtown. Is that an apartment building, now?"

"It's a church," she said.

The redheaded fellow three seats down the bar gave a snort. He stayed seated but I could tell he was tall and skinny. Probably taller than me, definitely skinnier. He wore a blue denim work shirt with the sleeves rolled up. The bottom half of a dragon tattoo peeked out from under the sleeve on one arm. He reached for the beer in front of him and drained half the bottle.

"Seems pretty quiet there tonight," I said.

"Oh, it starts to pick up around eight or nine during the week," the skinny guy said. "You lookin' to *worship?*"

"Jesse," said the fellow sitting next to him. "Shut your mouth, you dumb fisherman."

"It's outrageous to call that place a church," said Jesse. "Those people ain't no Christians of any type."

Becca stepped out of the kitchen with my dinner and gave Jesse the evil eye.

"Don't you talk that way," she said. "It don't do to say such things."

Jesse drank some more beer and went back to his barbecue and cornbread.

The pulled pork was good. Better than good. It was laced with a vinegar sauce that had a trace of mustard. I ate it and the coleslaw and a piece of the best cornbread I'd ever tasted. I asked for a second piece.

I paid the bill, left a generous tip, and stepped outside to my Nissan. It was time to visit *Sidoni.*

8

I drove back toward the center of town and looked for a parking space on the street. Nothing was available near the old courthouse. I parked around the corner and walked back on the sidewalk under a long line of tall, mossy Spanish oaks. A thick lawn spread from the base of the courthouse to the cross-street fifty yards to the north and from the main street in front to the wide slow river that bent its way behind the building. Several speedboats bobbed next to a dock beyond the lawn. I looked at the cars parked on the street and saw that most had license plates from other counties. Some were from other states: Florida, South Carolina, Alabama.

The waitress at the barbecue joint had called it a church but there was no marquee announcing the subject of Sunday's sermon and no invitation anywhere for the public to join for worship services.

Two men stood at the main entrance. One of the guys was my height—about six-three—with a full red beard. The other guy was a bit under six feet with a deep cleft in his chin. He was trying to grow a mustache but suffering from crop failure. His blond hair hindered the effort. Red Beard probably had thirty pounds on me, Crop Failure was thirty pounds the other way. Each wore a thin maroon cassock.

People entering the building approached the men, showed an ID card, and hurried through the lit entryway. Some laughed lightly as they entered. A few others rushed in as if a big dog was about to bite them in the hindquarters.

I climbed the steps to the front door, fished around in my wallet for my driver's license, and approached the two men. Red Beard held out a paw and I handed him my license. He looked at it and wrinkled his forehead.

"What do you want?" he asked.

"I'm looking for a girl."

Crop Failure picked up a telephone inside the door.

"Were you invited to worship?" said the big guy. "You must be invited to worship."

"I want to see Dorothea Millet. I understand she's here."

"There is nobody here by that name."

Another fellow walked to the door from down the hall. The guy was slender—about six-one—and had olive skin, black hair, three days' worth of beard, and thick eyebrows. He wore a light gray herringbone suit instead of a cassock and looked a lot like the guy I'd seen in the passport photo. Clint McCord.

"I know the woman of which he speaks," he said. "He refers to Shaysan Ri."

Crop Failure nodded.

"I'd like to see her," I said.

McCord shook his head.

"I just want to say 'Hello.'"

Another man approached the door with his card and McCord indicated for me to walk back down the front steps. I did and he followed me. The man with the card walked inside.

"Shaysan Ri is in focused meditation," he said. He put his hands together, the fingers barely intertwined, and held them to his chin. "It would be detrimental to her progress for her to be disturbed."

I pride myself on having a sensitive BS meter. This guy pegged its needle into the red.

"Her father is a Detective Constable in the British Virgin Islands," I said. "She left home suddenly and without a word and he's concerned about her. He wants me to talk to her. Just to make sure she's okay."

He shrugged.

"I'm sorry. She can't be disturbed. And the presence of an infidel such as yourself would disrupt the services and upset our followers."

"I understand," I said. "But the Constable won't. If I don't see her tonight, he'll call one of his buddies at the FBI field office in Atlanta tomorrow morning."

I let the lie sink in.

"A whole lot of infidels might come around to ask about her. They might even get a search warrant. That'll disrupt your services and disturb your faithful followers a helluva lot more than I could."

McCord stiffened at the threat.

"How about I just talk to Dorothea for a few moments and we can be done with it?" I said.

"This is the sanctuary for the Rahm Sahn Sidoni. Unbelievers are not allowed."

"I don't need to go in. Bring her out and let me talk with her out here on the lawn for a couple minutes. Then I'm gone."

The wheels turned for a moment. A light rain began to fall.

"I need to speak with the High Master," he said.

"Of course," I said. "That goes without saying."

McCord motioned for me to follow him back up to the entryway. He left me with Red Beard and Crop Failure and walked down the hallway.

I could see inside from the entryway. Ornate metal sconces lined a central hallway. Flickering light bulbs imitated dozens of lit candles. Pan pipe music played from a room at the end of the hallway. It reminded me of music collections sold on late-night television years ago when I was a kid. Before I'd outgrown television.

I watched the devotees as they passed the two fellows at the door. Most were men. All of them well-dressed. They showed their cards, walked down the long hallway, and disappeared around a corner. A stack of pamphlets sat on an antique sideboard in the entryway. I grabbed one and looked it over.

The pamphlet was professionally printed in multiple colors on thick shiny stock. *The Way to Joy* was printed by an organization calling itself *Aum Sidoni*. The booklet was short but well-written. The first few pages seemed heavy on Greek philosophy with a few New Testament scriptures thrown in for good measure. Their philosophy mentioned a Phoenician goddess named Astarte.

I remembered something about the Phoenicians from my high school world history class. They were sailors. Some of the best. I read on.

I couldn't tell whether *Sidoni* was an organized religion or just a movement and ideology until I got to the back page. The closing paragraph stated that adherents to *Sidoni* considered it less of a rigorous faith in deity and more of a way of life. The pamphlet, however, contained no direct references to sailing. Posers.

McCord returned a few minutes later and led me to a door about thirty feet down the hallway. I opened the door to find a lovely woman in a red leather armchair. Her dark brown hair was tied back with a silver ribbon. She wore an off-white sleeveless gown that draped to the floor and a large ring with a green stone on the middle finger of her right hand. She stared at the stone.

I almost didn't recognize her.

9

"DOROTHEA?" I said.

She looked up at me with clear eyes.

"Mr. Greene," she said. "It is so very good to see you."

I turned to McCord.

"Can you leave us alone for a minute?"

He smiled and shook his head. I turned back to Dorothea.

"How are you doing?"

"I am well."

"You left the island rather suddenly. You didn't even say goodbye."

"I was worried that my father's friends would try to keep me on the island," she said.

Her speech was measured and relaxed as if she were required to conform to a rigid rhythm. Her face was pale but her eyes were clear and bright; pupils about the right size. No signs of panic or anxiety, no runny nose, no nervous sweats. She didn't appear to be drugged.

"Your parents miss you," I said.

"That is regrettable."

"They'd like you to call them. You can use my phone."

I pulled my phone from my pocket and held it out to her. Dorothea looked at it.

"Call them," I said. "They only want to hear your voice. They just want to know you're all right."

"I will bear that in mind, Mr. Greene."

A British friend once told me that phrase was shorthand for

'screw you.'

"Would you like me to take you home?" I asked.

McCord stiffened.

"No," she said. "I am exactly where I wish to be."

I thought for a moment of what to say next. Dorothea beat me to it.

"I am here of my own free will," she said, "and I wish to stay here with my brothers and sisters of *Sidoni*."

She stood and held out her hand. McCord moved a little closer to her.

"It was very nice to see you," she said. "But I would like you to leave, Mr. Greene. Please give my regards to my parents."

I said goodbye, shook her hand, and followed McCord back to the courthouse entry.

"I trust that we have resolved your concerns," he said.

"Yes, I think you've done that."

"Then you'll be leaving now."

It wasn't a question.

"Sure," I said. "Sorry to have disturbed your *chakra* or whatever."

He left me at the door and returned to the room where I'd spoken with Dorothea. I switched off the digital recording pen I had in my pocket and walked back to my car wondering why a church would need a guy who carried a holstered pistol under his herringbone jacket.

It was getting late and I needed a place to bunk for the night. I pulled back onto Riverside Drive and turned south to look for the motel the car's nav system claimed I would find. I drove past the BBQ joint and a cluster of old homes onto a bridge that spanned the same river that flowed behind *Sidoni*. It was a wide river at that point; one that had probably carried three centuries' worth of cotton bales to the sea. On the other side of the bridge was a motel advertising cheap rates, clean rooms, free Wi-Fi, and 24-hour cable TV.

Seek and ye shall find.

I rang a bell on the counter to summon the night clerk. A short sandy-haired fellow in his early twenties walked out of a room at the back of the office. He didn't seem to appreciate my interrupting his favorite TV show.

"Just you?" he asked.

I nodded.

"No bags?"

I held up my duffel.

"Just one night?"

"Yep," I said.

He looked at me and squinted.

"What happened to your nose?" he asked.

Perhaps this line of questioning was the locally accepted, if less urbane, manner of initiating small talk or maybe they didn't see many former amateur boxers passing through Serenity. I didn't feel like telling him how I broke it and I was too tired for small-town conversation.

"I used it to beat an inquisitive motel clerk to death last week," I said.

He cocked his head about fifteen degrees to the right and shook it slightly.

"It's $69.95 for the room plus hotel tax and city tax," he said.

His voice labored with the boredom born of constant repetition.

I handed him my credit card and driver's license. He examined the license and wrinkled his forehead.

"Where the hell is this from?" he asked.

"British Virgin Islands," I said.

"Where the hell is that?"

"Caribbean," I said. "East of Puerto Rico. Just run the card. It's good and I'm tired."

He picked up a phone and called the credit card company to make sure this "foreigner" wasn't trying to pull a fast one. The company must have had good things to say about me because he hung up the phone and ran my card through the machine. A moment later, he handed me the card, my license, and one of those plastic programmable door keys.

"Room 212. It's up one floor in the elevator and to your right. Checkout time is eleven. The Wi-Fi login and password are posted in the room. Ice machine and vending down the hall. Use channel fourteen on the TV to check out."

He walked back to his television without asking if I needed help with my bag. At least he didn't ask for a tip. I found my room, tossed my duffel onto the desk, and picked up my phone.

10

"I'M in Georgia."

"That's too far away to do me any good," said Marie. "Did you find Dorothea Millet?"

"Safe and sound. At least, she appears to be."

"Followed a fellow home, did she?"

"There is a guy involved but the motivation seems religious."

"Which religion?"

"One I've never heard of before. But it's old enough to consider me an infidel."

"Was she religious on Tortola?"

"Not especially. But I suppose that could strike a person at any age."

"She's probably more interested in the guy than the religion," said Marie. Then her voice got a little sultry. "I understand the guy part."

"Yeah, I hear your boyfriend is quite the stud."

"He thinks so."

"And he thinks you could fly down to Savannah tomorrow. I'll pick you up at the airport and we can have a fun weekend together."

"That sounds wonderful, but I'm in meetings most of the day with faculty members and the acting chair of the dissertation committee."

"I'm not exactly sure what that means," I said. "But I am seriously missing you."

"It means that if all goes as planned, I will fly down before the next semester starts and visit you on your lovely little boat. Just a couple more weeks."

Her voice carried more than a hint of promise.

"I'd like that," I said. "I'd like that a lot."

We talked a little longer. Nothing consequential. I just wanted to keep hearing her voice. We hung up when she said we both needed sleep.

Except I couldn't sleep. Questions about Dorothea and the *Sidoni* church kept rolling around in my head. Why the fake email to her parents? Why did this McCord guy feel the need to carry a gun in church? I clicked on the television to dilute the questions with late-night entertainment drivel. I caught the last ten minutes of a fairly funny talk show. After that, however, it was exactly as Springsteen had sung when I was a teenager: "fifty-seven channels and nothing on." I clicked through them anyway.

An international charity I'd never heard of encouraged me to donate money to feed and clothe people in need. Scenes of starving and nearly naked children were interspersed with celebrity talking heads. It was heartrending and compelling but the last thing I wanted were new problems to think about. Click.

A home shopping channel. Click.

Another home shopping channel. Click.

A preacher's religious revival channel. Fast click.

A BBC special on political unrest in sub-Saharan Africa briefly caught my interest. Video clips of irregular lines of armed men marching down dirt roads were overlaid with a reporter's narration of religious and political differences, kidnapped children, destroyed villages, and child brides for fanatic warriors. The rival factions, for the most part, were rag-tag groups with well-worn AK-47s. One group had newer equipment and appeared to be better organized. The eventual winner seemed obvious.

At half-past midnight, I made my final click and went to bed.

I slept well in spite of the dull continuous drone of the room's window air conditioner. My internal alarm clock woke me at five-thirty. I strapped on my running shoes, tucked the room's card key into my shorts pocket, and jogged down to an asphalt running trail skirting the river's edge.

The trail led me downriver past tall red maple trees and massive oaks. A pair of whitetail deer—a doe and her fawn—scampered into the shrubbery as I ran past them. Everything smelled of jasmine and new rain and it was quite pleasant. Bugs buzzed in the bushes and the trees. I thought about Dorothea and why she'd come here.

Was she truly seeking a new spiritual experience? Why the secrecy? Why run away unannounced? How did she meet Clint McCord? Why send the odd email to her parents with the concocted story of a Colorado vacation?

The more I thought about it, the more questions popped up. But it all boiled down to her being old enough to make her own mistakes and her telling me she wanted to be there. I had no case to take to the local cops. She was an adult woman following the dictates of her own conscience. But I still had to fly back to the BVI and give bad news to the Millet family.

The river made a sharp bend a mile and a half downstream as it meandered toward the ocean. It was probably a hundred yards wide at that point. A chain link fence blocked the path and I stopped. A metal sign from the Georgia Department of Natural Resources warned: "DANGER: Crocodile Study Area. No Trespassing." The warning included the usual threats of fines and imprisonment. Thick trees and shrubs stood beyond the fence.

I turned to see an old aluminum fishing boat anchored upstream near the shore under a large tree that stretched over the river. An old man and a young boy, probably a grandson, sat there with poles in their hands.

"How's the fishing?" I asked.

"Fair," said the older man.

"It's the catchin' that ain't so good," said the boy.

"Do the crocodiles get all the fish?" I asked.

"There ain't no crocs in Georgia," said the older man. "Plenty of 'gators, though. 'Nuff of them to make a handbag for every woman in this state, I suppose. But there ain't no 'croc-oh-dahles' north of Miami."

"No, grandpa," said the boy. "They found a small group of crocs near the mouth of the river and they set aside that area so the government could study 'em."

"My favorite fishin' hole was down that way," said the man. "But they done closed it off and we can't even take our boat in there. They say we might disturb the 'croc-oh-dahles' habitat or some such."

The sound of high-revving large-displacement engines approached us from down river.

"Damn kids and their speedboats," said the older man. "How come the government doesn't stop *them* from bothering the crocs?"

A speedboat blasted around the bend downstream and headed up the river toward us. The boat had a deep "V" offshore racing hull, probably thirty feet long. Dual supercharged inboard engines wailed with a thousand combined horsepower. The fellow at the helm drove the boat like he'd been born on that river.

The driver looked over at us as the boat approached and our eyes locked. It was Clint McCord. He hastily turned his gaze upstream and continued piloting the vessel.

"That idiot races by here all the time," said the older fellow. "Ruins the fishin'."

"You know him?" I asked.

"Nah. He's just one of those stupid rich kids 'round here that's got more dollars than sense."

I ran upstream back toward the motel and thought about what I was going to tell Constable Millet and his wife. There wasn't much to give them. Just the assurance that Dorothea was alive and doing what she wanted. I could also give them an address to which they could send the occasional letter.

I returned to the motel, showered, shaved, and put on a clean shirt. A card on top of the television described the complimentary continental breakfast but the prose didn't draw me in. I decided to find something more substantial on the road. I checked out using the motel's TV channel, left the card key on the bedside table, and headed down the stairs and out the door with my duffel. Two cops stood near my rental car.

They wore dark blue uniforms with dark blue Mountie hats. Twenty-first century Tasers hung from their hips while 1970's mirrored aviator glasses perched on the bridges of their noses. RoboCop meets Buford Pusser.

The senior officer was maybe fifty years old and had a bit of belly fat. Little bronze Sergeant's chevrons perched on the lapels of his dark blue uniform shirt. His mustache, streaked with gray, could have been a required element under the local police uniform guide. A radio microphone hung from the neck of his shirt with the coiled cord stretching down to his duty belt. Two pens poked out of the corner of his left breast pocket.

He stood in front of a new white Chevy Tahoe. A full-size light bar with blue lenses sat on the roof and the word "POLICE" in big red letters covered most of the front door. The words "Shift Commander" sat in smaller gray letters a little farther down.

I recognized the younger cop as Crop Failure from the previous night's visit to Sidoni. He looked smaller without his cassock. He stood in front of an older white Ford Police Interceptor.

Old Mustache turned his mirrored glasses toward me.

"This your car?" he said.

"No, sir."

"You sure about that?"

"Absolutely. It belongs to Avis. I rented it from them yesterday in Savannah."

"Why?"

"Because they were a couple of bucks cheaper."

He rested his hand on the handle of his police baton. It looked exactly like the PR-24 I'd carried years earlier.

"I meant why did you come down here from Savannah?" he

asked.

"I'm a traveling Bible salesman."

Crop Failure looked into my car through the windows checking the backseat and rear hatch areas.

"I don't see no Bibles," he said.

Old Mustache cocked his head to the right.

"My associate, here, says he don't see no Bibles."

"I'm a damned good Bible salesman."

Old Mustache smiled like a happy little reptile.

"Your little rental car here has a busted taillight. That's a violation of Georgia state vehicle code, O.C.G.A. forty-dash-eight-dash-twenty-three subparagraph 'e', which requires that all lenses on all taillights be maintained and in good repair at all times."

I looked over at the left rear tail light and saw that most of the lens was missing. Shards of broken red plastic lay on the ground only a foot or so away from Crop Failure's right boot.

"Looks like somebody belted it with a PR-24," I said. "Wonder how that could have happened?"

Old Mustache smiled again.

"May I see some identification, please?" he said.

I handed him my BVI driver's license.

"British Virgin Islands?" he said. "Where the hell is that?"

"South of here," I said. "About fifteen hundred miles. It's so far south, we call you guys Yankees."

"You don't sound foreign. You sound like an American."

"I was raised in California."

"Then why the hell do you have a driver's license from..." He looked at the license again as if he'd forgotten its origin. "... the British Virgin Islands?"

"My Swiss license expired last year," I said. "Had to get a new one."

He handed my license to Crop Failure.

"Write it," he said.

The younger cop grinned at me like he had a bent coat hanger stuck in his mouth. He pulled out a ticket book and wrote for a few minutes without saying anything. He approached, asked me to sign the ticket, handed me a copy, and returned my driver's license. I noticed the name tag on his uniform said 'M. Danforth.'

"You know where the BVI is, don't you Mitch? It's only fifty miles north of St. Croix."

His mouth dropped open a little and he looked at Old Mustache. Neither looked amused.

"You get that taillight fixed," said the old cop, "or you get out of my town."

"Can I stay long enough to buy a T-shirt?"

Old Mustache scowled at me, got into his Tahoe, and drove away behind his mirrored sunglasses. Danforth dutifully followed. I put my driver's license back into my wallet and tossed the ticket into a trash bin next to the Nissan. *Let them track me down in the BVI.*

I placed my bag onto the back seat, slid behind the wheel, and drove back onto the highway toward Savannah. I kept an eye in the rear view mirror on my way out of town and wondered what had happened to Southern hospitality.

11

"MILLET hasn't been around in a while," said Al.

"It's been a rough couple of weeks for him."

Al and I were sitting in my office listening to a baseball game and wishing there were more tourists around to hire us. But it was the hot slow season. Nothing to do but wait it out.

"How'd they take the news?"

"The Constable was stoic," I said. "You know, the basic British stiff upper lip and all that. His wife, on the other hand…"

I shrugged. Al reached under the desk and pulled a beer from the mini-fridge. He nodded at me and I shook my head.

"She's having a hard time understanding how Dorothea has the right to screw up her life and join some weird religious cult."

"Ah, yes," he said. "The dreaded 'weird religious cult' out to steal our babies. Isn't that what we always call any religion we don't understand?"

"What do you mean?"

"Every religion looks strange from the outside. Jews believe the Red Sea parted before Moses, Hindus believe in an eight-armed goddess, and Christians believe a man died in a horribly brutal way and came back to life three days later. Every religious belief sounds weird to those standing outside it. Yet, each is completely accepted as fact by the adherent."

"Which means…."

"Every 'weird religious cult' is in the eye of the beholder."

"Well, it seemed pretty strange to me," I said. "And Dorothea's mom didn't take it well."

"Gina's got a lot of French blood in her. A strong emotional reaction should not be unexpected."

"French? She's from South Africa."

"French Huguenot," said Al. "Her people were driven from France three hundred years ago because they were Protestants. The Catholics in power considered Protestants to be a 'weird religious cult' and persecuted them accordingly."

"How do you know all this stuff?"

"I taught history, remember?"

That was the part of Al that was easy to forget. The part that followed his career as a Navy SEAL. He was the guy with a Silver Star, a Purple Heart, and, oddly, a Ph.D. A fellow who could kill a man with a knife in close-quarters combat in the early morning and read Locke or Sophocles that evening.

"Anyhow, the Huguenots migrated six thousand miles to the south and settled in the *Franchhoek*, the French Quarter of South Africa. Gina Millet comes from tough stock."

"She wanted me to go back and kidnap Dorothea," I said. "She thought you might assist me."

Al shook his head slowly from side to side.

"I gave up kidnapping years ago."

He finished his beer and tossed the empty into the trash can. The bottle clanked against several of its depleted brethren.

"So, when do Eryn's friends fly in?" asked Al.

"Late tonight."

"She excited?"

"Big time," I said. "She's at her desk right now planning every detail, every anchorage, each day's activities. We're going to Bobby's in a bit to pick up the food."

"Any of those girls know how to sail or are you on your own?"

"Just Captain Sim," I said.

He shook his head and let a thin smile slip across his face.

"What?" I asked.

"You and six single college girls on a chartered catamaran for a week," he said. "You should be ashamed of yourself for what I'm thinking."

"I am a one-woman man. Even if I weren't, I'm too old for her. Barely."

Eryn's footsteps approached and Al responded accordingly.

"Well, how about them Dodgers?" he said.

She poked her nose around the doorway.

"How come you guys are always talking about baseball when I walk into the room?"

"We like baseball," said Al. "Are you looking forward to a week of sailing?"

"I am so excited," said Eryn. "Most of my friends have never been down here and they are so going to love it."

"You still want to go diving Tuesday and Friday?" asked Al.

"Absolutely."

"I'll bring *In Depth II* and all the gear," he said. "Just get me their sizes and such."

Eryn smiled.

"Oh, Al. You are such a dear," she said. "Always thinking of us."

Eryn saw only the good in people. She turned to me.

"You ready to go shopping?" she said.

We walked outside to my truck and left Al to wait by the phone for non-existent customers. We turned onto Blackburn Highway toward Road Town and Bobby's Market Place. Traffic was light. It was hot and humid and most of the local folk had the good sense to stay inside.

"I'm so glad you could get that catamaran. Are you sure it isn't any trouble for you to skipper the boat?"

"None at all," I said. "Business is dead right now anyway."

"My uncle offered to skipper for us but some of the girls didn't want him around. He's taken care of me since my parents passed and he's a bit protective. The others felt he'd put a damper on the party, if you know what I mean."

I laughed.

We arrived at Bobby's and I turned into the parking lot. A clump of trees stood about forty yards from the store's entrance and I parked in their shade hoping my truck wouldn't melt while we were inside. We each grabbed a cart as we entered the store.

I watched Eryn as she pulled items off the shelves and marked them off a checklist. She didn't ask my opinion; she didn't need it. She chose quality items and avoided pre-packaged convenience foods. I was going to eat well on this trip. She put three cases of Ting in my cart but completely bypassed the liquor aisle.

"You know, most people use that stuff to make Flamingos or Palomas. But you haven't bought any tequila or rum."

"Ting is just fine all by itself," she said. "And none of us drink, Sim."

"None of you?" I asked. "No booze at all?"

"Get some Coronas for yourself, if you feel the need, but don't buy any for us."

"No, no. I'm good."

Forty minutes later, both carts were full. The checker tallied up the items and bagged them for us. Eryn handed her a credit card.

We pushed the carts out of the store and into the parking lot.

"Hey mon."

I turned to see Dale wearing the T-shirt I'd bought him in Savannah. Light blue with a giant peach on the chest and the words "Sweet Georgia Peach" underneath. There hadn't been a lot of shirts in his size at the factory outlet. His was about the size of a two-man tent.

"How are you doing?" I asked.

"Fine, Mistah Greene. Dale be doin' just fine," he said. "De charter business is slow right now but we still have lots to do in the off-season."

I threw Eryn the key to my truck and she left me with the two carts by the entrance. I watched her walk away in that hip-swingy fashion that is always somehow enhanced by loose knee-length shorts. A couple of local guys in a Mitsubishi drove into the parking lot. They slowed down to appreciate the view.

"That big cat gonna be ready for me in the morning?" I asked.

"De mainsail is a little worn and de port diesel burns some oil but she got a new generator and new air-conditioning units last week. 'S all workin' fine, mon."

That was what I wanted to hear.

I glanced over to my truck and saw Eryn open the door. She sat down in the driver's seat, pulled her legs into the cab, and disappeared in a ball of white flame. The shock wave crushed my chest and the world ended in a furious split-second roar that died instantly.

12

I couldn't tell if I was lying on my back in a dark room or suspended in a universe of black ink. I wondered if this were the afterlife my mom had talked about. I couldn't feel my arms or legs but I could sense people around me. An eagle carried me to a city in the sky. Towers with crenelated battlements looked out over puffy clouds. Huge mountains stood in the distance. I knew I was dreaming but I liked the clouds and the mountains. The ocean was a thousand miles away and I missed it, but I liked the clouds and towers and mountains anyway.

I sensed somebody staring at me but I couldn't open my eyes to see who it was. People spoke but a high-pitched whine rang in my ears and drowned out their voices. After some time, one voice stood out and I recognized it. I wanted to talk to her, to look at her. To touch her.

"He moved his finger," said Marie.

Another voice joined the first. It was distant—maybe ten or twelve miles away—but it boomed through the background noise like a bull entering the ring intent on dismembering a toreador.

"Can he hear us?" asked Al.

Something touched my right shoulder and then my hand. I tried to speak but somebody had their hands around my throat. They were trying to suffocate me.

"He's fighting it," said another voice. "We need to calm him down."

I didn't want to calm down. I wanted to scream. I wanted to get the hands off my throat. I wanted to breathe. A warm sensation traveled up my right arm.

The mountains and clouds returned for a moment and then a thick dark blue mist rolled in and covered it all.

————

My eyes opened to a grey world lit by dim fluorescent lights. A thin steel pole, polished and gleaming, stretched toward the ceiling. A crossbar with bent curled ends supported a clear plastic bag. A thin tube trailed out the bottom. Somebody slept in a chair next to my bed but all I could see was long black hair cascading down the side of a face and partially covering a shoulder. My eyes moved to the slender arm and the thin fingers.

Marie.

My throat was lined with sandpaper. I croaked a little but Marie did not wake. Sleep crept in on me again and the dim light in the grey room faded to black.

I woke the next morning to the unmistakable and oddly comforting sound of Al arguing with a somebody.

"He's awake," said a voice.

I tried to talk but only a thin rasp came out. A man in a white coat leaned over me and looked in my eyes with a penlight.

"Good morning, sunshine," he said. He gave a wide smile. "I am Dr. Vihaan Khatri and you are in hospital. Don't try to talk. You've been on a ventilator for some time and your throat is quite swollen. Just nod you head if you can understand."

I had no idea what he was talking about but nodded my head anyway.

"Your job is to rest in this bed and to let your body heal."

He examined my left arm and hand. I couldn't feel it when he touched them.

"Try to move the fingers of your left hand," he said.

I couldn't. My arm felt like dead meat hanging off my shoulder.

The man made a few notes on a chart and exited the room without saying anything more. Al put a glass of water in my right hand and I took a sip. I tried to remember the last time he'd handed me a glass filled with anything so benign.

"You're in the hospital in Charlotte Amalie," said Al. "Intensive Care Unit. It's Friday morning. You've been in a medically-induced coma for six days."

I nodded and looked around the room. We were alone.

"Do you remember anything?"

I shook my head.

"Your truck exploded and you got hit in the chest by a piece of your left rear tire," he said. "It broke five of your ribs and collapsed both lungs. Something else put a dent in your left shoulder. It didn't break anything in there but they think you may have a pinched nerve or something. You weren't breathing and had no pulse when the EMTs got there. They got your heart started."

I took another sip of water. My chest felt like a dump truck had parked there overnight. Al saw the question in my face.

"Eryn was killed instantly," he said. "You don't want the details."

I actually did but I couldn't ask.

"Dale was thrown against the building and hit his head on the cinder block wall. He never regained consciousness."

Anger welled up inside but it wasn't the time or place.

"Two other men in a nearby car were killed, too. One was the Deputy Secretary to the Ministry of Finance."

I sipped a little more water.

"It's all over the news up and down the Caribbean," he said. "People are saying it was terrorists after government officials. One of the local newsies is speculating that you and I are CIA operatives."

That must have hurt Al. I knew how he felt about the CIA.

"I found parts of the device," said Al. "We'll talk about that later. When you can talk."

I nodded.

"When you're ready," he said.

I looked in his eyes and saw it. The look of a predatory animal ready for the hunt. I nodded again.

"No hurries, okay?" he said.

Marie entered the room and walked over to my right side.

"I'll leave you two alone," said Al.

He walked out into the hallway. Marie leaned over the bed and hugged me gently.

"At least your nose hasn't changed," she said.

I smiled and lifted my right hand. I made a motion with it as if writing with a pen. She opened her bag and dug around in it. She found a pen and a small pad of yellow paper. She held the pad while I wrote.

Are you okay?

"I'm fine. You're the one in the ICU."

When do I get out?

"The doctor hasn't told us. It's only been six days since the accident."

It wasn't an accident. I knew it wasn't an accident.

Eryn's family?

"Her uncle flew down on Monday to…" She swallowed hard. "…to get her and take her home."

Funeral?

"It's tomorrow. In Stamford. I'm flying back tonight."

My pulse began to race and the light started to fade in the room. Marie ran out to the hallway.

My eyes opened later—I have no idea when—to see another doctor hovering over me. Marie and Al stood at the end of the bed. The paper and pen were gone. The bed sheet had been pulled down to my waist. Clear plastic tubes stuck out of my armpits. Streaks of red stained the inside of the tubes.

"You are a very sick man," said the doctor. "You had bi-lateral hemothoraces caused by broken ribs that tore into your lungs and blood vessels."

I had no idea what he was talking about but it sounded bad.

"I know it hurts a great deal to do so but you need to breathe as fully and deeply as possible."

He checked the tubes and looked over at a screen to my right. He turned to Al and Marie.

"He needs to rest," said the doctor. "Having you both in here does not facilitate that."

I gathered up my strength and took in a deep breath. Speaking hurt like mad but I had to say it. They had to hear me. It was little more than a croak.

"Tell the papers I didn't make it."

Al smiled.

"I already did, Sim. We're holding your funeral tomorrow."

13

THEY took the tubes out of my left side Saturday morning and watched me to see if that lung would collapse. I focused my energy on breathing, sleeping, and eating. My strength began to return in small increments. By evening, the numbness in my left side had receded and was replaced with the sensation of hot needles being jabbed into my forearm. Dr. Khatri called it "transient paresthesia" and was quite enthusiastic. I did not share his glee.

The needles left Sunday morning, replaced by a dull ache affecting my entire left arm. They pulled out the rest of my chest tubes that afternoon and moved me to a regular room. Al came in to see how I was doing. He brought a small cardboard box and a copy of the local paper. He showed me the short write-up on page two that announced my death. An adjoining article brought the island reader up-to-date on the police investigation surrounding the deaths of three "belongers" and two visiting American workers. It was clear the investigation had not progressed far.

"Had your funeral yesterday," said Al. "You would have liked it."

"You are so enjoying this."

Al smiled.

"Erv Parmenter and I took his speedboat out to Anegada and scattered your ashes off Pomato Point."

I wondered where they got the ashes but didn't dare ask.

"Anybody else show up to pay their respects?"

"Henry brought his runabout. Brought some cold beer, too."

"Nice of him," I said. "So who am I, now?"

"Everybody in here but Dr. Khatri knows you as 'Stewart Glasgow.' You're a tourist from Connecticut who got hit in the chest by the boom of a fifty-footer during an unintentional gybe."

"You think of everything."

"Millet's idea, actually."

He opened the box and pulled out a thin red wire with a small piece of a brown cardboard tube dangling from it. The tube was an eighth-inch in diameter and a quarter-inch long.

"I found this hanging from a tree branch twenty yards from where your truck had been. It's a piece of a squib. A detonator."

He reached into the box again and pulled out a short length of black wire attached to a small piece of broken glass.

"Part of a mercury switch," said Al. "It was on the ground thirty feet from your truck."

"Does Constable Millet know about those?"

"Yes, but I've asked him to keep it quiet."

"You suddenly trust him?"

"He ordered a police helicopter to fly you to this hospital," said Al. "Put his job on the line, I think, in doing so. I'm pretty sure your funeral would've been real had he not done that. He's earned a bit of my trust."

I nodded.

"Both these little gems are military grade, Sim. Somebody with training and access to this kind of gear blew up your truck and killed Eryn."

"And three others," I said.

Al nodded.

"Any ideas?" he asked.

"What is Millet doing?"

"Everything he can, which is, for the most part, nothing. The RVIP isn't geared up for this kind of investigation. He told the press he believes it was a terrorist bombing aimed at the Ministry of Finance but nobody has come out and taken credit for it. As far as anybody in the BVI knows, Eryn, Dale, and you were unintended victims."

I drank some water. My throat felt better but talking still hurt.

"I'm not buying that," I said. "Why rig my truck to blow if you want to kill two people in another car? How could anybody possibly know some government officials would park nearby?"

"So who did it?"

"Beats me. An angry Venezuelan drug lord getting back at me for what happened a year and a half ago? Somebody connected to that guy in California? A furious husband who thought it was *your* truck?"

Al smiled.

"It was somebody who knew how to use Mil-Spec explosives and detonators," he said. "Probably not an indignant husband but maybe a killer for the cartels or the folks in California."

"How much longer am I going to be in this bed?"

"Dr. Khatri says you're healing quickly. Something about the good physical shape you were in. You could be out in a day or two but you'll need another solid month or more for those ribs to heal."

A stabbing pain attacked my left side and I must have winced.

"How's the shoulder?"

"My whole left arm hurts and I have no strength in the hand. My grip wouldn't dent a peeled banana."

"Pain is weakness leaving the body."

"No, Al. Pain is the body telling you something is very wrong."

"Let's talk in a couple of days," he said.

Al left and a nurse came in and fussed with me a bit. Another nurse brought me dinner, if a guy could honestly call it that. A third nurse gave me medicine which, I am pretty certain, included a sleeping pill. A fourth nurse woke me around three in the morning to take my blood pressure and give me more pills.

On Monday morning, a big orderly helped me out of bed and into the bathroom. It was the first time I'd walked in nearly a week and a half and the muscles in my chest screamed in protest while my left shoulder and lower back sang a matching chorus. The orderly promised to drag me out of bed three times a day whether I liked it or not.

Constable Millet and Al walked in just before noon. Millet handed me a photocopy of a crudely-written letter.

"This arrived in the morning mail," he said. "Somebody seems to be taking the credit."

The letter referred to the "struggle of the common man" and proclaimed victory over "imperialist forces intent on globalization and capitalist hegemony." It was signed by Epanastatikos Agonas.

"Who is this 'Agonas' guy?" I asked.

"It's more of a what," said Al. "Translated, the name means 'Revolutionary Struggle.' It's been designated a terrorist group by both the U.S. and Greek governments."

I wondered how my truck had become a symbol of capitalist hegemony.

"A few months ago, they detonated a car bomb outside an office of the Bank of Greece," said Millet. "They used 75 kilos of explosives and nearly flattened the building."

"Why would they want to pop my car?"

"I have no idea. Did you see any unusual people near your truck or in the parking lot?"

"Just those two guys in the Mitsubishi. What are you going to do with that letter?"

"We'll keep it quiet as long as possible. We have people researching this organization, of course, but we're relying quite a bit on your FBI. Given that a U.S. citizen was killed…"

"Two," I said. "Don't forget about me."

"Yes, of course, two U.S. citizens. As I was saying, your FBI is working the case, too. Do you want to speak with them?"

"I'm dead. Let's keep it that way for now. It's not like I have anything useful to tell them anyway."

I read the letter again and it made just as little sense as it had the first time.

"Did the FBI ask for any samples of explosive residue?" I said.

"They sent one of their technicians over from Puerto Rico and he examined the wreckage."

"Most explosives have chemical markers. They should be able to track down the manufacturer."

"And they may share that information with me," he said, "if it is politically expedient. Or they may not. I'll do what I can on my own."

"I might be able to help, but I'll need some information from you."

I told him what I needed and he took notes.

"This may take me several days," he said.

"I'm not going anywhere soon."

14

MARIE walked into my room on Tuesday afternoon and threw her arms around me. My spirits rose more than a notch or two.

"How are you doing on that doctorate?"

Marie was open-mouthed.

"You're in a hospital bed ten days after dying and you're asking about my education?"

"It's important to you. That makes it important to me."

I was about to say something suggestive about other things important to me when a tall blond fellow with piercing blue eyes walked in. The man didn't appear to be a doctor and he wasn't a tourist, either. In the heat of a Caribbean summer, he wore a light blue button-down long-sleeved shirt and dark blue twill pants. He must have welcomed the relative cool of my hospital room. I didn't recognize him at all but the eyes looked vaguely familiar.

Marie turned toward him.

"Sim, this is Orson Flake," she said. "Eryn's uncle."

He stuck out his hand and I shook it.

"I am very sorry," I said.

"Constable Millet tells me that you bear no responsibility for what happened."

"Somebody does," I said.

"Mr. Flake and I are bringing you home to Stamford, tomorrow," said Marie. "The doctors say you'll be well enough to leave and all you need is rest and rehabilitative therapy for your arm and shoulder."

"We have excellent facilities in Stamford."

"I don't think I'd last the plane ride to JFK," I said. "And I'd like to keep a low profile right now."

"My plane has a very comfortable couch you can rest on," said Flake. "And nobody needs to know you're on it. We fly direct to Stamford tomorrow afternoon."

Flake could see the reluctance in my eyes.

"Marie, can Sim and I talk privately for a minute?"

She looked confused but agreed and walked out into the hallway. Flake pulled a chair to the right side of my bed and sat down. He waited a few moments as if rehearsing a speech he'd prepared earlier in the day.

"You knew Eryn," he said. "You knew how wonderful she was. How completely innocent and free of guile."

"Yes, I do."

"She was my late brother's daughter. We took her in when her parents passed."

He fidgeted in the chair.

"I've been quite successful in business and I have significant resources," he said. "I want to find out who did this and I want them brought to justice."

He stood up and walked over to the sink. He grabbed one of those little wrapped plastic cups they always keep for people who get thirsty. He tore off the wrapping, filled the cup, and drank the whole thing as if it were something more comforting than water.

"I've done some research, Mr. Greene. I know about your past."

"You shouldn't believe everything you read in a police report."

He smiled and filled the cup again.

"I'm putting together a team of trained investigators to locate the guilty parties. I want you to lead that team."

"I can barely brush my teeth. I don't see how I can be much help."

"Like I told you," he said. "I've done my research and I know who you are."

"I'm glad one of us does." I shook my head. He opened his mouth to speak but I cut him off. "What happens when you make a mistake in your business, Mr. Flake?"

"I've been doing it long enough that I don't make a lot of mistakes. But if something bad happens, well, maybe I'll lose some money. And somebody else might lose their job."

He sat back down in the chair.

"This is a different kind of enterprise," I said. "You make a mistake in *this* business, even a little one, and people die. Sometimes they are innocent people."

"That is why I need your help."

I shook my head again.

He looked down at his hands. We were quiet for nearly a half minute. A half minute can be a long time when you're grieving.

"What sort of business are you in?" I asked.

He raised his head.

"I own a leasing company. Machinery, airplanes, rolling stock. Some mid-sized business somewhere needs to expand their operations and they need new equipment. Maybe they don't want to tie up their capital or maybe they see a tax advantage in leasing. They call my company and we put the deal together."

"Have you put any deals together in Greece?"

His brow furrowed.

"No," he said. "Why?"

"Some Greek revolutionaries are claiming responsibility for the bomb. Something about the common man's struggle against capitalists."

He looked down at the floor.

"You say you've been successful in your business. Have you made any enemies along the way?"

He shook his head.

"They weren't trying to kill Eryn," he said. "Nobody would want to do that. And they weren't trying to get back at me for anything, either. It has nothing to do with my niece or my business. I've never even been to Greece. Not even on vacation."

I'd come to the same conclusion.

"They were trying to kill you." He leaned back in the chair and crossed his legs. "Do *you* have any idea who would want to do that?"

I took a deep breath. It hurt to breathe like that but the nurses insisted I do it and I didn't dare argue with them.

"I've been lying here on this bed for the last couple of days going through a list in my head. Names and faces from the past. Trying to think of anybody who would want me dead and gone."

My throat was dry and I reached over to the table for my glass of water.

"I honestly can't think of anyone." I took a drink from the glass. "Yet."

Flake cradled his left hand in his right and rubbed it while staring at a spot on the floor. He screwed up his nerve and looked back up at me.

"I've set aside some money. A fund we can use to find the people who killed my niece."

He told me how much.

"You could fund a small army with that," I said.

"I want you to be a part of that effort."

"I don't want your money. I'm not a paid killer."

He shook his head vigorously and stood up.

"I don't want them killed. I want these people captured and prosecuted and I want you to lead the team. My team."

The "team" aspect of Flake's proposal didn't appeal to me. I'd been a team player in high school but grew out of it.

"Right now, I can't even touch my toes. I can barely sit up in this bed without screaming from the pain in my chest."

He stood up and put his cup on the counter near the sink.

"But if you can give me some time to get patched up and can keep my survival a secret, I'll take you up on your offer. And I'll find those bastards."

He handed me a business card and walked out into the hallway.

15

MARIE walked back in, leaned over my hospital bed, and kissed me a second time. It felt good and real and worth living for.

"Don't they let you shave?" she asked.

"I'm in a hospital. A shave and a haircut costs fifteen hundred bucks."

"We'll take care of that when we get you back home in Stamford."

She stood up, dragged a chair closer to the bed, and sat down.

"How'd your meeting with the doctoral committee go?"

"They reviewed my draft and questioned some of my conclusions regarding home-schooled high-school students but it went well. There is more work to do before it'll be ready, though."

"I always thought home-schooling was for weirdos and misfits."

"Many of them do quite well," said Marie. "Eryn was one of my case studies. She was quite brilliant…"

I reached out and held her hand.

"I'm sorry," she said. "I'm still expecting her to walk through that door all bright and bouncing with joy."

There wasn't anything to say.

"I only hope they find the people who did this," she said. Her grip on my hand tightened. "I don't mean you, of course. That's not your job. Let the police track them down and deal with them."

"C'mon, you know me. I've never been much of a fighter."

"That's the problem," she said. "I *do* know you."

"I'm no knight in shining armor. And I'm still trying to learn how to breathe. Anyway, Constable Millet wants me out of the way so he can solve this on his own. I'm in no position to argue."

Another nurse walked into the room and fussed with me. Dr. Khatri followed a few minutes later and picked up a clipboard.

"How is he doing?" said Marie.

"His vital signs are remarkably robust for a dead man."

He wasn't looking at either Marie or me. He appeared to be talking to the clipboard while occasionally glancing at a machine that hummed and clicked on the other side of the bed. Checking my oxygen levels and blood pressure; reading about how much I'd eaten; seeing how much I'd peed.

"How are you feeling this morning, Mr. Glasgow?"

There was the slightest hint of conspiracy in his smile.

"Great," I said. "Is there a golf course nearby?"

"There is but you will not be on it for several months. Those ribs need time to heal." He looked at the clipboard again. "We can't splint them, of course. You can only rest and let them knit on their own. You now have an excellent opportunity to catch up on your reading."

"I read when I can."

He picked up the book that sat on the swing-away table and opened it.

"'Achilles' baneful wrath resound, O Goddess, that impos'd infinite sorrows on the Greeks, and many brave souls los'd from breasts heroic; sent them far to that invisible cave that no light comforts; and their limbs to dogs and vultures gave.'" He put the book back down. "That seems rather dark."

"A friend brought it. He's always trying to get me to read what he calls 'the good stuff.'"

"Come Friday morning, you may sit in your comfortable chair back on Tortola and read all you like."

"You're letting me out?"

"Tomorrow afternoon, if you continue to improve at this rate. Maybe the next day. I'd like to see you do a little better on your breathing performance and lung capacity, however."

"It hurts like mad to breathe."

"As it should," he said. "The lower lobes of both your lungs collapsed. Deep breathing helps those recover. But it's your choice. You can either endure serious but temporary pain now or get pneumonia and feel much worse for the rest of your life. Which may be shortened thereby."

A smile crossed Marie's lips.

"You can bring your book to Stamford," she said.

The doctor's brow furrowed.

"Not unless he's going by boat. While he has recovered quite nicely so far, the damage to his lungs was very serious. So there will be no flying, no SCUBA diving, no mountain climbing. Nothing particularly strenuous for several months and all of it at sea level."

Marie's smile faded.

16

FLAKE flew home that night in his jet. Marie hung around a bit longer but her life had to regain some normalcy and she flew home commercially Thursday morning. I couldn't blame her.

They released me late that afternoon but wouldn't let me walk out of the hospital. I had to leave in a wheelchair and a nurse had to push it all the way to the parking lot. She said it had something to do with liability insurance and lawyers. It made me wonder how many people died walking out of a hospital.

Al brought me back from St. Thomas on *In Depth II*. It was a smooth ride through Long Bay as Al opened up the big turbocharged diesel and brought our dive boat up on a plane. The open sea was a little rougher as we flew past the charter boats and ferry traffic in the evening twilight and my ribs hurt from the jarring ride. Nobody seemed to notice that Al hadn't bothered to clear either of us through customs and immigration. After all, Sim Greene was dead.

Al throttled down as we approached Sea Cow Bay and I was glad to see my boat exactly where I'd left her that Saturday morning before the world ended in a white hot flash. Al nudged the boat next to *Figaro* and I grabbed her starboard shrouds with my good hand and stepped aboard her side deck.

"I'll be back in an hour or so," said Al.

I nodded and Al goosed the throttle and waddled out of Sea Cow Bay.

A boat doesn't like to be ignored. After a while, she gets upset.

She'll shake her boom back and forth and start to dance around her anchor. She might get lonely and allow algae and barnacles to set up housekeeping on the hull. Mold could take up residency in the bilges. Entropy is magnified by the sea.

I unlocked the companionway hatch, went below, and flicked on the cabin lights. The air below was musty so I opened the forward hatch and let in the faint breeze. By chance, I hadn't left much food in the boat's fridge—just a chunk of hard salami and three slices of blue-green bread—or the cabin would have reeked. I tossed the bread into the trash and moved on to check the electrical panel.

On the bulkhead next to the electrical panel hung a small five-by-seven picture of my parents and two sisters sitting on the lawn in the backyard. Mom had sent me the photo nearly twenty years earlier when I was still a young seaman in the Navy. It arrived a week before the accident.

"I haven't joined you all, yet."

I checked the voltage in the two house batteries and smiled at the news. Even though it had been nearly two weeks without running the engine, the solar panels I'd installed months earlier had kept the batteries charged. I grabbed a flashlight and went back up on deck.

Figaro had fared well in my absence with only a little extra bird guano on her topsides and some chafe on the anchor snubbing line. I had the urge to grab my bucket and brush and clean her off but I didn't have the strength and I didn't want my flashlight to attract attention from shore. Sim Greene was dead and he needed to stay that way.

I sat in the darkness of the cockpit and listened to the sounds of the ocean. It felt good to be out of the hospital and back on my own boat.

Al returned in my dinghy with two bags of groceries. He clambered over the port lifelines and I tied the dinghy off to a stern cleat one-handed. Al took the bags below and I started *Figaro*'s diesel engine. We weighed anchor and motored out to sea. Al raised the mainsail and unfurled the jib as I turned *Figaro* to the southwest.

"You're almost useful for a power boater," I said.

"Yeah, I'm a real Renaissance man."

He went below and returned with two cold bottles of beer.

"I can't have any alcohol while on these pain meds," I said.

"That's why I only brought two. Shall we head to Norman Island?"

"Too crowded. And the boys over at the *Willie-T* would recognize *Figaro* in a heartbeat. There's that little harbor on Peter Island. The one without any moorings."

Al nodded.

"How long are you gonna hide out?"

"I have no idea. My left arm is tingly and weak; nearly dead weight. Dr. Khatri says I need therapy and rest."

"It'll all come back," he said. "You just need time."

The night sky was clear and crisp and the northeast breeze steady as we sailed to Peter Island.

"I need to use the head," said Al. "You okay?"

I nodded and Al went below. Normally, in conditions like these and under this point of sail, *Figaro*'s helm would be light with little or no tendency to round up to weather. Fingertip sailing. Tonight, however, it was all I could do to keep her on course. My ribs ached and my left arm was useless. The wind increased slightly as we got farther from Tortola and the helm felt heavier. After a few minutes, I was sweating under the effort; effort I wouldn't normally feel.

A puff of wind hit and the force tore *Figaro*'s wheel from my hand. She heeled over and rounded up into the wind. I could hear things falling and being thrown about the cabin. Al clambered up into the cockpit, eased the mainsheet, and got us back on course.

"What the hell? I barely had time to do my business."

"I can't even sail my own boat."

"Take it easy on yourself. You were dead a few days ago."

"I'm still dead. Or, at least, just as useful."

Forty minutes later, Al dropped the bow anchor in twelve feet of water east of two unoccupied sailboats. The existing vessels were situated stern-to the beach with lines running aft and tied to trees that stretched over the water. Al pulled *Figaro*'s stern line into the dinghy, rowed ashore in the dark, and tied the line to another stout trunk. He came back and I watched him adjust the lines fore and aft until *Figaro* lay abreast of the other two vessels. Three old fiberglass sailboats sitting in the dark.

Al grabbed a flashlight, turned it on, and examined my face.

"You don't look so great," he said. "You gonna be all right out here? Are you good for a couple of days?"

"Where there are no alternatives, there are no problems."

"I'll come out Sunday and bring you some more grub." He pulled a cell phone out of his pocket and handed it to me. "New number; new identity. Call me if you're having problems or need anything special."

I nodded.

Al clambered back down into the dinghy, fired up the outboard, and scooted out into the Sir Francis Drake Channel toward Road Town four miles away. It was nearly eleven at night. I stepped down into the cabin, lay down on the starboard settee, and let *Figaro* rock me to sleep. It took seconds.

17

I slept like a dead man until the sun rose high enough to punch its way through the companionway and into my eyes. My ribs were sore and my left arm ached but I managed to get up to find some cheese, crackers, and an apple to eat. That simple task wore me out and I sat back on the settee to catch my breath. The summer sun beat down on *Figaro* and the cabin became a sauna. I grabbed a bottle of water, climbed into the cockpit, sat under the bimini and listened to a goat kid on the shore cry for its mother.

After a few minutes, I felt strong enough to let myself down the boarding ladder and into the water. I swam around *Figaro* on my back sculling with my right arm and frog-kicking with my legs. My left arm trailed in the water. But the water was cool and I felt better floating in it. I tried to pull myself back onto the boarding ladder but couldn't do it. Searing pain shot through my left side and I could almost hear pieces of my broken ribs grinding against each other. I looped my right arm around one of the rungs of the ladder and floated there feeling stupid for having bitten off more than I could chew.

After some rest, I sculled over to the beach and crawled into the shade of a sea grape tree. The damp, cool sand felt good on my back. Marie joined me moments later lying next to me on the sand and I wondered how this could be. She looked at me with those deep brown eyes framed by jet black hair and spoke words I couldn't understand. She kissed my cheek. I woke to a wild island goat sniffing my face. I yelled in surprise and the goat scampered off into the trees and up the hill.

Dark red sea grapes hung from the tree above me and I remembered an old islander extolling their medicinal qualities. I reached up, grabbed a few, and ate them. They were mostly pit but still tasted good. I lay back down in the sand and fell asleep.

The sun had arced quite a bit during my nap but sleep had brought additional strength and I was able to stand. I walked over to where Al had tied *Figaro*'s stern line and checked the knots. It was an unnecessary exercise in caution; Al was a superlative seaman. But years of living on a boat had taught me to recheck tied lines.

I reentered the water and swam back to *Figaro*. My left arm felt a little better and I was able to grasp the boarding ladder with my fingers. It hurt to board the boat but I made it. I stood in the cockpit, dropped my shorts, and rinsed off the salt water. A dull ache and nausea spread across my body and I had to lie down on a cockpit bench to catch my breath. I lay there for about twenty minutes before I had the strength to go below and put on dry clothes.

I grabbed my new phone.

"D.C. Millet. How may I help you?"

"Stewart Glasgow, here."

"What? Oh, I didn't recognize the number."

"New name, new phone, new number. Any progress on that info I need?"

"You asked for it two days ago."

"And?"

"And these things take time," he said. "But I will follow up on it. You should focus on recovering from your injuries, my friend."

I told the usual lies—I felt great; I didn't need anything; my recovery was coming along fine—and we hung up.

A squall blew in and I closed hatches and dogged ports to keep the rain out. As a precaution, I checked the usual things down below: seacocks, water level in the tanks, bilge dry and pump operating. The batteries were still in the green arc but I'd need to charge them in the morning. Waiting was fine with me. I didn't feel like climbing into the cockpit to start the engine. But it was also too early for bed. I reached for my new phone again. She picked up on the second ring.

"How are you this afternoon?" I asked.

"Sim?" said Marie. "Did you get a new phone number?"

"Yes. But please don't spread it around."

There was a long pause on her end.

"Because you're hiding."

"My current survival strategy."

"How are you feeling?"

"Doctor Khatri says I'll recover. But right now I'm completely wiped out."

"We sort of missed that early August vacation, didn't we?"

"We can make up for it later."

"I'm going to talk to my doctoral mentor and see if I can take some time off. I want to come down there and take care of you."

"Bad idea. You've got to finish what you started. How much longer will it take you?"

"I don't know. The research and analysis is all done. I just need to turn it all into a coherent dissertation. Then I have to stand there in front of these stuffy professors and defend the thing."

"Can you get all that done by Thanksgiving?"

"Maybe."

"No problem, then. You focus on finishing your doctoral stuff and I'll focus on building a new rib cage. Then you fly down for the holidays."

"Okay," she said. "Thanks for supporting me."

We said our goodbyes and hung up.

The squall moved southwest and I reopened the hatches to get some ventilation down below. I wondered about the other two boats in the anchorage. Neither had shown an anchor light or cabin lights the previous night and I'd not seen any crew aboard. As far as I could tell, they both were empty. No complaints, here. Solitude was my friend.

I wanted to get in the water again to cool off but feared I might not be able to get back aboard. The sun set behind the hill west of me and the sea grape trees grew dark. A line of shadows climbed the hill across the harbor.

Hunger returned and I went below to make dinner. Al had bought premium stuff the previous night and I looked forward to it. I needed protein to heal so I opened a package of smoked turkey and ate it with water crackers and a can of apricot halves.

Out of habit, I tuned *Figaro's* shortwave receiver to the weather report. Iron Mike—NOAA's computer-synthesized weatherman—announced the formation of a new tropical depression west of the Cape Verde islands in the Atlantic. He referred to it by its assigned number and I realized I'd missed two big tropical storms in the two weeks since the explosion. Explosion? Not the right word for it. It wasn't just an explosion. That could happen by accident. This had been well-planned and expertly executed.

All those thoughts ran through my head while Iron Mike described the new tropical depression. His mechanical voice predicted that the Eastern Caribbean would be unaffected. He promised further information as it became available.

I shut off the radio and the cabin lights and crawled off to bed thinking of the unavoidable hurricane on its way. The one building up inside me.

18

SATURDAY was much like Friday. I slept in longer than usual and ate tinned fish with instant coffee. Protein and caffeine; breakfast of champions. I normally made French press—Al says I'm a "coffee snob"—but grappling with a *cafetière à piston* and a pot of boiling water with only one good arm didn't seem like a great idea. Thankfully, the instant coffee I had was an upscale variety a friend had sent from Germany. It wasn't the best—it tasted earthy; like old cow manure with chocolate overtones—but it was better than nothing and it washed the fish down.

I climbed into the cockpit and started *Figaro*'s engine to top off the batteries. It's a two-hour task so I grabbed one of the books Al had loaned me and sat down in the cockpit to read. The author had lived through the horror of the holocaust. Having seen a lot of death at both Auschwitz and Dachau, he still had some good things to say about life. The story was amazing and shocking and riveting all at once and I became so engrossed in his account that I almost forgot to shut off the engine at the appointed time.

I hit the halfway point of the book and fell asleep in the cockpit. Hours later, a rain storm blew into the harbor and soaked me. The cooling breeze felt invigorating and I grabbed the boat brush to scrub *Figaro*'s topsides. The storm moved on and took the breeze with it. Heat and humidity returned and sweat rolled off my back and down my legs. But I'd overestimated my stamina and made it only halfway down the port side deck before exhaustion set in. Back in the cockpit, I sat down in the shade of the bimini with my back against the cabin bulkhead.

Figaro moved a little and a hand reached up from the boarding ladder. A young woman climbed into the cockpit and sat on the bench across from me. I recognized her and wanted to speak but couldn't. It was Eryn. But it wasn't the tanned, animated, happy Eryn I'd seen weeks earlier. She was pasty white with worry spread across her face. Her head shook back and forth as she stared into my eyes.

The sound of twin diesel engines drew my attention and I turned to see a large catamaran enter the harbor; off-season charterers looking for a decent place to drop the hook. I looked back toward Eryn but she was gone.

I went below and splashed water in my face.

You're hallucinating, Sim. Eryn is dead and what's left of her is buried somewhere in Connecticut. She's not climbing into anybody's boat.

I poured some more water into a glass and drank it. I'd been stressed by overexertion but felt fine now. I climbed back up into the cockpit. The chartered cat was gone.

I was about to swim ashore when my phone rang.

"I'm coming out Monday afternoon," said Al. "Are you good until then?"

"Sure."

"You need anything?"

I told him what to bring and he agreed.

"How are you feeling?"

"Good, I guess."

"You guess?"

"I saw Eryn a few minutes ago. Right here in *Figaro*'s cockpit."

Al was quiet a moment.

"What pills did that doctor give you for pain?"

I told him.

"Take it easy on the pills."

"I'm not taking any more than he prescribed."

"Cut back anyway. There's no advantage to hallucinating

visitations from the dead."

"Okay."

"Are you good until Monday? Or do I need to get out there tonight?"

"I'll be fine," I said. "See you Monday."

I made a sandwich, drank some water, and listened to the weather report again. Nothing new to worry about. I turned off the radio and sat down on the settee.

A ship's horn sounded and I woke with a start. It was dark outside the companionway. I looked at my watch and realized I'd slept over four hours. My ribs hurt as I sat up but I needed to give the boat a last check before turning in. The anchor chain forward and stern line aft were both secure, the halyards bungeed away from the mast, and the mainsail tied tight against the boom. Everything shipshape.

I went below, turned on the anchor light, and made my bed on the starboard settee. Despite napping most of the day, I fell asleep almost instantly.

I woke shortly after sunrise Sunday morning feeling two hundred percent better than I had the previous day. My left arm felt stronger but my ribs still hurt like mad when I did my breathing exercises. I turned on the radio and set to crafting a real breakfast. I cooked a half-pound of bacon, fried three eggs in the fat, and toasted a couple slices of bread in the greasy pan. I pulled a pint of milk out of the fridge and carried it all over to the dinette.

A preacher came on the radio and launched into his sermon with a vigor rarely heard in the States. There was no question about it. He had the Caribbean fire and he was going to shake the hell out of his listeners. Forgiveness was good; revenge bad. Jacob cheated Esau out of his birthright and Esau was hopping mad about it. He fumed and he waited and he plotted the death of his brother. Jacob's momma heard about these goings-on and she told Jacob to pack it up and get out of town. It broke up the whole family. The preacher closed out the tale by concluding that even if we thought we had the moral right to get even—to get some delicious and deserved payback—we shouldn't ever do it. It would ruin our souls in the end.

I had to change the channel. I'd committed myself to the revenge business the moment Al showed me the bits of military-grade hardware somebody had used to kill Eryn. No well-meaning fire-and-brimstone Caribbean preacher was going to slow me down.

Well, Sim, I thought, *if you're going into the revenge business, you'd better get in shape for it.*

I washed and dried the breakfast dishes, climbed into the cockpit, and dove into the water. I felt stronger and swam to the beach and back three times. I went ashore, picked several bunches of sea grapes, and ended my workout by swimming back to *Figaro* a fourth time. The boarding ladder was not nearly the obstacle it had been the day before. I went below and napped again.

The sun was out and wispy clouds floated across the sky. A light breeze took the edge off the heat but did nothing to abate the humidity. I felt strong enough to go up on deck and finish cleaning *Figaro's* topsides. My left hand and arm still hurt but painful use was better than no use at all. And I had this inner suspicion that the pain helped somehow.

After two hours of laboring in the thick heat, the deck gleamed and I felt more alive than I had in weeks. My ribs still hurt but I was able to let myself down the boarding ladder again and let the sea hold me. I hooked my feet under the stern line and floated on my back with my ears under the water. Clouds formed and floated over the harbor and out to sea in complete silence. I heard no motors or birds or insects. No slapping of halyards against masts. No people babbling nonsense. I thought how good it was to be alive and wondered how long it would take for me to fully recover.

I boarded my boat, made dinner, and ate it in the cockpit. Night fell and darkness settled over the small harbor. The lights of Tortola flickered on one by one and the pinpricks of a trillion stars flickered in the black sky. I lay on the port cockpit bench and looked at the stars.

The vision of Eryn climbing into my truck came back, however, and the pool of white hot anger I'd fought back while in the hospital returned. Somebody had killed my friend and I had to find those responsible. There were things to do and a trail to follow; a trail that cooled with every day I sat in that anchorage.

19

I slept in the next morning but the summer sun rose high and the heat soon drove me off the boat and into the water. I felt good so I swam the three hundred yards to the opposite shore, rested a few minutes, and swam back. A minor squall blew into the anchorage as I climbed back into *Figaro*'s cockpit. Rain fell in sheets. I grabbed a bar of soap out of the head and showered on deck. The rain moved on and I toweled dry, went below, and made a sandwich.

Just when I thought the day might kill me with boredom, the monotony was interrupted by the sound of *In Depth II* blasting into the harbor. Al and Constable Millet came aboard with several bags of food and three six-packs of beer. Al stowed the provisions and then brought up several cold ones from the cabin. We sat under the bimini and drank. Millet handed me a small thumb drive.

"I had to call in more than a few personal favors to get this for you."

"Is it all there?"

"Everything you asked for. Even the cruise ship manifests."

I took it below and plugged it into my laptop. The thumb drive was filled with scanned Customs and Immigration documents. Entry forms, passport scans, daily reports. I created a new subdirectory on my laptop and named it "Eryn." I highlighted all of the files on the thumb drive, set them to be copied over, and climbed up into the cockpit.

"Customs and Immigration would be very displeased if they knew I had brought these records out to you."

"Let's not tell them."

He leaned back against the cockpit coaming and drank some of his beer and we talked about me recovering and getting stronger.

"I'm only interested in your getting well," he said. "I don't want to know what you and Mr. Higgins intend to do with the information I just gave you."

"Of course," I said. "How's the investigation going?"

"Not a single lead. Your FBI sent two fellows down to look around but all they did was complain about how we'd failed to preserve the crime scene to their liking. They found nothing, gave up, and flew home."

"That's it? Seriously?"

"That doesn't sound like the FBI to me," said Al.

"It was disappointing to say the least," said Millet.

A beep sounded; the files had transferred. I went below, retrieved the thumb drive, and gave it back to the Constable.

"Well," said Millet. "I suppose I should get back to Road Town."

He and Al handed me their empties as they stepped back aboard *In Depth II.*

"Sim," said Millet. "I do want to find the people who killed Dale and Eryn and the others and will help you in any way I can."

"But without really knowing about it," I said. "Right?"

Al laughed and Millet shrugged. The boat's big turbocharged diesel roared into life and Al piloted the boat out of *Figaro's* little harbor. I went below to look at what Millet had brought me.

The information included subdirectories for each Customs and Immigration entry point into and out of the BVI: the main airport at Trellis Bay, the ferry terminal at West End, the head office in Road Town, the Virgin Gorda Airport, and the smaller offices at Spanish Town, Gun Creek, and Great Harbour. Each of these subdirectories contained additional folders organized by date. They spanned the period from six days before the attack to three days after. Seven offices worth of international visitors over a ten-day period.

Most of the folders held hundreds of files. Each file consisted of an entry or exit document, a photograph or two, and a scanned print of a passport's main page. I added up the files in my head and realized that, even in the slow summer months, the BVI attracted over a thousand tourists a day. That number didn't include the tourists arriving by cruise ship: another ten thousand over the nine-day period. I put those on the back burner because the cruise ships rarely stayed more than one night. An assassin, however, would need to spend a few days tracking me down and observing my habits.

The information was thorough. Purpose of visit, length of stay, hotel or boat name (if chartering), and in-country contact info were all listed on the entry documents. Over ten thousand people, each with multiple documents and pictures, to examine.

Every project demands a process. I opened a spreadsheet on my laptop and created a row of labels at the top: name, entry date, intended length of stay, lodging, exit date, and probability score. The last was a number I assigned between one and ten.

Single travelers got a high score. So did visitors from California and South America. Boat charterers staying seven days or more earned low numbers. Families earned a low score, too. Assassins don't generally bring their kids along on a hit job. The same logic extended to large groups traveling together. But there are outliers and everybody would be entered into the spreadsheet. It was all about the process.

Playing the odds, I started with the first day of files from the West End office. I figured it would be easier for a killer to bring explosives into the country on a ferry than an airliner. I took my time reviewing the pictures and the documents and entering the data into the spreadsheet. There was no reason to hurry.

Nothing stood out in that first group of files. Nothing struck a chord. No familiar faces. No names from the past.

My eyes started to blur around ten o'clock that first night and I figured it would be better to knock off and get some sleep rather than risk missing an important connection. I shut down the laptop and crawled into my berth.

I woke with a strengthened resolve to continue the process of profiling tourists. When I finished with one customs and immigration office for a particular day, I moved on to a different entry point. It was slow tedious work and *Figaro*'s cabin got hotter and more humid as the day wore on despite having every port and hatch open. But I stayed focused on the project. I didn't know exactly who or what I was looking for but I resisted the urge to rush things. I didn't want to miss anything important.

The process turned into a routine. Wake early, swim, eat, and read through customs files hoping to find an assassin. It was a subjective and flawed process but it was something to do; something that might reveal the murderer. It was aggravating and mind-numbing work and I couldn't do it for more than an hour at a time. When my head got too full of pictures and documents, I'd take another swim or make a meal or clean up the boat. I became frustrated at the slow pace. At night, I dreamed of immigration records and passports.

I found what I was looking for Thursday morning.

20

HE almost slipped past me. I'd looked at Jacques Dehlin's passport photo, reviewed his entry documents, and gave him a high probability score. I was about to enter it into my spreadsheet and move on to the next file when the little voice piped up. I took another, longer look at the photo and got a strong visceral feeling deep down in my reptilian brain that Mr. Dehlin was a guy I should examine more closely.

He'd arrived in a chartered aircraft two days before the attack. A smart move. Nobody screens your luggage, pats you down, or has their dog sniff your carry-on when you're getting on a chartered plane in the States. The BVI has two airports with Customs offices. His plane had landed at the airport on Virgin Gorda avoiding the larger international airport at Trellis Bay. He'd probably taken the local ferry to Road Town.

Getting past the local Customs and Immigration folks on Virgin Gorda wouldn't be much of a trick. A guy could hide enough C-4 to destroy a truck inside a hollowed-out salami. The detonation materials and switches could be shoved into the bottom of a camera case hidden under all the cords, chargers, and batteries packed by the typical tourist.

That's probably how Al would have done it.

Still, I didn't know for sure this guy was responsible. I needed more.

He'd come into the country with one other passenger; a guy named Hunter Reynolds. I reviewed their exit documents and found that both of them had flown to Puerto Rico on the same commercial flight from Trellis Bay. That flight left only an hour after I'd been rolled into the hospital in St. Thomas. There was no reason they couldn't fly commercially, of course. They'd already used the explosives.

Their travel and entry documents indicated they were both from Texas. Who in Texas wanted to kill me? They listed a bed and breakfast on their entry forms as their local address. It was a nice place near Cane Garden Bay.

I grabbed my cell phone and punched number two on the speed dial.

"Whassup?"

"I think there were two of them," I said.

"Yes."

"Yes what?"

"Yes, I'm in," said Al. "I want a piece of this. Who are they?"

I told him about the bed and breakfast near Cane Garden Bay and asked him to find out if they'd actually stayed there and, if so, to get as much information about them as possible. I transferred the passport photos to my phone and texted them to him. I could hear the increased excitement in his voice before we hung up. He was all in.

I scrolled through my contacts list and made another call.

"Sim?"

"I may have found them."

I heard a small intake of breath.

"Who did it?" asked Constable Millet. "And why?"

"I'm not sure. But I'm certain they aren't local. So I'll be travelling soon."

"You won't just hand it over to the authorities?"

"It's too thin. I have to build a case for them. The immediate problem is that I can't use my U.S. passport. I'm dead, you see."

"I can see how that *would* present a problem."

"So I need a BVI passport. One for Stewart Glasgow but with my photo. A different name, perhaps, but the initials will match my monogrammed shirts."

"I don't believe I have ever seen you wear a monogrammed shirt."

"Well, you get the idea. I need a new passport."

"You are asking me to do something that violates international law. I won't do that."

"Screw international law. I'm on the trail of these killers and I want to follow it."

"I should report this to the FBI."

"You could. It might even be a fine idea. But they didn't seem all that interested a few days ago."

He didn't have an answer to that.

"These killers murdered two of your government officials as well as Eryn and Dale. That doesn't motivate you to bend a few rules?"

"I will not violate international law. I can't help you."

And he hung up.

I sat down and tried to think of any connections I still had who could get me a decent fake passport. The latest improvements in technology were a significant hindrance. Barcodes, holographic seals, and banks of internationally-networked computers compounded the problem. Gone were the days when a guy could find a usable counterfeit passport from a talented forger in a Tijuana back alley.

Maybe Al had a source. He could get his hands on almost anything.

He called me three hours later.

"I drove over to that B&B in Cane Garden. Those two guys didn't have reservations there and the owner never saw them. So I drove over to the airport and showed their pictures to the usual crowd of taxi drivers."

"And?"

"And none of them remember picking up those two guys."

"Great."

"But Briney—you remember him, right?"

"The older guy who picks up charter groups?"

"Yeah," said Al. "He told me the RVIP found a stolen car at the airport the morning after the explosion. It was a white Jeep owned by a lady who runs a B&B near Josiah's Bay. So I drove over to her place and showed her the pictures."

"What'd you find out?"

"Jacques Dehlin and Hunter Reynolds checked into separate rooms a few hours after they landed on Virgin Gorda. I took photos of the room registration documents."

"Does the owner remember anything about them?"

"They rented her Jeep at twice the going rate and kept it for three days. They left it at the airport Saturday afternoon with the keys in the glove box. When they didn't return the car, she reported it stolen. The cops found it but the guys had left three hundred-dollar bills next to the car keys and the owner suddenly felt better about things. She decided it was no big deal and the cops dropped it."

"How about the credit card they used to reserve the room?"

"Counterfeit. But they paid for the rooms in cash so the owner called it good. No skin off her nose, right?"

Al texted me the pictures he'd taken of the hotel registration documents and I loaded them onto my laptop. They both gave addresses from The Woodlands, Texas, and both listed their occupations as "Research Scientist."

Nice try, guys, but it didn't work. We are going to find you.

An idea popped into my head.

I opened my laptop again and pulled up Jacques Dehlin's passport photo. What if the guy had dyed his hair and restyled it before the trip? What if he had shaved off any facial hair? What if he didn't really wear glasses?

Before I could afford an electronic chart plotter, I used paper charts and thin sketching paper to plot *Figaro's* courses and positions. Electronic gizmos occasionally die, so I keep my old paper charts rolled up in a piece of plastic pipe and stored under my quarter berth. I located the pipe, unrolled the charts, and found a few pieces of the old sketching paper lodged between two charts.

I enlarged Jacques Dehlin's photo on my laptop, taped the paper over the screen, and used a pencil to trace the photo onto the paper. I pulled it off the screen, erased the glasses, and changed the hair a little. I experimented with beards and mustaches.

Despite my lack of artistic skills, the real culprit emerged. He'd done his best to alter his appearance but he couldn't do much to hide the cleft in his chin.

I grabbed my phone.

"I figured out who one of those guys is."

"Who is he?" said Al.

"He wrote me a fix-it ticket in Georgia."

"Seriously?"

I told him about Mitch Danforth: local cop and *Sidoni* doorman.

"Why would he go after you?"

"Must've been something I said."

"What's the plan?"

"I haven't got one, yet."

"We've got time," said Al. "Business couldn't be slower. August is already crap and I don't think September or October will be any better. We'd probably save money by closing up shop until after the tourists start coming down around Thanksgiving."

He was right about business being slow during the summer. Even if we had been busy, though, it wouldn't have mattered. We both had our priorities straight and knew what had to be done.

"We need to think this through," I said.

"Let's take our time and do it right. Identify the target, plan the mission, and execute the plan."

"What about Liv? Will she be okay with this?"

"She's in New Zealand with her dad. He's got pancreatic cancer and will probably be gone by Christmas. She went home to take care of him. I suppose she'll want to stay and settle his affairs when it's over." He paused a moment. "And we're taking a little break, anyway."

I hadn't seen that one coming.

"Sorry to hear about all that. I had no idea."

"You've been out of the loop."

"That's one way of putting it."

I ended the call with him and redialed the Constable. I told him about my two suspects. I told him how they'd come into the country on a chartered plane and how they'd smuggled in plastic explosives and a detonating mechanism with a mercury switch.

"I'm pretty sure these assassins came from Serenity, Georgia; from that church your daughter joined."

"I should report this to the FBI."

"If my theory is right, your daughter is with some dangerous people. People who know how to kill and aren't the least bit reluctant to do so. If you contact the FBI, word could get back to that church. That would put Dorothea in extreme danger."

Millet was silent.

"The best way to protect your daughter is to keep Sim Greene dead. They have to believe they got away with killing me. I need that passport."

He was conflicted; torn between the law and his family.

"I will have it for you early next week."

"One more thing. Did anything unusual or newsworthy happen in St. Croix the day your daughter flew to the States?"

"I could call my counterpart over in Christiansted. She would know. But what are you looking for?"

"I don't know. I've just got a hunch."

My mind raced through several different possible scenarios. Different ways of approaching the problem. Each option had its strengths and weaknesses. All of them had one thing in common, though; the need for more information—intel we didn't have.

I thought of somebody who could help and called him. He asked a lot of questions. I answered some of them. In the end, he agreed to get me what I needed.

21

I woke the next morning with the pleasant realization that while my ribs still hurt, my left arm felt normal and functioned properly. I celebrated by eating breakfast, swimming to the beach, and resting under the sea grape tree.

The familiar drone of our dive boat grew louder as it approached the little harbor. I walked into the water and swam toward *Figaro* as Al tied up to her starboard rail. Dr. Khatri appeared and stepped onto my boat as I reached the boarding ladder.

"I must say that I am surprised to see you swimming so easily, Mr. Glasgow. Do you need any assistance getting out?"

I shook my head as I climbed the boarding ladder and stepped into the cockpit.

"Doctors now cross international borders to make house calls?"

"Mr. Higgins insisted that I come out to examine you. He can be, shall we say, rather persuasive."

Al smiled as he transferred several bags of provisions from *In Depth II*'s deck to *Figaro*'s galley. I grabbed a towel, dried off, and sat down on the port cockpit bench.

"Go for it," I said.

Dr. Khatri sat on the bench across from me and pulled a stethoscope and blood pressure cuff from a small canvas bag. He put the cuff around my good arm, pumped it, and listened to the stethoscope as he released pressure and loosened the cuff. He asked me to take deep breaths and listened to various areas of my chest and back. He examined ears, throat, and eyes; he spent a lot of time looking at my eyes. He probed and prodded my limbs testing strength, coordination, and reflexes. He asked about pain and I realized that my ribs did not hurt nearly as much as they had the previous day.

"What have you been doing to recuperate?"

"Swimming, reading, sleeping. Taking those pills you gave me. Am I doing the right things?"

"Apparently. Quite frankly, you're in much better physical shape than I expected."

"Sorry to disappoint you," I said.

"Disappointed? Delighted would be a better word."

"He's doing well?" asked Al.

"Amazingly so," he said. The doctor turned back to me. "You were dead three weeks ago. You were barely well enough for us to release you from the hospital eight days ago. And now here you are swimming in the ocean and climbing a ladder into this boat and not complaining nearly as much about pain as I'd expect. You're suffering the lingering side effects of a concussion but you are in astoundingly good physical shape and I have no medical explanation for it."

"Clean hands and a pure heart."

"Hah," said Al.

"Whatever it is you're doing, please continue."

Doctor Khatri was still shaking his head when Al helped him aboard *In Depth II* and cast off the boat's lines. I watched them leave the harbor and turn back toward St. Thomas.

My phone rang as I stepped down the companionway into the cabin.

"How are you doing?" asked Marie.

"I just saw the doctor. He says I'm recovering faster than he'd anticipated."

"That's wonderful. Has Constable Millet found the people who did this?"

"I don't think he has a single lead. He doesn't have the resources for this kind of investigation. He says the FBI is working on it but I don't think they have their hearts in it."

"Dad knows people in the FBI. Should I ask him to check into it?"

"I thought he was on the defense side of things."

"He oversaw white-collar prosecutions at the DOJ. He worked with the FBI all the time. I'm sure he still knows people there and he'd do anything for you."

"Does he even know I'm still alive?"

"Yes," she said. "I told him. I had to. You're one of his absolute favorite people and he was heartbroken. Did I do the wrong thing?"

"He's a lawyer. He knows how to keep a secret."

"Unlike his daughter, I suppose."

"Don't bug him about it," I said. "The FBI knows how to do their thing."

"He'd love to hear from you. How long will you be hiding out on your little boat?"

Is it wrong to tell a lie if you are trying to protect somebody else? Telling the truth could certainly put Al and me in danger. But, if my theory were correct, it could also endanger Dorothea.

"Al thinks I should take *Figaro* outside the hurricane zone and get some rest while the cops sort it all out. Maybe go as far south as Carriacou or Grenada. Tyrell Bay wouldn't be such a bad place to chill for a few months."

"I'll come down and go with you. I can sail the boat while you rest."

"That would be marvelous but Al says he can help me. And you've got to finish your thesis or dissertation or whatever."

We talked more about her dissertation and us getting together for Thanksgiving. When the conversation trailed off, we did the adult thing and hung up. Being an adult can be difficult.

Very early in my naval career, an experienced Chief Petty Officer told me the ocean didn't hate me or love me or even notice me. It didn't "give a rip"—his exact words—who I was or what I thought.

But it would smack me hard if I didn't pay attention, take everything into account, and make sure my vessel was seaworthy and prepared for the worst the sea could dish out.

Figaro had a long sail ahead of her and I needed to check every piece of her gear from stem to stern. I found only a few issues: the headsail furling drum had a corroded cotter pin, a few hose clamps needed tightening, and the crankcase was a half-quart low. All were easy fixes. Even Kyle—my faithful self-steering windvane—got a little extra grease in his gears.

Marie's words came back to me several times during the day. By dinnertime, I'd talked myself into calling her dad.

"This is David."

"Remember me?" I said.

"Of course. Are you okay?"

"Feeling much better."

"We were shocked at the news. I can't tell you how relieved I was to hear you survived."

"I nearly didn't."

"Marie says you are, shall we say, keeping a low profile?"

"Absolutely. Are you still an attorney?"

"I hate it when friends ask me that. It means they're in trouble. Which jail are you calling from?"

"Funny, but I'm not in jail. I need a favor. Do you still have friends in the FBI?"

"Yes."

I heard a metric ton of caution in that one word.

"I was a Deputy Attorney General, a political appointee, for six years. I worked with good, talented career people."

"Okay," I said.

"What's this about? Why are you asking me about my time in the Justice Department?"

"This is going to sound odd, but I'd like you to ask around about a church in Georgia. It's called *Sidoni*." I spelled it for him.

"A church? In Georgia? Does this have anything to do with your accident?"

"The guy who saved my life has a daughter who joined *Sidoni* and he's not sure it's legit. He's worried about her and I owe him."

"I'll check into it."

"Don't mention me or the BVI at all. Part of that low profile, okay?"

"Entirely confidential," he said. "All part of the attorney-client privilege."

"Thanks."

"When do we see you next?"

"Not for a while. I'm going to lie low for a couple of months."

"Marie has suggested that we bring *D'Artagnan* down for Thanksgiving and Christmas."

D'Artagnan was David's sixty-foot wooden schooner. Completely rebuilt at tremendous expense, she combined classic old-world looks with the most modern amenities.

"I can't imagine any better place to be for the holidays," I said.

"Agreed. We shall see you then."

I spent Saturday and Sunday attending to the things I hadn't finished on Friday and scrubbing the hull with a piece of old carpet. That task wore me out quickly, though, and I had to break it up into several sessions. But the work got done. By Sunday night, *Figaro* was ready.

Al called Monday morning. We talked about the trip and decided on what we needed to get underway. The list was short. He promised to bring the extra provisions and fuel in the evening and hung up. I tried to call Marie. Her line went directly to voice mail.

"I'm feeling good right now and just wanted you to know," I said. "Al and I set sail tomorrow morning and you might not hear from me for some time. But I'll be okay. And I love you."

My phone rang an hour later. I recognized the number.

"It's my favorite lawyer," I said.

"Calling his favorite single-handed sailor."

"What's up, counselor?"

"It's about that church you mentioned," said David. "One of my former colleagues at the DOJ says it's legitimate. 'Weird but legitimate' were her exact words."

"Thanks. That might help my friend rest a little easier."

He asked me where I was sailing next and I told him the same lies I'd told Marie about Carriacou and Grenada. I didn't feel great about lying, especially to people I really cared about, but the truth couldn't be shared.

Al showed up an hour after sunset with food, drink, and enough plastic Jerry jugs of water and diesel fuel to top off *Figaro*'s tanks. He also brought Constable Millet.

"I have a few things for Mr. Stewart Glasgow," he said.

He handed me a shiny new pre-stamped British Overseas Territory Citizen passport and a sealed envelope. I looked at the envelope.

"What's this?"

"You'll need that to enter the United States. It is a 'Certificate of Good Standing' indicating that Mr. Stewart Glasgow has no criminal record."

"Not yet, anyway."

"There's one more thing," said Millet. "I called Lieutenant Williams in Christiansted on Friday. She told me that a fourteen-year old girl disappeared the same day Dorothea left."

"Did they ever find her?"

"No. She is presumed to have drowned."

"Presumed?"

"Her body never turned up but they found her things on the beach."

"They found *some* of her things on the beach," I said.

"You think something else happened?"

"I have my suspicions."

Millet gave a look of dismissal.

"For the record, I have no knowledge of what you two are planning to do," he said. "But I trust that someday you'll tell me and that I won't be disappointed."

With that, Millet started *In Depth II's* engine and roared back toward Road Town. Al and I stowed the provisions he had brought and then sat in the cockpit to discuss the next steps. He tapped his phone and pulled up a passport photo.

"This guy looks familiar to me," said Al.

"You know Hunter Reynolds?"

He shook his head.

"Not by that name. It's the face. And a feeling."

"Does that change anything?"

"Nope."

"So, you're just going to disappear tomorrow?" I asked. "Won't people ask questions?"

"That's all taken care of. The Constable will leave *In Depth II* tied up at our dock tonight. I told Perry I was flying to New Zealand to join Liv and he said he'd keep an eye on things while I was gone. I told him to keep it a secret."

"Perry can't keep a secret."

"That's why I told him."

"Nice of him to watch the boat."

"He's been badgering me to sell him your half of the business," said Al. "You know, you being dead and all that." He smiled and winked. "You ready for this?"

"My ribs still hurt but the arm is stronger. I'm ready."

"I suppose we'll find out."

22

A sailboat's departure represents a choice between the safety of a protected harbor and the promise of the ocean. This time it felt like a duty.

We left two hours before sunrise and sailed around the west end of Tortola in the dark. Only a few lights from Soper's Hole beamed across the water as we sailed past. Less than a year after Irma, Soper's Hole was still a ghost town. While my favorite beach bar on Tortola got a catamaran jammed into its ceiling, the second floor of the most popular restaurant at Soper's Hole caught a flying pickup truck. The place still hadn't been rebuilt.

Dimmer lights illuminated footpaths to the few houses that still stood like mountain goats on the steep walls of the West End. Halfway through the narrow channel between the West End and Great Thatch Island, I looked south to see only a handful of anchor lights in Leinster Bay on St. John. It was the slow season, of course, but there still should have been a lot more charter boats hanging off the mooring balls in that lovely bay. I wondered if the islands would fully recover.

Clear of Great Thatch, I set a course to the northwest that bypassed the Turks and Caicos. *Figaro* and I had been there with Marie and I didn't want to run the risk of being recognized so we headed directly to San Salvador in the Bahamas. We established an alternating watch schedule; four-hour shifts from 0600 to 2200 and two-hour watches until 0600 the next morning.

Al and I talked a fair amount the first day but by the middle of the second, there wasn't much to say. Conversation aboard dwindled to the man going off-watch informing the other of changes in weather or issues with the boat. Neither of us wanted to rob the other of needed sack time so we put a reef in the main every night and shook it out in the morning. Furling the jib was a one-man affair so it was easy to shorten sail if a squall blew through.

The passage took longer than I expected. The normally steady east-southeast winds died during each of the last three nights leaving us to wallow in the swells, making only a knot or two for hours at a time. The occasional squall would sneak in behind us at night and push us along at hull speed while dousing us with warm rain. But the squalls were quick to dissipate.

Large commercial vessels passed us two or three times a day. A lump on the horizon ten or twelve miles away would grow into a container ship, tanker, or bulk cargo vessel. Occasionally, we'd see a cruise ship. Like a distant city in the desert, their glow emanated from below the horizon. As they approached, they grew brighter until, like a Las Vegas hotel, they completely defeated the darkness. Al swore he could read a book on a moonless night as long as a cruise ship was within four miles. The other vessels showed only the minimum required lighting and snuck around us in the darkness.

We spotted San Salvador early in the morning on the sixth day. The island's small marina with its narrow entrance looked as if it had been carved out of the island's rock with dynamite. A large powerboat—nearly sixty feet long—had been dragged onto the shore years before. It listed to port east of the concrete dock where we tied up. We raised the yellow quarantine flag and took our passports and *Figaro*'s documentation to the Bahamian customs office at the airport.

It was quiet that time of year and we were the only ones in line. But we waited while a large customs officer finished a sandwich. A sign on the wall read "No Eating and No Bags With Fish." A rule obviously not meant for government officials. Ultimately, he took our money, stamped our passports, and let us go. We returned to *Figaro*, went below, opened all the hatches and ports to get some air flowing, and sacked out for the afternoon.

Neither of us felt like cooking that evening so we walked up the Queen's Highway to a resort north of the marina. San Salvador, too, was still struggling to recover from hurricane damage. Torn roads and uprooted trees told of the storm's ferocity but the air conditioning in the resort's restaurant seemed fine. And the steamed grouper was delicious.

A tall sun-burnt fellow in a loud shirt walked in, sat at the bar, and ordered a mojito. He downed half of it while looking around the room. His eyes stopped at our table and he set his drink back down on the bar.

"Well, I'll be dipped," he said. "Al Higgins? Man, I haven't seen you in forever and a day."

Al's head spun around like an owl.

"Wally McConnell? What are you doing here?"

The man grabbed his drink and walked over.

"I fly a little bizjet for a small cosmetics company. The CEO and his wife wanted to visit the Club Med here and go diving so I got tasked with flying them down. I can't complain, though. The bonefishing's pretty good and the drinks are on his tab."

"Sit down, Wally, and meet Stewart Glasgow."

Wally dragged a chair over from another table and shook my hand.

"I can't believe you're still alive."

"Alive and kicking."

"You're a brave man, Stewart. Hanging around this fellow can get you in some serious trouble."

"Those days are long over," said Al.

"What are you drinking, guys?"

"Caribs and Heinekens," said Al.

Wally waved at the bartender. He acknowledged the request and hurried about preparing the drinks.

"Back in the day," continued Wally, "when I was flying U-28s with the 318th, I'd slip us onto a flat piece of dirt somewhere in-country and Al and his guys would bolt out the door and run off into the bush."

"Most of that is best forgotten," said Al. "Or, at least, not discussed."

"I'd stick with the plane and wait for 'em. Just me, my M4, and a briefcase full of cash in some third-world hell hole. They always came back, though, with either big grins on their faces or some guy wearing a black hood and zip ties."

The bartender brought fresh beers for Al and me and another mojito for Wally.

"I'm not sure our former employer would appreciate us talking about it."

"Hardly matters. I'm sure all the details of those ops are in hacked emails given to the Kremlin. And our old bosses are writing books about it, anyway." Wally paused to finish his second mojito. "I thought we were gonna lose you on that last trip, man."

"It was no big deal."

"No big deal?" Wally shook his head back and forth. "I had to clean all that blood out of my airplane. Your blood. I thought you were gonna leave that U-28 in a body bag. Or, at least, lose the leg."

"What can I say? We had the best medic. But that was a long time ago. It's not worth talking about."

"So what are you doing here?"

"We're delivering a boat up north."

"You deliver boats now?" asked Wally. "Seems like weak sauce for a guy like you."

"It keeps me busy."

"You guys want to go fishing with me tomorrow?"

"We're on a tight deadline," said Al. "The new owner wants his boat at his home yard in New England for some restoration work. How long are you gonna be here?"

"Three more days. Less if that storm gets any closer."

"Aren't you worried about that?" I asked.

"I'd think you guys would be more concerned," he said. "I can load up the boss and be wheels up in an hour. Three hours later I'll be touching down in Dallas. How far away can you get in four hours?"

Al shrugged. "It'll turn north."

We talked for another half-hour or so. Wally tried to talk about old times but Al avoided most of it. He maneuvered the conversation toward Wally's life. Did he ever get married? How did he like flying corporate jets? Anything to divert him from talking about Al's prior occupation as a warrior. Finally, Al complained of being tired and we said our goodbyes. Wally's boss, unknowingly, paid our dinner bill and we walked back to *Figaro*.

"You're not tired," I said.

"Tired of a guy who should keep his mouth shut but can't."

"Is that how you got that scar on your leg? During that last trip with Wally?"

"I didn't get it shaving."

We walked down the concrete dock toward *Figaro*. The owners of a large sport fishing boat across the marina from us were hosting a loud party. Music, drink, laughter, dancing.

"Let's get the hell out of here," said Al.

23

WE cast off the mooring lines and left San Salvador just after midnight setting a course due west to the southern tip of Cat Island. There wasn't much wind so I started *Figaro*'s diesel. It was the first time since leaving Tortola that I'd had to run the engine for longer than an hour or two to charge the batteries. The wind kicked in around sunrise and our sails began to pull in earnest. I killed the engine. By noon we were making seven knots off the southwest point of Cat Island. Al came up to stand his watch so I could get some sleep.

"I just checked the forecast. That tropical storm Wally was talking about is going to pass north and east of us. But it could get close enough to cause us some grief. You think we should find a spot where we can hole up for a while?"

I went below and checked the chart.

"We can make Fernandez Bay in about two hours," I said. "It's well protected from the north, east, and south."

"Sounds perfect."

We put two reefs in the main, furled about half the jib, and turned north. Fernandez Bay is a small bight of water bounded by a short rock spit to the north and a shallow river mouth to the south. A half-mile long scimitar of white sand beach recessed into Cat Island. Beyond the beaches lay dozens of thatched-roof resort buildings, empty in the slow hot season.

We found good holding in hard sand east of the rock spit. In anticipation of shifting winds, we laid a Bahamian moor with two anchors so *Figaro* could swing a short arc around a fixed point.

I dove over the side, swam north to the beach, and walked across the hot sand toward a large coconut palm. I sat with my back to the trunk and watched Al dig around in *Figaro's* lazarette. He pulled out my pole spear, a mesh sack, and my snorkeling gear. I watched him swim to the small rock jetty. He dove ten or twelve times; a minute or so below followed by a few minutes on the surface. I swam back to the boat when I saw him turn away from the jetty.

I attached *Figaro's* small barbecue to the pushpit, hooked up the propane tank, and lit the grill while Al prepared the lobsters. He slit each bug down the middle lengthwise, cleaned out the unpleasant bits, and laid the halves open-side down on the grill. I went below to retrieve two beers. We could only cook one lobster at a time but that was fine; the second lobster cooked while we ate the first, the third while we ate the second.

"What's our mission?" asked Al. "What are our objectives?"

A squall blew in across the island and rain bounced off the bimini above us.

"Bring the people responsible for Eryn's murder to justice and bring Dorothea back home to Tortola."

"How do we know those guys did it? How do we even know they're from Georgia? All you've got is a hunch and a piece of tracing paper."

I didn't have an answer.

"Fine," he said. "Let's say those two guys planted the bomb and we find them in Georgia. Easy solution. I fly up there on a Friday, take them both out Saturday, and get back to Road Town in time for the Sunday cricket match."

It had been nearly two years since I'd seen that side of Al—the well-trained, highly capable, killer—and his coolness briefly caught me by surprise.

"Two guys don't just grab some Mil-Spec explosives, fly down to the Caribbean, and kill people on their own dime. It's bigger than that. There's something evil in that church."

"Which you can't articulate," said Al.

"Dorothea disappears, somebody sends a fake email to her parents, and I track them down to a church in Georgia. Another girl disappears in St. Croix…"

"She drowned."

"…or was given a fake drivers' license and flown to Georgia with Mitch, Clint, and Dorothea. You don't need a passport to fly to the states from St. Thomas."

The rain increased in intensity and the wind played a light tune in the rigging.

"It's still an indistinct mission with nonspecific objectives. There is no better recipe for failure."

"Go on."

"I was trained to plan and execute limited direct-action missions with specific objectives. We rescued hostages, snatched people for interrogation, and neutralized bad guys our country wanted deported off the planet. You were a Master-at-Arms. You arrested drunk sailors, handled security, investigated minor crimes, and solved a couple of murders NCIS couldn't be bothered with."

"And your point is?"

"We don't have the skill set to bring down an entire organization. We have no infrastructure, no intelligence network, no friendly insurgents in the target area, no relevant training, and no assets. We don't even know who we're up against."

I could feel heat in the back of my neck.

"You don't have to do a thing," said Al. "I can find those two guys and I can take them out all by myself. I'll even throw in the dude who lured Dorothea away."

"Clint?"

"Yeah, sure. Call it a trifecta."

I knew anger wouldn't help; wouldn't get me closer to my objective.

"Why did you even come on this trip?" I asked. "We're halfway there and now you want to abort the mission."

"You needed the therapy. You needed a reason to get back. You needed to get away from Tortola and sail your damned boat."

"And now?"

"Now we take our time and sail *Figaro* back home," said Al. "We roll into Road Town and you miraculously return to the land of the living while I go hunting in Georgia."

From Al's perspective, his was the perfect plan. Short, specific, and lethal. But I needed more.

"You are the best friend I have and I appreciate your advice. But I am rejecting it."

"I figured you might." He took another bite of lobster. "It doesn't matter. I'm still with you, buddy. Right or wrong, I've got your back."

Lobster is the most delicious thing on the planet but I'd suddenly lost my taste for it. Al was too close to being correct in his assessment.

"We'll know more once we get to Fort Lauderdale," I said. "Stick with me that long, okay?"

"What's so special about Fort Lauderdale?"

"Trust me."

Al watched me push away my plate of lobster.

"You're not gonna eat that?"

Strong east winds filled with rain blew in over the palm trees that evening. I set up a tarp to funnel the rain into *Figaro's* water tanks. I slept on the starboard settee that night and got up a couple times to make sure our anchors were holding. The Bahamian moor worked like a charm as the storm's winds clocked around to the north. By mid-morning, we had strong northwest winds which, unfortunately, came directly from the direction we intended to sail. So we spent another day at anchor.

Al speared some fish behind the rock spit while I swam to the beach and back. Neither of us spoke much. We read, we ate, we listened to the weather report.

The next morning found us still facing a northwest wind but it was lighter and we didn't feel like waiting any longer. We weighed anchor and sailed close-hauled on a starboard tack for five hours and then motored into the wind to reach Little San Salvador. A cruise ship company had bought the island years earlier, renamed it "Half Moon Cay," and declared it off-limits to non-paying visitors. So we dropped the hook in a protected spot close to the west end of the island well away from their facilities.

The night sky had that perfectly transparent quality it gets at sea after a storm, clarity you don't see elsewhere. We sat in the cockpit, drank the last of our beer, and watched a thunderstorm pummel the earth southwest of us. Daggers of lightning, probably ten a minute, glowed from beneath the horizon.

We left the next morning and sailed all day keeping Eleuthera at least five miles to port. Cruise ship sightings increased in number but those ugly giants stayed farther offshore and we didn't worry too much about them. The hand line fishing rig I'd tied to the pushpit jumped and the cord holding the black plastic yo-yo went taut as we approached the northernmost arm of Eleuthera. Al barely turned from the book he was reading.

"Your watch, your fish."

I grabbed the hand line, reeled it in, and pulled a small dorado into the cockpit. Al poured a shot of rum into its gills and the fish died instantly. I went below, retrieved my filleting knife, and quickly separated two fresh fillets from the carcass, the former going into the fridge, the latter overboard. A few buckets of sea water erased all sign of the carnage.

"Your arm seems to be all the way back. How are the ribs?"

Everything still ached but I'd noticed definite progress.

"Much better."

Al went below, splashed a little oil into a frying pan, cooked one of the fillets, and brought it back to the cockpit with some sliced limes.

"We're out of beer," he said.

"It's a wonder we don't sink."

We turned west-northwest as the sun set. The Man Island lighthouse flashed its three white beams every fifteen seconds. *Figaro* continued dead downwind to pass the lights of Spanish Wells at a steady, if sedate, five knots. Hours later, we spotted the Hole-in-the-Wall light flashing from the southern-most headland of Great Abaco.

We reached the northern Berry Islands around ten o'clock on Saturday morning and found good holding ground in ten feet of water between Great Stirrup Cay and Little Stirrup Cay. We sacked out until sunset and enjoyed a quiet evening with more fresh mahi on the barbecue.

"We'll be in Fort Lauderdale day after tomorrow," said Al. "Last chance to back out and sail home."

"If Stewart Glasgow's passport will get me past Customs, I want to see this through."

24

WE weighed anchor the next morning and continued on our westward course. The winds were light out of the southeast and I set *Figaro's* nylon drifter on a port tack. The main/drifter combination worked fine, carrying us along at between five and six knots, until we hit the Gulf Stream and had to turn a bit south to avoid being set by the northerly current. We made Ft. Lauderdale under power and dragged our salt-sprayed boat into the main channel around three the following afternoon. Hot and humid, it was the typical summer day one finds in south Florida in early September.

Almost all of the big hotels near the water have marina facilities and most have guest docks. We picked the fanciest—it would be the last place anybody would look for a couple of fellows intending to make trouble—and had *Figaro* secured in her slip by four o'clock.

Al and I took the marina's courtesy car, along with the boat's documents and our passports, to the customs office in Port Everglades. The officer looked at my new British passport and read the Certificate of Good Standing. He turned back to the cover examining the British coat of arms surrounded by a lion, crown, and unicorn. He pointed at the French phrase beneath it.

"What does *'Dieu et mon droit'* mean?" he asked.

"'God and my right,' I believe."

"I always thought it meant 'Do it on Monday,'" said Al.

The officer smiled and stamped our passports. Al stopped at a liquor store and picked up a six-pack of his favorite Heinekens.

When we got back to the marina, I checked my email and found the usual amount of useless spam, a message from Orson Flake, and some delightful correspondence from Marie.

I opened Marie's email first, of course. She was making progress with her dissertation and had persuaded her father to bring their boat down to the BVI for Thanksgiving. She made suggestive remarks about what I could look forward to. Nice. Flake's email was shorter and less romantic. I read it and made a quiet fist pump.

After nearly a month of living entirely on my boat, the marina's showers were an absolute luxury and the hotel restaurant's New York strip steak—I'd eaten enough seafood over the last few weeks— a sensual, if pricey, delight. The warm sourdough bread was amazing and the coffee unspeakably good.

The sun set and was replaced by harbor lights. The red and green navigation lights of smaller boats motored past the hotel while we ate. A massive motoryacht, large enough to carry a helicopter on a landing pad near its stern, pulled up to the long concrete quay east of the hotel. We watched as a dozen of the ship's crew scurried about setting massive fenders and handling thick mooring lines. It wore me out just watching them.

Al paid the bill for dinner in cash and we walked back to *Figaro*.

The Heinekens had cooled properly in the fridge during dinner and Al broke out a pair as we sat in the cockpit and watched a party of beautiful people walk from the massive yacht to the hotel.

"Flake came through," I said. "His lawyer is holding a package for us in their Miami office."

"Is that what you were talking about last week on Cat Island?"

"Uh-huh."

"What's in the package?" he asked.

"A lot, I hope."

"Let's not take the car for that trip. It's probably got a GPS transponder so the hotel can track it."

"So what?"

"If they can track it, they can track us driving to that law firm," said Al. "Small details add up to major consequences."

We talked of other things and then, finally, stepped down to crawl into our respective bunks. The boat hadn't been this still for weeks and, even though my bunk was not pitching or rolling at all, I felt my head rolling back and forth as if it were. It's a well-known phenomenon—rolling in a stationary bunk—experienced by those who sail.

Figaro's galley is directly across the cabin from my quarterberth so the sounds and smells of Al's cooking were unavoidable. My ears told me he was slaughtering a farm animal bare-handed but my nostrils suggested we'd be having fried ham and scrambled eggs for breakfast. I crawled out of my bunk as Al finished setting the table with toast and jam. Timing is everything.

I locked up *Figaro* after breakfast and we walked to a bus stop. We rode to the Tri-Rail station and then took the train south to the Metrorail. We transferred to the Green Line and continued on another forty minutes. It wasn't hard to find the law firm's office; their name was at the top of a fifteen-story building in red, ten-foot-high letters. We rode the elevator to the top where we were escorted to a conference room.

The room was smaller than a hockey rink but not by much. The view through the floor-to-ceiling windows revealed an expanse of Miami residences to the east dotted by swimming pools. The gleaming blue water of Biscayne Bay lay another three or four miles beyond.

A serious woman in a pink shirt and dark skirt/jacket combination walked into the conference room. A younger man followed her carrying a cardboard box. He tried to look serious. She probably could have carried the box—it wasn't much larger than the ones her Ferragamo shoes came in—but she was not the kind of person who carried such things into a conference room.

"I'm Kathryn Cole," she said. "I represent Mr. Flake in his leasing and litigation interests in Florida."

The young man put the box on the conference room table and

introduced himself as an associate.

"And this box is for me," I said.

"Yes," said Kathryn. "Can I have your name so we can tell Mr. Flake who picked it up?"

"No."

She looked uncomfortable.

"We need your name for our records," she said. "I just can't hand over a client's property without some identification."

"Sure you can," I said. "Call Mr. Flake and tell him a man with a broken nose came to pick up the box. Ask if he needs further identification. I'll bet you dinner he won't."

She looked puzzled but smiled and left the room. The younger man stayed to make sure we didn't steal the box. But he was uncomfortable in the room with Al and me, and decided to attempt some small talk.

"So, did you guys just come in on a boat?" he asked.

"Why do you ask?"

"You both have that look. Like you've been at sea for a few days."

"We're fishermen," I lied.

"We don't get a lot of fishermen in our offices."

"Time to step up your marketing."

Al laughed and the young man stopped asking questions. Kathryn returned a few minutes later.

"Mr. Flake authorized me to release the box to you. He would like you to contact him at your earliest opportunity."

I thanked her, grabbed the box, and headed for the elevator. Al and I reversed our tracks back to Fort Lauderdale. The heat of the day had built and some thundershowers rolled in from the west and pummeled the harbor. We were soaked to the skin before we got back to *Figaro*.

Al pulled two more beers from the fridge and popped the tops as I sat down to open the package Orson Flake had sent me.

25

CRUMPLED newspaper sat atop a red canvas bag. I unzipped the bag to find strap-sorted stacks of crisp U.S. currency. Under the cash lay a small red USB thumb drive and four thick three-ring binders. The binders were labeled "Economic Analysis," "Demographic/Market Characteristics," "Movers & Shakers," and "Political Extract." I pulled the binders out and started reading.

Al counted out the stacks of hundred- and fifty-dollar bills.

"There's enough cash here to buy a half-dozen Afghan warlords," he said. "How much did you ask him for?"

"Only two warlords' worth."

"You got a raise. This kind of cash gives us options."

He put the money back in the red bag, grabbed a binder, and moved over to *Figaro's* dinette to read it.

"Intel," he said. "Fairly decent intel."

"It seems Flake regularly hires a research outfit to produce a detailed analysis of any market he may want to enter."

Al put the binder he'd been thumbing through down and picked up the Movers & Shakers.

"Nice," he said.

I plugged the thumb drive into my laptop and saw a list of source files for the contents of the binders and subdirectories filled with pictures. I copied it all to a new subfolder, left the laptop on *Figaro's* navigation table, and picked up the Political Extract binder. I took it to the starboard settee and made myself comfortable for careful reading.

"Did you say the guy who lured Dorothea away is named Clint McCord?" said Al.

"Yep."

"This says he's Vice President of the local longshoremen's association and a member of the Serenity City Council."

He turned the binder around to show me a picture of Clint McCord walking out of an office building.

"That's him," I said.

Al went back to the binder and turned the page.

"Look at this guy!"

It was a picture of a bare-chested Clint standing in a boxing ring with his left arm raised in victory. Al turned the binder back.

"It says here he fights amateur Mixed Martial Arts. Middleweight class; six-one; one hundred eighty-five pounds; seventeen wins, five losses. Nice abs."

Al grabbed his phone and punched his fingers at the screen. I soon heard what sounded like a boxing match.

"What's that?"

"A video of Clint McCord's latest fight."

"Is he any good?"

"He doesn't punch a lot," said Al. "Seems to favor the round-house kick and getting his opponent on the ground. He's good, though."

"Are you developing a man-crush on an adversary?"

"No. I'm just wondering how a longshoreman in his early thirties who fights MMA and recruits for a church gets elected to the City Council."

He shut off the video and went back to the binder. He stopped at one page and stared at it.

"You got any idea who this is talking to Clint?" he asked.

He turned to binder toward me and pointed at a post-fight picture of Clint McCord with a cut under his eye. He was talking to a guy in a tight black T-shirt. It wasn't a great picture but the face looked familiar. I went back to the navigation table, opened the laptop, and found the picture I wanted. I showed it to Al.

"Same guy?" I asked.

Al looked at it and nodded.

"He's one of the guys who came to the BVI and tried to kill me," I said. "Hunter Reynolds."

"I'm not so sure of that," said Al.

"Here's his passport," I said.

Al pointed at the page in the binder.

"Is this photo on your laptop?" he asked.

I navigated through the subfolders, found the photo, and turned it toward Al. He studied it for a long minute.

"I think our group worked with this guy in Africa. He was a private contractor; former British SAS."

"You worked with Hunter Reynolds?"

"That's not his name if it's the guy I'm thinking of. But I heard he was killed years ago."

Al used the zoom feature to expand the photo until the screen centered on the man's left ear.

"You see that?" he asked.

An earring, a small silver dagger framed by silver flames, sat on the man's earlobe.

"SAS," he said.

He scrolled the picture to show the man's jaw. A small scar stretched across the left side.

"He told us he got that in Afghanistan before he went private."

"How well did you know this guy?" I asked.

"His real name is Trevor Hickey. Most of the guys in our squad thought he was a real bad ass. I just thought he was a corrupt bastard and a little crazy. He bragged about cutting the liver out of a dead Taliban fighter, cooking it, and eating the damned thing."

"I'd say that's more than a *little* crazy."

"Oh, yeah, that's totally nuts. The dead guy could have had hepatitis or cholera or any number of STDs."

"Of course," I said.

As if those were the only reasons not to eat a dead man's liver.

"It's also a war crime," said Al. "Word was that the SAS gave him the boot because of it. And that's when he went private."

"But you say he's dead?"

"I didn't see it happen but it didn't hurt my feelings to hear of it."

"You didn't like him?" I asked.

"We were handing out cash like it was candy and I suspected him of pocketing a big chunk of it. I confronted the guy and he tried to turn it on me. Then I got shot up during an operation—you heard about that a few days ago—and was sent home. The last thing I heard was that Hickey got his ass blown up in a truck in Mali."

"Does this change our plan?"

"As far as I can tell we don't have a plan." He continued reading the binder in front of him. "But if this guy is involved we are sure as hell going to need one."

He closed the laptop and handed it back to me. I left it on the navigation table and went back to my settee. We read our respective binders for a few minutes in silence before Al started laughing.

"You're not going to believe this," he said.

He turned the binder for me to look and I gasped. The face in the picture could have been a still from a cheap horror movie. Half of the man's long, skinny, hairless skull was forehead. An exaggerated brow bone protruded over small eyes and a long, pointed nose. What teeth he had were spiky, almost fang-like. His long ears were pointed at the tips.

"Give me that," I said. "This has got to be some sort of joke." I read the paragraph adjacent to the photo. "Duncan McCord, High Master of *Sidoni.* Clint's younger brother?"

"That's what the binder says but I don't think they're even in the same phylum."

"It says here the guy suffers from 'Christ-Siemens Touraine' syndrome...'"

"Whatever the hell that is," said Al.

"The writer says it's a 'rare condition where one is born without—and fails to develop—sweat glands, hair, fingernails or teeth.' Seems like there's more than that going on there."

"Let's hope that thing hasn't laid any eggs."

26

WE spent the rest of the day studying the materials Flake had sent us. Al was more diligent and focused than I. My slacking was something I attributed to having been blown up five weeks earlier. I forgave myself and crawled into my quarterberth early that evening.

Al was still reading when I woke up the next morning.

"*Sidoni* seems more like a doomsday cult than a religion," he said. "They've got a messianic leader preaching apocalyptic sermons."

"How so?"

"This Duncan McCord, the church's founder, claims to be the 'last prophet' and calls himself the 'High Master.' So, he's the boss and he claims Queen Astarte will come to accept those who are purified and saved."

"The rest of us just go straight to Hell?"

"That's about it."

"How does one become 'saved,' according to the High Master?"

"Seems to be a three-step plan," said Al. "First, you must believe in Queen Astarte. Second, you must strive towards immortality by purifying yourself with ritual sex..."

"You are such a lying sack of..."

Al shoved the binder towards me.

"No, seriously," he said. "Read this."

I did. *Wow.*

"Well, that certainly isn't your grandma's boring religion."

He retrieved the binder and continued.

"Finally, you must remain loyal to *Sidoni*. This appears to be a function of monetary donations and missionary work."

"Ah, the monetary Yin to the purifying sex Yang."

Al shook his head in disgust.

"I'm not sure it's a real thing," he said.

"What do you mean?"

"The tenets are completely modern creations. They profess some ancient roots on the surface but all they do is idolize love and compassion. And money. There is no responsibility or accountability, no instruction or depth."

"When did you become a theologian?"

"I've cracked open a book or two on the subject. In any case, I'm starting to come around to your way of thinking. *Sidoni* controls the local power structure. Police, city, unions—everything but the local PTA."

"And..."

"You said there was something evil in that church. I think you're right."

"Where do you get all that?"

"Read the binders. It's in there between the lines. And there's Trevor Hickey, of course. If he's involved, it's evil."

He kept reading. I went topside to give the boat its morning inspection. Al joined me in the cockpit a few minutes later.

"There's nothing in there about the other guy who came to kill you. Jacques Dehlin? The guy you say is really Mitch Danforth. There are no photos in these binders that look anything like either that passport photo or your pencil sketch."

"Danforth is only a local cop. Flake's researchers wouldn't bother looking at him."

He thought for a minute.

"You need to drive me to the train station," he said. "And I'm taking the money with me."

"Okay," I said.

"You want to know why?"

"You want to do your own recon?"

"I've got a sliver of an idea and I want to run with it."

We talked about some possible approaches during breakfast. Afterward, Al grabbed his duffel, shoved the money into it, and slipped on his boat shoes. I locked up *Figaro* and we walked down the concrete path to the concierge and the courtesy car. We drove down 17th Street to a mobile phone shop, exchanged some of Flake's money for two prepaid "burner" cell phones, and continued on to the train station.

"I took the thumb drive with me," said Al. "I left the binders for you. Study those over the next few days and meet me in Jacksonville any time after noon on Tuesday."

"Will do."

"You still against me just taking those three guys out?"

"Yep."

"You trust me?"

He was a cold-blooded killer but his skills and instinct had saved my neck several times.

"Completely," I said.

"What were you wearing when you went to Georgia?"

"Shorts, short-sleeve shirt, boat shoes," I said. "What I pretty much always wear."

"Serenity is predominantly working class. Longshoremen, mechanics, rednecks, and the like. You got any jeans? Any boots."

"Jeans."

"Stick 'em in your duffel when you get to Jacksonville." He thought for a half-minute. "Are you gonna be okay single-handing *Figaro* up north?"

"A hundred percent."

"Okay," he said. "I'll see you in six days."

He grabbed his duffel and slammed the door shut. I watched him walk under a red Amtrak awning and into the station. And then Al was gone and I was on my own. I turned the car around and headed back toward the harbor. I stopped at a Winn-Dixie and bought a week's worth of provisions. For one. They barely filled the little cart the hotel provides to boaters so they can get their stuff down to the dock.

I spent the afternoon reading from the four binders. When I got sick of reading, I coiled lines and put away dishes and filled *Figaro's* water and diesel tanks. Then I read some more.

According to Flake's research, Serenity had been a somewhat sleepy agricultural town until six years earlier. That was when Andrew Grier Stephens moved back. He'd come from modest roots—an old southern family whose wealth and power had declined substantially after the abolition of slavery—and left town at seventeen to make his fortune. He returned with enough money to buy the old Poplar Manor and convert it into one of the state's most exclusive oceanfront resorts.

When he first arrived, there were questions about how he'd made his money—some claimed he'd sold vacuum cleaners to people with dirt floors—but "Andy" was elected mayor a year later and he worked tirelessly to expand Serenity's economic base. He'd brought in investors who improved the city's bulk shipping facilities and built a new roll-on/roll-off dockyard to handle automobile shipments.

Ships filled with wheat, wood pulp, and heavy machinery sailed into Serenity's port. Those same ships left laden with corn, limestone, and oats. High-end European cars destined for dealerships along the eastern seaboard drove onto Serenity's docks from specially-designed roll-on/roll-off "RORO" ships; American-built cars and trucks rolled back on.

Even though Serenity had fewer than thirty thousand full-time residents, the influx of investment capital created thousands of new jobs and the area's tax base grew substantially. The International Longshoremen's local had negotiated well and the city had a thriving working class. Unemployment was nearly non-existent.

The mayor managed to score a federal grant to expand the local airport. The runway was improved and extended to eight thousand feet. A control tower was erected and staffed and a small passenger terminal built. The new Stephens Field attracted the interest of a small regional carrier and they soon offered three flights a week.

As the economy flourished, the crime rate dropped. There simply was no serious crime in Cass county and the FBI listed the area as having the lowest crime rate in the country by a wide margin. A recent AARP article about small town retirement touted Serenity's safety, free senior services, a Meals-on-Wheels program, and other senior-oriented interests.

Mayor Stephens was credited with these successes and he easily won reelection. Nobody was surprised at rumors of a possible Senate run.

Flake's research contained detailed information about *Sidoni*, too. Duncan McCord, the younger of the two McCord brothers, started *Sidoni* around the same time Serenity began enjoying its economic rebirth. *Sidoni* had raised money to purchase the old courthouse from the county and then donated additional funds for construction of the new county court and city office complex.

The church had grown to include a multimedia presence. Audio podcasts had grown into a weekly livestream video sermon. A number of high-profile celebrities followed *Sidoni* and most of the local city leaders had become devout adherents to the new faith. A member of the British Royal Family came, on rare occasion, to attend services. The church even kept a business jet at the local airfield.

The light in the cabin grew dim as the sun arced closer to the horizon. I put away the folders and walked to the hotel restaurant to have my last—for some time, at least—really good steak. Halfway through it, I remembered a phone call I needed to make. I finished dinner, paid my bill, and made my way to the concierge.

"I need to make a collect telephone call."

His face fell.

"Is that still a thing?" he asked.

I shrugged. He led me to a room behind the reception counter and pointed me toward a small desk with a landline. I dialed "0" and followed the automated prompts. When asked for my name, I said "Tortola."

"Who is this?" asked Orson Flake.

"Exactly who you think it is."

"Didn't I send you enough money to purchase a cell phone?"

"Oh, there was plenty of that. I'd just rather not leave a trail."

"How are you feeling?"

"Almost a hundred percent and ready to seek a little justice."

"Excellent. My lawyer tells me *two* men showed up to receive the package. Who is this other fellow?"

"A team member."

"I don't know anything about this person."

"I do."

"How do I know he's qualified?"

I thought about the night Al and I had rescued Liv from a hostage situation. It hadn't gone well for four hardened gang members.

"He's qualified," I said.

"Whatever. I have four good men ready to join you. Where should we meet?"

"Slow down," I said. "Who is leading this effort?"

"You are."

"Then I need to pick people I know and trust."

"I can send you their résumés. What's your email?"

"It doesn't work like that, Mr. Flake. And I am no longer using email."

"Well, I'll need your phone number so I can call you."

"No. This team needs to be both silent and invisible. You have to understand the importance of that."

"How will I get in touch with you?" he asked.

"You won't. I will get in touch with you."

"How will I know if my money is being spent properly?"

"I'll provide a complete report with a full accounting once the project is finished."

There was a deep sigh on the other end of the line.

"I'm not in the habit of funding major projects in the blind," said Flake.

"Do you fund a lot of projects like this? Seriously?"

He was quiet and thinking.

"You've got to trust me," I said. "I know what to do and I know how to do it. But this kind of mission does not lend itself to top-down long-distance management. By the way, the information you provided us was very thorough. Thank you for that."

"Glad I can do something right."

"These measures are for your safety as well as mine."

We ended the call on a positive note and I walked back to *Figaro*. I went below, grabbed a cold beer, and climbed back into the cockpit to relax. Boats of every description plied the channel under the 17th Street bridge. Red, green, and white navigation and steaming lights reflected off the harbor waters as they motored past.

Across the harbor to the north was an older marina that, by all appearances, catered to a much less wealthy group of boaters. Two men sat on folding chairs tending a barbecue on the stern of an old sportfishing boat that looked like it hadn't been scrubbed since Ft. Lauderdale became a city. Flickering lights from another old vessel betrayed the owner's devotion to that cultural desert known as television.

Another man, grieving for his niece, sat in a comfortable room over a thousand miles away wondering whether or not he should have given money and information to a strange lone sailor and an unknown accomplice to begin his latest "project."

Too late for second thoughts.

I finished my beer, stepped down into *Figaro*'s cabin, and crawled into my quarterberth. My ribs hurt only a little as I thought about the long days ahead of me.

27

I woke up an hour before sunrise and rigged *Figaro* for single-handed sailing: rolling out my jacklines, fixing them to padeyes fore and aft, and putting on my safety harness. It was supposed to be a fine day for sailing but I would be alone on this trip. If I went overboard, there wouldn't be anybody there to throw me a line. I felt real excitement: the satisfaction of a fundamental need to sail my boat away from the nonsense ashore.

The weather report predicted southwest winds at fifteen knots and three-foot swells, perfect conditions for where I was headed. I reviewed my charts and decided on a spot seventy nautical miles east-northeast of Ft. Lauderdale—a place on the edge of the Little Bahama Bank where I could hang out unnoticed for a couple of days while Al did whatever it was he needed to do. A heading due east would get us there once the northerly set of the Gulf Stream kicked in.

The morning sun found me motoring out the main channel toward the Gulf Stream. North of the channel entrance was a strange sight: a large cargo ship stranded on a sand bar and listing slightly to starboard. A pair of tugs loitered nearby, waiting for high tide so they could drag the ship to deeper water. I grabbed my binoculars and read the name *Alang Fanang* on the stern. Somebody had grown complacent and, despite all their expensive electronics, had lost their situational awareness.

Leaving early guaranteed that I'd get to my intended anchorage with enough daylight to make it through the shallows and drop the hook without meeting the same fate as the *Alang Fanang*.

My ribs ached as I raised the mainsail, unfurled the jib, and set Kyle to steer *Figaro* on an easterly heading. We quickly gathered way on a broad reach toward the Gulf Stream. I trimmed the sails and shut down the engine.

We entered the Gulf Stream only a couple miles out of Fort Lauderdale and the combined effort of wind and current sent *Figaro* crabbing along a diagonal path toward the Little Bahama Bank. With high hopes, I put a pink and silver flat-headed lure on my handline rig and let out fifty yards of line off the plastic yo-yo.

The high rises of South Florida's beach condos—perhaps the tallest objects in the state—disappeared over the horizon after a few hours. No land or buildings in sight, I focused on the steady stream of maritime traffic—freighters, cruise ships, and smaller private vessels—heading to and from the Bahamas.

A cloud, filled to the brim with rain and wind, grew dark south of *Figaro* and headed toward us. I put two reefs in the main and furled about half the jib. The sky turned gray and strong gusts hit us as the squall approached. Visibility dropped to only a few miles as rain fell in sheets and bounced off the deck. I went below and turned on the radar so I could track any nearby vessels.

The squall passed and grey skies gave way to white puffy clouds marching across a sheet of clear blue crystal. The ocean, too, changed to that deep cobalt color I love. I let out the reefs in the main, hoisted it to full height, and unfurled the jib. *Figaro* took the bit in her teeth and raced off once again.

Moments later, my handline sprang as tight as a guitar string and I grabbed the yo-yo. Nothing seemed to be fighting on the other end and I figured I'd snagged some flotsam or a piece of sargassum. I brought the line in hand-over-hand and was surprised to find a small blackfin tuna on the hook. Soon, the fridge held three pounds of fresh fillets in two plastic bags.

I grabbed a Coke and sat in the cockpit under the bimini watching Kyle steer my boat. Every twenty minutes or so, I'd stand up and look around for traffic but I was alone and safe. I spotted the little island at four o'clock.

It was small—less than a quarter-mile long and only a few hundred feet wide—and uninhabited. With rocks to the west and shallow water to the south and east, it was inhospitable to larger boats. My chart, however, showed a clear channel and ten feet of water a few hundred yards northeast of the island. I hoped the wind and current would be mild in its lee and that nobody would bother me there. Bypassing Bahamian customs—I didn't want to press my luck reentering the United States as Stewart Glasgow again—was the essential task.

I had the sails furled and the hook down in short order. The northerly current was light but steady. I fished a hundred feet of yellow floating line and a boat fender out of the lazarette and tossed them astern. If I somehow fell overboard, I'd have a line I could use to pull myself back to the boat. Without that, the current would have a fair chance of carrying me—still not the strongest swimmer—out into the deep Atlantic.

Another squall headed toward us out of the south and I stripped to shower in the warm rain. Rain fell for nearly half an hour and the cool breeze drove away the heat of the day. It was invigorating and I suddenly felt an increase in appetite. I went below, dressed, grabbed some fresh tuna, and returned topside to light the grill.

My ribs ached only a little as I cooked the tuna. I ate my fish dinner and sat down to read more of Flake's research material.

Local preachers had been reluctant to welcome *Sidoni* into their city. But the church had sponsored an opioid rehab program for local addicts and the program worked. Addiction in Serenity dropped to almost nothing—an amazing achievement by any measure—and drug-related crime became virtually nonexistent. The police got their share of the credit. They had worked hard to arrest the dealers and shut down the drug labs that had made Serenity their home.

But all was not rosy. Stories of young adult women being

brainwashed and persuaded to join *Sidoni* began to surface shortly after the church was established. The issue came to a head when a group of parents from neighboring states travelled to Serenity to "rescue" their children from the church. A local preacher helped organize protests but the demonstrations became violent and arrests were made. Mayor Stephens used his influence to calm the situation and restore peace. *Sidoni* thrived.

The day's sail had worn me out and I caught myself nodding off in the middle of sentences as I read them. I put a bookmark in the binder and stepped up on deck to check my anchor. All was well with the boat so I went below and crawled into my quarterberth.

I spent the next few days reading, swimming, eating, and sleeping. At night, I'd lie back on the port cockpit bench, look at the stars, and listen to waves crashing on the rocks. The clear night sky spoke of peace but the waves roared in anger and I knew how they felt. But mine wasn't a hot wild anger. It was a cold dispassionate need to avenge Eryn's death and, if possible, save Dorothea.

Figaro gained a following while anchored off the small island. Sea turtles and spotted eagle rays swam near her during the day and tarpon with glowing eyes circled around her stern at night. The water was clear enough that I could see lobsters hiding under nearby rocks as I swam around the boat.

On Sunday, I got out the charts and planned my trip to Jacksonville. The mouth of the St. Johns River lay about two hundred and fifty nautical miles to the northwest. The Gulf Stream and the southerly winds would turn *Figaro* into a speedster. I decided to head north dead downwind for the first hundred and fifty miles, then turn west on a broad reach. The Gulf Stream would still set me north after the turn west but at a decreasing rate as I left the main flow of the current and approached Jacksonville. The final push—powering up river to the city—would add two hours to the trip. To get there Tuesday afternoon, I'd have to leave an hour before sunrise Monday morning. I set the alarm on my phone and fell asleep in the cockpit with the moon staring down at me and the wind washing over my face.

28

THE outermost sea buoy for the St. Johns River lay four nautical miles offshore. I passed it a few minutes before noon on Tuesday and turned to port, toward the channel entrance. The wind had clocked around and *Figaro* was now pointed almost directly into it so I started her engine, furled the genoa, and dropped the main. We plodded on at almost five knots.

My phone signaled an incoming text as we motored into range of the nearest tower. From Al's burner, the message was short and simple including only the latitude, longitude, and name of the marina he'd found for *Figaro*. I looked at my chart and realized I'd be motoring upstream another three hours. I texted Al my ETA.

The river was wide and deep and, though crowded with larger ships, trouble-free. The tower at Jacksonville Beach appeared as we approached and, later, the big red-and-white checkerboard water tank of Naval Station Mayport.

The marina was neither large nor modern but it was well off the main flow of the St. Johns River. A great spot to hide a boat among sport fishers, runabouts, and sailboats from the seventies and eighties. A whole lot of faded fiberglass. It was a low-key place and *Figaro* fit right in.

A large older woman met me at my slip and greeted me with an excess of hospitality. She said my friend had paid three months' rent in advance. I adjusted *Figaro's* mooring lines and boat fenders, hooked up the shore power, and generally made everything shipshape while waiting for Al's call. *Figaro* had completed her task.

She'd gotten Al and me into the U.S. outside the video cameras, away from TSA's watchful eyes, and off the more common lists of travelers entering the country.

The sky grew dark and clouds closed in on the marina. Buckets of rain drove me back down into the cabin. Lightning seared the sky and thunder cracked overhead. I lay on the starboard settee and listened to the storm as the cell passed to the east. My phone rang as the rain stopped.

"I'm in a white Chevy van outside the gate. Say good-bye to your boat and bring your gear."

I grabbed my duffel, locked *Figaro,* and trotted up the dock to see Al behind the wheel of a used full-size cargo van. Al turned the ignition as I climbed into the passenger seat.

"Nice wheels," I said.

"Bought it from a plumber. The price was under the magic number and it fits right into the herd of hundreds like it. Nearly invisible."

"Magic number?"

"Any cash payment over ten thousand dollars is reported to the government. Best to stay under the radar." He turned onto the main drag outside the marina. "Your trip go well? How are the ribs?"

"The trip was great and the ribs feel much better."

"You've worked hard," he said. "Glad to see it's paying off."

"I'm fit enough to single-hand again. Is *Figaro* okay in that spot?"

"I paid the dock master in advance and hired a diver to keep the bottom clean."

"One less thing for me to worry about."

"You can't come back here until it's over, you know. No traces."

"Yeah, I guess so."

I looked in the rear to see a dozen plastic tubs and cardboard boxes filling the van's cargo area.

"What's all this stuff?"

"Mission gear."

"What'd you do?" I asked. "Spend all of Flake's money in six days?"

"Not even close. But I have made a few tactical assessments and some key acquisitions while you were out sailing. You hungry?"

"Starving."

He drove a few miles to a bakery/deli that sold me a six-dollar Reuben sandwich for ten bucks. Al ordered a Cuban. It looked a lot better than my Reuben and I put that bit of knowledge away for later use. He grabbed a cup of water.

"No beer?" I asked.

"We are downrange, my friend. No hostilities, yet, but we are still downrange. So, no alcohol."

"I'm trying to remember the last time I saw you *without* a beer."

"Like I said, we are downrange and, therefore, dry."

"You're serious, aren't you?"

He nodded.

"So, what have you been up to?" I asked.

"I took the train to Tampa, bought that van out there, and headed north. I spent a day in Serenity doing supplemental recon then drove to Tallahassee."

"What'd you do in Tallahassee?"

"I went to the state capitol, filled out their little forms, and started a business."

"What?"

"Eat your sandwich."

We finished our late lunch and walked back out to the van. The September heat and humidity—something I'd grown accustomed to aboard *Figaro*—suddenly seemed oppressive in comparison to the air-conditioned delicatessen. Al drove onto I-95 northbound and into rush-hour traffic.

"Tell me about this business you started."

"You rejected my one-day solution so I started to plan an extended campaign. For that, we needed a Combat Outpost. But you can't rent office space unless you have a business. No business, no COP."

"So you started one."

"On paper."

"Did you open up a bank account, too?"

"Banks ask for too much information these days."

Al drove onto the ramp that led to Jacksonville International Airport. After a few minutes, he turned onto a side street leading to an industrial park filled with newer one-story buildings of varying sizes. Each unit stood behind a screen of trees at the street. Attractive, upscale, and reasonably private. He turned into the driveway of a mid-sized building.

"Welcome to the COP," said Al. "We've got thirty-two hundred feet of industrial space. Three offices, a conference room, bathroom with shower, and a kitchenette. Comes with A/C, security system, and high-speed internet access. Not a lot of windows and no swimming pool but, for the most part, all the comforts of home."

"Landlords around here take cash with no questions asked?"

Al pressed a button on the visor of the van and a large industrial-sized garage door began to roll up.

"Landlords all over the world take cash," said Al. "Especially when you hand them six months' rent in advance and two months' rent as a security deposit. But you still need the legal docs and you have to pass a credit check. You still gotta look legit."

Al turned the van around, backed into the garage bay, and pressed the button again. We waited until the door closed before getting out. Heavy-duty industrial shelving laden with boxes lined half of a wall. A silver Dodge minivan stood against the other wall in back.

"You buy that, too?"

"From a soccer mom." He stretched his arm out in a sweeping motion. "For the record, we're a small R&D subsidiary of a major tech company that prefers to remain anonymous."

"Wait a minute. You passed a credit check?"

"Not me. Bart McDaniel."

He saw the question on my face.

"I added a team member."

The door to one of the offices opened and a fellow with wavy, white hair walked out. He wore an orange T-shirt, tan shorts, and a prosthetic leg below the left knee.

"Sim Greene," said Al. "Meet Bart McDaniel."

"Pleased to meet you," he said. "Call me 'Mac.'"

Mac stuck out his hand and shook mine.

"I wasn't sure when you guys would get here so I went out and got a pizza, some sodas, and a key lime pie," said Mac. "You hungry?"

"We ate," said Al.

"Well, I haven't," said Mac.

We followed him into the office and sat down at a small conference table. Mac started in on the pizza.

"Mac was a Green Beret combat medic before he lost his leg," said Al. "And he cross-trained as a sniper back in the day."

"That 'day' was a long time ago," said Mac.

"Well, it's good to meet you," I said. "As they say, 'any friend of Al's,' right?" I turned to Al. "Can we talk for a minute?"

Al and I walked through the open office door and I closed it behind us.

"Do we need a third guy?"

"Mac's here for logistical support. Tech, intel, and guns."

He could tell I wasn't sold on the idea.

"For what you want to accomplish, we need a team. You and I could handle a single strike and take out the bad guys who killed Eryn but, as I recall, your intention is to destroy *Sidoni*, expose local corruption, and free Dorothea if she's still alive. Am I right?"

"Yeah."

"That's more of a sustained campaign, not a single attack. It'll require a few things: insertion, intelligence gathering, infiltration, and a fair chunk of unconventional warfare. The two of us don't have the bandwidth to do all that."

"And adding a disabled ex-comrade brings our team up to full capability?"

Al laughed.

"I wouldn't use that D-word around him."

"I'm still not feeling great about this."

"Me, neither. I'd be happier if we had a platoon. But we haven't got the time to do much recruiting. And Mac might look harmless to you but he's got skills."

"Skills."

"We are less than fifty miles from the battlefield. We've got two nondescript, easily camouflaged vehicles that will get us there and back. We've got a Combat Outpost and matériel. We've got the intel Flake sent us but that's only a start. It needs fleshing out. In addition to his other qualities, Mac has some tech skills with the internet and computers and stuff. He's set us up with state-of-the-art gear and he knows how to develop intel. Who knows? We may even need a sniper."

He was making his point.

"You got a better idea, Sim?"

I shook my head.

"No, but I should have been included in this decision. I'm going to have to think about this."

"Fine. Let's go back in, have a slice of pie, and give you a bit of a makeover."

29

I'VE always been a sucker for good key lime pie and this one was delicious. Between bites, Al explained what intel we needed to round-out the information Flake had given us. Photos, maps, locations of key infrastructure.

"And one more thing," said Al. "You said you met a guy in a barbecue joint who didn't much care for *Sidoni*. Think you can find him? Some local knowledge would be helpful."

"Don't you think I run the risk of being recognized?"

"Time for that makeover I mentioned."

"I think he should go for the blond look," said Mac.

"Yeah," said Al. "Combine that with the bit of beard he's grown and he'd be a different guy altogether."

"What about my broken nose?"

"Nothing we can do about that. But Sim Greene died in the BVI. Nobody is expecting to see him in Georgia."

Al handed me a hair coloring kit and I took it into the bathroom to try it out while he and Mac unloaded the van and organized the equipment they'd bought. By the time they were finished, I was a sandy blond with a light brown beard.

"That'll work," said Al. "Wish we could make you shorter, though."

"Hunching down would be obvious, don't you think?"

"I suppose," said Al. "Mac and I are heading out to do some more shopping."

"Shopping? You've already got a ton of stuff here."

"We're contemplating a small-scale military offensive. If it comes to that, we'll need this gear. And more."

"More?"

"Specialized gear," said Mac. "Electronics you won't find at Best Buy, guns they don't sell at Cabelas, and drugs you can't buy at Rite-Aid."

"We'll take the Chevy and be back in five or six days," said Al. "And we talked about the intel we need. You okay going outside the wire on a recon job?"

"I can handle it."

"Distant recon only. Don't get too close. You don't want to be spotted."

"We've got three computers set up in the conference room," said Mac. "One of those is yours and you can use it as much as you like. Our local network is chaining two separate VPNs with the last one routed through a secure server in Finland."

"I have no idea what that means," I said.

"Virtual Private Network. It keeps you invisible and untraceable. Even the best hackers can't track you."

They drove off in the Chevy and, suddenly, it was just me and the minivan.

The kitchenette and three small offices, set up as bedrooms, occupied one wall of the COP. Mine was at the end of the hall. The contents—bed frame, mattress, end table, and dresser—were still in their cardboard boxes labeled with Swedish names. A stack of linens sat on the floor in a corner. I had to build my furniture before I could unpack my duffel.

I woke up the next morning knowing I had to fill in some holes in Flake's research. I spent an hour online looking for answers but a lot of those holes had to be filled by on-the-ground legwork. I walked into the garage and started the minivan.

Al had cleaned the car out pretty well but it still bore the wounds inflicted by a young family. Little shoes had scuffed the dash in front of the passenger seat, various food items stained the carpet, and an ancient fragment of red licorice lay petrifying inside the glove box. Touches of realism if I ever got pulled over.

I found my way to I-95 and turned north. There was no hurry and, more importantly, no need to draw the attention of law enforcement so I observed the seventy-mile-per-hour speed limit. Tall longleaf pines flanked both sides of the highway. The "Thank You for Visiting Florida" sign appeared in due course and was quickly followed by a bridge over the St. Marys River and a "Welcome to Georgia" sign with its giant peach and the governor's name printed at the bottom.

Twenty minutes later I exited the highway and drove into Serenity. I passed the motel I'd stayed at two months and a lifetime earlier, crossed the river, and passed the barbecue joint with the marvelous cornbread. Continuing on, I passed the bank, offices, and the fine old homes before reaching the old downtown area surrounding *Sidoni*. Nothing seemed to have changed. I drove on until I reached the new city complex at the north end of town.

My boots-on-the-ground recon started in the Serenity public library. I quickly located several books on the town's history and found some good pictures of the old county courthouse. A book on local antebellum architecture yielded the building's original floor plan. I photographed the page with the phone I'd bought in Ft. Lauderdale.

The periodicals section held a comprehensive collection of past issues of the Serenity Herald. I focused on the police beat section and found only a few major crimes in the last four years. Local fishermen had found a girl's body on the shore of the river south of town three years earlier. Her throat had been slashed. She was from Ohio and her parents had reported her missing, possibly abducted, the year before. The police said her body had probably been dropped from the bridge upstream. I realized that I had jogged by the spot only a few months earlier.

Several issues covered the religious unrest and public demonstrations against *Sidoni* earlier in the year. Flake's researchers had missed some interesting details and I photographed the relevant sections of those articles, too.

In February, a woman showed up in Serenity looking for her runaway daughter. She made a lot of noise. She wrote her Senator and her Congressman and even called the White House. Solana Bradford, an Army veteran who had served during Desert Storm, had made it plain to anybody who would listen that she wasn't leaving town without her sixteen-year-old daughter.

A news crew from the NBC affiliate in Washington, D.C. drove down to interview her and to investigate the situation. But some hooligans trashed their van and ruined their equipment in the hotel parking lot. Some other unknown fellows beat and robbed two members of the crew outside a bar that same night. The team folded up and went home without a story. Two days later, Solana Bradford was killed in a crosswalk by a hit-and-run driver. Her death merited only a few short sentences in the Herald.

Another group of protests and demonstrations broke out a month later but it was quickly quashed.

I left the library and drove toward the center of town. Mac had given me a wireless video interceptor and tasked me with locating every video camera within a half-mile of *Sidoni*. The device looked like a small computer tablet but was thicker with a couple of three-inch antennae sticking out the top. I drove around the area and parked near businesses and intersections and recorded camera locations on a street map. I also noted the locations of city-owned traffic cameras, finding only three within a mile of *Sidoni*. I highlighted areas on the map where traffic was affected by road work and confirmed the locations of police and fire department buildings. I was glad to learn the local cops didn't have a helicopter.

I drove back to the COP and spent the evening compiling the information I'd gathered and reading from the binders Flake had sent me.

30

MORNING traffic heading north from the COP was light. But Jacksonville pulled in workers from all over and commuters driving into town had a different experience. A few stressed drivers honked their horns.

The folks in Serenity, however, seemed devoid of stress. I hadn't fully noticed it the previous day but now it stood out in stark reality. People in the town seemed happy and cheerful. Folks in the stores and on the streets were lively and content. A portrait of small-town bliss.

I, on the other hand, had worked late the previous evening and needed something stout to wake me up. I drove directly to Fully Woke, the coffee shop across from the old courthouse.

Fully Woke. Yeah, that's what I need right there.

The place had a homey look with white wooden-paneled wainscoting and bright yellow wallpaper. Black-and-white pictures of crusty old men with large fish hung on the walls. Signs on the walls advertised ethically-grown, fair-trade coffee beans sourced directly from the farmer.

I ordered their light roast Hammerhead—a drip coffee with a shot of espresso. The smiling barista took my money and promised to call my name. A table in the corner next to the window overlooked *Sidoni*. Perfect. A younger couple in their twenties sat across the room from me. I thought of Marie and wished I could enjoy a cup with her that morning.

A green Subaru parked at the curb outside Fully Woke. The

driver was a blonde in her mid-40s. Neatly dressed with a camera strap around her neck. She took a couple of pictures of the old courthouse.

Two of *Sidoni's* maroon-robed priests walked out the front door of the church with another man and the blonde lifted her camera. One of the priests spotted her and stared. She put the camera down and the trio went back inside.

The barista called the name I'd given her and I almost didn't recognize it. I'd been Sim my whole life, Stewart for only a few weeks. I retrieved my Hammerhead and returned to my table. The coffee was excellent and I decided I'd need to learn how to reproduce the combination aboard *Figaro*.

The priest who had spotted the blonde and another guy walked out *Sidoni's* front door and stared at the Subaru. A white Chevy police Tahoe with its blue lights flashing pulled up and double-parked beside the green car. Old Mustache—the same guy who'd run me out of town months earlier—exited the Tahoe and approached the blonde. Bystanders who had seemed initially interested in what was going on left the area once they saw him.

I couldn't hear the conversation but I could tell the blonde and Old Mustache had met before. They weren't friends. The old cop reached into the car and grabbed the woman's camera. She protested as he opened the camera, removed the memory card, and put it in the shirt pocket of his uniform. Then he slammed the camera onto the pavement, breaking it into two pieces. He picked up the pieces and handed them to the woman.

Smiling, Old Mustache walked back to his Tahoe, got in, and backed up. The woman started her Subaru and drove off. The car had yellow Virginia plates that read "Don't Tread on Me" at the bottom. The Tahoe didn't follow.

The priest and the other man with him approached the police car. As they got closer, I recognized Clint McCord and a wave of anger washed over me. The policeman handed the camera's memory card to Clint. He clapped the old cop on the shoulder in a gesture that clearly showed who was in charge.

I walked out Fully Woke's back door, got into the silver Dodge, and drove down Riverside toward the south end of town in the same direction the woman had gone.

I found the green Subaru with the yellow Virginia plates at the restaurant I'd visited during my first trip to Serenity. I parked next to the Subaru and walked in.

The blonde sat in a booth near a wall with no windows and talked into a cell phone. I paid for a piece of cornbread, took it to the woman's table, and sat down across from her.

"I've got to call you back," she said as she ended the call and put her phone in her purse. "Who are you?"

"Call me Stewart."

"I'm not calling you anything. If you don't leave this minute, however, I'll call the police."

"I doubt that. They just broke your camera."

The hard look on her face softened.

"Why did they do that?" I asked.

"Who are you?"

"A friend."

"Do you live here?" she asked. "Do you even understand what is going on in this town?"

"I'm here on business. I was just surprised at how that cop treated you. Why did he do that? And why take the memory card?"

"Because I know what is going on in that church. Because I am trying to get the government to do something about it. Because I call my ..."

She stopped mid-sentence when she saw the waitress bringing her food. She continued after the waitress left.

"Because I call my senators every day. And because I want my daughter back."

Her name was Grace Kinney and she was a nurse from Charlottesville, Virginia. Her daughter had disappeared over a year earlier and a private detective had tracked her to *Sidoni*.

"Is the government doing anything about it?" I asked.

"My senators are hacks. They won't talk to me. I've called the FBI, too, but they just tell me *Sidoni* is protected by the First Amendment and isn't violating any federal laws because my daughter is an adult."

"And the local police are something less than hospitable?"

She sat and stared at her plate.

"Do you have anybody who will listen to you?"

"For a while there, the news people were interested but they don't care anymore. Even her father doesn't care. He's just tickled she's eighteen and he no longer has to pay child support."

"So, you fight a one-woman battle?" I asked.

"No, there are more of us. We had a social media page with over two hundred members. Some were parents worried about their children. Some just wanted to support us. We were trying to raise awareness about what is going on in there but we got shut down in January. They said we were promoting intolerance and hate speech. Then Solana got killed. Now there's only a handful of us and we're reduced to sending group emails."

"Who were you taking pictures of?"

"I thought I saw a celebrity coming out of there," she said. "An actor and his wife."

"What do you hope to gain with that?"

"I don't know. Maybe one of the tabloids will print an exposé and my story will get some traction."

"Seems like a long shot," I said.

"I'm all out of good ideas. That was the best I could think of."

"Aren't there any locals who agree with you? Anybody who wants to help?"

"One person," she said. "A local preacher. But she's more frightened now than I am."

I thought about it for a moment and weighed my options.

"There might be others," I said. "Others willing to do something substantive."

Grace got visibly shaken and stood to leave.

"I don't even know you. I have no idea why I opened up to you about all this but I am done with expecting a white knight to just fly in here and help me." She reached into her purse and handed me a business card. "But if you meet any such people, give me a call. Until then, I am out of here."

She walked out.

The waitress noticed and walked over.

"Is everything all right?" she asked.

"I must have said something wrong."

She smiled as she put the bill on the table in front of me.

"It happens."

I walked to the register to pay for Grace's meal. Taped on the wall next to the cash register hung a piece of copy paper with a headline reading "Have You Seen Jesse?" Under the headline was a picture of the redheaded fellow I'd seen in that same restaurant months earlier. The same guy who had spouted off about *Sidoni*. The text indicated he'd been last seen taking his fishing boat out to sea the last week of July; only a few days before Eryn was killed.

31

I spent the rest of the day scouting the locations of the longshoreman's union office, the local bank, shipyards, public works yards, and the city power plant. I drove the bridges leading to and from the resorts on the barrier islands and identified a few gated communities set aside for the upper crust.

Darkness fell and I drove back toward the old courthouse. I parked a block away under a tree and took my night-vision goggles into the back seat behind the tinted side windows.

Cars drove in and filled the parking spaces and side streets near *Sidoni*. Most had either out-of-state license plates or Georgia plates from different counties. There were few locals.

At eight o'clock, *Sidoni's* thick wooden doors opened and a steady stream of people, mostly men but some couples, began to move from the parked cars toward the building. They climbed the stairs, showed their ID cards to the maroon-robed priests at the door, and walked into the building. The doors closed promptly at nine and nobody entered or left after that.

Two hours later, a man left the building through a side door and walked toward a big pickup truck parked under a streetlight. He was large but not tall and kept his long hair in a ponytail that trailed out behind his cowboy hat. He wore jeans and work boots and a black T-shirt. He carried a small red canvas bag.

The truck was one of those lifted diesel pickups with huge tires on giant black wheels. Twin smokestacks stuck up behind the cab. It probably had enough torque to pull an aircraft carrier. Two plumes of smoke erupted into the sky as the man started the truck and two more stabbed the air as he accelerated away from the courthouse. The rattle-rumble sound of a turbocharged diesel was unmistakable.

Two priests opened the doors again at one in the morning and *Sidoni*'s adherents trickled out in small groups and drove away. The last stragglers stepped out at one-thirty and the maroon-robed men closed the doors behind them and turned out the lights.

Friday night was a to-the-minute replay of what I'd observed the previous evening complete with the pony-tailed cowboy in the truck with the red bag and *Sidoni*'s faithful leaving well after midnight. I expected the same pattern for Saturday but there was one major difference. After the doors opened and the devout started entering the building, a large white passenger van drove around from behind the church and turned north onto Riverside. A robed priest drove the van and another sat in the passenger seat. A half-dozen young women sat in the back. As it passed, I caught a glimpse of the young woman sitting directly behind the driver. It was Dorothea.

The van continued north through town. I started the Dodge, made a U-turn, and followed from a discreet distance. Ideas of how I could possibly rescue Dorothea ran through my head: everything from running the van off the road to rear-ending it at a stop light. But then what? Overpower the priests? Grab Dorothea and make an escape? I tested each scenario in my head and realized that I was probably outnumbered and almost certainly outgunned.

Two miles later, the van turned right onto a small highway and crossed the bridge leading to the twin barrier islands of King George and St. Paul. A T-intersection presented a binary choice and the van turned left toward King George Island. After another half-mile, it turned right and stopped at a guard house near a sign for the Plantation Estates and Country Club. The gate opened moments later and the van disappeared behind a thick stand of trees.

A uniformed man stepped out of the guard house and looked at my minivan as if nobody beyond the gate would ever own such a thing. I turned the car around and returned to *Sidoni* while cursing my own ineffectiveness.

The pony-tailed cowboy left at the usual time with the usual noise. *Sidoni's* doors again opened at one. A blond fellow came out the side door a half-hour later and walked toward a black limousine. I recognized him in the green tint of my NVGs as he turned to get into the car. The urge to shoot Mitch Danforth right then and there rolled over me like a wave. But the wave passed and I watched the limo back out of the parking lot, turn onto Riverside, and drive south.

Al had cautioned me to avoid short-range reconnaissance but I had to follow the guy who'd tried to kill me on Tortola. Still, there wasn't a lot of traffic in Serenity at that hour and I had to stay back quite a distance. The limo continued south on Riverside for about a mile and a half and turned left into a residential neighborhood. I killed the headlights as I approached Persimmon Street and nosed the unlit minivan into the intersection until I could see the limo's taillights receding in the distance. I counted the streetlights Danforth passed until he turned left.

I flipped the car's headlights back on and drove down Persimmon. Danforth had turned into a driveway leading to the rear parking lot of a row of newer two-story townhouses set against a small forest of tall pine trees. The units had different façades intended to hide identical floor plans. They had different window trims and different colored front doors but each unit featured identical brown brick climbing halfway up the front topped by beige vinyl siding. They looked like something that belonged in a cheaper area of New England, not southern Georgia.

I drove a hundred yards or so past the townhouses, turned the car around, and killed the ignition.

A light came on in the top floor of the second unit closest to me. I started the minivan, drove back toward the townhouses, and turned into the parking area. The black limo sat in a carport bearing the same address as the unit with the second-floor light. I wrote down the license number.

I left the townhouses, found my way back to Riverside Drive, and headed southwest toward I-95. Serenity had gone to bed hours earlier and the road was as empty as a college kid's bank account. Headlights pulled onto the highway behind me as I left the city limits. Blue flashing beacons came on moments later.

Damn.

I pulled over and slowed as the police car approached. It pulled around me, continued on at high speed, and disappeared around the next corner. Relieved, I continued on to I-95 and took the onramp heading south to Jacksonville.

Four miles later, I rounded a corner and spotted a vehicle fire a half-mile ahead. Bright orange flames rose into the sky. Emergency vehicles stood in front of the accident. Red and blue lights painted the trees on either side of the highway.

A cop stood in the middle of the highway waving a flashlight. I stopped and he walked up as I rolled the window down. It was Old Mustache, the police sergeant who had beaten my rental car's tail light to shards with his nightstick and, only days earlier, had broken Grace Kinney's camera. He shined the light in my face.

"We've got a truck on fire up ahead and it's filled with propane bottles," he said. "This road is goin' to be closed for several hours. Where are you headed?"

"Gainesville," I lied.

One of the propane bottles exploded. It was like a bomb had gone off and Old Mustache ducked involuntarily. He pointed his light at a short dirt strip connecting the north- and south-bound sides of the divided highway.

"Well, you can turn around here at that emergency access and get on the other side of the highway. Go back about a mile to the next off ramp and then west about four miles to Ocean Highway. Head south and you'll see Salt Bluff Road in about ten more miles.

That'll put you back on ninety-five southbound."

He turned the light back toward me and looked at me with an inquisitive eye.

"Do I know you, son?" he said.

"I can't imagine how you would, officer."

Another propane bottle touched off and one of the truck's doors flew twenty feet in the air. Two more bottles exploded in quick succession and Old Mustache ducked at each blast.

"Thanks, officer," I said. "I'll get out of your way."

I drove onto the access road and turned into the northbound lanes. The sergeant turned his flashlight as another car approached from the north.

32

I slept in Sunday morning. The previous night's close call with Old Mustache had spooked me so I stayed in the COP re-reading Flake's intel as well as the research I'd collected. At noon, I took a break and drove the minivan to a spot where I could see *Figaro* lying in the marina. She looked fine through my binoculars but I wanted to run down there and check her out myself despite Al's warning. I resisted the temptation.

Knowing the COP fridge was bare I headed into the wilderness of Jacksonville's strip malls to forage for fast food, took my lunch back to the COP, and ate it at the conference table. The big commercial door rolled up as I finished eating and the Chevy backed in. Al grinned from the passenger seat.

"We got some good stuff."

"And I spotted Dorothea last night."

I shared the details of my recon exercise and how I had followed the church van to a gated community.

"She was in the van. I'm sure of it. I also spotted Mitch Danforth and followed him home."

"Too close," said Al. "You got way too close."

Mac approached with a duffel in his hand.

"You guys ready to go?" he asked.

"Go?" I said. "You just got back."

"Mac and I think some training might be in order," said Al.

"We picked up some new toys to play with," said Mac.

"Where can we do that?" I asked.

"On the old family farm," said Mac.

Forty minutes later, we were headed west on Interstate 10.

"My family owned a fair piece of Alabama back in the day and I still have the house," said Mac. "It's a bit rustic and we're down to a little over two hundred acres, now, but that's plenty for what we need to accomplish."

Al drove while Mac navigated. I sat on the floor behind Mac perched on a pile of sleeping bags. Stacks of gun cases, boxes of ammunition, and our duffel bags occupied the rest of the van's floor space.

"Won't the neighbors complain about the noise?" I asked.

"I doubt any of them will even see us. The cabin is in some dense woods. And the place is only a few miles from Fort Rucker. So, the neighbors already hear plenty of military racket. We've got suppressors, too, so whatever sound we make won't be heard past the trees."

"Al told me about your military service. What have you been doing since?"

"After the Army cut me loose with a permanent disability, I did a personal azimuth check to figure out what to do with the rest of my life. Once I got over feeling sorry for myself, I signed up for a computer class and met folks who were getting deep into the tech side of things. Things clicked and we started a security consulting business. Hacking clients' systems to keep hackers away. We sold the business two years ago for way too much money and I retired again. Now I blog about shooting and weapons."

We drove on in near silence and I fell asleep among the duffels, sleeping bags, and other gear. I woke as Al turned the van off a narrow asphalt road onto a single-lane dirt track. Our headlights pierced a forest of long-leaf pine trees rising out of tall grass. We lumbered and swayed on the rough road for nearly ten minutes before an old farmhouse appeared before us in the twin high beams.

The house sat on a stone foundation with an old brick chimney on one end. The vertical board siding had been painted once, probably during the Truman administration. Windows appeared to be intact but the front porch exhibited a profound list to starboard. A rusted metal roof covered the structure.

"Air conditioning?" I asked. It never hurts to be hopeful.

"No. And last month it was hotter'n a goat's ass in a pepper patch. But it's cooled off a bit. We'll survive."

He stopped the van, hopped out, and walked up a short lane to the front door. He opened it and turned on the lights.

"Electricity!" I said.

"Don't be a smart-ass," said Al. He got out and walked around to the back of the van. "And give me a hand with this gear."

I got out the side door and walked to the back of the van. Al handed me two soft guitar cases emblazoned with Fender and Gibson logos. He grabbed two more and we followed Mac into the cabin. Al went back to the van for another two cases.

"What did you guys do?" I asked. "Start a southern rock tribute band? I didn't even know you could play."

Mac unzipped a Gibson case. Inside was a scoped, M4-style carbine with a short, threaded barrel and four magazines. A longer, fatter tube occupied a fabric sleeve next to the barrel.

"It's called a 'Blackout,'" said Mac. "It shoots .30-caliber, subsonic ammo. Holographic red-dot sights for daytime use and infrared designators for use with NVGs at night. Fairly quiet with the suppressor but still quite lethal."

"Expensive, too," said Al. "The shotguns were cheaper." He opened a box and pulled out a foot-long rectangle of black metal. "But their suppressors cost three times as much."

"That's some serious firepower."

"Hey," said Al. "If you wanna dance, you gotta bring some music."

Mac grabbed another case—long and skinny, hard-shelled, with four metal latches—obviously holding a high-end hunting rifle.

"This one is my personal favorite," said Mac. He unlatched the case and picked up a rather plain-looking, bolt-action rifle with a sling and a very large scope. "It's a .300 Winchester magnum; built it myself. Custom action, barrel, trigger, stock, and scope. You can't buy a rifle this accurate at your local sporting goods store. I call her the 'Neurosurgeon.'"

"He can wipe a gnat's ass with that thing at a thousand yards," said Al.

"Al is somewhat prone to exaggeration," said Mac.

"The 'Neurosurgeon?'" I asked.

"Mac taught FBI snipers how to hit hostage takers within a two-inch impact circle centered on the bridge of the nose—they call that the 'no-reflex zone'—at two hundred yards. You still that good, Mac?"

"Two weeks ago, I was shooting five-inch gongs at eight hundred yards with this baby. But head shots are for video games. You should always aim for center mass."

We emptied the van of several dozen brown cardboard boxes of varying sizes and shapes and weights.

"What else did you guys get?"

"A little bit of everything," said Mac. He spoke as he opened up the boxes. "Sidearms, ammo, load-bearing vests with body armor, ballistic helmets, PRC-148 encrypted radios, some state-of-the-art listening gear, extra license plates for the vans, a police scanner, and..."

He reached into a box and pulled out something that looked like a long, thick sausage.

"...a case of Emulex. This piece right here would vaporize this cabin."

"You guys planning to blow a bank vault?" I asked.

Mac smiled and Al shrugged.

"You never know," said Al.

"Here's something you've probably never seen before," said Mac. "Make a guess."

He reached into a box, pulled out a little chrome and black device about the size of a fingernail, and handed it to me. It had a USB computer connection on one end and a small black plastic cap on the other.

"Looks like the little thingie that comes with a wireless mouse and keyboard. The one I always lose."

"Well, it actually *is* a USB receiver for a wireless mouse and keyboard. And it will work with almost every wireless mouse and keyboard on the market. It is also a listening device and keystroke logger with its own memory storage." He reached into the box and pulled out two clear plastic bags filled with them. "Each one has its own IP address. I can log onto any one of them from anywhere in the world and download the audio and key-logging files any time I want. And because they never really transmit anything over radio frequencies, they can't be detected with a traditional bug detector."

I was impressed.

"So, what'd you do while we were gone?" asked Al.

"I filled in some of the gaps in our intel."

Al listened as I told him.

33

AL and I dragged ourselves out of the cabin before first light for a morning run.

"Tell me more about Mac," I said.

"He's legit. He doesn't crow about it but he did three tours in Afghanistan as an SF combat medic. Got there right after nine-eleven. He rode horses with Ismail Khan in the valleys between Herat and the Iraqi border. Mac carried tens of thousands of dollars in his saddlebags to pay off tribal warlords and buy information on Taliban positions. He set up medical clinics, treated villagers, and gathered a ton of intel about how al-Qaeda operated and which of their leaders hid in what caves."

I was getting a bit winded—that whole broken rib thing—so I let Al talk away.

"A family brought in their young daughter one day. Their crappy gas stove exploded and burned the girl badly. Mac sedated her and debrided her wounds. He worked on her for hours and then sat with her for nearly two days until they could transport her to a burn unit where she got skin grafts. He brought her back to her family and her grandfather was so grateful, he told Mac where he could find one of Bin Laden's top lieutenants. Mac and his A-Team dropped what they were doing, found the right caves, and took out the bad guy along with a couple dozen other baddies. The intelligence techniques Mac developed are now taught at West Point."

"What does he bring to our team?"

"Who's the toughest guy you know?"

"You," I said. "What's your point?"

"Who's the smartest guy you know?"

"I don't know. You're pretty far up on the list, though."

"Mac is the toughest person *I* know," said Al. "*And* the smartest."

"Okay."

"Don't feel bad. You're pretty tough, yourself. You had your chest caved in and you fought your way back. But Mac is a different breed of cat."

"That stuff in Afghanistan. The clinics, the horses, and the caves. Were you involved in any of that?"

"No. Mac and I never served together."

"Then how do you know all this?"

Al paused a moment.

"I've known Mac my whole life. We grew up a few blocks from each other in Lynchburg and we've kept in touch."

"You're happy with him," I said. "And he's obviously got skills. I can't argue with that. But how deep into this operation does *he* want to be?"

We spent the rest of the week in weapons training. We shoulder-fired the Blackouts in Close Quarters Battle drills both in daylight using the red-dots and in darkness with the night-vision goggles. We fired thousands of rounds of ammunition both with and without the suppressors attached. The suppressors weren't Hollywood movie quiet—the hiss we hear when a spy fires his silenced Walther—but the chunky, thumping sound of the rifle's action was quiet enough that we could practice without hearing protection.

His pistol range got a workout, too. We practiced holding a solid thumbs-forward grip with locked elbows in an isosceles stance while focusing on the top of the front sight. We drew from holsters, practiced switching from rifle to pistol, and dropped and reloaded multiple magazines in rapid fire 'El Presidente' drills. We put thousands of holes in dozens of paper targets and added a lot of dents to Mac's steel gongs. Mac was a skilled instructor and he brought Al and me up to speed in record time.

"Surprise, speed, and violence of action," said Mac. "Those are the three things we bring to an engagement."

I spent my spare time working out. I found a tree limb the perfect height and thickness for a chin-up bar and a path through the woods to run as an obstacle course. My ribs still ached, of course, but I felt myself getting stronger and hurting less every day.

We reviewed the maps and pictures I'd acquired during my recon and pored through the binders of research Flake sent to Ft. Lauderdale. Then we did it all again. We memorized street names and the locations of the police and fire stations, city offices, electrical substations, public works lots, shipping facilities, and union buildings.

On Saturday night, I noticed a tension in the air I hadn't felt before.

In Al's opinion, Alabama was not "downrange" and post-training beer was acceptable. We'd taken a few cold ones out onto the front porch. The only light came from the ultra-violet bulb in the bug zapper Mac had hung from the rafters in one corner. Happy, jolly Mac got deadly serious.

"Two weeks ago, Al told me about this mission," he said. "I understood the motivation but was skeptical about the probability of a favorable outcome. Now I want to be a part of it. If you want me."

"Seems like you're already in it," I said.

"I've just been training you and organizing gear. Logistical support. But now I want in as a full team member."

I looked at Al. He shrugged. It was my decision.

"I know what motivates Al," I said. "He wants to kill the people who murdered an innocent young girl on Tortola. But why do you want a piece of this?"

"On Monday, I started verifying the intel we have. It's rock solid. On Wednesday, I hacked into the Cass County Coroner's files and found the autopsy for that girl they found in the river three years ago."

"Fifteen years old," said Al. "Throat slashed."

"That's the problem," said Mac. "The ME's report describes a deep and long incised neck injury starting below the left ear and continuing to the right side across the trachea. Arteries on both sides severed. The report concluded she'd been attacked from behind by a right-handed killer. But it also said the lungs showed no aspiration of blood."

"Okay."

"Not okay. I saw more than my share of these in Afghanistan and the lungs almost always suck in some blood. And there were no pictures in the file. That's unheard of for a homicide-related autopsy. So I dug around. As it happens, she had rich parents. They ordered a private autopsy back home in Ohio. I hacked into that one, too. Their examiner concluded she'd suffered a short deep cut below the jawline severing two arteries and her left vagus nerve. No damage to the trachea. And the pictures he took showed a cut less than six centimeters long."

"Why is that important?"

"You can't inflict that type of wound from behind with the right hand. No Medical Examiner could see those wounds and write a report like the first one. Her attacker was left-handed and somebody is covering that up."

Al nodded.

"*Sidoni* has the political pull," said Mac. "They run the county. They use religion, violence, and mind games to control the population. I saw all that in Afghanistan. But now it's happening right here in *my* country. In *my* freakin' backyard. It has to stop. We have to destroy it."

"You could get killed," I said. "Or worse. Why take that risk at your age?"

Al finished his beer and sat back with a grin.

"At my age?" said Mac. "Don't confuse my hair color with a white flag of surrender. I know what I'm doing and I know the risks."

"Okay, Mac, you're in."

He smiled, walked into the cabin, and returned with three more cold bottles. The deal was sealed.

On Monday, Mac announced he was tired of our cooking. He suggested a place for dinner in a city a couple towns away. The sun set as the van reached the narrow highway and turned north.

Wide parkways of mown grass separated the highway from the tall long-leaf pine trees on either side. I wondered how many drunk drivers owed their lives to the Alabama DOT's vigilance against vegetation.

The drive was shorter than I thought it would be given Mac's estimate of "a couple towns away." But his definition of a town was minimalist at best. Apparently, if there was a church, a used-car lot, or a water tower with a name on it, the place qualified as a town. A 'city,' however, included a bank branch, an elementary school, and a Family Dollar store.

Across from the Family Dollar was an abandoned gas station with an orange and white Gulf sign. Three men sat on one of the empty pump islands. They were of a type: gaunt, ratty clothes, open sores, and nasty teeth. They looked twenty years older than they were and wore paranoia on their faces like a badge of honor.

"Damned tweakers," said Mac. "Sitting around waiting for the next chance to get fried."

The restaurant sat toward the end of a small strip mall at the far end of town. Mac parked under a streetlight and we walked in.

"Don't let the decor fool you," he said. "The food is delicious."

The dining area was maybe twenty feet wide and a bit longer with a kitchen area located behind a cash register and a row of bar stools. Prints of civil war soldiers, red and pink camellia blooms, and John Wayne hung from the walls in plastic wood-grained picture frames. The floor was a checkerboard of brown and beige vinyl tiles. A waitress waved a hand indicating we could sit anywhere we liked and Al picked a booth that looked out over the parking lot.

"What's good here?" I asked.

"It's all good," said Mac. "For me, it's a tossup between the grilled shrimp and the catfish with cheese grits. And the red velvet cupcakes are to die for. Tessa loved the baked chicken and the banana pudding."

"I had no idea you were married," I said.

"Lost her nine years ago in the same car crash that took my leg." Al stood up.

"I gotta hit the head, guys."

He walked toward the back of the restaurant.

"I assumed you lost your leg in combat."

"I'd just returned from an eighteen-month tour. We were coming home from dinner out and a drunk driver ran a red light and T-boned us. Tessa died on the way to the hospital."

"I am so sorry."

"It's been nine years. I'm okay, more or less. Still eats at Al, though."

"How come?"

Mac's eyebrows rose.

"Tessa was Al's little sister. He didn't tell you I'm his brother-in-law?"

"He sure didn't."

"We were best friends growing up. Al joined the Navy after high school and became a SEAL. I joined the Army, went on to Ranger school and the Q course, and wore a green hat most of my career. Tessa and I got married along the way."

Al returned from the bathroom in time to hear the last bit of Mac's explanation.

"I never knew you had a sister."

"Yeah, she was a real sweetheart before she married this loser."

Mac smiled. A waitress arrived to take our drink orders and it effectively ended that conversation. Mac started a new one after she left.

"We need to talk about our mission problem," said Mac.

"Problem?" I said.

"Al was trained for DA missions. Infiltrating hostile territory, performing a specific task, and getting out alive. Direct action with a targeted result. But what we've been talking about all week is unconventional warfare; a sustained counterinsurgency."

"So we should call in the Marines?" I said.

"The Marines are America's pit bulls. SEALs like Al just want to swim onto a beach, break things, and kill people. Counterinsurgency is where Special Forces training excels. We're like the Peace Corps but with grenade launchers and submachine guns."

"The Peace Corps?" said Al.

"They might not welcome the comparison. But we learned the language, culture, and customs of the locals. We built relationships with local leaders and taught them how to fight. Then we fought alongside them. Force multiplication."

"We know where the one guy lives," said Al. "We could take him out quietly with a single shot from the back of the van. We also know they keep the girls in the old courthouse. Sim and I could bust in, shoot up the bad guys, free the prisoners, and Hotel Alpha."

"Did I mention that SEALs just want to kill somebody?" said Mac.

Al shrugged.

"Direct action won't work on its own because it won't last. The surviving bad guys will rebuild and continue their operation. We have to destroy the organization and render the geography toxic to them. Classic counterinsurgency applying diplomatic, military, economic, and information principles."

"So how do we go about doing this?" I asked.

Al leaned forward.

"Destroying an entrenched organization is a revolutionary act," he said. "And a revolution is eighty percent political and only twenty percent military. Mao said 'the people are the sea in which the revolutionary swims.'"

"When did you become a devotee of Chairman Mao?" I asked.

"Mao was a Grade-A rat bastard but he knew how to win," said Al. "I like winning."

The waitress returned with our drinks and took our dinner orders. Mac waited until she was out of earshot.

"Our objectives are to defeat a small organized group of insurgents, free their captives, neutralize their leaders, and permanently isolate any surviving leftovers from the population. That last part—the isolation part—has to come from within the community itself. We have to build a political machine from the population upward.

"From what I've read in Flake's reports, there could be a small group of friendlies; people upset about what is going on. The vast majority are neutrals. We must consider everybody in the local power structure, however, to be dirty and hostile."

"There's something I don't get," I said. "Something I am missing. Why do the simple, God-fearing folks of Serenity tolerate a dangerous, religious cult in their midst and the corrupt police who protect it? Why are there so many neutrals?"

"Fear," said Mac. "It worked for Hitler, Stalin, and Pol Pot. It's what keeps the North Korean people in check today."

"Fear isn't enough," said Al. "Dictators have to control the flow of information while eliminating dissent. Ignorance is strength, right?"

"What do you mean?"

"Look at what happened during the Arab Spring. Tunisia, Libya, and Egypt were ruled by brutal totalitarian regimes that used fear to control their people. But those regimes were swept away by information spread through smart phones and social media."

"I didn't see a lot of fear in the faces of people walking around Serenity. There's something else going on."

"Either way, we must get the locals to support us," said Mac. "We start with the active friendly minority and then work to influence public opinion against *Sidoni*. We feed information to the neutrals and build support at the grass-roots level. This will erode the enemy's political power and, eventually, either destroy or drive out the insurgent elements."

"Sounds like our first objective," said Al, "is to identify that active friendly minority."

The waitress brought our food and all talk of counterinsurgency ended. The pork chop I ordered was hot and tender with a sweet glaze on it. It could have been the best pork chop I'd ever eaten or, maybe, I was just tired of cabin cuisine. The food disappeared quickly. I was almost down to the bone on my pork chop when Mac spoke up.

"Trouble," he said.

I looked out the window and saw a skinny fellow, one of the three men at the old Gulf station, loitering near the front of the van.

"He's the lookout," said Al. He stood up to go outside. "Pay the bill, Mac. We're outta here."

I followed Al out the door and toward the van.

The lookout whistled as we approached and the other two guys came around the side to meet us. The lookout stood back. One of the other fellows had a tire iron. The third guy produced a knife and moved toward Al.

"What's the matter, Shorty?" the man said.

"You're gonna look awful funny trying to crap that thing," said Al.

The guy with the tire iron moved to swing it at me but I stepped inside his arc, grabbed his left arm, and jammed my right elbow into his neck. He dropped the weapon and reached for my throat with his right hand. My left arm blocked him and I put my right fist into his gut. He bent over from the punch and I followed with a left hook to his jaw. The punch connected halfway between his ear and chin and the guy's head spun to his left as his knees folded. A small glass pipe fell out of his shirt pocket and shattered on the asphalt.

I looked over at Al. He stood there with a knife in his hand; his attacker slumped over on the ground.

"Did you kill him?" I asked.

"No reason to," he said. "Just another stupid addict."

Mac walked up.

"The lookout ran down the street," he said. "Did I miss all the fun?"

"We'd better skate before the cops arrive," I said.

Mac started the van and got us back on the highway.

"Stupid meth heads," he said. "The politicians talk about opioid abuse in the cities but the problem out here is cheap Mexican meth. The junk is ruining our country. Every small town in this state is plagued with it and the cops can't stop it. They can't even slow it down."

Mac drove at a sedate pace retracing our line back to the cabin.

"You know that active friendly minority we were talking about?" I said. "I may have an idea."

They listened.

34

I sat in a wooden folding chair and listened to a key turn in a lock. The door opened and Reverend Sharpe entered the front room of the living quarters attached to the back of Serenity's AME Church.

"Don't turn on the light," I said.

She froze in the doorway.

"You are in the Lord's house, brother," she said. "You better have a damned good reason for breakin' in here."

"Please sit down."

"Who the hell are you?" she said. She pulled a cell phone out of her bag. "I got 911 on speed dial."

"Just listen to what I have to say before you call the cops."

She paused a moment, closed the front door, and sat in the chair across from me. She kept the cell phone in her hand.

"You were arrested six months ago," I said.

"And I went to court and pled guilty to a charge of Disorderly Conduct. I paid the fine, too, and did twenty-four hours of 'community service.' Ain't that rich? My whole life *is* community service."

"And then somebody stole your car and set it on fire down by the river," I said. "That was supposed to be a message, wasn't it?"

"Did they send you here to kill me?"

"No. I'm here to help you."

"Sure you are," she said. "So, what's with the mask?"

"It's for my safety. And yours."

"If you want somethin' from me, then get to it."

"I read about your situation in the newspaper," I said. "You and your members were protesting outside *Sidoni* and the police showed up. Somebody slugged a policeman and they grabbed you."

"Nobody slugged any policeman. It was a peaceful demonstration against old-time blasphemy and modern-day slavery. But they arrested me and sent two of our members to the hospital."

"How does your congregation feel about that?"

"Not good," she said.

"What do you mean?"

"I've got some angry young men in my ministry who are about to lose it. Sometimes they talk about doing things that are very un-Christian. And that would not be good at all."

"Are you planning on doing anything about it?"

"I called the ACLU and a couple other do-gooder groups up north but none of them seemed to be particularly interested. I'm not planning on doing anything else."

"Would you like to see *Sidoni* stopped?" I said.

She looked at me quietly for a moment and then shook her head.

"A guy breaks into my church and sits here waiting for me in the dark. He wears a mask so's I can't see his face. He's got a smooth tone in his voice and acts supportive and understanding but I don't really know who this guy is or why he's asking me questions."

"Assume that I'm a friend who wants to help. A friend who has no connection with the authorities."

"I'm not ready to make a lot of assumptions," she said. "Those people who burned my car might decide to do it again. But they also might lock me in the trunk first."

"I want to help you expose *Sidoni* for what it is. But I can't do it alone."

"If you're about to ask me to enter my little flock of believers into a fight they're gonna lose, then you can pound sand. That just ain't gonna happen, brother."

"Nothing like that. No fighting at all."

"Who am I talkin' to?" she asked. "Who exactly?"

"I'm part of a group that wants to expose the evil going on in that old courthouse. I'm sorry I can't be any more detailed than that."

"What's in it for you?"

"We want to shut down *Sidoni* and free the girls inside."

"You think they're being held captive? You think they're being held against their will?"

"You called it modern-day slavery."

"They got the police, the city men, the union bosses, and all the politicians," she said. "Every last one of 'em is in it up to their hindquarters."

"And it all needs to come down."

She laughed.

"Like you gonna do all that?"

"Not alone," I said.

"And that's where you think we come in?"

I opened my mouth to respond but she held her hand toward me palm forward.

"Sorry, brother, I'm not going to put my congregation at risk simply 'cause a masked, smooth-talking, white dude can figure out how to break into my church."

"Like I told you, no fighting, no guns, and no protests. Just eyes and ears."

"I don't follow you," she said.

"All we want is for people to keep their eyes and ears open. All we want is information. And we want it to come through you."

She sat there stone-faced with her arms folded.

"Maybe that level of involvement will keep the young men in your congregation from making a bad impulsive decision," I said. "Think about it."

"Okay, I'll think about it. But how am I supposed to know you're really going to step up to the plate?"

"Watch the news and read the paper. You'll know in a few days." I handed her a piece of notepaper with an email address on it. "If you like what you see and want to help, send me an email saying you're interested in the used tires I advertised on Craigslist. If you don't want to hear from me again, send an email thanking me for dinner but that you 'just want to be friends.' Either way, you shouldn't tell anybody about our meeting. Not even members of your congregation. It could be dangerous for you."

"What are you gonna do?"

"You'll see it soon enough. You'll know it was us."

She nodded and I stood up to leave.

"One more question," she said. "When you bought that mask, why'd you pick LBJ? That dude was one scary cracker."

"It was on sale."

35

THE barista at Fully Woke handed me my dark roast and I walked over to my usual seat near the window to enjoy the coffee and watch *Sidoni*. I didn't see Grace Kinney or her green Subaru. I didn't see Old Mustache or his white police Tahoe. I didn't see any maroon-robed priests. I did see a lot of happy people walking along the sidewalks and going about their business. I dialed the number for Mac's burner.

"It's all good."

Moments later, he parked our cargo van in front of the sign announcing the future home of the Sidoni Multi-Media Center. A small area of dirt and weeds, remnants of a flower garden when the home had been occupied, lay to one side of the sign. Al, shielded from *Sidoni* by the van, stepped out and placed a softball-sized fake rock in the dirt next to a few other rocks. He got back in and the van pulled away.

"We good?" asked Mac.

"Nobody following."

"How's the feed?"

I pressed the icon for the camera's app on my tablet. A clear view of *Sidoni's* main entrance and south side door filled the screen.

"Picture perfect."

Mac had set the camera to record only when it detected motion. To reduce the chance of being discovered, he'd set it to transmit recorded video segments only when summoned by the camera's app on his tablet. The need to be within range meant we would become regular customers at Fully Woke.

A dark blue Volvo crossover with tinted windows and Connecticut plates drove slowly past the old courthouse several cars behind the van.

"Possible tail. Blue Volvo."

"I see him," said Mac. "We'll head north and lose him."

"Roger."

The Volvo drove by again five minutes later. Two minutes after that, it returned from the opposite direction, turned around, and parked in front of the sandwich shop next door.

The driver pulled out a pair of binoculars and scanned the old courthouse. After a couple of minutes he put the binoculars away, pulled out a cell phone, and made a call. It was a short call. Moments later, he opened the car's door and stepped out. I dialed Mac's phone again.

"That Volvo is no factor."

"We'll be in the parking lot out back in ten minutes."

The Volvo guy was big; probably six-two and a little over three hundred pounds. Seriously overdressed. He looked around, closed the car's door, and walked into the sandwich shop. I opened the internet browser on my tablet. It took me a few minutes but I eventually found a place that looked promising. I wrote the address on a napkin. Above the address, I wrote:

> *I am the guy you're looking for but you being here doesn't work for me. We need to talk. Be at Bonnie's at 4 pm or the mission is off and I disappear. Your boss wouldn't like that.*

I finished my coffee and walked over to the sandwich shop. Mr. Big sat at a table with a soda in his hand. I walked up to him, tucked the napkin into his shirt pocket, and left out the back door.

―――――

I'd never been to Bonnie's Diner before but the map on my

phone had put it forty-five miles east of Serenity; basically, in the middle of nowhere. Exactly what I wanted. The nearest town was three miles away and it was a very small town. The last two of those three miles were on a sandy dirt road. The billboard on the main highway made the first turn easy but subsequent signs weren't so obvious and we had to hunt around to find the place. The road ended in a wide dirt parking lot in front of what appeared to be an old tobacco house retro-fitted with large plate-glass windows. A thick stand of trees, mostly hickory and ash, surrounded the place and stretched up onto a short hill behind the restaurant.

We'd come an hour early to scope out the area and look for anything suspicious or worrisome. We walked into the diner twenty minutes early and found a place decorated almost exclusively with old tin road signs, beer-branded mirrors, pages from old Sears catalogs, and other ephemera from past decades. The wall opposite the entry held a huge fireplace topped with a massive copper chimney.

Al chose a booth next to a large window overlooking the parking lot. I ordered a large plate of fried shrimp and Cokes for Al and me. The shrimp arrived and I was able to eat a few before the big guy walked in. He saw me, walked over, and sat down.

"I'm Jack Harkness," he said. "What do you mean my being here doesn't work for you?"

"Because you are obvious and, therefore, a danger to us," I said. "Saying you stand out like a sore thumb is an insult to thumbs everywhere."

"I know my job."

"And you'll get yourself killed before starting it."

"Listen, bucko, I'm forty-five and I'm still alive."

"Like they say on the prospectus, 'past performance is no guarantee of future results.'"

"Orson Flake sent me to check up on you guys. So I'm checking up."

"Prove it."

He pulled out a cell phone and stabbed at the screen a couple of times. I could hear the phone ringing and a voice answer. He handed the phone to me.

"Who is this?" I asked.

"Sim? This is Orson Flake."

I recognized the voice.

"Why are we talking right now, Mr. Flake?"

"I hadn't heard from you and I want a progress report. It's been three weeks since you picked up my money in Ft. Lauderdale and I've heard nothing from you. I have no idea what you are doing with my money."

"This is the wrong time for this conversation. The situation is dangerous and Mr. Harkness has been compromised."

"What do you mean 'compromised?'"

"I spotted him fifteen minutes after he got into town. And I'll bet you twenty bucks they've noticed him, too."

"What makes you so sure?"

"A car with Connecticut plates stops across from the hostile target's headquarters and the driver starts glassing it with binoculars. Then the driver gets out wearing an over-stuffed tailored suit on a hot day in Georgia. You think he won't be noticed?"

"I need to know what's going on there," said Flake. "I want information and if you won't give it to me, then I'll send people who will."

"We are making progress and I'll call you tonight with more details. But this project is outside your scope of competence and what you don't understand about this process will get people killed. I won't run that risk. If I see this guy in town again or anybody like him, I'll call off this operation and return whatever funds we haven't spent."

"But..."

"There is no more to discuss. Those are my terms and they are inviolable."

I ended the phone call with him in mid-protest and handed the phone back to Harkness.

"You need to get out of here, my friend. And don't go home by way of Serenity."

"I'm a big boy," he said.

"No kidding," said Al.

Harkness gave Al a dirty look, walked out, and drove away.

Al grabbed the last two shrimp while I paid the bill and left a tip in the jar. We walked out toward the minivan.

"Amateurs," said Al.

———

Sailors establish routines at sea. They test bilge pumps and batteries, look for loose gear and chafed lines, and check fuel and water tank levels. They get updated weather reports twice a day. These become habits.

By habit, I checked the nightly NOAA online weather report. A depression off West Africa had grown into Tropical Storm Six and was expected to dump heavy rain on the southern Cape Verde islands. Being dry islands, Tropical Storm Six would come as welcome relief. It was nothing I needed to worry about.

But Orson Flake was.

36

I sat on the ground in the shadows of moonlight twenty feet from Longstreet Avenue with a beer in my hand and my back against a thick, rough, old oak tree. I had a few minutes and was thinking about what Al had told me about "Old Pete" Longstreet. Apparently, he was Robert E. Lee's principal subordinate. Lee called him his "Old War Horse" and put him in command of the right wing at Gettysburg. Old Pete saw the futility of Pickett's Charge but still carried out the order. That mistake, easily one of the biggest tactical errors made during any battle, was a big part of the South's loss at Gettysburg, a psychological defeat from which they never recovered. Al said Longstreet was the best corps commander in the war on either side. It didn't seem to help him much at Gettysburg.

It's strange, the stuff you think about while waiting in ambush.

That night, I wore an old beat-up overcoat and tried to look like a local bum while waiting for one of *Sidoni's* most trusted adherents: the guy who took the church's donations to the night deposit box at the local bank. I'd watched him two weeks earlier and we had figured Saturday night was their biggest draw, so I sat there on Longstreet Avenue with a can of beer in my hand and the Civil War in my head. Our target would be there soon. He was a creature of habit and always left the old courthouse at eleven.

We chose that spot because there were no businesses nearby with security cameras and because the only streetlight on the block wasn't working. It broke when Al shot it earlier that evening with a suppressed pistol.

Mac had picked the lock to a third-floor office suite overlooking the street. That spot, about two hundred yards away, gave him the best angle for the shot we needed. He waited there with the Neurosurgeon.

Al sat in the minivan half a block away with the engine idling.

It would be hard not to see our target and impossible to avoid hearing him. His truck was supremely efficient at converting fuel into noise.

"Target has made the turn toward you, Bravo."

Mac's voice rang in my earpiece but his radio call was superfluous. Al and I could already hear the truck approaching with its whining turbochargers and loud vertical exhaust pipes. The neighbors must hate all that racket so late at night.

"Transport is in place," said Al.

"Bravo is ready," I said. "Your call, Delta."

"Delta sees no other traffic," said Mac. "It is a go."

The big truck approached in full voice. I heard the pop of Mac's mostly-silenced rifle and the truck rolled to a stop as its left rear tire deflated. Mac had timed it perfectly and the truck stopped only thirty feet away from me.

"Target is static," said Mac. "Continuing overwatch."

The big guy with the ponytail and cowboy hat got out of his truck and cursed as he walked to the back and looked at his tire. I hunched a bit as I walked toward him. It had the effect of making me look both older and shorter, something I would want him or any other observer to remember.

"You need any help, friend?" I asked.

"Git outta here an' go let your pups suck," he said, "or I'll knock you into next week, you old geezer."

I pulled the Taser out of my pocket.

"You're not very nice," I said.

His eyes grew big and he swore as I pulled the trigger. I watched the metal barbs shoot through his XXXL T-shirt and he hit the ground writhing in pain as 50,000 volts coursed through his body.

It's an awful thing to feel but an amazing thing to watch. The manufacturers call it electro muscular disruption but it's more like a full-body charley horse.

I put a black bag over his head, rolled him over onto his stomach, and fastened his thick arms together at the wrists with three extra-large zip ties. Al pulled up in the minivan—the passenger-side sliding door already open—and jumped out. We heaved the big thug into the spot where the middle row of seats had once been, the spot where somebody's children had once dropped melting popsicles from their kiddie seats. Al reached over and shoved a syringe into one of the guy's arms while I zip-tied his legs together and slid the door closed.

Three red bags lay on the front seat of the truck. I reached into the open driver's door and grabbed them. Red canvas bags sized to fit into a bank's night deposit drop. I tossed them into the gap between the front seats of the minivan.

A large aluminum fuel tank sat in the back of the truck behind the cab. I set my beer can on top of it and hopped into the passenger side of the minivan. Al pulled away at a sedate pace.

"On the road, Delta," I said.

"Covering fire terminated," said Mac. "En route to extraction."

Al turned the corner, drove back on a parallel street one block over, and stopped at the agreed-upon spot. I climbed into the back and Mac walked out between two parked cars. He slid into the passenger seat with his gun case and looked at his watch as Al drove off.

"Two minutes and seven seconds from flat-tire to extraction," said Mac. "Not bad."

"Half that time was waiting for Bubba, here, to get out of his truck," I said.

"No more talk," said Al. "I'm not sure he's completely out."

I searched our captive and found a Colt .45 pistol, a cell phone, a cheap watch, an old pocket knife, and a studded leather wallet on a chain. I pulled the memory and SIM cards from the phone, wiped off my fingerprints, and tossed it out Mac's window. The rest went into a small brown duffel.

Once I was sure Bubba was out, I took the black bag off his head and replaced it with a pair of blacked-out ski goggles and some industrial ear muffs. See no evil; hear no evil. The ride back into Florida was uneventful. No roadblocks. No sirens. Not a single cop car. Al pressed the garage door button and drove into the COP.

"You guys need any help?" asked Mac.

We told him we didn't. He grabbed the three bags and his rifle case and carried it all to the office.

"I'll count the winnings and clean my weapon," he said. "Let me know if you need anything."

Al and I half-carried, half-dragged the big man to a steel chair at the back of the garage. We zip-tied his arms and legs to the chair.

"What'd you put him out with?" I asked.

"Fifty milligrams of Benadryl, five milligrams of Haldol, and two milligrams of Ativan. We call it a 'B-52.' Puts even the biggest boys to sleep. But he'll be coming out of it soon so it's time for the masks."

"Can't we just keep the goggles on him?"

"I want him to see us. The stuff I've got works better if the subject isn't completely disoriented. Goggles tend to goof things up."

Al walked over to a bookshelf that faced Bubba and pushed the record button on a hidden video camera. I opened a duffel and pulled out two Guy Fawkes masks and a pair of black hoodies. We put them on and Al pulled the muffs and goggles off Bubba. He was already awake.

"You think those masks y'all wearin' are funny?" he said. "You guys are dead men."

Al reached into the duffel and pulled out a clear plastic bag with a syringe and two small bottles of clear liquid. He inserted the needle into one of the vials and pulled out the plunger. The liquid filled the syringe.

"What the hell are you doing?" said Bubba.

His eyes went wide and he struggled to get out of the chair.

"You seem angry, brother," said Al. "Let's give you a little happy juice."

Al shoved the needle into the man's right thigh and pressed the syringe's plunger. The man protested and swore like he had on the street, his limited vocabulary unburdened by excess creativity.

"Let's give him a few minutes to relax," said Al. "I need a drink."

Al and I walked back to the office and got a couple of Cokes. Mac was dutifully cleaning his rifle.

"How'd we do?" asked Al.

"You're not going to believe this. There are twenty-five bundles of hundred-dollar bills. Ten thousand dollars per bundle. A quarter-million dollars."

Al let out a low whistle.

"Are you sure they're all hundreds?" I asked.

"Every one," said Mac. "Fresh and crisp, too."

"That's a lot of dough for a church fundraiser," said Al. "Let's ask our guest about it. He should be ready by now."

"What'd you give that guy?" I asked.

"Sodium thiopental," said Al. "They used it on St. Thomas to keep you in a medically-induced coma. It's also a decent truth serum. I grabbed some while nobody was looking."

Always the opportunist.

"Think he'll tell the truth?"

"Like Abraham Lincoln being waterboarded."

Al finished his Coke, crushed the can, and tossed it into the trash.

"Mac, give me about ten minutes with the guy and then send in the Super Chief."

"Sure thing."

"That first dose should have softened him up by now," said Al. "Time to get a little intel."

We walked back out wearing our masks and hoodies and Bubba glared at us. Al dragged a chair closer to him and sat down. I leaned against the wall.

"How you feelin', man?" asked Al.

"Just great," he said. "I just love being tied to a stinkin' chair."

"Yeah, that's unfortunate," said Al. "What's your name? My friend and I are tired of calling you 'Bubba.'"

"Harley," he said. "Harley Augustus Lee."

I looked through Harley's wallet and nodded.

"Nice truck you got there," said Al. "Very trick ride."

"Best truck in the whole state of Georgia."

"Where'd you get it?"

"A buddy done give it to me. Best damned truck in the whole South."

"A friend gave you that truck? Nice friend."

"Well, some dude got arrested and the city took his truck. One of my cop friends fixed it so's I could get it."

"Well, you use it to make deposits for the church. I figured it was their truck."

Harley chuckled a little. "It's mine, jackass."

Harley gave Al the evil eye.

"Do you know how much money you were taking to the bank tonight?"

"I don't ask and they don't tell. It's usually just a single bag; sometimes two or three. I just put 'em in the bank's drop box and run on home."

"They had a quarter-million in those three bags."

Harley's eyes got big.

"Where do you suppose all that money comes from, Harley?"

"Donations, I guess."

"That's a pretty successful church."

Harley grinned.

"What's so funny?" asked Al.

Harley laughed. "You guys are about as sharp as a bowling ball. You think *Sidoni's* a church?"

"If it isn't a church, what is it?"

"They call it a way of life but my grandpa woulda called it a fancy cathouse. The best cathouse there is, too. New young kittens all the time, brother. They call 'em 'Priestesses.'"

He laughed.

"Where do these priestesses come from?"

Harley opened his mouth but didn't say anything. He shrugged his shoulders. Al asked him again but got the same response. He pulled out the syringe and reloaded it.

"Booster shot," said Al.

He pumped the drug into Harley's upper arm.

"Are you still with me, Harley?"

"Yeah."

"We were talking about the young women at the church. Where do they come from?"

"All over, man. No more Americans, though. Not anymore. Did that for a while but some of their folks started gettin' wind of where their girls ran off to and it caused a bunch of trouble."

"How do the girls wind up at *Sidoni?*" asked Al.

"Clint and Mitch bring 'em in. They're good lookin' dudes and just as smooth as an otter's belly. They just snake them gals away like it's nothin' at all."

"Aren't you afraid the cops will see a missing person's report and recognize one of the girls?"

Harley laughed.

"Cops? Mitch *is* a cop. He's the guy who got me my truck. The rest of 'em get paid off or come in once in a while to 'worship' for free."

"So Mitch is the boss?" asked Al. "He calls the shots?"

"He's up there, all right, but the High Master is in charge. Mitch tells us what the High Master wants done and we do it."

"The High Master. That's Duncan McCord, right?"

"Yeah. Who'd you think I was talking about?"

"Are the girls happy at *Sidoni?*"

"We have to slap 'em around a bit at first but they get with the program pretty quick."

"What about that girl who wound up in the river three years ago? Did you slap her around, too?"

"I ain't been here that long. I don't know what you're talking about."

"Do any of the girls ever try to go home?"

"After a while, they don't want to leave. They love it, man. They love us. They think we're all freakin' awesome."

Al looked at me and shook his head.

"Aren't you afraid word will get out? That somebody might turn you in?"

He smiled.

"You guys don't know whether to scratch your watch or wind your butt. I told ya, man. The cops know all about it. And so do their bosses. We're protected."

"Different question. Who is Hunter Reynolds?"

Harley shrugged. "Ain't never heard of him."

A railroad train's horn blew in the distance as if it were heading toward us at high speed. It blew again as it approached a nearby crossing. The nearest rails were over two miles away but it sounded as if they were just outside the building. Rail cars clacked over seams in the tracks. It was a long train and Al waited for the sound to diminish.

"He's from Europe," said Al. "Tough guy. Has an earring in his left ear."

"A couple of guys got earrings. It don't mean nothin'."

"His is kinda special, though. A small silver dagger with flames on either side."

Harley's brow wrinkled. "Trevor?"

"Tell me about him."

"He don't talk much. And he ain't American. One of the guys said he was some sort of English Green Beret or somethin'. That dude's ornery as hell, though. You don't want to rile him."

"Is he right- or left-handed?" asked Al.

"How would I know?"

"He carries a gun, doesn't he?"

"Yeah."

"And he wears it inside the waistband behind his left hip."

Harley thought a moment. "Yeah, I guess he does."

"So, he's left-handed."

"I guess so."

"Can you tell me anything about the priests at *Sidoni?*"

He shrugged.

"How do you become a priest? Do you need to be a long-standing member? Do you need to take any vows?"

Harley laughed.

"Vows? No, it ain't like that. They don't have to believe. They just gotta be ex-military and have skills. And they've got to know Trevor."

"Are they armed?"

"They all carry nines," said Harley. "Every one of 'em."

"Just the pistols?"

"Yeah. We got some HK MP5s in a closet, but they'd only bust those out if things got real. It don't ever get real."

Harley blinked his eyes and looked as if he were about to fall asleep.

"Stay with me, Harley," said Al. "Prostitution is still illegal in Georgia. The townspeople can't be happy about it. Why don't they ask the state police to close it down?"

"The townies love us. We're like Disneyland for adults, man. People roll into town and spend their dough and have a great time. And we do good stuff, too. Churchy stuff. *Sidoni's* got its own drug rehab and they sponsor a boy's club, too. The High Master even bought new uniforms for the high school football team last year."

"But some outsiders tried to shut it down," said Al.

"Yeah. See what it got them?"

"Are you talking about Solana Bradford?"

"Who?" said Harley.

"She came here last March to get her daughter back. She brought a news crew with her, too. But she got hit by a car while crossing the street."

Harley shook his head.

"It was a truck, man. Best damned truck in the whole state of Georgia."

"Your truck?"

Harley laughed.

"Mitch told me to do it. Didn't even dent my bumper."

He'd killed a woman and was proud of it. That bothered me. Al was unfazed.

"Well, Harley, it's Sunday morning in Serenity. Is anybody expecting you back at *Sidoni?*"

"No, man. It's closed up tight on Sundays. It ain't right to run a whorehouse on a Sunday."

Al put the black bag over Harley's head and we walked back to the office.

"So what should we do with the body?" asked Al.

"We're not going to kill him."

"Are you kidding me? After what you heard about Solana Bradford?"

"I've got a better idea."

37

ZIP ties are quick and convenient but they aren't permanent. We secured Harley to a cast iron drain pipe with two pairs of steel handcuffs. To keep things quiet, we shoved a rag into his mouth and secured it with a couple lengths of duct tape. Al added ear muffs and a black bag over his head. See no evil, hear no evil, speak no evil.

We rolled into Serenity about five in the morning. I'd pulled Harley's security card key from his wallet and Al had coaxed him into telling us how many priests would be in the building on a Sunday morning. Harley said the girls all stayed on the second floor. We now had a game plan.

Mac put together a decent disguise on short notice. He took off his prosthetic limb, folded up the left pant leg of his blue overalls, pinned it inside by the knee, and grabbed a pair of crutches. He rubbed dirt on his face and messed up his hair. Al and I put on dark face paint and body armor.

"Our top priority is to rescue Dorothea," said Mac. "Gathering intel is secondary. Non-lethal force is preferred."

"And if these bean bags don't drop them?"

"Hit them center mass and the shock will knock them out. They won't even remember what hit them."

"If they resist?"

"You have your pistols."

We tested the radios and dropped Mac off a block west of *Sidoni*. Al drove south and parked the van around the corner and out of sight of the courthouse. We put on helmets with night vision goggles, grabbed our suppressed shotguns, and made our way to a spot across the street from the back door of the old building. A security camera hung above the door. A black metal card reader perched on the wall next to the handle.

"It is a go, Delta," said Al.

"Roger that," said Mac. "Surprise, speed, violence of action. Make it happen."

A few seconds later, we heard Mac pounding on the front door with one of his crutches. We soon heard the sound of the front door opening over Mac's radio. I pulled a green laser pointer from my pocket and trained it on the camera's lens. With the camera now blind, Al ran up, pulled a baggie out of his pocket, and smeared peanut butter across the lens. He waved and I shut off the laser.

"What do you want?" said a voice over Mac's radio.

"It's Sunday morning," said Mac. He sounded drunk. "Why isn't this church open? And where's the damned preacher?"

Al pressed Harley's card key against the reader and the door made a dull buzzing sound. Al pulled the door open and I entered with my shotgun at my shoulder.

"We're in, Delta," said Al. "Keep him occupied."

In the green hue of the NVGs I saw a room with a steel kitchen table in the center and a refrigerator in one corner. I found the building's electrical panel next to the refrigerator and switched off the master breaker. Al moved forward to the door opposite me and I assumed the number two position. It opened to a wide hallway leading through the center of the building. I recognized the ornate sconces I'd seen nearly three months earlier. But there were no flickering light bulbs or any pan pipe music. We could hear Mac over the radio as he continued his act at the front door.

"I'm in a bad way," he said. "You're a church, aren't ya? I need some help, man."

"You're at the wrong church. This is the sanctuary for Rahm Sahn Sidoni."

"What?"

"It's the sanctuary for Rahm Sahn Sidoni."

"I don't care if it's the wetsuit room at the Ron Jon Surf Shop," said Mac. "I just need a little somethin' to get me by, you know? You got any wine or anything?"

A robed figure entered the hallway from a room about twenty feet ahead of us. I saw the green line of Al's infrared designator move to the priest's chest. Al fired and the figure went down. I zip-tied the man's wrists together and duct-taped his mouth shut.

"One hostile down," Al whispered.

I looked into the room the man had left and saw a desk with a computer and three blank monitors. A bank of now inert electronic equipment occupied a rack to the right of the desk. Al pointed down the hall in the direction he wanted to go. I shook my head and entered the room. Al covered the hallway.

On the desk in front of the center monitor was a mug of coffee and a half-eaten sandwich. Killing the power to the building had interrupted our friend's breakfast. I slipped one of Mac's USB gizmos into a slot at the back of the computer. A stack of DVD cases, organized by date, stood on the right side of the desk. It looked like I could fit six of them in the pouch on my vest so I grabbed the most recent discs and joined Al in the hallway.

"C'mon, man. You gotta help me," said Mac over the radio.

"Get the hell outta here, ya lush."

"Fine way to treat a veteran."

The front door slammed.

"Delta heading to vehicle," said Mac. "Stand by for incoming hostile."

I heard footsteps coming down the hallway from the front door. A male figure appeared from around a corner ten yards away, stopped, and reached for his hip. I fired for center mass and the bag hit him square in the chest. He slumped to the floor. I kicked his pistol down the hallway and gave him the zip-tie and duct tape treatment.

"Number two hostile down," I said.

We moved quickly down the hall toward the main meeting room.

"Delta," said Al. "You read me?"

"Five-by-five," said Mac. "Almost to the van."

"Roger that."

We entered what appeared to be a chapel with a dais and an altar at one end and a wide staircase against the opposite wall. I headed up the staircase with Al behind me. We reached the second floor landing and a robed figure rounded the corner less than a yard in front of me. I threw a left hook and got a lot of my shoulder and chest into it. It wasn't the prettiest punch I'd ever thrown but it connected well with the man's jaw and snapped his head around. He dropped like a sack of wet sand. I found a pistol under his robe, tucked it into my belt, and stepped over the man to cover the upstairs hallway. Al tied the man's wrists and taped his mouth.

"Three down," he said.

"Delta is idling and ready for extraction," said Mac. "No hostiles in view."

The girls' quarters were supposed to be off the second floor hallway. The Close Quarters Battle training Mac had drilled into us paid off. When Al entered a room as the number one man, I covered his blind side as number two. We switched off positions and moved from room to room searching for Dorothea. But we couldn't find her or any of the other girls. Except for the three priests we'd seen, the place was empty.

"We have activity on the police scanner," said Mac. "Hostiles are incoming. Time to make haste."

We made our way down the stairs and toward the door we'd entered. I heard Al's shotgun chunk out two rounds behind me in quick succession.

"Fourth hostile no factor," he said.

We ran out the back door. The Chevy sat idling by the corner with its sliding door open. Al and I piled in and Mac took off. Our exit route took us past Harley's truck, still inert by the side of the road. Al grabbed a small radio transmitter.

"Fire in the hole," he said.

He pushed a button and the beer can I'd set on Harley's fuel tank ignited. Filled with thermite, it quickly achieved something north of 4,000 degrees Fahrenheit. White flames illuminated the street behind us as we drove away. Within seconds, the intense heat melted a hole in the top of the fuel tank and heated the diesel fuel beyond its flash point. A tower of flames rose from the tank. In less than half a minute, somebody else's truck became the "best damned truck in the whole state of Georgia."

"Ya gotta love thermite," said Al.

Mac turned a corner and slowed down to normal speed as he headed toward the freeway. Sirens blared in the distance as police cars headed toward *Sidoni* and we rolled down the southbound onramp toward Jacksonville.

"Did you see any of the girls?" said Mac.

"No," I said. "Every room we checked was empty."

"Plenty of beds in those rooms," said Al. "And nobody in 'em. A total bust."

I reached into my vest pocket and pulled out the half-dozen DVDs I'd taken.

"Not so sure about that. We've got six days of security camera video."

"So, what?"

"They've got cameras in all the rooms," I said. "The video might be useful."

Forty minutes later, Mac pulled the van into the COP and the garage door rolled down behind us. Al replaced the Georgia license plates with a pair from South Carolina while I stripped the cable company's vinyl lettering from the sides and back of the Chevy. Harley heard us and started making as much noise as a guy could with a rag in his mouth. Al grabbed a syringe and pumped the contents into one of his fat thighs.

"And now," said Al, "you're gonna tell us why that church building was nearly empty."

38

AL was patient and thorough. Harley put up some resistance, at first, but he eventually told us that there had been a private party "off-campus." Mac had downloaded video from our rock/camera while Al and I were raiding *Sidoni* but the only thing on it were the church's two white passenger vans driving past the courthouse three hours before we'd arrived.

Al asked Harley about the vans and Plantation Estates and his eyes lit up. He told us that both Clint and Mayor Stephens owned homes there and that Clint held parties at his place. We kept the big guy sedated for the rest of the day.

Social media in Serenity went nuts Monday morning. A few of the city's employees trickled into work early and noticed an odd addition to the statue of General John B. Gordon. It was a fine bronze statue of the former Confederate general and Georgia governor sitting astride his horse. It was the pride of Serenity standing in a prominent spot in front of the new City Hall. But somebody had spread a blue tarp over it during the wee hours of the morning and secured it with duct tape.

The first maintenance worker sent out to cut the tarp away discovered an unconscious Harley. We'd set the big guy on the bronze horse behind the general. Short lengths of duct tape covered his mouth while longer pieces stretched his arms around the general's waist. Harley was naked as the day he was born but not nearly as cute. The worker snapped a photo on his phone and posted it to Instagram with a grinning-face emoji. Within moments, somebody reposted the photo to Facebook. It went viral in minutes. Somebody altered the original photo into a humorously-captioned meme and it traveled coast-to-coast before the cops arrived to free Harley. By the time he came to and the police had finished peppering him with questions, the story had been picked up by the BBC and Russia Today.

The Serenity Herald reported on their website that security camera video from the previous night showed a short man in a Guy Fawkes mask walking up to each of the City Hall's outside security cameras and, one by one, shooting them with a suppressed pistol. A subsequent article reported a daring robbery of "church funds" over the weekend and a break-in at a local house of worship. There was no mention of gunfire or of any priests being injured. Chief Bill Willardson, leader of Serenity's finest, was quoted as stating that there was "nothing worse than scoundrels who would steal donations from a church." He vowed to catch us.

A secure server in Finland uploaded four high-resolution videos to a popular internet video site during the wee hours of Tuesday morning. The videos—definitely not safe for work—showed several of Serenity's city councilmen, a police lieutenant, and the Speaker *Pro Tempore* of the Georgia House of Representatives all enjoying the rather unusual "worship services" offered at *Sidoni.*

The videos were only a few minutes long but each ended with the promise of more to come. The site took them down within the hour—the videos violated their corporate standards—but not before enthusiastic users around the world had copied and posted them for all to see on a half-dozen other video sites, ones with less-stringent standards.

An anonymous email account in Switzerland sent copies of all four videos to email addresses at Fox News, ABC, the Washington Post, and the FBI. A separate anonymous email account sent copies to the Governor's office, the state Attorney General, and to all those on the membership rosters of both the Georgia Federation of Women's Clubs and the United Daughters of the Confederacy.

Telephone circuits among the state's elite started to burn up that afternoon and numerous claims of fraud and false editing were made along with threats to catch the miscreants who were slandering the Peach State's rich and powerful.

Word of the videos built throughout the morning. Writers for late-night talk shows—keen to make jokes about a religion strange to them, essentially any religion—worked to turn allegations of prostitution and white slavery into a smiling host's one-liner worthy of a few laughs. Parents of some of the girls who had left their families to join *Sidoni* made social media pleas to their elected officials. The President tweeted. The Senate Majority Leader assured reporters that the issue was being "looked into."

I didn't realize how much traction the videos were getting nationwide until a couple of news vans rolled into Serenity and set up their satellite feeds. We watched the results on Jacksonville's local ABC and NBC affiliates.

The respective correspondents started with the usual reporter-holds-a-mike-in-front-of-a-building-while-talking-to-the-camera routine but moved on to some man-on-the-street interviews with locals. All of those interviewed either claimed ignorance of the church or said something vacuous about tolerance of other faiths. And then, as if on cue, the heavy wooden courthouse doors swung open.

Duncan McCord, clad in a dark green robe and looking like Nosferatu, walked out of the courthouse flanked by two maroon-robed priests. Four women in white gowns followed behind them. Duncan walked directly to the closest camera/reporter team. The other team joined them.

"My name is Duncan McCord," he said. "I am the High Master of *Sidoni* and will be glad to answer any legitimate questions you might have."

"Have you seen the videos posted this morning on the internet?" asked a correspondent.

"Some of them. They're obviously doctored. Sadly, there are

those who hate us and who choose to distort and mock our sacred rites."

"Some say your church is nothing more than a sex cult."

"That is a massive distortion of our beliefs, our worship, and our ceremonies. We are an ancient religion and we worship Queen Astarte. She is the goddess of universal love. The same love which joins man with woman also joins virtue with truth. Love destroys war, poverty, hatred, and disease. Queen Astarte brings us happiness, beauty, marriage, and laughter."

"Are the girls in your church being held as sex slaves?"

Duncan turned to the first young woman to his left.

"Priestess Adara-Calista, are you being held against your will?"

"No, High Master," she said.

"And you Kaia-si-Nara? Are you here against your will?"

"No, High Master," said the second young woman.

Duncan turned back to the cameras.

"We only wish to be left alone to exercise our First Amendment rights and to worship as we please," he said.

With that, he and his entourage turned and walked back into the old courthouse. The first on-site correspondent turned to his camera.

"You have heard it directly from the High Master of *Sidoni*," he said. "His church is, in his words, just a normal religion practiced by the devotees of Queen Astarte."

The correspondent was about to cut back to the news anchor when a black Mercedes rolled up into the field of view and Dr. Jennifer Boulton got out.

The Dr. Jen show, a nationally-syndicated radio program based in New York, had just broken into the Talkers' Heavy Hundred and was gaining nationwide recognition. A clinical psychologist, she was known for pithy, off-the-cuff, common sense remarks that sometimes embarrassed her callers. Marie is a fan of the show; I am a fan of Marie. The reporters recognized her immediately and rushed to interview her. She was a short woman who compensated for that with a commanding voice that pierced any background noise.

The cameras kept rolling.

"*Sidoni* preys upon young women and uses them for illegal purposes," she said. "I'm here to call for the release of these girls."

"The High Master of *Sidoni* claims theirs is a legitimate religion with ancient roots," said the first correspondent. "And the young women say they live here willingly."

"So any human behavior can be justified by claiming it's a religious practice?" she said. "That is ludicrous. And that man is lying. Those women are brainwashed and being held against their will."

"The police don't seem to agree with you," said the second correspondent.

"The parents of these young women need to gather here and raise their voices until the authorities—local, state, and federal—take note and start enforcing the laws that protect women from this kind of abuse."

She finished the interview, got back into her Mercedes and drove off.

"Hey, Mac," I said. "I think we may have found another local to assist us."

"She's from New York. That's not local."

"Don't get technical."

I pulled a fresh burner out of the box and called Dr. Jen's radio station in New York. They put me in touch with her producer who said she would make a few calls. The burner's number rang about fifteen minutes later.

"This is Dr. Jennifer Boulton. My producer tells me you have information regarding the videos coming out of Serenity, Georgia."

"I do."

"What can you tell me?"

"Lots. But nothing over the phone."

"Well, how do I get the information you so badly want to

provide me?"

"Are you staying here locally?" I said. "We could meet for dinner."

"I'm in Savannah."

"I have a car."

"And I already have plans for this evening."

"Breakfast, then?"

"That'll work. Meet me in the lobby of the Hyatt Regency at ten in the morning. We'll have brunch and you can tell me all about it. How will I recognize you?"

"I'll recognize you."

"Sheesh. How cloak and dagger can you get?"

She hung up. I got in the minivan, drove the two hours to Savannah, and parked on a side street a couple of blocks away from her hotel. She walked out of the lobby a little after nine, turned east behind the old City Hall building, and continued along the riverfront plaza past the antique-looking ferry boats moored there. I watched to see if she were being followed and was pleased to find I was the only one tailing her. She walked into a club that looked like an old warehouse. I gave her a few minutes and followed her inside.

She sat alone at a table for two set against the wall with her eyes on the club's small stage. A three-piece blues band offered a tight rendition of Stevie Ray Vaughn's "Pride and Joy." I ordered a local draft porter at the bar and took it over to join her.

"Sorry," I said. "I couldn't wait until tomorrow morning."

"What? Who are you?"

"We were supposed to meet for brunch. I got impatient."

"How did you know I'd be here?"

"I didn't. But a friend of mine loves your show and I've heard it quite a bit. You talk about your love of live music and I figured there was a good chance you'd sneak out tonight."

"And you didn't want me to tape our conversation or alert any third parties before you showed up tomorrow morning."

"Caution has become a driving force in my life."

"What's your name?"

"Call me 'Stewart.'"

"Because you won't tell me your real name. Okay, what *will* you tell me?"

"That *Sidoni* is a front for sex trafficking. They lure in young women and underage girls over the internet and get them into the business. The clientele are rich and powerful and the goods are sweet and young. It's an illicit cash cow in the shape of a church. You saw the videos, right?"

She nodded.

"We have more," I said. "And we'll add names to the customers' faces before we make them public."

"Why are you telling me this?"

"We need somebody in the media. Somebody we can trust. Somebody who can light a fire under popular opinion and keep it burning."

"Why me?"

"Why did you show up at *Sidoni* today?"

"I was here for a conference and was going to fly home this morning, but I saw those videos and decided to get involved."

"Why?"

She took a sip from her drink.

"Two years ago, before my show took off and I still had my private practice, a sixteen-year-old patient ran away from home. Her parents had money and they did everything they could to find her. A private detective tracked her down to Serenity, Georgia. He reported to them that she had joined *Sidoni* and was being held against her will."

"Did he have any evidence?" I asked.

"He said he did. But he disappeared before he could share it with the parents."

"Disappeared."

She shrugged.

228 | ROB AVERY

"They never heard back from him. He closed his office."

"What happened after that?"

"The parents contacted the local police but they did nothing. Then the state Attorney General's office. They did nothing. Then the FBI who, as you may have already guessed, did nothing."

"She was sixteen," I said. "Some Assistant U.S. Attorney should have gotten carpal tunnel syndrome from typing up all the violations of federal law."

"Are you implying corruption all the way to the top? How are you going to prove that?"

"I probably won't. I just want to shine some light on it. I want to start feeding you information."

"What kind of information."

"Proof that politically powerful people are raping young girls at *Sidoni*."

"Proof?"

"Pictures, names, dates. License plates of private cars. Perhaps a short video clip or two you could put on your website."

"I'll need to clear *that* with my legal department first. It's a bit creepy and could be illegal."

"Is it as creepy as wrinkled old politicians paying money to have teenage girls? As creepy as a local power structure built around that sort of evil?"

She thought for a moment.

"We can kill this thing, Doctor. We can kill it dead."

She took a drink from her glass and thought a minute. The band launched into "Sweet Home Chicago" and she moved her head with the music.

"I'm in," she said. "And you should probably call me 'Jen.'"

39

AN email arrived Wednesday afternoon indicating a potential buyer's interest in a set of used tires I did not own and had not advertised. The interested party wanted to see them that evening.

We grabbed some gear, hopped in the minivan, and hit the road north. The sun set before we arrived and street lamps cast their cones of orange light to the ground. We drove up and down nearby streets looking for anything unusual—any reason to abort the mission—but saw nothing alarming. Mac stopped the van a block away under a large oak tree and I grabbed my bag and got out. I walked toward the AME church trying to stay in the shadows without being obvious about it. The earphone of my radio crackled.

"You read, Bravo?" said Al.

"Five by five, Alpha. *Et moi?*"

"*Recevoir cinq sur cinq, chéri.*"

The front door was unlocked this time. I walked into the foyer and put on my mask. The lights were off and I waited a minute for my eyes to adjust. Two large black men walked out of the foyer's corners on either side of me.

"The church is closed for the night," said one of the men.

"I'm sorry. The door was open."

"You here for a reason?"

"The Reverend expressed an interest in purchasing some used tires."

"What's in the bag?" asked the other man.

"Tires."

He stared at me for a minute and then jerked his head to the side.

"Follow me, masked man."

"*You okay, Bravo?*" said Al.

"Of course," I said.

I followed the first man down the central aisle of the chapel. The second fellow locked the front door and dropped in behind me. We reached the lectern and turned left toward a room set into the wall. Reverend Tabitha Sharpe sat at a desk and motioned for me to sit down. The two other men joined us.

"Still sportin' the LBJ look?"

"Reverend, we should probably dismiss these gentlemen," I said.

"They're my brothers. They can hear this."

"I understand you trust them and everything but…"

"No," she said. "They really *are* my brothers, Trent and Terry. Our parents liked the letter 'T' for some reason."

"Okay."

"Are you the guy behind those internet videos?" asked Trent.

"It was a team effort."

"You guys actually broke into *Sidoni* and robbed the place?"

I didn't answer. He took that to be a 'yes' and shook his head in disbelief.

"You got some guts, brother. I'll give you that, but you're takin' on an awful big 'gator. And that 'gator don't like having its tail slapped. And there's a lot more evil in this town than sits in that old building."

"I'm starting to understand that," I said. "But there is more I need to know. And we're going to need some help."

"I was wondering when you'd be getting to that," said Reverend Sharpe.

She sat back in her chair and stared at me. Trent and Terry folded their arms across their chests.

"What do you want from us?" she said. "And, please, be specific."

"I need two things from you. If you are willing."

"Go on."

"First, I need information. Facts I can't get in the library, stuff I can't pull up on Google. Second, I need some people. People we can trust."

Reverend Sharpe sat up straight.

"You're not getting any foot soldiers, brother. My people aren't expendable bullet-catchers who are gonna lay it down for some outside team of do-gooders. That ain't happening."

"That's not what I've got in mind," I said. "I don't want to put any of your parishioners in danger. But we can talk about that later. My first need is information."

She nodded.

"Who is behind *Sidoni*? Who runs it?"

"Duncan McCord runs it," she said. "But the whole town is behind it."

"Not the whole town," said Trent. "But the police, the town men, and union bosses are all lined up right behind it. Everybody from the mayor and police chief down to the guy who runs the local Piggly Wiggly. And they'll burn your backside if you cross them."

Reverend Sharpe nodded.

"Who isn't behind it?" I said.

"Lots of people," she said. "Good, God-fearing people who work hard, treat their families right, and go to church on Sunday. But they're quiet people, too. They might think something is going on in there with *Sidoni* and that the police are corrupt, but they don't talk about it. Maybe those videos of yours will change some minds."

"I don't know," said Terry. "As corrupt as the town men and the police are, the people here still consider themselves secure and safe from violent crime. Safe from outside evils."

"So they tolerate a local evil because they fear a greater one from the outside?" I asked.

"You know how many tweakers and heroin addicts there are in this town?" asked the Reverend.

I thought about the three guys in Alabama who'd tried to jack our van.

"Zero," she said. "Not a single one."

"Okay."

"Not a single meth lab, either."

"Hell," said Trent. "We don't even have any homeless people in this town. If the cops or the city men find any addicts or vagrants or other 'undesirables,' they run 'em out of town. Or worse. And the cops are always on the lookout for undesirables."

"That brings me to my second need. I am guessing you have members in your church working in the police station, the union offices, and the city hall."

"My girlfriend runs the company that cleans the police chief's house," said Terry.

"We got people everywhere," said Trent.

I opened up the bag I'd brought and pulled out the plastic box containing Mac's little USB bugs. They listened as I explained our plan.

40

THE Dr. Jen show aired every weekday from noon to three p.m. Eastern time. On Thursday, she spent the third hour discussing the beliefs and practices of *Sidoni*. She referred to it as "America's newest and most controversial religion."

She talked about the videos, child abuse, and a city filled with people who did nothing about it. She said she wanted to know what her listeners thought about the issue. Within minutes, the station's switchboards were full.

A listener from Newark, New Jersey, got fairly heated about the subject suggesting that if the government wasn't going to do anything, the parents might want to take the law into their own hands. Another listener, a first-year law student from the Boston area, suggested that *Sidoni's* practices were religious beliefs protected by the First Amendment. The hour was filled with opinions, justifications, and expressions of shock and horror. Dr. Jen's last call of the day came from a grieving mother.

"Madison was the most beautiful and talented girl you'd ever meet. Then one Saturday she said she was going to the mall with a friend. But she didn't come back. We called the police but they wouldn't even take a missing persons report. They said she'd probably come back in a few days."

"Did she come back?"

"No. But we got into her email account and found a four-month stream of emails between her and a man named Jackson. We saw how, over time, he drew her away from us. He invited her to live with his 'church family' and bought her a ticket to Savannah, Georgia."

"Were the police able to track her down after reaching Savannah?"

"Our local police received no help at all and the Savannah police wouldn't even talk to us."

"Do you think your daughter joined *Sidoni*?"

"We recognized her in one of those videos on Tuesday. I know it's her."

The caller began to sob and Dr. Jen did what she could to comfort her in the last few minutes of the show. The bumper music faded in.

"Is this what we're going to do all day?" said Al. "Sit around and listen to psycho-babble on the radio?"

Mac turned from his computer to face me.

"Al may be feeling some frustration from not having shot somebody for four whole days."

I sat back to watch the family feud.

"We're not getting anywhere," said Al. "We drive into town, drink coffee, download video from a fake rock, and listen to radio shows. Zero progress."

"There are decades where nothing happens, and there are weeks where decades happen."

"So, now you're quoting Lenin?"

"Revolution travels at a slow pace, Comrade."

"You're hilarious, Mac."

"We're building the ranks of the friendly minority. That takes time. And it's not like we're spinning our wheels. We're gathering resources and building up intel."

"What intel?"

"Whenever I find something new, I print it out and put it in the box right here. And as the USB bugs go online, I add them to the list."

Al walked over and started reading through the short stack of papers.

"We have a bug in the Public Works department and another in the control tower at the local airport? Whoopee."

"And a third in Clint McCord's office at the longshoreman's union."

"What about the one Sim placed in the *Sidoni* security room?"

"Nobody ever talks in that room or even uses the keyboard. We're getting zilch from it."

Al grabbed another sheet from the stack.

"Hey, the City Park's department approved a permit for kid's soccer. That's some heavy-duty intel right there."

"I'm not saying every bit of information we grab is earth-shattering news, Al."

"And Mayor Stephens is playing in a fundraiser golf tournament Saturday. Hoo boy!"

"Big golf addict. Plays three times a week at his country club and every Saturday morning at Sea Pines in Hilton Head. Has a regular eight-forty-two tee time. And that limo Sim spotted is the mayor's official city car."

Al gave Mac the finger and walked out of the room.

"I think you're number one, too, Al."

As it turned out, Reverend Sharpe hadn't wasted any time handing out the little USB bugs. More of them came on line Thursday night and Friday morning. The bugs had been pre-programmed to record conversations, separate them into individual audio files, and surreptitiously email them to Mac's VPN account. By ten in the morning, we had received audio files from a dozen computers in the City Hall, the Police Department, several minor government offices, and Clint McCord's computer in his union office. But nothing from within *Sidoni*.

Mac wrangled the audio files while Al and I reviewed our collection of *Sidoni's* security videos. The video files were high-resolution clips in living color and the content would have made Stanley Kubrick blush. We focused on matching the faces of *Sidoni's* "worshippers" with the names of respected local politicians and business people for future internet posts.

At noon, Mac called us over to his computer.

"We just got a new clip," he said. "And you're going to want to hear it."

We sat down next to him and he clicked on a file.

"*Clint,*" said a slow raspy voice. "*It seems as if you're having difficulties over at the church.*"

"*Willardson thinks it's a follow-up to what happened six months ago.*"

"*What do you think?*"

"*That was a small, ineffective protest,*" said Clint. "*This group used a Taser on Harley. They had night-vision goggles, suppressed shotguns, and bean-bag rounds. The local churchies never had that kind of firepower.*"

"*Any fingerprints?*"

"*Nothing. Not even a partial on the empty shells they left. We think they wore medical gloves. They were pros. Do you know anybody who would try something like this? Competitors who want to take the business?*"

"*Nobody that stupid. Nobody who would come in tossing bean bags. What is Willardson doing?*"

"*He's following some leads. Harley said they kept him in a railway warehouse. And one of our people spotted a guy who doesn't fit. Big fellow who is neither a local nor a tourist.*"

"*Have Trevor handle the interrogation. I want to know who is behind this.*"

The caller was silent a moment.

"*I got a call this morning from one of our friends, a Senator. He is concerned about the optics.*"

"*The videos? They're not online anymore.*"

"*How many did they get?*" asked Raspy.

"*Two weeks' worth.*"

"*We kept those as leverage. Now they're gone and somebody else has the leverage.*"

"*We still have months of files in my safe. And we haven't had a Senator here since the August recess. They don't need to worry about it.*"

"They worry about everything, Clint. That's why they are in office. And that's why they help us."

Raspy-voice hung up and the audio stream ended.

"Looks like we've made an impression," said Mac.

"Not a good one," said Al. He looked at me. "Are you the big fellow they're looking for?"

"Maybe I should stay out of Serenity for a while."

"We could always jump to Plan B. Shoot, loot, and scoot."

Mac and I ignored the comment.

"Do you have any idea who he was talking to?" asked Al.

"Not a clue," said Mac. "He sounds old and foreign but I can't place the accent."

"Haven't you got some sort of voice recognition software?" asked Al.

"You think I'm the NSA or something?"

Mac went back to his audio files while Al and I reviewed more of *Sidoni's* purloined security camera footage.

41

DR. Jen's Friday show featured a discussion of how abused women can become psychologically bonded to their captors. She interviewed a prominent professor of psychiatry about Stockholm Syndrome. Listeners called in to talk about their own abuse and responses and the professor offered very general advice.

During the last hour, she played snippets of the recording I'd sent her of Harley's interview. The audience heard his description of *Sidoni* as "a fancy cathouse" with "new young kittens." They heard how Clint and Mitch lured them from their families and how the girls, after being "slapped around," didn't want to go home. They thought the priests at *Sidoni* were "freakin' awesome."

"I can't give a professional opinion about any one person," said the professor. "But in those few sentences we are hearing of serious abuse and of victims exhibiting some of the classic signs of Stockholm Syndrome. These girls have been tricked away from their families and then physically abused. And after all of that, they exhibit positive feelings toward the very people who abuse them."

"Is this why we haven't heard of any *Sidoni* priestesses trying to escape?" asked Dr. Jen.

"That is certainly possible."

The bumper music started to fade in but Dr. Jen continued. "We'll continue discussing *Sidoni* on Monday. Until then, ask yourself why the FBI has not shut down *Sidoni*. Who, exactly, is protecting this sex cult?"

"Are we heading into Serenity tonight?" I asked. "More recon?"

"You're not," said Al. "You're the big guy they're looking for."

"You're kidding."

"Mac and I can handle it. Just stay here and chill."

They left a few minutes later.

I considered going out for a run but figured it might attract attention in an office park. I did some push-ups, ate some dinner, and re-read portions of Flake's research material.

Living on land in the COP had weaned me of my nightly weather reports; I'd gone a week without one. That rubbed against my natural routine so I sat down at the computer to see what NOAA had forecast. The tropical storm that had pounded the Cape Verdes had grown stronger as it marched across the Central Atlantic and NOAA upgraded it to named-storm status. Tropical Storm Julius was now east-southeast of Bermuda with 65-knot winds. Still, it was over sixteen hundred miles away and moving slowly. I figured it would blow itself out.

Mac and Al returned about eight o'clock. They brought the tablet into the conference room.

"You gotta see this," said Mac.

He tapped on the tablet and a video popped up showing the south side of the courthouse. Two vans pulled up to the curb and a group of young women left the building and got into the vans. One of them looked like Dorothea. They had all traded in their long white dresses for more stylish skirts, jeans, or shorts. The vans left and the building's door closed.

"How long ago was this?"

"Time-stamp says six thirty-five," said Mac. "We downloaded it an hour ago."

"Are they making a break for it? Things getting too hot in Serenity?"

"Maybe they're going to another 'private party,'" said Al.

Mac smiled.

"You guys tired of sitting around?" he said.

42

"HE just turned off the lights," said Mac.

"Should be walking out any minute, Alpha."

"Roger that."

The door to the townhouse opened and a figure walked down the stairs toward the parking lot. He pulled a key fob out of his pocket as he approached the black Lincoln limousine. The lights blinked, he opened the door, and sat down behind the wheel.

"Turn around and you're dead," said Al. His voice came in loud and clear over the radio. "That's a pistol barrel pressed against the back of your skull."

"What the hell is going on?" the driver whispered.

"Just back the car up slowly and drive north on Riverside. Stay calm and drive normally. Don't make me nervous. Don't attract anyone's attention. It's only a little nine-millimeter bullet but it's enough to blow all your gray matter out your eye sockets."

"Okay, man. I'm not doing anything stupid."

We watched the limo back up and turn onto Persimmon Street toward Riverside Drive. Mac started the van and we followed fifty yards behind.

"Is this some sort of joke? Is somebody in the crew messing with me? This is bullshit."

"No joke, Mitch. And no questions."

Mitch turned onto the highway.

"There's a car following us. What do I do if it's a cop?"

"Just drive, Mitch. Drive carefully. And live."

"I know where there's fifty grand hidden away. I can get you some money, man."

"We don't need money," said Al. "We need you to shut up and drive. Don't make me put a hole in your head."

Mitch stopped talking and kept driving north into town.

"Pull into the Piggly-Wiggly and drive around back."

"That car is following me."

"As it should. Park under that tree next to the dumpster."

He did as Al instructed. I put on a wrestling mask, opened the door, and pulled Mitch from behind the wheel. Al got out, grabbed Mitch, and spun him around.

"I have a few questions," he said.

"I'm not going to answer any of your fu…"

Al grabbed Mitch's crotch with his left hand and squeezed. Mitch opened his mouth in surprise and Al put the barrel of his pistol inside.

"I have a few questions, Mitch. You are going to answer them."

Mitch tried to nod.

"Now, I'll pull this gun from your mouth but I am going to stick it in your ear. If I don't like the answer I get from every question I ask, I'll either squeeze my left hand really hard or my right finger really soft. Do you understand?"

"Yes."

"Good answer," said Al. "Does the guard at Plantation Estates make you stop the car when you come in to pick up the mayor?"

"Not the regular guy. He knows the car. But sometimes there's a different guard if the regular guy is off."

"What about the exit gate?"

"It's automatic. It opens when you're a hundred feet away."

"What's the routine when you get to the mayor's house?"

"What do you mean?" said Mitch.

Al tightened his left hand grip and Mitch stood up on his toes.

"Do you pull up into the driveway?"

"No. I park on the street and he walks out. He says the headlights in the driveway wake up his wife."

"Does he bring his clubs or do you get them for him?"

"They're already in the trunk. It's just him."

"Glad to hear it," said Al.

He let loose of Mitch's tender parts and pulled the pistol away.

Mitch wore a light jacket and a Serenity Seagulls bill cap. I took both. We cuffed him, duct-taped his mouth shut, and put a bag over his head. I took his keys, opened the trunk, and pulled out the mayor's golf bag. Al shoved Mitch in. He mumbled through the duct tape. Al grabbed a syringe, stuck the needle in Mitch's arm, and pushed the plunger.

"Get some sleep, Mitch."

The mayor's clubs looked expensive. They went in the dumpster.

We transferred our gear from the van to the backseat of the limo. Al drove the van to a side street three blocks away and parked it next to a small plumbing shop. Mac and I followed in the limo.

"You almost look like him in that jacket and cap," said Al.

He and Mac got in the back seat and prepped the gear. I drove north on Riverside and turned right toward King George Island and Plantation Estates. Al smashed the car's dome light with the butt of his gun.

"Nice dark windows," said Mac. "The guard can't see in. But what if it's not the regular guy? What if he stops us?"

"Then he can sleep in the trunk with Mitch," said Al.

But it was the regular Saturday morning guard and the heavy steel gate began to open when we were still fifty yards away. I slowed down and the guard waved us through from his desk in the gatehouse.

"His lucky day," said Al.

"Turn left," said Mac. "Then make a right at the fourth street."

Mac had hacked into the county's land records and located Mayor Stephens' and Clint McCord's homes in the Plantation Estates community. The properties backed up against each other in neighboring waterfront cul-de-sacs. Satellite imagery revealed that Clint's lot was larger than most with several outside pavilions and a dock stretching into the channel behind King George Island.

"Turn here. The mayor's place is at the end on the right."

The street was narrow and lined with loblolly pines. The lots were large; half of them still empty. Most of the homes were raised above ground level, presumably to guard against hurricane storm surge. And they were private, hidden from each other with saw palms and thick hedges of holly.

I parked at the curb in front of the house. A light clicked off in the front room and Mayor Stephens walked out the front door. He opened the limo's back door and hopped in to find Al's pistol pointed at his head.

"Hi, I'm Derek. I'll be your kidnapper this morning," said Al.

I turned the limo around, drove halfway down the street, and parked in front of an empty lot.

"What the hell is…?"

"Mayor," said Al. "You are a hostage. You can cooperate and be useful to us or you can die. Two options."

He looked at Mac and then at me.

"I'll cooperate."

"Get us into Clint's house."

"I don't think I can."

"Why?"

"Nobody's there. And I don't know the pass code to his alarm system."

"Bullshit," said Al. "We saw them loading up the vans for a party last night."

"Not at Clint's," said Stephens. "I would have heard it. And I would have been invited. And I'd be over there right now sleeping it off."

Mac and Al and I looked at each other.

"You're the guys who busted into *Sidoni*, aren't you?"

Nobody answered.

"What a bunch of screw-ups," he said.

"Where are the girls?" asked Al.

"How should I know?"

Mac gave him the zip-tie, duct tape, and black bag treatment.

"He could be lying," said Al. "Drive over to Clint's."

It took less than a minute. Clint's was a large two-story brick and stucco French country house. An expansive brick staircase led up to the main floor from a circular driveway. There were no cars on the street or in the driveway and no lights on inside.

"Not much of a party," said Al.

"It's an hour before sunrise," said Mac. "Maybe they're all hungover."

"How'd they get here? Do you see any vans? Any cars at all?"

"We've been skunked," I said. "Again."

"This sucks," said Al.

I drove back toward the guardhouse and we made it past the gate without any drama. The van was still where we'd left it. Al stayed in the limo and guarded the mayor while I drove west on a two-lane highway. Mac followed in the van. Eight miles out of town, we turned right onto a dirt road and drove over a small bridge. I found a good spot behind a copse of trees, parked the limo, and walked back to open the trunk.

We transferred them into the van one at a time. Zip ties, black bags, and ear muffs. Al gave each a shot of B-52 to keep them quiet. I wedged a quarter-tube of Emulex and a timed fuse against the limo's fuel tank and got back into the van.

Mac turned the van around and drove back to the highway. A bright light flashed behind us as we drove east toward I-95. The sound of the exploding limo followed moments later.

"The mayor's not going to be happy about that," said Mac.

43

"COOL masks, guys," said the Mayor. "Call me 'Andy.'"

He sat there zip-tied to the chair grinning like a happy dog. It was as if the joy juice were double-strength.

"Okay, Andy," said Al. "I have a bunch of questions about the *Sidoni* church and your little town."

"*Sidoni* is the best thing that ever happened to me. I've never been happier."

"How long have you been a member?"

"Oh, hell, guys. I dang near started the thing."

"We thought Duncan McCord started it," said Al.

"I met Duncan when I was on vacation in Jamaica. We met at a Nyabinghi."

"What's a Nyabi...." I said.

"It's an all-nighter held by Rastafarians," said Al. "Helluva party. Don't interrupt."

He turned back to the mayor.

"We're interested, Andy. Tell us more about it."

"Yeah, right. Duncan told me of an idea he had about a new church. He'd had a vision."

Andy looked around. We waited.

"Queen Astarte came to him in a dream. She told him to start a church for her. She said it had to be on the coast. I guess water is important to Queen Astarte; it's super powerful." He licked his lips. "Can I get a drink of water?"

Al nodded and I left the room to get a bottle from the fridge.

"…my home town had everything he needed," Andy said as I returned.

"That must have cost a lot of money," said Al. "Buying the courthouse, building a new one for the county."

"Oh, yeah, but Duncan had the connections. People he knew popped up out of nowhere to contribute. They even rebuilt the docks, the airport, and all the other infrastructure. Serenity is an entirely different town, now."

"We thought you did all that."

"No," he said. "Duncan brought all that in. He just let me get the credit."

"Who were these connections?"

"What?"

"Give me some names."

He looked down and his ears and neck flushed red.

"I never actually met them. The money just kinda rolled in."

Al continued another half-hour with Mayor Andy but he didn't have much else to say. Nothing valuable. We moved him back to the cast iron drain pipe with the bag over his head and the ear muffs and retrieved Mitch.

"You think those masks are funny?" he said.

"Everybody says so," said Al.

He was much less compliant than the mayor. It was a replay of our question-and-answer session with Harley complete with a "What the hell are you doing?" when Mitch spotted Al with the syringe. Al ignored him and pumped in the "happy juice" amid Mitch's empty threats. We gave him a few minutes alone while the drug kicked in. Once again, Al asked the questions.

"I'm honored to meet you, Mitch."

"Whuh?"

"You're kind of a big deal at *Sidoni*, aren't you? Real tight with the boss."

A confused look crossed Mitch's face.

"I do what I'm told, I guess."

"No, you're Duncan McCord's right-hand man. You're the number two guy there."

Mitch looked dumbfounded.

"Duncan ain't the boss," he said.

"That's not what the mayor said."

"The mayor knows almost nothing."

"It's not what Harley said, either."

"Harley? That stupid bag of guts? He never knew anything. And look what it got him."

"You mean his horseback ride behind General Gordon?" asked Al.

"I ain't sayin'."

Al paused to wait him out.

"He got more than that."

"I don't know what you mean," said Al.

"He got a dinner date with Papa Croc."

He giggled as if he'd told a joke.

"Who's Papa Croc?"

"The crocodiles, man. Mayor Stephens got that spot near the river mouth set aside as a crocodile refuge. I think they're all gators, though."

Al waited again. He knew Mitch had more to say.

"We call it a dinner date with Papa Croc."

"Who has dinner with Papa Croc?" asked Al.

"Anybody who doesn't play nice. Anybody who screws up. Trevor gets the word and he takes 'em down there in the boat. He slits their throat, slaps on a weight belt, and tosses 'em in the river. Papa Croc gets his dinner."

"And Trevor did that to Harley?"

"Yeah."

"Do any of the young women have dinner with Papa Croc?"

He looked down at the floor.

"The girls, Mitch?"

"If they're too much trouble," he said. "Or get too old and not worth selling."

"Selling?"

"We train 'em, keep 'em a while, and then sell them to the industry."

"The sex industry?"

Mitch nodded.

"Let's get back to Papa Croc," said Al. "Who tells Trevor to arrange these dinner dates?"

"That's all Clint. He runs the show."

"Not the High Master?"

He shook his head and giggled.

"Duncan's a joke, man," he said. "He's the public face of *Sidoni* and what a face." He laughed. "He's a one-man freak show."

"But Duncan sent you and Trevor down to the BVI to blow up that guy in his truck, didn't he?"

"No, no, no. Clint sent us. Trevor rigged the bomb. I only went to point out the target."

The sound of the Super Chief came again and put a pause on the interrogation. Al looked at his watch and waited for the sound to dissipate.

"Where'd the girls go last night?" he asked.

"Major private party," said Mitch.

"Where?'"

"We've got a member who won't come to town. A high roller who doesn't want to be seen so he sends a jet over once in a while. It's a freakin' airliner. It came in Friday afternoon and flew the girls out to 'purify' him and his buddies over the weekend." Mitch smiled at the word 'purify.' "We're a church that makes house calls."

Al looked at his watch again.

"The morning's half gone, Mitch. I need some breakfast. And we need to figure out what to do with you two."

He put the black bag over Mitch's head.

"What do you mean?" said Mitch.

Al walked over to the shelf opposite Mitch, switched off the video camera, and continued toward the office. I followed.

"I dunno," said Al. "We'll think of something. Maybe we'll put you guys on some statues and let Trevor schedule dinner with Papa Croc."

"You can't do that, man!"

Mac had cooked sausage and eggs for us during Mitch's interrogation. They were still warm. Al turned on the local news to see if it had anything to say about the mayor and his cooked limo. There was much more.

The first few "outsiders" had arrived on the *Sidoni* church grounds early that morning. But they weren't the outsiders Serenity welcomed, the people who spent money at the local restaurants and bars before a little evening "worship" at the old courthouse. These folks had a different agenda and they'd brought bull-horns and banners with them. News vans arrived minutes later and the cameras rolled as the protesters got into full swing.

At most, there were fifty of them. Some were parents wanting their daughters back. Some were outraged high school students from out of town. Some were semi-pro protesters—the eternally-outraged warriors—aching for more time in the spotlight. The news crews supplied those spotlights and careful camera placement exaggerated the protesters' numbers.

The three of us watched it all unfold on the big screen hanging from the COP's conference room wall.

"None of those network idiots gave a damn about these girls before we showed up," said Al.

"That's the general nature of a cover-up," said Mac.

"Smart ass."

Chief Willardson showed up on site with a dozen local cops in riot gear and his own bull-horn. The cameras caught the exchange.

"This is an unlawful assembly," said Willardson. "Those who do not disperse within five minutes will be arrested and prosecuted."

"We have every right to be here," said a middle-aged woman. "We're on a public sidewalk and our assembly *is* peaceful. Our voices *will* be heard."

Willardson responded and the screaming back and forth grew in volume. Sidoni's large wooden doors opened and the High Master walked out flanked by two maroon-robed priests.

The protesters quieted down as Duncan McCord raised his arms and prepared to address the crowd. Five gun shots rang out in rapid succession and one of the priests collapsed on the grass. People screamed and cameras turned toward the source of the shots. Duncan and the other priest hurriedly dragged their fallen brother back into the courthouse. A camera caught a blue Volvo speeding from the area.

People ran in all directions. The police arrested those who had been the most vocal.

News of the attack outside *Sidoni* spread like a Southern California wildfire in a Santa Ana wind. Within minutes, hastily composed stories—complete with audio and video clips from the various news crews—appeared on network news websites.

Every nationwide news hour that evening featured footage of the attack. High Master McCord called in to the local station to answer the local anchor's questions and to report that the injured priest had only been hit in the leg by a single bullet. Every cable and television network played the audio clip of Duncan's phone call.

By Sunday morning, *Sidoni* was a bonafide victim of religious intolerance. Their teflon shield had been restored.

The well-dressed talking heads on the Sunday morning talk shows featured heated political conversations about the *Sidoni* protests and the subsequent church shooting. Discussion focused on First Amendment religious rights and the pervasive ownership of "assault-style" rifles. Nothing was said about young women being brainwashed or held against their will. *Sidoni* had masterfully switched the narrative.

On Sunday afternoon, the Serenity Herald website reported that local police had attempted to stop a blue Volvo with Connecticut license plates. A high-speed chase ensued but ended when the driver lost control and crashed into a bridge abutment. The car's fuel tank ignited in the crash and the driver was immolated. A picture showed several officers and firemen milling about a blazing vehicle. The article indicated that the driver was the prime suspect in the church shooting. A picture of Jack Harkness, lifted from his driver's license, followed the article.

I'd warned the guy. I knew they'd spot him. Still, the reality of what happened made me sick to my stomach.

I picked up my burner and punched in the number I wanted.

"Hello."

"Jen, it's Stewart from Savannah," I said.

She laughed.

"You sound more like somebody calling into my radio show than a secret informant."

"Would you like some more secrets?"

"Absolutely," she said. "My show topped the charts on Friday. Highest ratings ever. If you've got more information I can put on the air, then gimme, gimme, gimme."

"I've got enough for three shows, Jen, but I can't give it to you yet."

"Now you are being a tease."

"What I have may score you a visit from federal authorities."

"I protect my sources, Stewart. You don't have to worry about me. We've got the First Amendment on our side and I have some marvelous and expensive attorneys."

"I'm sure that's true, but it's not quite ready for you."

"So, why did you call?"

"Do you have an affiliate in Charleston, South Carolina? Somebody you trust?"

"Absolutely," she said.

"I have a couple of guys who need protection."

"I'm not sure what you mean."

"Right now, *Sidoni* is trying to make themselves look like victims of intolerance. They're trying to gain the moral high ground. I have two witnesses who can tell the feds more than they ever wanted to know about *Sidoni*; how they get the girls, who they are blackmailing, and who they kill to keep things quiet. But the folks who pull the strings in Serenity will kill them if they get a chance."

"Give them to the FBI. They'll put them in a witness protection program."

"Unless one of those feds is on *Sidoni*'s payroll and my informants suddenly hang themselves."

I told her what I had in mind and she agreed to help out.

"What do you call yourselves? Does your group have a name? An identity?"

"We haven't given it much thought."

"Every cause needs a name and a tag line," she said. "I'll come up with something."

"Knock yourself out. By the way, that fellow who was burned to death in his car down here? The guy they say took a few shots at Duncan McCord? He wasn't one of us."

"What do you know about him?" asked Dr. Jen.

"Not much."

"Keep me posted, Stewart."

"Will do, Jen."

44

WE trussed Mitch and the mayor up with zip ties, fastened the black bags over their heads, and laid them on the van's floor. Al gave each a shot of B-52 and, once asleep, covered them with moving blankets. We had a four-hour drive ahead of us.

"Do we seriously have to go all the way to Charleston?" said Al.

"It's the smart thing to do," said Mac.

"How do we even know what the smart thing to do is? We've tried two DA ops with specific objectives and failed at both."

"We've been skinny on intel," said Mac. "We don't have any satellites, analysts, high-altitude drones, radio intercepts, or informants. We're stuck with doing the best we can with what we have."

"Charleston is the best we have? Why?"

"The FBI office there is less likely to be tainted by the corruption in Serenity. And Charleston is well away from our COP. It'll throw 'em off our trail and make them think we bunk in north Georgia. And South Carolina still has blue laws. Charleston closes down early on a Sunday night."

Al gave us both a dirty look but he got in the van.

"Drive carefully," said Mac. "And keep in touch."

"Roger," said Al.

I punched the button on the garage door opener and drove out into the night while Mac walked back into the office. Al sat in the passenger seat with a small flashlight reading a book by Edmund Burke. Our cargo stayed quiet under their blankets.

We couldn't blame either of them for not wanting to go back to Serenity. Nobody wants to have dinner with Papa Croc. Prison had much greater appeal.

Al turned off his light and put his book away as we passed the last off-ramp to Savannah.

"You really gonna let that bastard go?" he asked. "The one who came to Road Town?"

"Giving him to the FBI isn't exactly letting him go, is it?"

"He killed Eryn. He tried to kill you."

"What are you suggesting?"

"There are swamps and bogs on both sides of I-95 up ahead. We could put a bullet in that bastard's head and be done with him. And the FBI still gets the mayor."

It was a thought. And it appealed to that morally thin part of me that screamed for revenge.

"The enemy won't miss him. Another will step up and take his place. He's more dangerous to them alive. Mitch knows a lot more than the mayor does and the FBI can get more out of him than we could."

Al shrugged.

We got to Charleston ahead of schedule and Chalmers Street was empty. Al called Mac as we made our first pass. I turned to circle the block.

"You ready?"

"Yep," said Mac. "Dr. Jen's pet network crew are anxiously awaiting my call. Their van is parked outside the old United States Custom House. They can't see the drop point from there but they're close enough to get there and set up their lights and cameras before the FBI shows. Just let me know when you leave the drop and I'll set it all in motion."

The van rocked a bit on the cobblestones as we pulled up to the building. An elliptical arch joined two tall octagonal pillars at the entrance to the Old Slave Mart museum. A heavy iron gate stretched across the entryway. I stopped the van and we dragged the

Mayor to the entry and zip-tied his wrists to one end of the iron gate. We zip-tied Mitch to the other end.

"How about I just kick him in the nuts as hard as I can?" asked Al. "If I can't make a touchdown, at least I could try for a field goal."

"Just get in the van."

He did and we drove off. Nobody was there to wonder why a couple of guys would be left sitting outside a slave museum with black bags on their heads. Al grabbed his burner.

"It's done," said Al. "Now en route to point Zulu."

"Roger that," said Mac.

The plan was for Mac to send a few snippets of Mitch's confession to Dr. Jen's media contact in Charleston via Mac's VPN email account. Then he'd call the FBI's Charleston office to let them know who was tied to the gate in front of the Old Slave Mart. Once the FBI was confirmed en route, he'd call Jen's people to let them know Mitch and the mayor were only four hundred yards away. If all went well, the FBI would get there moments after the cameras and news people were ready to document everything. The cell phone buzzed.

"The FBI are on their way."

The most direct route from their field office to the Old Slave Mart sent them south on Morrison Drive. We parked on a cross-street eighty yards west of Morrison.

"Let me know when you see them," said Mac.

"Will do."

"Oh, and I got some info on that private airliner Mitch was talking about."

"What?"

"Yeah, remember that bug of ours that found its way into the Stephens Field tower? I checked the feed for Friday night. A Boeing 737 landed there just after six. It took off an hour later."

"Whose Boeing 737?" I asked.

"No idea. All I got is a tail number with a C6 prefix. So it's Bahamian registered and won't show up on the FAA database."

A caravan of six obviously government vehicles blasted past the intersection on Morrison.

"We have eyes on the feds," said Al.

"Roger that," said Mac. "I'll call the newsies."

I started the van, turned around, and found our way back to Route 17.

We got back to the COP in the wee hours of Monday morning, crawled into our beds, and slept in. Mac started yelling at us about ten o'clock.

"Guys, you gotta hear this," he said. "It's from Clint McCord's office."

Al and I gathered around Mac's desk while he unplugged his headphones and turned up the speaker volume. We heard a door swing open.

"We know who is behind all of this."

There was a slight British accent to the voice.

"You got something from that Harkness fellow?"

"Absolutely. Good information, too. He was sent down here to supervise a group of operatives hired by a fellow named Flake."

"That's him," said Al. "Trevor Hickey. The guy who tried to kill you in Road Town. I recognize the voice."

"Shhh," said Mac.

"Who is this 'Flake' guy?" said Clint.

"Orson Flake is the uncle of that girl who died with Greene down in the Virgin Islands."

"Collateral damage."

"Flake is wealthy and has somehow deduced that Sidoni is behind his daughter's death," said Trevor. *"He decided to come after us."*

"So he hired some gunnies?"

"So it appears."

"What did Harkness tell you?"

"He said there were eight of them. And he thought they were foreign mercenaries."

"Like you?"

"*Funny.*"

"*Where are they now?*" asked Clint.

"*He didn't know. He had no way of reaching them.*"

"*That's ridiculous. Unbelievable. Are you losing your touch?*"

"*There's nothing wrong with my technique. He was in extreme pain and knew more was coming. He would have told me had he known.*"

"*I don't buy it. Would you trust that guy to supervise a team of mercs?*"

"*Not at all. But I'm not Flake,*" said Trevor.

"*And how do you supervise a team if you can't reach them?*"

"*He relied on them contacting him. It was a security measure they insisted upon.*"

"*And you checked his cell phone?*"

"*There were several calls to Flake but nothing to or from anybody who could be part of this team.*"

"*Did you get any details? Names? Descriptions? The cars they drive?*"

"*Nothing specific. He only said they were trained professionals and extremely expensive.*"

"*We need to crush this thing. Send Crowe and Peters to grab Flake and his family and bring them back here. Have them take the jet. I want you here hunting the mercs.*"

"*I'm already working on it.*"

"*Once we get Flake, we can get the information we need to make it all go away. Flake, his family, the mercs. All gone. You got that?*"

"*Got it.*"

"*Have you heard anything from Mitch or Andy?*"

"*Not a thing. And these mercs left no evidence at all in Andy's car. What's left of it.*"

"*They'll slip up,*" said Clint. "*And we'll get them. Shooting Wilson in the leg from that guy's car was a good move. It linked him to the protests and made Sidoni look like the victim. It made the trouble-makers and reporters all look stupid.*"

"*Do you want me to do anything special with the mercs when we find them?*"

"*No. Just shoot them and toss 'em to the gators.*"

"They're probably still full from chewing on Harley," said Trevor.

They both laughed and the conversation ended with footsteps leaving the room. Mac closed the audio file.

"Sounds like he did us a solid," said Al. "Eight of us? Foreigners?"

"Nice diversion," said Mac. "Sad he had to go through all that."

"What kind of jet do they have?" I asked.

"Gulfstream," said Mac. "Five hundred knots or so."

"How old is this conversation?" I asked.

"Just over an hour," said Mac.

"They could be landing in Connecticut right now."

45

I picked up my burner and dialed the number Orson Flake had given me. It was a business line and the call went to voice mail.

"Don't leave a message," said Al. "It could compromise us."

I hung up and dialed Marie's number. She answered.

"Marie, this is Sim."

"I don't usually pick up calls from anonymous phone numbers. I'm glad I did this time."

"Me, too. But I don't have time to talk. I need Orson Flake's cell number."

"I haven't heard from you in six weeks. And your voice mail is full."

"I'm not using that phone right now. Look, I'm sorry for not calling you but I've had good reasons. Trust me. Right now, I need to contact Flake and the number he gave me isn't working. Do you have his cell?"

"No," she said. "But I have his wife's number. Do you have a few minutes? I am kinda missing you. And we need to talk."

"I wish I could. Please believe me. But I can't spare even a minute and I can't tell you why. Sorry."

She gave me the phone number but was less than a good sport about letting me go. I hung up and dialed Lisa Flake. She put Orson on the phone.

"Mr. Flake, things have gone bad in Serenity. They killed Jack Harkness."

Flake gasped.

"Who killed him?"

"*Sidoni.* They caught him and tortured him. He told them you hired him. "

"Is this some sort of joke?"

"It's no joke. It's a serious problem and you need to get yourself and your family far away."

"I hired you to solve a problem and now you've made it worse? Is that what you are telling me?"

"I told you to get that guy out of Georgia and he stuck around anyway and got himself caught. Now he's dead and you are a target. We don't have time to argue about it. You need to get out of Stamford before they find you."

"We're in Colorado on a family vacation at our cabin."

"That gives you a decent head start but they'll find that cabin. Is there anywhere else you can hide?"

"I have a cousin in…"

"Don't tell me where. Just pack up your family and get there as soon as possible. Don't tell anybody where you've gone. Just get there. And shut off all your phones and disable your social media accounts while you are at it."

"You can't be serious about this," he said.

"This is as serious as I ever get. These men intend to kill you and your family. You are in grave danger."

"Should I fly out of the country?"

"Your jet is on one of those flight tracking websites. Do you have a car, there?"

"We keep an old Suburban here at the cabin," said Flake. "Should we rent something else?"

"No. Rental cars can be tracked, too. But don't waste any time. Get your family some place where you won't be found."

We hung up and Al shook his head.

"That guy is toast," he said. "He couldn't hide a golf ball in a snowbank."

"Let's hope he can hide his family."

"Damned shame," said Mac.

An hour later, my cell phone, the burner with the number nobody knew, rang. The caller ID said 'Anonymous.' I looked at Al and he shrugged. I touched the button with the little green handset on it and pressed it to my ear.

"Sim?" said a voice. "Sim Greene?"

"Sorry, wrong number."

"C'mon, Sim. Don't ghost me. This is your old friend Spencer from Miami."

My old friend? I'd seen him twice in my life. The first time had been in one of the TSA's airport interview rooms in Puerto Rico. He'd walked in, casually offered me a suppressed .45 pistol with subsonic ammo, and suggested I use it to kill a very bad man on Tortola. Then he'd handed me his business card; one that clearly showed a federal seal but failed to list either a last name or the agency he represented. The second time I'd seen him had been at the docks in Fort Burt Marina only days after somebody had slit the bad man's throat. Spencer was all smiles.

"Sorry to disappoint you, Mr. Spencer, but Sim is dead."

"Yeah, we heard all about that," he said. "Killed by terrorists in Road Town. Sad to hear of it. I was a big fan of his work."

"What do you want?" I asked.

"My boss and I want to meet with you."

"Why?"

"We'd like to talk you out of doing something stupid, okay? How does lunch work for you?"

"I'm booked."

"Dinner then? I don't want to go to the trouble of tracking you down."

I thought for a minute. Were we blown? How did Spencer know? Who else knew?

"There's a restaurant forty-five miles west of Serenity. It's on a dirt road north of the main highway; rather rustic but the pie will change your life." I gave him the name of the place. "Get a table near the kitchen and be there no later than six-fifteen."

"I understand that you need to check everything out ahead of time, but don't make us wait too long," he said.

"Only as long as I need to, Mr. Spencer."

"What do you want to drink?"

"I'll have a Coke."

"And what would Al like?"

"Who's Al?"

"Ha!" he said. "That's hilarious. See you tonight, my friend."

I hung up. Al grabbed my phone, pulled off its back cover, and removed the battery and SIM card.

"It's a trap," said Mac.

"I don't like it," said Al.

"Well, I'm not over here doing handsprings."

We talked about it and agreed that we needed to find out how Spencer and his people, whoever they were, knew about us.

46

BONNIE'S Diner hadn't moved much in the last ten days; the thick stand of ash and hickory trees still standing guard. Al parked the minivan on a dirt road five hundred yards north of the restaurant and we walked through the trees toward the diner's rear. We circled around and picked a spot from where we could watch the parking lot and waited.

Nothing appeared to be out of the ordinary. The late lunch crowd—locals, mostly—walked out into the parking lot, climbed into their pickups, and drove off. A few early dinner customers started to dribble in around five-thirty. At five after six, a white GMC Yukon with deeply tinted windows pulled into the lot and parked near the diner's entrance. The man I knew as Spencer got out of the driver's side and walked into the diner alone. He came out a few minutes later and opened the passenger door. A short older woman got out and walked into the diner ahead of Spencer. There appeared to be no other agents; no suspicious cars or vans. We waited there and watched the diner for another fifteen minutes.

"Looks pretty clean," said Al.

"Yep."

"You know what to do if things get sideways?"

"Through the kitchen and out the back door."

Al nodded.

"Keep in touch," he said.

Al walked back through the woods to the minivan. I walked into Bonnie's and found my dinner dates at the booth I'd requested. They sat against the wall near the kitchen watching the front door.

There were only three other small groups of people in the place. It was probably known more for its breakfast and lunch fare. I walked over to the feds' booth and sat across from them. The wall opposite me was a mini-memorial to southern drinking. It featured a large red antique tin Coke sign and a Jack Daniels "Old No. 7" mirror. I sat where I could see the front door in the mirror.

The waitress spotted me from behind the counter, walked over with a Coke, and set it down in front of me.

"Did y'all come back for some more shrimp?"

"You've got quite the memory."

"Some guys look like they'd be worth rememberin'."

"Can you give us a little more time to study the menu?" said Spencer.

The waitress shrugged and left.

"The blond look works for you," he said. "Not sure about the beard, though."

"Beards are an acquired taste. Don't like my beard? Acquire some taste." I looked at my watch. "You have ten minutes of my time. Don't waste it."

"I'd like to introduce you to Sondra. She is my supervisor at the agency."

"And what agency *is* that?"

Spencer looked at Sondra. She sat stone-faced.

"We heard your truck exploded a few months ago back in Road Town," he said. "Heard you got toasted in the process. That made me kinda sad. Then you and Mr. Higgins pop up here in Georgia."

I drank some of my Coke.

"We know what you two have been doing. We think we know why."

"Do you want to help us?"

"We want you to stop. We want you to go back to Tortola and your little SCUBA diving business and forget all about Serenity, Georgia."

"These people are killers and pimps," I said. "They abduct young girls, use them as prostitutes, and sell them when they are finished. Somebody gets in the way? They kill them."

"That is simply not true," said Spencer.

"They murdered Solana Bradford eight months ago. I have a recorded confession. They tried to kill me but screwed up and killed a sweet young woman. And they tortured and killed Jack Harkness over the weekend."

"*Sidoni* is a legitimate religious entity. And those girls know what they're doing."

"I can't tell if you are willfully ignorant or suffering from some sort of federal agency political groupthink."

Sondra decided to enter the conversation.

"You and your friend are going to leave *Sidoni* alone. You *will* leave Georgia immediately."

"Let me check my Magic 8-Ball." I rotated an imaginary ball in the air, flipped it over, and stared at the imaginary bottom. "It says 'Outlook Not So Good.'"

Neither of them smiled.

"I'll check again," I said. I rotated the invisible ball some more and looked a second time. "'Very Doubtful.'" I shrugged.

"Funny," said Spencer. "Do you have any idea how much trouble you are in?"

"Educate me."

"Well, let's see. You broke into a church and you shot some people."

"The newspaper didn't mention a single casualty," I said.

"Then you stole video and other electronic information and shared it over the internet."

"Those would be state and local crimes. Why would you feds be interested?"

"Mr. Greene," said Sondra. "There are enough violations of federal law here to keep an Assistant U.S. Attorney busy for months. The video postings are almost certainly violations of the

Computer Fraud and Abuse Act. And we could add in a few domestic terrorism charges and a criminal RICO action into the mix. You and your friend could spend the rest of your days in a federal prison."

"And, yet, here I am enjoying a Coke without the encumbrance of handcuffs."

Spencer and Sondra exchanged a look.

"You think you know what is going on here," said Spencer. "But you don't have a clue. The McCords are friends of ours. Unsavory friends, perhaps, but useful ones."

"We have a mutually beneficial arrangement and we don't want it ruined by you and your abrasive friend," said Sondra. "And despite what you may think, we have control over the situation."

Two policemen walked through the front door. They spotted us in the back booth and headed toward us.

"Do either of you own that white Yukon?" asked one of the cops.

"That car is ours, officer," said Spencer.

"The registration is expired. May I see your identification?"

Spencer produced a driver's license and handed it to the cop in charge.

"Maryland? Well, you're a long way from home, aren't you?"

Another policeman walked in and headed toward us. But it wasn't a policeman. It was Trevor Hickey in a police uniform. He pulled the pistol from his holster and leveled it at Spencer.

"That vehicle is stolen. You are all under arrest. Keep your hands where I can see them."

The other patrons in the restaurant quickly got up and headed for the front door.

"There must be some mistake," said Spencer. "We're with the federal government and any questions you may have can be resolved with a single phone call to Washington."

Spencer moved to stand up and Hickey shot him in the right shoulder. Spencer screamed in pain as Hickey grabbed him and pulled him out of the booth. The acrid smell of cordite filled the air.

One of the other officers pulled out some military-grade double-cuff plastic restraints exactly like the ones I'd used in the Navy, yanked Spencer's arms behind him, and tightened the cuffs on his wrists. The other cop cuffed Sondra.

I was pulled out of the booth next.

Hickey looked at me closely as the other two cops cuffed me. He had a silver earring in his left ear. A silver dagger wreathed in flames. I watched as a look of recognition washed over his face.

"Wait a moment," he said. "Do I know you?"

"Not so well."

"You're dead." He had a slight British accent but you had to listen for it. "You bought it months ago."

"Don't believe everything you read in the papers."

"Where's your friend?"

"I like to think I have more than one."

Hickey slapped me across the face. Then he stepped in close and lowered his voice.

"Al," he said. "Where can I find Al Higgins?"

"Who?"

"Your buddy. The fellow with whom you run that diving operation. I knew him in Africa and I saw him on that island with you. I would have taken him out, too, but it wasn't in the plan. There wasn't time. Is he here in Georgia?"

"He's right behind you," I said.

He turned his head and I shoved my knee into the crotch of his blue police pants. He dropped his pistol and went down gasping.

"My mistake," I said. "Must've been somebody else."

The cop behind me hit me in the kidneys with his PR-24 and I dropped to my knees. Hickey recovered from the sucker kick, holstered his pistol, lifted me to my feet, and grabbed me by the throat.

"I am so going to enjoy killing you."

"You've haven't been so good at it."

"And then I will track down your little friend and finish what I started years ago."

They marched us out of the restaurant.

"Everybody needs to calm down," said Sondra. "We'll straighten this all out once we get to the police station."

"They're not police," I said. "They work for your unsavory but useful friends."

Hickey looked directly at Sondra.

"We know who you are," he said. "We don't care."

They walked us toward a blue service van backed into a parking space reserved for disabled access. A Serenity Police car sat next to it. A black Cadillac Escalade pulled up and stopped in front of the van. The driver got out and opened the right rear door.

Duncan McCord stepped out in his dark green robe and stared at us. The picture Flake had given us didn't do him justice. In reality, he was much more hideous. He walked up to me and studied me with dark, soulless eyes as if I were a rare, unusual insect.

"Nice robe," I said. "Does it come in any men's sizes?"

He drew a short, claw-like knife and held it to my throat. I felt the blade press against my skin and wondered if I were already bleeding.

"Why do you attack *Sidoni?*"

"You brainwash girls, sell them to high-rollers, and kill anybody who gets in your way. You could prove me wrong by letting me go."

"How many are with you?" he asked.

"Two dozen in Serenity. Hundreds more to take our place when we are gone."

He pulled the knife away and turned to Hickey.

"These people are enemies of Queen Astarte and must be removed."

"Yes, High Master. It will be done."

Duncan returned to the back seat of the Escalade and it drove off.

"I demand a telephone call from the police station," said Spencer.

"Do you really think you're going to a police station?" said

Hickey.

One of the officers opened the sliding side door of the van. They shoved us onto the floor and slid the door shut. Spencer moaned in pain. The other officer got into the passenger seat in front while Hickey and the first cop walked over to the driver's side.

"You know where to take the two feds, right?" said Hickey. "Slice them up properly and toss them to the alligators. But leave the tall, mouthy one for me. He'll lead us to the others. And I want to hear him beg for death."

We heard Hickey get into his police car and drive away.

"What's going on here?" asked Sondra. She tried to work herself into a sitting position.

"Shut up," I said. "And stay down. Flat on the floor."

The cop behind the wheel started the van and reached up to shift it into gear.

"We're all low," I said. "No more than two feet off the floor."

"Who cares?" said the driver.

A cacophony of shattering glass ensued as bullets tore through the side windows and sheet metal of the van. Blood, brain matter, and skull fragments from the two cops flew across the inside of the van sticking to the headliner, the dash, and the windshield. The mayhem stopped and I looked up to see two corpses slumped forward against the dashboard.

Moments later, Al opened the sliding door. A suppressed Blackout hung barrel-down across his torso. He pulled us out of the van, drew his knife, and cut our zip-tie restraints. Mac walked around from the driver's side.

"That minute or so of stalling was all we needed," he said. "It made all the difference. And that line about Duncan's robe was freakin' hilarious."

I removed the microphone and transmitter I'd been wearing and turned to Spencer.

"You still think the McCords are just unsavory friends?" I said. "You still think you have the situation under control?"

"There must be some mistake."

"There was and you made it. You decided to try and find me. But somebody in your organization told Clint McCord where you were going and who you were meeting. Clint sent his professional killers to take us all out. One of your coworkers—perhaps your own boss—was willing to sacrifice the two of you so the McCords could get me and Al. Let that sink in for a moment."

Spencer shook his head.

"How'd you find me?" I asked.

"We tracked your phone call to Marie."

"Did you ping the phone?" asked Al. "Did you figure out where we were?"

He shook his head. It wasn't convincing. Al put his thumb in Spencer's bullet wound and squeezed. Spencer howled.

"I need an honest 'yes' or 'no' answer. Does anybody in your organization know where you called?"

"NO!" he said. "We didn't have time for that. Just the pen register on the phone. You'd better dump it if you don't want to be tracked."

"How do we know you're not lying to us?" I asked.

Spencer whispered something I couldn't hear.

"What?" I said.

"HartKampf Logistics," said Spencer.

"What the hell does that mean?"

"Follow HartKampf Logistics."

Sondra helped Spencer into the passenger side of the Yukon and walked around in front to the driver's side.

"You boys do whatever you think you need to do," she said. "But you are on your own. Spencer and I were never here. We never met with you and we never talked with you. You got that?"

"Sure," I said. "None of this happened. But you'd better get Spencer to a friendly doctor and have him look at that shoulder. Maybe he'll chart it as an extreme tennis injury."

She started the Yukon, jammed it into gear, and took off in a cloud of dust as if the big white SUV really were stolen.

47

"YOU think we're cutting it too close, guys?"

"Maybe," said Al.

I noticed that he was rubbing his right leg through his jeans over the scar.

"Jack Harkness gets taken, tortured, and torched. They tie him to us and claim he tried to assassinate the Holy High Master. Then they track us down and spot me. I'm not liking it."

"Progress isn't always a straight line," said Al.

"What the hell?" I said. "Look who's Dr. Norman Vincent Peale all of a sudden."

"We planned the mission," said Mac. "We make adjustments but we keep working the plan."

"I propose a slight adjustment," said Al. "You loan me that .300 Win Mag of yours and I blow Hickey's head off."

"I think that would just blow up our plan," said Mac.

"That SOB said he wanted to finish what he started years ago. He tried to get me killed in Africa. He admitted it. He bragged about it."

"Why didn't you take him back at Bonnies?" I asked.

"We were outnumbered five to two," said Al. "And you and those two feds would have been the first to bleed out. It wasn't prudent."

"Thank you for your uncharacteristic display of self-control," I said.

Mac laughed.

"I'll have that guy's British ass on a plaque," said Al.

Mac pulled into a gas station. I filled the tank while Al tossed our old phones into the trash and programmed three new burners. We got back onto highway 23 toward Jacksonville and the conversation dried up. We drove in silence for nearly an hour. Mac finally broke it.

"How did Hickey know where to find us?" asked Mac.

"Somebody in Spencer's agency—whatever agency that may be—is on *Sidoni*'s payroll," said Al.

"Is that why the FBI seems to be doing nothing about *Sidoni*?" asked Mac.

"The FBI *always* seems to be doing nothing," said Al. "They don't say anything until they have a suspect in hand. And they don't take anybody into custody until they have a case locked up tight."

"Either of you ever hear of 'HartKampf Logistics' before?" I asked. "Spencer said we should look there."

"Nope," said Mac.

"Try Googling it," said Al.

"I just did but the closest thing that comes up is some doctor who does cosmetic surgery."

"If it ain't on Google, it doesn't exist," said Al.

"No," said Mac. "You're wrong there. You're not even close. Google sees only a tiny sliver of the worldwide web."

"What do you mean?"

"Google indexes the Surface Web."

He could tell we weren't following him.

"What's the deepest spot in the Atlantic Ocean?" he asked.

"The Puerto Rico Trench. It's about as deep as Mt. Everest is tall."

"The first ten feet down is the Surface Web," said Mac. "Google sees that. The rest of that abyss, all the way down to 28,000 feet, is the Deep Web. That is where the hidden stuff is; private encrypted databases, content kept behind pay walls, and any number of password-protected pages or websites. Most of the Deep Web is legit. But a fair-sized chunk is what we call the Dark Web."

"And that is?" said Al.

"That's where the sinister stuff is located. You want to hire a hit man? You'll find him on the Dark Web. Looking for drugs or stolen credit card numbers? On the Dark Web. Want to buy or sell illegal stuff of any kind? Dark Web, again. Google doesn't get anywhere close to the Dark Web."

"I don't get it," said Al. "If you hide something on the Dark Web—if it's really meant to be invisible—then how does anybody find the hit man, the drugs, or the stolen credit card numbers?"

"TOR."

"Who's that?" asked Al. "Some Norse god?"

Mac sighed.

"It's T-O-R; short for 'The Onion Router.' Never mind the details. One of my former business partners knows more about Dark Web access than anybody else I know. I'll make some inquiries."

"Dark Web," said Al. "Who comes up with this crap?"

"Think of it as high-tech anarchy," said Mac. "But it's the best idea I can think of to try and find out what that fed was talking about."

"What about Jack Penn?" said Al. "The 'Cracker' knows something about everything. You think he's still over at Mayport?"

"One way to find out."

I punched Penn's number into my new burner. He picked up on the second ring.

"Hello, Mr. Penn. Do you remember this voice?" I asked.

There was a long pause on the other end of the line.

"I think so. But we heard he died a few months ago."

"Yes. It was very sad. But before he died he said he wanted me to ask you a question."

"I'm not sure what the game is, here, but go ahead."

"Have you ever heard of HartKampf Logistics," I asked.

"Don't call me back."

Then he hung up.

―――――

I woke up before dawn, threw on my shorts and T-shirt, and grabbed the keys to the minivan. I drove down to the beltway, turned east, and crossed the Dames Point Bridge. I'd visited the Cracker at his apartment nearly two years earlier and was pretty sure he hadn't moved. He was a Navy spook—cryptologic technician, signals intelligence—and knew stuff nobody should. He was also a creature of deeply-ingrained habits.

He walked out of his apartment at six thirty-five and stepped into a brown ex-government Crown Victoria. I followed him for a few miles and watched the car pull into a Starbucks parking lot. I continued to the next driveway and parked on the other side of the Starbucks. I guessed he wouldn't recognize me with the beard and the longer, lighter hair.

Jack sat at a small two-person table reading *The Guardian* on his iPad. I ordered a large dark roast, added some cream and sugar, and sat down at the table next to Jack's facing him.

"Tell me what you know about HartKampf Logistics and I promise to leave you alone."

He looked up from his iPad. He was open-mouthed. He saw past the hair and beard.

"You're dead," he said. "You're supposed to be dead."

"Not so much, actually."

"I can't talk to you about this."

"Yesterday, I was having lunch with a guy who carries a very federal-looking government business card that lists only one name, a DC phone number, and no agency," I said. "His boss was there, too. Our lunch was interrupted by three bad guys. One of the bad guys shot the fed in the shoulder. Then the three tried to abduct us. Their attempt failed with two of the baddies going down very hard."

"Why are you telling me this?"

"Mr. 'One-Name-Only' said two words to me before he and his boss scooted their slick little backsides back to DC. He was bleeding at the time and he was earnest. He said 'HartKampf Logistics' as if it should mean something to me. It doesn't. But your behavior tells me that it means something to you."

He made a move to get up.

"Don't," I said. "I'll just follow you."

"All the way back to my office at the base? How will you get past the guard?"

"I'll stand at the gate and yell 'HartKampf Logistics' over and over until somebody asks me why I'm yelling. Then I'll tell them you're my best friend and that you promised to tell me all about it."

He thought about that and sat down.

"Okay, okay," he said. "Shut up and I'll tell you what I know. Then you'll leave me alone forever, right?"

I nodded.

"I don't know anything."

"Not fair. You've heard the name."

"Yes. And I can't tell you the context in which I heard it. But I can tell you that I don't know exactly what they do or how they do it or who runs it."

"What do you *think* they do?"

"I *think* they move things."

"What kinds of things?"

"I have no idea. Honestly. But it could be stuff that can't be openly moved with bills of lading and customs forms and the usual documentation."

"Smuggling?"

He shrugged.

"Who are the people behind this outfit?" I asked. "Who runs it and where can I find them?"

"Again, I don't know."

"Yes, you do and you're going to tell me."

"Don't try to threaten me, Sim. I don't know and I don't want to know. We had an analyst who stumbled across the name and started asking questions. He disappeared."

"Disappeared?"

"He got reassigned, I think. Probably somewhere very remote. Didn't have time to say good-bye."

"Jack, you need to listen to me. I travelled up here from my comfortable digs in the Caribbean to rescue a young girl who was abducted by some very bad people. The same people who tried to kill me. This name came up during my inquiries and I need to know everything about it, the people involved, and how it ties in to a high-grade whorehouse in Serenity, Georgia."

He thought for a few moments.

"You're not going to let go of this, are you?"

"What do you think?"

"I think you're going to get yourself killed."

"That's the beauty of it, Jack. I'm already dead. I've got nothing to lose."

"I'll need a little time to get you what you want."

"Don't try to stall me."

He thought for a moment.

"Do you know how to get into an old locked Crown Victoria without beating the car up too badly?"

"I grew up in California," I said. "There are certain skills that go with the territory."

He pointed toward a group of trees across the parking lot.

"I will be entering that Best Buy at ten o'clock tomorrow morning. I will spend exactly one hour in that store and my car will be parked under one of those trees away from the security cameras. It will be locked. If somebody breaks into it and steals anything, even so much as a single manila folder left on the front seat, I will call the police and they may even take fingerprints. And if they catch whoever did it, I will make certain the prosecutor presses charges."

"I'll owe you, Jack."

"I'll add it to your tab. And interest will be compounded monthly."

"Oh, one last thing," I said. "Who are these people with one name on the card and no agency?"

He shook his head, held his hands out palms forward, stood up, and walked out to his car. He didn't burn the Crown Vic's tires on his way out of the parking lot but he came close.

48

I headed back toward the COP wondering what I'd find in Jack's car the next morning. When I got there, I found Mac and Al eating bacon and eggs. They were as quiet as an old married couple who'd been fighting all morning. I grabbed some bacon and a glass of orange juice and sat down.

"What's wrong?"

"We need to go back into Serenity," said Mac. "And Al doesn't like it."

"Reverend Sharpe sent a message through her key logger this morning. Says she needs to meet with you."

"So?" I asked.

"So it's a trap," said Al.

"And you know this how?"

Al pounded a fist into his chest.

"Even if it isn't," said Mac, "you can't go. You're both compromised. They know you're alive."

"Mac picked up an APB on the Serenity police frequency," said Al. "They downloaded our pictures from our shop's website and uploaded them to every cop car in town. So every single hostile in Serenity is looking for the two of us. We are both useless in Serenity."

"I could wait until dark."

"She says you have to meet her at the church and be there at noon," said Al. "A specific place at a specific time in broad daylight. That's a sure sign of a trap."

"You're both toast if you show your faces in Serenity," said Mac. "Which means it is up to me."

"That's not going to work," I said.

"Why not?"

"For starters," said Al, "you're exactly one leg short of a full complement."

"Do I need to kick your ass with my prosthesis to prove I can do it?"

A fair amount of heated wrangling ensued but we eventually figured out how we could make certain it wasn't a trap. We worked out the details during our drive north.

We arrived in Serenity a little after nine and parked the minivan a block away and across the street from Reverend Sharpe's church. Her brother Trent walked in the side door at nine-thirty. We saw no suspicious traffic or unusual cars. At ten-thirty, Mac moved to get out of the van. As he opened the door, however, Reverend Sharpe exited the building with her two brothers and got into a newer Toyota Camry.

We followed their car into an older section of town. They parked in front of a coffee shop next to an old S. H. Kress store and walked in. We parked fifty yards south.

"Here goes nothing," said Mac.

We watched him walk toward the coffee shop in that slightly mechanical gait of his.

"You read me, Bravo?" he said.

"Five by five, Delta."

Al sat in the back seat with his Blackout. I kept the engine running in case we had to extract Mac. We saw him walk in and heard him order black coffee to go. It came, he paid, and we heard him walk across a tile floor.

"Sorry to crash your party," he said.

"This is a private booth, friend," said one of the brothers. There was tension in his voice.

"I'm here for a mutual friend," said Mac. "You said you wanted to see him."

"I don't know who you could be talking about," said Reverend Sharpe. "But if I wanted to meet with somebody else, why would that person send you?"

"He hates wearing a mask in public," said Mac. "But you can talk to him yourself."

We heard the sound of Mac handing an ear bud to Reverend Sharpe.

"Go ahead, Bravo."

"It's me, Reverend. I can't be there. I know that might seem unusual, but you've got to trust me on this."

"Your voice is a little strange over this radio," she said. "How do I know it's you?"

"My voice would sound a lot more like LBJ's in person."

"You were supposed to come at noon."

"That didn't fit into my calendar."

"Okay."

"Talk to my friend, Reverend. Tell him whatever it was you wanted me to hear."

She gave the ear bud back to Mac.

"One of my congregation called me this morning," she said. "You're gonna want to know what he said."

49

WE drove back to the COP and I went online to live stream the Dr. Jen Show. I was anxious to see if the files we'd given her added any fuel to her fire. They had.

Her bumper music faded under short excerpts of Harley and Mitch admitting to awful deeds they'd done for *Sidoni*.

"Welcome to the Dr. Jen show. Hopefully, you don't know these two men. They are operatives of the *Sidoni* church in Serenity, Georgia. A church that has managed to weather some serious accusations over the last eight days by fashioning themselves as victims of religious intolerance. That claim, however, is far from the truth.

"During this hour, we'll discuss the efforts of the Alice Paul Society in exposing the illegal activities of the *Sidoni* church. We'll also share the recorded video interviews of two men who worked for that church; men who killed for it.

Al and Mac walked into the room carrying three guitar cases and a fisherman's tackle box as the radio commercials began to play.

"What's the Alice Paul Society?" asked Mac.

"I think it's us."

They put the guitar cases on our conference/kitchen/workshop table and unzipped them.

"Alice Paul?" said Al. "Is that what you get if McCartney wears face paint and carries a boa constrictor on stage?"

I looked up "Alice Paul" on Wikipedia.

Mac handed me a Blackout. Al opened the tackle box and pulled out the bore snakes and the bottles of bore cleaner and lubricating oil.

"I just love the smell of bore cleaner," said Mac.

"I used to put a dab behind each ear before going on a date," said Al.

"Probably drove the ladies wild down at the trailer park."

Al shook his head as he broke down his Blackout.

"You think this kind of thing—this talk show stuff—really helps at all?" asked Al.

"It's exactly the kind of publicity we want," said Mac. "It's a strong card and Dr. Jen is playing it for us."

Dr. Jen returned and we listened to her as we cleaned our weapons. She played sections of the audio from the Harley and Mitch interrogations. She spent a lot of time on Mitch's admission that Harley had been murdered and fed to alligators by *Sidoni*. She revealed that "sources within the Alice Paul Society" told her Mitch was one of the mystery men who had been turned over to the FBI in Charleston with the media present and cameras rolling.

She said her staff had contacted the U.S. Attorney's Office for the Southern District of Georgia to discuss *Sidoni* and the evidence against them. The feds had declined to respond. She started taking listener calls and the floodgates of public outrage swung wide open.

"That's what I'm talking about," said Mac. "These people are the sea in which our revolution will swim."

"I'd still just as soon bust into that courthouse and shoot every maroon-robed priest I see," said Al.

"Again, we see the primary SEAL response," said Mac.

I grabbed a fresh burner at the end of the second hour and, moments later, was bumped to the head of Dr. Jen's caller line. I was suddenly on national radio.

"For those just joining us for the third hour, we are discussing the *Sidoni* religion and the allegations of their involvement in kidnapping, murder, and sex trafficking. We now have a representative from the Alice Paul Society on the line to discuss these issues. Good afternoon, Stewart. What can you tell us?"

"We've uncovered a religious cult with leaders who trick young girls into joining them, prostitute the girls out to wealthy and powerful people, and then kill anybody who gets in their way. Your listeners have heard strong evidence of these allegations during this show."

"Do you have any more for us today?"

"There is a private airliner that flies into Serenity to pick up girls for private parties. Did you get the email I sent about that?"

"Yes, we did. And we have new information about that airplane."

She talked about Mitch's statements regarding the wealthy mystery man who flew the young women of *Sidoni* to the Bahamas on his own 737 for private "purification" services. She cited the tail number Mac had found and revealed the airplane's owner; a billionaire hedge fund manager.

"Stewart, we appreciate your efforts in uncovering these crimes. Can you keep us posted as you discover new information?"

"Will do. And thank you for raising national awareness of this issue on your show."

With that, the line went dead and Dr. Jen continued.

"I know the days of hard-hitting investigative journalism are nearly over in this country," she said. "But if there are any in the media who still have the guts and the wherewithal, they should take a hard look at *Sidoni* and find out more about the billionaire who flies underage girls to his island in the Bahamas for 'private parties.'"

The show ended and Mac let out a low whistle.

"Gutsy chick," said Al.

"You're in the Alice Paul Society. 'Gutsy chick' is not within the scope of accepted language."

Mac laughed.

"These guys don't take prisoners," said Al, "and that kind of talk—what she's saying over the air right now—that could get her killed. I call that gutsy."

An hour later, the news reported that a mountain cabin near

Aspen, Colorado, had exploded and burned to the ground. Early investigations indicated that a leaking propane tank caused the explosion. While no bodies had been recovered, it was believed that the family who owned the cabin had been staying there and all were presumed dead. A picture flashed on the screen showing Orson Flake, a red-headed woman of similar age, and three teenage children.

"Dammit," said Al.

50

AL was cooking dinner when Mac rushed in and told us we had another conversation to listen to.

"It's from Chief Willardson's office," he said. "It's an hour old."

We went into the conference room and Mac clicked on his mouse.

We heard a door open.

"Come in, Hickey, and sit down."

Steps clacked on tile and a chair scraped across the floor.

"Have you heard anything back from your FBI?" said Trevor Hickey.

We heard the muted beep of a telephone button being pushed.

"Jacobson, you get anything back from the feds on those fingerprints?"

"They report no matches, sir."

"Weren't those prints any good?" said Willardson.

"Yes, sir. The rest of the van was a mess but we got three sets of solid, clean prints off the floor. I submitted them last night but the report came back negative. I called my contact at the bureau this morning and he said they don't have anything close, not even a partial."

"How can that be? There's gotta be a hundred million fingerprints in their database."

"That's what they told me, sir."

"Okay, that's all."

"Something's dodgy," said Hickey. *"The big guy we had in the van was that bloke from Tortola. Sim Greene. He was U.S. Navy for twenty years. His fingerprints are in that database."*

"Maybe you were mistaken. Anyhow, I thought you and Mitch blew

him up months ago."

"That is what the news reported. But I saw him in that restaurant. And I've got this feeling he is getting help from a former Navy SEAL. A slippery little bugger. Very tough to kill, apparently."

"Then we'll need to find both of them. Did you tell Clint we should be turning over every railway warehouse in the county looking for these guys?"

"Harley said a train went by while they were grilling him."

"It's a waste of time. Those guys could be anywhere. And burning that detective in his car was stupid. It's attracting attention we don't need."

"Clint wanted to send a message," said Hickey. "So people would know what happens when somebody makes a run at us."

A telephone rang.

"Chief, I have Sergeant Crowe on the line."

"Put him through."

Another beep sounded.

"Willardson."

"We can't find Flake. He told a neighbor in Stamford they'd be at their cabin in Snowmass for a week. We watched the cabin and saw no sign of them so we blew it this morning thinking it might bring them in. But they didn't show. Flake may have been tipped off."

"What about his plane?"

"It's here parked at the airfield. And he hasn't rented a car."

"Hang on a second."

We heard another beep of a button being pushed.

"Are your men really that incompetent?" asked Hickey.

"You can do better?"

"No question about it."

Another beep sounded.

"Crowe?"

"Yes, sir."

"Get back here immediately. Hickey will take over this assignment."

"Yes, sir."

Willardson hung up.

"There it is, Hickey. Your big chance to prove you're the hotshot you claim to be."

"I'll find him."

"Clint isn't getting his money's worth out of you," said Willardson. *"You screwed up the job in Tortola and you screwed up the job yesterday. And you got two of my men killed in the process."*

Hickey swore at Willardson. Footsteps walked away and a door slammed.

"Unrest within the opposing forces?" said Mac. "Dissension among the troops? We are making headway."

"And Flake is taking Sim's advice," said Al. "High stakes hide-and-seek."

51

"IT'S two in the morning," said Al. "How do we know they're gonna be on this road?"

"Reverend Sharpe seemed confident," I said.

"How do we know there's any value to this target?"

"We don't. We're trusting the Reverend and her source."

"Could it be a trap?" said Mac.

"You think she'd come out here with her brothers if she thought it was a trap?"

"I still don't like it," said Al. "Three of them and three of us."

"We're on the same side."

"How do you know?" said Mac. "It wouldn't be the first green-on-blue attack I've seen."

"Didn't you guys act on information you got from locals?"

"Sure we did," said Al. "But we never brought the informants along on a mission. And the leads were always vetted and the info backed up by other reliable intel."

"Well, we are fresh out of spy satellites. And there is no way the three of us could handle this operation on our own."

Mac tensed up.

"Wait a minute," he said. "I see something." He looked down at the tablet in his lap. "Headlights just over two miles away."

"How many sets? There are supposed to be eight of them."

"Can't tell, yet. It's a string of vehicles, though. They're entering that small forest section. We've got four minutes, max."

I looked up at the drone above us with its dimmed red and green navigation lights.

"Okay, I've got eight sets of headlights in a tight pack coming out of the trees," said Mac. "There's a lot of dust but no traffic behind them."

I walked across the dirt road to talk to the Reverend.

"They're nearly here," I said. "Keep your masks on. Stay inside the treeline until the last vehicle stops. And don't say a word. Somebody might recognize your voice."

"Ninety seconds, Bravo."

"Alright, Delta, get that thing down."

The buzzing we'd heard before grew louder as the drone dropped and landed next to Mac. He put the tablet down and picked up his Blackout. Headlights flickered on the dirt road around the corner only two hundred feet away.

The first van rounded the corner and Al shot the left front tire with his suppressed Blackout. The van swerved and stopped even with my position in the woods. The other vans stopped as the first driver got out to look at his tire.

"What the hell?" he said.

At that point six masked individuals stepped out of the woods and shot out the tires on all eight vans. The Reverend and her brothers had our suppressed shotguns—we didn't have enough Blackouts to go around—and the sound was significantly less than deafening and only momentary. Anybody more than a half-mile away wouldn't have given it a second thought.

"Get out of the vehicles," I yelled. "Move slowly and keep your hands up."

The eight drivers got out. There were no passengers.

"Get on your bellies," I said. "Clasp your hands behind your neck. Nothing tricky. Nobody wants to kill you."

The men complied. Al went from driver to driver with zip-tie handcuffs while Mac and I held our Blackouts on the prone men.

"If you want the vans," said the lead driver, "you just take 'em and let us go."

"What's in them?"

"I have no idea, mister. We're just drivers."

"Where did you get them?"

"A warehouse outside Columbus. Our shop steward said these had to be on a RO-RO by six o'clock this morning and we'd each get a bonus to go up there and bring 'em down to the docks."

"Which RO-RO?"

He told me the name of the ship.

"Which warehouse outside Columbus?"

"I couldn't tell you one warehouse from another," he said. "But he texted me the address and these vans were right outside the loading bays."

I reached into his pocket and grabbed his cell phone. He gave me the password and I went through his texts. I wrote down the address for the pickup point.

"And you have no idea what's in the vans?"

"The boxes say parts," he said. "But that bonus was pretty big."

"We'll find out," I said. "And we'll let you go soon enough."

Once Al finished handcuffing the prone men, he helped the lead driver to his feet and put a black hood over his head. Trent and Terry hooded the other drivers and helped them up. Then they walked all eight down the road to where we'd parked our vehicles.

Mac picked up his tablet and sent the drone up to watch for traffic.

"Nothing coming either way, Bravo."

I walked up to the first van and opened the sliding side door. The interior was packed with wooden crates labeled "Automotive Parts." Each crate bore an odd logo featuring a two-headed eagle with an ornate "T" on a coat of arms. Al returned with a small video camera to record the action as I went to one of the larger boxes with a pry bar. I pulled off a couple of slats on one side and a stack of M4 carbines and extra magazines slid onto the ground surrounded by foam peanuts. I opened another crate to find neatly-packed M3 MAAWS rifles and three-inch diameter shells.

"Well, Alpha," I said. "There's something you don't see every day."

"Whisky Tango Foxtrot," said Mac. "I haven't seen a Carl Gustav since I left Afghanistan."

"What have we got here, Bravo?"

"Eight vans; four crates of M4s per van; thirty rifles in each crate. That's nearly a thousand M4 carbines. And these are the selective-fire military grade models. Add in sixteen crates of MAAWS with ammo."

"Enough for a large battalion," said Al.

"What's near Columbus, Georgia?"

"Fort Benning."

"I'm guessing the Army is missing some gear," I said.

Smaller crates held 5.56 millimeter military-grade ammunition; hundreds of thousands of rounds. We didn't bother opening them all. We didn't have time. All total, we spent twenty minutes examining the boxes and recording the contents on video. Al also recorded the vans' license plates and VINs. We grabbed a few rifles for later examination.

Al searched the lead van and returned with a manila envelope thick with hundred dollar bills.

"Jackpot," he said. "Thirty grand in bonus money."

We doused the vans with gasoline and dropped a timed igniter into the middle of each one. It would all be gone in minutes.

"Let's hit the road," I said.

There were fourteen of us in three vehicles. We heard the muffled thumps of the exploding vans from two miles away. We continued in silence until we were three miles from Serenity. We stopped at a spot we'd checked out earlier that evening and led the drivers on foot into a meadow.

"Lie down," I said.

"You're going to shoot us," said one of the drivers.

"I'd rather not. What's your name?"

"Jerry."

"It might be your lucky day, Jerry. I'm going to cut your cuffs off and drop a pair of dull scissors a few feet away from you. Your job is to stay on your belly with your arms at your sides and that hood on. Then count to a thousand. Count it out about as fast as you'd count sheep jumping over a dead man's ass. Not one bit faster. Then you can grope around for the scissors, cut your hood off, and free your buddies. But if you count too fast and I see you move while I'm still here, then I'll have to shoot all of you. I won't like it but that'll be the natural consequence of your failure to follow directions. Do you understand me, Jerry?"

"You guys got some balls," said Jerry.

"I suppose we do."

"Somebody might just feed them to you."

"Your shop steward?" I asked.

"No. But I think the guy who paid him might give it a try."

"It's not happening this morning, Jerry. Now count out a thousand slow sheep. And, remember, speed kills."

We walked back to the cars where Reverend Sharpe and her brothers had been waiting. They'd taken off their masks.

"You guys did well," I said. "Very professional, very tight."

"Not all of us are guys," said the Reverend. "Just sayin'."

"We gonna see you without that mask, Mister Badass?"

"Not if I know what's good for me."

Trent and Terry smiled and the three got in their cars. We got back into our van and watched them drive away.

"You think we should head to Columbus?" said Mac. "That's nearly five hours west."

"I think we should get some breakfast," said Al.

"Can you find out who owns that warehouse?"

"It's all on the internet, gentlemen," said Mac. "Just gotta dig for it."

"I still think we should get some breakfast," repeated Al.

We stopped at a Waffle House off I-95 just north of the Florida state line. The place was small; thirty diners max. Al walked toward a booth at the far right near the restrooms. He sat where he could see the entrance. Mac and I followed. Plastic-coated menus waited for us at the table.

The staff was admirably swift. A portly young black woman with false eyelashes curling outward and upward a full inch approached us. The tag on her uniform said "Aletha."

"What can I get for you this morning, gentlemen?"

"I'll have the All-Star with ham, eggs fried, runny yolks, and coffee," said Mac.

"Same," said Al.

"Same," I said. "But with sausage on top of the ham."

"Then it really ain't the same, is it?" said Aletha. She smiled.

"Okay, I'll have an All-Star with sausage, eggs…"

"I got it," she said. "I got it."

She left and took the notes she'd made to a man standing in front of a large gas stove. He pulled a ladle from a canister and dumped the contents into a small frying pan, poured the liquid from the pan back into the canister, and put the pan on a burner. He cracked two eggs one-handed with a dexterity that only comes after cracking ten thousand eggs one-handed. He repeated the process two more times with two more pans. The ham steaks and sausage patties got similar swift, professional treatment. Another staff member ladled batter into three waffle makers. Excess batter bubbled out and onto the stainless steel counter.

Our coffee arrived quickly; the food moments later. Al ate with zest and an admirable level of dedication while keeping an eye on the door. Chain restaurant breakfast had never tasted so good.

"You got any idea what that shipment was worth?" I asked.

"I don't know the going black-market rate for MAAWS units and US-made selective fire M4s but I'm guessing we torched around ten million dollars' worth of guns and ammo."

"A fair piece of change."

"Somebody was expecting those guns," said Al. "And somebody else was expecting ten million extra dollars. There will be a response."

"And that ship the fellow mentioned?" said Mac. "We need to figure out who owns it and who is running this stuff."

Other patrons walked in and sat down. By six a.m., the place was packed. The staff turned everything up a notch as breakfast orders were taken, eggs cracked, waffle irons loaded, toast cut and buttered. It was as if somebody had spun the volume to ten and doubled the tempo. The diners in the booth next to us started talking about Tropical Storm Julius.

"Are you following that one?" asked Mac.

"Last I checked, Julius was twelve hundred miles straight east of us. NOAA says it's becoming better organized and building into a Category 2 hurricane."

"Worried about your boat?" said Al.

"Absolutely. I may sneak down there and double her lines if it gets any closer."

"Did you know that FEMA monitors hurricanes by checking on Waffle House locations?" said Mac.

Al looked at Mac like he'd just stepped off the moon.

"Seriously, they have a Waffle House Index they use to track storm-caused destruction."

"You're pulling my chain," said Al.

"Not at all. If a Waffle House is closed, FEMA knows it's really bad there and gives it a red dot on their map. If they're open but only offering a reduced menu, the location gets a yellow dot. If it's fully open, then it's all good and gets a green dot."

"And why do we need to know this?" I said.

"As you said, there's a hurricane headed our way. It seems relevant."

We finished breakfast and stood to go. Four people waiting near the door quickly grabbed our booth. I took the check and two twenties to the cashier while Al and Mac walked to the van.

52

I trusted Jack Penn but still felt the need to exercise caution. His skill in deciphering codes, understanding intel, and gathering information from unconventional sources was well-known but his devotion to the Navy and military protocol was lifelong. I showed up two hours early, parked on the other side of the shopping center's massive lot, and glassed the security cameras, building roofs, and other vehicles in the area. A cop car drove in shortly after nine o'clock and parked near the Starbucks. A lone policeman entered the store and, ten minutes later, exited with a pastry and a large paper cup. Had there been a donut shop in the area, I'd be fretting over a constant stream of snack-hungry law enforcement.

At five minutes to ten, the Crown Vic rolled in and parked under the tree Jack had specified. He got out, looked around, and walked into the Best Buy store. I waited twenty minutes. No cop cars, no shooters on rooftops, nothing out-of-the-ordinary to concern me.

My earbud buzzed.

"Bravo, we have a clear field from this angle. No threats apparent."

"Roger that, Alpha."

I drove the minivan through the parking lot at a sedate pace and parked next to the Cracker's car. I got out, slid the slim jim into the slot between the passenger window and the door, hooked the lever to the door's locking mechanism, and pulled up. The door unlocked and I opened it. A thin manila folder sat on the passenger seat. I grabbed it, closed the door, and drove away peeling the latex gloves off my hands as I negotiated the lot's speed bumps.

"Bravo, we have a bogie at your two o'clock position."

I looked to see another Jacksonville police car enter the lot and turn directly toward me. Thirty yards away, it turned onto a parallel course heading through empty parking lanes toward the Starbucks. I continued.

"Bogie is now parked and walking in to get a cup, Bravo. You can stop biting bullet holes in your boxer shorts."

"Roger that, Alpha."

We returned to the COP to find Mac tapping away at his keyboard.

"What have you been up to?"

"I made some more videos and uploaded them to that server in Finland. One of them features three congressmen, a Senator from Virginia, and Serenity's own Police Chief William 'Bill' Willardson. The other has some more clips of our interrogations."

He clicked an icon on his screen. The video started with the title "Who Killed Solana Bradford?" and included a logo with a picture of Alice Paul juxtaposed against a pink Venus symbol.

"Where'd you get the logo?" asked Al.

"I bought it on a site for freelance artists. Super cheap."

"Doesn't that leave some sort of paper trail?"

"I used Mayor Andy's city credit card."

Al smiled and nodded. "Nice touch."

"Now I'm loading the TAILS OS."

"Tails?" said Al.

"It's an acronym for 'The Amnesiac Incognito Live System.'"

Mac earned two blank stares.

"It'll let me drop down below the Surface Web without leaving any electronic fingerprints. Trust me."

Al opened the manila folder I'd retrieved from Jack Penn's car and pulled out a single sheet of paper.

"Well, this was certainly worth the trouble," he said.

I took the paper from him and read the few typed words:

Tesseract; Samota GmbH.

"I say we drive back there and kick his ass," said Al.

"Not part of our mission profile."

Mac took the sheet from me and read it.

"Gimme a minute."

"A minute," said Al. He looked at his dive watch.

"A few hours, then. A few quiet, uninterrupted hours."

Mac walked into the conference room, sat down at his computer, and started poking away at the keyboard. Al and I hopped in the minivan.

"What's bugging him?" I asked.

"He's been up all night and he's frustrated. So am I. We grab people, interrogate them, get useless intel, and achieve nothing."

"We toasted some illegal guns last night."

"And how did that further our mission to eliminate *Sidoni?*"

"I don't know."

"And the feds are zero help. In fact, they've turned against us."

"Maybe they're working the case behind the scenes," I said.

"You give them way too much credit. And we are getting nowhere. We're just stirring up a big hornets' nest and every time we step closer thinking we're going to destroy it, the nest gets bigger and the hornets more deadly. It's not meaningful progress." He looked up as I turned south onto I-95. "And where the hell are we going now?"

"NOAA upgraded Julius to a full-fledged hurricane," I said. "I need to check on *Figaro.*"

"Risky," said Al.

"If she sinks, the marina staff will come looking for me. What's the greater risk?"

Al nodded.

"Okay," he said. "Do what you gotta do. I'll provide cover from the van."

I drove to the marina where *Figaro* had waited patiently for nearly a month. A few other owners were down on the docks checking their boat's mooring lines and looking for signs of chafing or other wear. Al stayed in the car.

Boats hate to be left alone. A boat owner who fails to take the proper precautions should, upon returning to his vessel, expect an olfactory assault from the sour smell of neglect. Humid environments breed mold and a sailor who leaves his boat in the water for weeks at a time better learn how to deal with it.

I opened the hatch and stepped down the companionway. All was well. The small dehumidifier I'd bought in Ft. Lauderdale did its magic, sucking water out of the air and draining it into the sink. I checked hatches and ports; all were as I'd left them—closed and secure. The bilge was dry. I climbed back up into the cockpit, dragged some extra lines out of the lazarette, and used them to double-up *Figaro's* mooring lines. I checked and retied her boat fenders.

A neighboring boat owner struggled at getting his mainsail off its mast so I went over and helped him. In return, he helped me detach *Figaro's* sails. I stowed them below. Checking again that all was secure, I locked up the boat and returned to the van.

"What'd you do?" said Al. "Wax the damned thing?"

"Back to the COP?" I asked.

"Serenity. We need to check our hidden camera rock. And Mac could probably use a little more 'alone time.'"

We continued north. I turned on the stereo and "It's Not My Cross to Bear" cued up on my playlist.

"That guy sure could sing the blues," said Al.

"How come your generation had such great music?"

"We let ugly people sing."

I laughed.

"How's Marie?"

"Upset, I suppose. I didn't call her for nearly two months and then, when I finally did, I didn't have time to talk."

"And you couldn't explain why."

"Yep. How's Liv?"

"Still in Australia. Her dad died three weeks ago and I wasn't there for her. I couldn't even answer my phone when she tried to reach me. So, I'm dead to her right now."

"She's a forgiving woman."

"I may have pushed it too far this time."

We passed the sign alerting us that Serenity was only five miles ahead.

"Once more unto the breach, dear friends," said Al. "Once more."

"Don't they have an APB out on us?"

"Wanted?" said Al. "Dead or alive?"

"Something like that."

"We are in the most innocuous and invisible vehicle on the planet. We'll be fine.

Minutes later, we continued north into Serenity. I parked the van behind the sandwich shop next to Fully Woke. Just close enough to get a connection and download the files from our hidden camera.

"There's nothing on this video," said Al.

"Nothing?"

"The camera records movement. If nothing moves, there's no video. Just a snapshot every hour. Nobody has gone in or out those doors in four days."

"Maybe we scared away the paying customers."

I started up the van and headed back toward the COP. Mac sent Al a text as we pulled onto I-95.

Good news, kids. Daddy hit the mother lode. Too much to text. Don't wake me when you get home. I'll be napping.

"What is that supposed to mean?"

"I don't know," said Al. "But it sounds good."

53

A few key people paid attention to Dr. Jen's Tuesday afternoon end-of-show challenge. On Thursday morning, the *Drudge Report* ran a link to a *Washington Times* piece about a billionaire hedge fund manager whose private airliner made numerous trips between Serenity, Georgia, and his private island in the Bahamas. An unnamed source—alleged to be one of the flight crew—asserted that numerous young girls had been on those flights. Three million people clicked on the link.

By noon, the *New York Times* and two major television networks reported confidential sources placing a governor, two sitting Senators, and a former President of the United States on that same billionaire's 737. Video clips they'd received from Mac's faux email account bolstered the claims. Within hours, every major news source in the US, and quite a few others, reported what they knew about the growing scandal.

The politicians in question quickly denied any knowledge of *Sidoni* or any impropriety taking place on the island. Several threatened libel suits.

"We're broadcasting today from an undisclosed location," said Dr. Jen. "We've received some serious threats over the last few days and, while I don't scare easily, I have ten employees I care about. So, we've moved out of the studio. But we are not shutting up."

"Saw that coming," said Al.

"Today, we have Dr. Salvatore Palilla joining us on a video feed. Dr. Palilla is the Beck Professor of Politics and International Affairs at Princeton University. Welcome to the show, Dr. Palilla."

"I'm delighted to be here, but I don't understand exactly why you've asked me to join you today."

"My apologies for that. I asked my producer to bring you in cold. We're not trying to put you on the spot. I just want your frank and unrehearsed opinions about some world political issues."

"That I can give you."

"You're an authority on political trends in Africa. What can you tell us about the fighting in West Africa and the governments involved."

"A lot, but you need to understand the history of Western Africa."

"Can you give our listeners some of that?"

He laughed. "I can give you two semesters' worth, but you'll need to enroll in my classes."

"We've only got about forty minutes," said Jen.

"Africa is filled with valuable, largely untapped, resources. Britain, France, Spain—all of Europe, really—realized that a hundred and fifty years ago. Back then, they were interested in rubber, cotton, dates, cocoa, things that don't grow well in Europe. They established colonies and, ultimately, took control of over three-fourths of the continent. Two world wars and a Great Depression, however, seriously damaged Europe's ability to control their colonies.

"There were uprisings and, one by one, the nations of Western Africa achieved independence. But that hasn't slowed foreign interest in Africa's resources. China has their One Belt One Road Strategy and a number of African countries are allowing China to invest there. But those investments have thick strings attached."

"I'm guessing that China isn't interested in cocoa and cotton," said Jen.

"Africa has half the world's gold, a third of the world's uranium, and ninety percent of the world's platinum and cobalt. There is also this mineral called 'coltan.' I have no idea what it is but it's used in nearly every electronic device on earth and Africa has three-fourths of the world's supply. They've also got two-and-a-half million square miles of uncultivated arable land; sixty percent of the global total. You want to feed the world? That could happen in Africa."

"That's worth fighting over," said Jen. "But isn't this just a new brand of colonialism?"

"Chinese colonialism? I suppose you could call it that. But many of the leaders of these countries—democratically elected, more or less—are eagerly entering into agreements with them."

"But not everyone is excited about it?"

"It is a tasty-looking pie and everybody wants a slice," said Sal. "Currently, there are ten separate armed conflicts in West Africa. Nigeria is embroiled in five of them. The Insurgency in the Maghreb—a conflict spanning two decades—currently involves eight separate African countries. Some of these wars appear to be byproducts of the same tribal and religious divisions that existed well before colonialism. But some factions only want control of the area's resources. They want to be the sellers."

"Does the U.S. government play any role in these conflicts?" asked Jen.

"Officially, U.S. foreign policy is focused on helping these countries combat corruption, spread democracy, protect civil rights, and promote peace and stability in the region."

"And unofficially?"

"You want my opinion?" asked Sal.

"Absolutely."

"There are hundreds of little armed conflicts all over the world in places your listeners have never heard of with names they probably couldn't spell. Most of these conflicts are small, hardly noticeable on a global scale. But one tinpot provincial leader in some unheard of spot in Mali or Burkina Faso might be more helpful to our country than the alternative tinpot."

"Okay."

"So our government picks sides in these little wars trying to help out the guys we like. We want to think they'll pay us back someday. But these people are rarely good people. Most have bad reputations or nasty habits. For many, our country's assistance would be embarrassing. For others, it could damage important diplomatic alliances. For some, it could be just plain illegal."

"The seedy side of government," said Jen. "Our tax dollars at work?"

"Precisely."

"How do these rebels get their weapons? Is anybody looking into that?"

"There is very little hard data in that area. Muammar Gaddafi had a massive and sophisticated arsenal in Libya. When his regime collapsed, a lot of that weaponry wound up on the black market. The larger and more complex weapons were shipped to factions in the Middle East. The more common firearms made their way to rebel forces and criminal groups in West Africa. But the U.N. believes that Gaddafi's weapons account for only a fraction of the total."

"So, we don't know where the guns come from?"

"We know China sells rifles and rocket-propelled grenades to various governments and some of these are stolen by or sold to rebels but they're hard to trace. Some of my peers believe that arms dealers from the Ukraine, Russia, and Lebanon are the prime suppliers of rebel forces but nobody has been able to prove it. There just isn't any conclusive data."

"What if I told you our own government was a source?" said Jen.

"I'd be surprised. And I'd want to see hard evidence of it."

There was a short pause in the conversation.

"I just emailed you some photos and a short video. Less than thirty-six hours ago, members of the Alice Paul Society intercepted and destroyed an illegal shipment of military-grade weaponry worth nearly ten million dollars on the black market."

The professor drew in a breath.

"That looks like some sort of anti-tank gun," he said.

"There were eight vans full of M4 carbines, M3 MAAWS rifles, and ammunition for both. These guns were en route to Serenity, Georgia, to be loaded onto a commercial vessel bound for West Africa."

"How would these arms get on that boat? Our shipping and anti-smuggling controls are the best in the world."

"Let me play this audio excerpt for you, Sal."

"Our shop steward said these had to be on a RO-RO by six o'clock this morning and we'd each get a bonus to go up there and bring 'em down to the docks."

"Which RO-RO?"

"The Sørøya Frakt."

"Here's where it gets good," said Mac.

"The *Sørøya Frakt* is owned and operated by Tesseract Shipping," said Jen. "That company operates a fleet of container ships, bulk freighters, and Roll-On, Roll-Off vehicle transports. These RO-ROs make regular runs from Serenity, Georgia, to Freetown, Sierra Leone. They continue south and east to Abidjan, Cotonou, and Lagos. From there, they sail north to Southhampton, England. Then back to Serenity.

"Tesseract is wholly-owned by Samota GmbH, a German company that also controls a subsidiary called HartKampf Logistics," she continued. "We have copies of manifests showing multi-million dollar payments to an entity called 'HKL' which, we believe, is shorthand for HartKampf Logistics. Samota, the parent company, is entirely owned by a fellow named Ewing McCord who happens to be the father of both Clint and Duncan McCord, the brothers who started the *Sidoni* church."

"A lot of this is well outside my realm of expertise, Jen, but how does a religion get involved in arms trafficking?"

"It's a three-way conspiracy. The U.S. government wants guns and ammunition quietly shipped to parties unknown in sub-Saharan Africa. Ewing McCord's ships transport the goods and keep the money. The cash is then laundered as tax-free religious donations to *Sidoni*.

"Keeping it quiet is easy. The McCords use *Sidoni*—and the world's oldest temptation—to lure in the rich and politically powerful. They surreptitiously film them *in flagrante delicto* and keep the footage so they can blackmail into silence anybody who might threaten to uncover the smuggling operation. The same federal agencies who provide the illicit arms provide cover for a human trafficking ring disguised as a new religion, *Sidoni*."

"What is your source for all these documents?" asked Sal.

"The Alice Paul Society. We received these documents yesterday afternoon. And we just sent an email to the Department of Justice laying out the entire scheme: ships, countries, deliveries, payments, and the corporations involved. Now that we've broken the story, we'll send copies to other media outlets."

The bumper music faded in and Dr. Jen closed the show.

"Boom," said Mac.

"So this whole thing—*Sidoni*, the girls, the videos—is just a front for smuggling guns to East Nambuzu and Butt-Crackistan?" said Al.

Mac nodded.

"How did we get ourselves in the middle of this steaming crapfest?" asked Al.

Mac tossed two manila folders onto the conference table.

"One for each of you," he said. "Enjoy."

Each folder held several stapled documents featuring different sections on Tesseract Shipping, Samota GmbH, HartKampf Logistics, and Ewing McCord. I started reading about HartKampf Logistics.

"Whoa!" said Al. "Get a load of this guy."

He'd gone straight to the section about Ewing McCord. The second page featured the picture of an older man with a round face, wide porcine nose, and small, evil eyes. He could have been a qualifier for a World's Ugliest Dog contest.

"This guy is almost as ugly as his kid," said Al.

"Well, he's certainly got a face for radio."

"And he fathered two children. How does that even happen?"

"C'mon, you're old enough to know the answer to that question."

"You know what I mean," said Al. "How does a guy that repulsive manage to attract a mate and successfully breed?"

"Like my dad used to say, 'There's an ass for every saddle.'"

————

An hour later, CNN reported that the Department of Homeland Security's Inspector General had announced an inquiry into possible violations of Customs and Immigration policies and procedures regarding a private airplane making multiple trips to and from the Bahamas. The FBI and Department of Justice had no comment.

The networks, however, were all over the story that evening. NBC reported the identity of a woman who allegedly procured escorts for flights to what was now being referred to as "Party Island." ABC interviewed a young woman who claimed she'd escaped from *Sidoni*. The BBC reported a confidential interview with a man who claimed he'd helped cover up *Sidoni* and a smuggling operation when he worked for the CIA. PBS found an expert to discuss America's clandestine involvement in foreign wars.

Politicians from both parties claimed it was fake news.

54

"WE have to dump Sidoni," said Clint.

His recorded voice was as clear and distinct as if we were all standing right there in Willardson's office.

"What do you mean 'dump Sidoni?'" said Willardson.

"Do you have any leads on these mercenaries; these Alice Paul Society people?"

"Nothing, yet. Can't your people in Washington figure out who they are?"

"My source in DC is ghosting me," said Clint. "He doesn't pick up the phone and he's not returning my messages."

"We'll find these guys and take 'em out."

"Not soon enough. Father says Sidoni's got to go. It was a great tool while it lasted but it's gained too much attention. It now threatens our core business. So we need to take Sidoni out of the picture. Permanently."

"How should we do that?" asked Willardson.

"You don't do anything. Hickey will take care of it when he gets back."

"And nobody will suspect a thing?"

"There's a hurricane headed our way. Sidoni is in an old brick building. The wind will blow and the building will collapse. Hickey will set charges to make sure it does. The Fire Department will blame the hurricane."

"What about the girls?"

"They go down with the building. Duncan, too."

"Your brother?"

"Duncan's a zealot. He's been eating his own dog food for so long he now believes all that crap about Queen Astarte. Like it's real or something."

"*And Ewing is okay with this?*" asked Willardson. "*Doing his own son?*"

"*Call him.*"

We heard somebody dialing a phone.

"*Yes?*" said a raspy voice.

"*Clint tells me you think Sidoni has become a liability and that you want to ditch it.*"

"*That is precisely what I want. These federal investigations are getting too close to me. I am having difficulty controlling them and am concerned.*"

"*You're shutting it all down?*"

"*We will move our American operations elsewhere. I have another port city in mind with equally useful and greedy politicians.*"

"*Can I talk to you alone, Ewing?*"

There was a pause in the conversation.

"*Will you excuse us, Clint?*"

A door opened and closed.

"*Clint says the building, the girls, and even Duncan need to go? That seems extreme.*"

"*What is that phrase you Americans use? To 'tie up loose ends,' is it?*"

"*Your son is a loose end?*"

"*He believes this ridiculous 'religion' we created. He thinks he is supreme and eternal but that conviction is now a liability. One I can no longer afford.*"

"*We go a long way back, Ewing. We've done a lot together.*"

"*Yes,*" said McCord. "*And?*"

"*I just texted you a picture. I want you to look at it before anybody in your organization decides I could be, as you called it, a loose end.*"

"*Is this some sort of threat?*"

"*No, Ewing. I just want you to think of our past and what it means.*"

There was silence but the microphone was sensitive enough to pick up a man's labored breathing.

"*You think you can blackmail me?*"

"*Blackmail? Not at all,*" said Willardson. "*Life insurance. You do whatever you want with your family. Just leave me and mine alone here* in Serenity."

"You've become too much of an American. And Americans overreact."

"I just want to make sure you don't overreact. If anything happens to me, Clint will get a delivery. A package with pictures and documents and my sworn statement. And that old journal in the picture will go to The Hague."

Silence.

"Ewing? You still there?"

Mac and Al and I just looked at each other for a few minutes. Al finally broke the silence.

"I'm supposing our collective resolve to wait this thing out has now dissipated."

It had. Mac went back to his computer while Al and I pulled out the courthouse floor plans again and started working out a plan.

NOAA issued hurricane updates twice a day. I checked their website for the morning update on Julius. It wasn't great news. Air Force WC-130s were flying into it, taking measurements, and relaying the data back to NOAA's National Hurricane Center. Julius had grown to Category 4 status with sustained winds near 140 miles per hour. The eye was less than four hundred miles south of Bermuda and barely nine hundred miles east-southeast of Jacksonville.

The five-day Hurricane Track Forecast Cone predicted landfall anywhere between Jacksonville and Wilmington, North Carolina. The governors in four states were starting to talk about coastal evacuations and possible emergency declarations. We were at the south end of the cone but it was little comfort.

Al peeked over my shoulder.

"You getting nervous about this storm and *Figaro?*"

"Yep."

"Let it go. The mission has to be top of mind. Nothing else. Your boat will be fine. Anyway, we've snagged enough dough in the last couple of weeks to buy you three sailboats."

"I suppose so."

Mac looked up from his computer. "Good news," he said.

"Do tell," said Al.

"I just intercepted a phone call between Clint and Trevor. He's not going to be blowing up the courthouse anytime soon. The FAA issued a TFR because of the hurricane. *Sidoni's* plane can't get back home until the Temporary Flight Restriction is lifted. That won't happen until well *after* the hurricane passes."

"That police captain could do it himself," said Al.

"We should do something about that."

55

A dozen high school students showed up in front of *Sidoni* early Saturday morning to protest. By nine o'clock, there were over fifty. Most held hand-painted signs. A news van from Jacksonville rolled up ten minutes later, a full twenty minutes before the police arrived. Al and I watched it all unfold on CNN's live feed.

"Free the *Sidoni* girls! No excuse for abuse!" the kids shouted.

"You are trespassing and must disperse immediately," yelled a police sergeant.

"Free the *Sidoni* girls! No excuse for abuse!"

"Disperse immediately!"

Four girls approached the sergeant.

"Don't you recognize me?" said one. "I'm the mayor's daughter."

"And I'm a councilman's daughter," said another.

The sergeant paused to think about possible consequences. Parents arrived. One man worked his way through the crowd and approached the officer. A woman followed him with her smart phone camera trained on the pair.

"These girls are not trespassing," said the man. "They are standing on a public sidewalk and lawfully exercising their constitutional rights to free speech."

"Who are you?" asked the policeman.

"I am Benjamin Abram. I am an attorney from Savannah and I represent the Free Youth from Serenity."

"Who are the 'Free Youth' of whatever?"

The lawyer waved his arm across the crowd of students. They

cheered.

The sergeant looked at the smart phone, the lawyer, the news cameras, the mayor's daughter, and the growing group of assembled parents. He turned and walked back to his vehicle. The other officers followed his cue.

"Looks like we're getting more traction with the locals," said Al.

"Kids, smart phones, and lawyers. Some of the more powerful forces in today's universe."

Mac walked into the conference room.

"How does it feel to be deaf?" he asked.

"Huh?"

"We have a major problem. They found our bugs and pulled 'em."

"All of them?"

"No, we still have the low-value bugs. So we can listen in on all the doings of the Georgia Youth Soccer Association, the local Elks' lodge, and the United Daughters of the Confederacy. And we can still listen in on the FAA tower."

"Which is closed, right?"

"Yep. But all the good stuff is shut down. So we are now flying around in the dark without instruments."

"So that's it?"

"I still have some clips that came in before it all went dark. Once I'm done with those, we won't be getting anything else."

"How'd that happen?" asked Al.

"I haven't got a clue but they started going off line early this morning. I am guessing somebody found one, figured out what it was, and put the word out."

"Are we compromised?" I asked. "Is there any way they can know where we are?"

Mac shrugged.

"I doubt it," he said. "The bugs are untraceable."

"Still, we have no idea when they're going to blow *Sidoni* and kill the girls and we have no way of finding out."

"We need to find another source of intel," said Mac.

"Improvise. Adapt. Overcome," said Al.

"That's Marine talk," said Mac.

"It works for them. It'll have to work for us."

We sat down around the conference table and brainstormed the problem.

At noon, the news reported a police shooting in the parking lot of a low-priced motel northwest of Serenity. Initial reports characterized it as a confrontation between local law enforcement and a gang of criminals. The story evolved during the day as more information came in and by the time the nine o'clock news played over the COP's television, they had finally got it right.

"A gunfight in the parking lot of a Georgia motel has left three men dead and two injured," said the lead news anchor. "Peter Kurten joins us from Serenity, Georgia, with more information."

The feed switched to a correspondent standing in front of Serenity's police building.

"Thank you, Brent. A task force within the Serenity Police Department has been conducting an intense investigation following the attack against the *Sidoni* church nearly two weeks ago. An anonymous tip led them to a motel ten miles outside the city limits. Three police officers and seven deputized citizens confronted the suspects this morning and a gunfight ensued. However, the eight suspects—six men and two women—were federal agents in the process of conducting their own investigation. This tragic case of mistaken identity resulted in the deaths of three men, including one policeman, all from Serenity, Georgia. Two FBI agents were also shot; one is in critical condition."

"Peter, have any of the local authorities indicated what led to this awful mistake?"

"Chief Willardson made a statement to the press about an hour ago."

The video cut to a pre-recorded segment featuring a portable podium set inside a ring of hastily erected lights outside Serenity

Police headquarters. Chief Willardson walked to the podium, blinked in the bright lights, and read a prepared statement into a cluster of microphones.

"Earlier today, an anonymous tip led our department's Special Crimes Unit to a motel outside Serenity, Georgia. Members of the unit confronted suspects in the motel parking lot who then opened fire on our officers and deputies. Our unit returned fire. Eventually, the suspects identified themselves as agents of the Federal Bureau of Investigation. Unfortunately, this identification was not made until three of our unit's members were killed. We are shocked at the loss of these wonderful men and have contacted the State Attorney General's office to request a complete investigation."

"Why would the FBI open fire on your officers, Chief?" asked one of the reporters.

"I will not be answering any questions."

The camera cut back to the news desk.

"We contacted the Federal Bureau of Investigation for comment and they released a statement twenty minutes ago," said the weekend anchor. The camera cut to a screen with the Department of Justice / FBI seal at the top. White letters scrolled up over a blue background.

> "Agents of the Federal Bureau of Investigation have been conducting an investigation regarding equipment stolen from military bases in the state of Georgia. Agents from the Bureau of Alcohol, Tobacco, Firearms and Explosives recently joined this task force. This morning, eight members of this joint investigative team were ambushed and fired upon by members of the Serenity Police Department and a number of local vigilantes. These individuals did not identify themselves until after our officers neutralized the threat. A complete investigation is ongoing."

The camera cut back to the news desk where the anchor reported about the earlier demonstrations in front of Sidoni. Al turned off the television.

"It's working," he said. "The feds are getting involved."

"And we're getting local support," said Mac.

"We still haven't rescued the girls."

The news also reported that Julius, now a full Category 5 hurricane, was less than seven hundred miles east of Jacksonville. NOAA predicted life-threatening storm surge and rainfall in portions of the Carolinas and mid-Atlantic. The news channel weather people filled the screen with five-day prediction cones. The cones from the European prediction model showed Julius marching toward the North Carolina/South Carolina border but NOAA's cones aimed it straight at the middle of Georgia. For once, I rooted for the Europeans.

56

I sat in the dark and listened to the tick-tock of the pendulum wall clock hanging in the next room. Large throw pillows sat in a stack on the floor beside me and a large oak armoire with a mirror on the door returned the faintest ghost of my reflection. The room was clean and tidy and smelled faintly of lavender.

The alarm app on her phone broke the morning silence and she turned on her side to reach over and shut it off. She clicked on the light and gasped. I put my hand over her mouth.

"Don't scream. It's me. The guy who usually wears a mask."

Reverend Sharpe's breathing eased and she calmed down. I took my hand away.

"What are you doing here?"

"Waiting to talk. Sorry if I startled you."

She pulled the sheet up around her.

"So, you're the guy they're all out there looking for?"

"Guess so."

"My brothers would beat your sorry backside if they saw you in here with me." She considered calling for help but decided against it. "Okay, you want to talk? Talk."

"Week before last, one of your brothers mentioned that his girlfriend cleaned Chief Willardson's house."

"Yeah."

"I need to talk with her. Can you arrange that?"

"What about?"

"The less you know, the safer you and your congregation will be."

She looked at me a long time as if trying to judge a book by its cover.

"You guys are making some headway."

"What do you mean?" I asked.

"Didn't you see what happened yesterday? People protested *Sidoni* and the police backed down."

"A battle won, perhaps, but the war isn't over."

"Everybody in this town is now talking about *Sidoni* and power and corruption. And good old immorality, too. People are coming to grips with how quiet they've been and how bad it's become. The collective conscience of this town's regular folk is getting a kick in the pants. And you folks made it happen."

"How so?"

"You brought the whole thing front-and-center. Videos, radio shows, news stories. You exposed the corruption—or, at least, a fair chunk of it—and people are responding. The preachers in this town talk to each other and just about every one of us is giving a sermon today on basic right versus wrong and the importance of civic activism. Of how we all need to live on the right side of sin and not be shy about it."

"You think your followers can bring about change?"

"We can't overthrow the cops or the city men by ourselves but we can support change when the time comes."

It seemed weak to me but I wasn't about to discourage her.

"Makayla," she said.

"What?"

She grabbed her phone off the bedside table.

"The girl you want to talk to. Her name is Makayla." She gave me the phone number. "I'll text her and tell her to expect a phone call from a stranger."

"It would be safer if I just showed up."

She shook her head.

"You show up at her place the way you showed up here and she would skin you alive."

"Tell her the Caller ID will show a restricted number."

"You know," she said. "You're a lot better looking without that mask."

"I sure hope so."

When I got back to the COP, I found Al sitting in front of the television with a mug of coffee and a warmed-up pork tamale for breakfast. Philistine.

"You're not gonna believe what's going on, Sim."

"Try me."

"The President sent out a few tweets this morning referring to our videos and blasting the locals for shooting at the FBI yesterday. He also complained about 'white slavery' going on at the *Sidoni* Sanctuary and blamed the 'lazy fake news media' for not reporting it. And he accused the 'deep state' of covering it all up."

"I guess he's got *that* right," I said. "But why now?"

"Think about it. We are only a couple of weeks from the mid-term elections. He's talking about *Sidoni* because the nation is talking about *Sidoni*. He's got to look like he's on top of this issue."

"Did he say he was going to do anything about it?"

"He called for the Attorney General and the Justice Department to conduct a complete investigation."

"Wow. Here I am agreeing with the guy. But nobody in DC is going to do anything about it. The deep state guys like Spencer and his ilk have too much at stake."

"You're an unrepentant cynic."

"Why would a cynic repent?" I said.

Al nodded and went back to his tamale. After a few minutes he changed the channel to one of the Sunday morning political talk shows and got up to get another mug of coffee while the commercials played. Mac walked in with his gun case and a cleaning kit.

"Seriously, guys. Are we going to sit around and watch television all day?" Mac asked. "We've been sitting on our hindquarters for days watching the news and calling radio shows and listening to bad guys plan the murder of a couple dozen young women."

"Getting antsy?" said Al.

"I'm sniper-trained. I'm like a mosquito in a nudist colony. I know what to do, I just don't know where to start."

"What have you got in mind?"

"I don't know. Go shoot up an old courthouse? Free some prisoners?"

"As you may recall," said Al, "our last direct attack on the courthouse was also on a Sunday and did not free any girls. So, what have we learned? And, more importantly, what do you think *they* have learned? Don't you suppose they've enhanced their security? And we are, as you pointed out, deaf. We have no new intel coming in."

"Quiet time is over, guys. I'm sick of sitting around."

"Let me make a phone call," I said.

57

SHEETS of plywood covered the windows at Serenity's Waffle House but it was still open with the full menu. A green dot on FEMA's Waffle House Index hurricane map. Julius had not arrived in full force but the city streets were still much less crowded than usual. Almost nobody walked around in the strong wind and heavy rain.

Makayla's information had been helpful; perfect, in fact. Chief Willardson walked out of the Waffle House precisely at eight a.m. Mac came out ten feet behind him with a bill cap on backwards and a gym bag in his left hand. He coughed and Willardson turned around. Mac smiled at him and Willardson, curiosity satisfied, turned back toward his car and pulled a set of keys out of his pants pocket.

Al stopped the van beside the Chief's car and Willardson looked up at him while Mac—still behind the Chief—pulled a device that looked like a short cattle prod out of his gym bag. He shoved the prongs of the unit into the small of Willardson's back and pulled the trigger as I slid the side door of the van open. The big cop fell to his knees and I dragged him into the van. Mac closed the side door and hopped into the passenger seat. Nobody inside the Waffle House saw it happen. Plywood makes a poor window.

"I hope he doesn't have a heart condition," said Al. "I'm not so good at getting useful intel from a corpse."

I duct taped and zip-tied the Chief's wrists and ankles like we had for Harley and Mitch and Mayor Andy. He got the black bag over his head, too. Al drove west while I searched our captive. I handed Willardson's car keys, wallet, pistol, and cell phone to Mac as Al pulled over to the side of the street near a city trash bin. Mac made the toss and Al drove off.

The Chief made a grunting sound as he recovered from the initial shock.

"What the hell..."

I slapped his face through the black bag.

"Shut up," I said.

Al picked a spot within a dense grove of magnolia trees near a river bottom. It wasn't the best place in the world for an interrogation during a hurricane—the trees creaked in the strong wind and small waves in the river rose and fell—but it was remote, if not quiet, and only ten minutes from the Waffle House. Time was not on our side and we had to do this quickly. We pulled the bag off Willardson's head.

"What the hell is going on here?" he said. "You think you can rob a Police Chief?"

"I will ask the questions," said Al. "You will answer them."

"The hell I will."

Mac pressed the cattle prod to Willardson's thigh and tapped the trigger. Willardson screamed.

"You ever use a Taser before?" asked Al. "Ever get Tased during training?"

Willardson's breathing came back to normal and he stared at Al with hate in his eyes.

"Tasers won't kill a healthy person," said Al. "They're weak sauce. But this thing is a hundred times more powerful. Riot cops in foreign countries use them for crowd-control. Ten seconds could stop your heart. So you will answer my questions."

"What do you want to know?"

"We want to know everything about Ewing McCord."

"He'll kill me if I say anything."

"He's going to kill you anyway," said Al. "And your family, too."

He pulled a small recorder from his shirt pocket and pressed a button.

"*Forget about Flake,*" said Ewing McCord. "*I need you to fly back here and get something from Willardson.*"

"*The FAA has closed the Eastern Seaboard.*"

"*Rent a car if you have to. Willardson has something of mine and I need you to get it from him. Then kill him and his family. Make him watch the family die.*"

"*With pleasure.*"

Willardson's eyes grew to the size of pie plates.

"Five seconds," said Al. "Then my friend over there gets all electric on your ass."

Mac pressed the cattle prod into the big man's thigh.

"Can you protect my family?"

"We'll do what we can," I said.

Willardson swallowed.

"Ewing McCord was born Stevnich Horvat. He was a mid-level officer in the Croatian Defense Forces during the Bosnian war. He ran the Dretelj prison camp. The prisoners were Serb civilians who hadn't done anything wrong and had never fought for either side. Horvat's soldiers tortured the men and raped the women. They killed hundreds and buried them in mass graves."

"Ethnic cleansing," said Mac.

"Whole families," said Willardson. "When the truth started to leak out, Horvat disappeared and became Ewing McCord."

"How do you know this?"

"I was a youth leader in the Croatian Party of Rights. I disappeared with him."

"And U.S. officials gave you both new identities so they could use you as a channel for illegal arms deals."

"Yes, but the proof I have will expose him," said Willardson. "If it ever got to the UN Security Council or The Hague, Stevnich Horvat would spend the rest of his life in prison."

"Where is this proof?"

"I scanned it. It's on my cloud account."

He gave us the account information. Mac logged onto it with his laptop and downloaded the files.

"How are they going to destroy *Sidoni?*" I asked.

"Multiple charges will go off at one o'clock Wednesday morning. That's when they think the hurricane will be at its strongest."

"Hurricanes don't cause explosions," said Mac.

"They've got video of the local fire chief. He'll say it was an accident. The building shifted, a gas line broke, and a spark from old wiring set the whole thing off."

"And everybody goes up in flames?" I asked.

"Three of my men work there as priests. They were told to get out at twelve-thirty. I think Clint wants to keep them around as ground troops for his next venture."

"But they won't tell Duncan about it?" asked Al.

"He knows. But he's nuts. He thinks it's some sort of 'religious purification' and that it'll make him stronger."

"And the girls will go with him?"

"Not willingly," said the chief. "But they'll go."

Mac's download ended and he opened some of the files. I looked over his shoulder.

"What's that picture, there?" I asked.

"I kept that for Clint," said Willardson. "It's locked up in my desk drawer at home."

"And?" I said.

"Clint was married. But Loretta disappeared two years ago. She was pregnant. It almost destroyed him. He looked for her, looked real hard. Hired a private investigator. They never found her."

"It happens," said Al.

"But I know what really happened," said Willardson.

He told us the story.

We drove to Willardson's house, picked up his family, and dropped them off at a hotel about two miles from the COP. Al and I returned an hour later with the minivan, a burner, and some cash.

"Drive west to Mobile, Biloxi, or Baton Rouge," Al told them. "Or south to Miami or Ft. Myers. Or pick another direction and keep driving. Throw away your phones, don't use your credit cards, and stay off social media."

Willardson's wife looked confused.

"When can we come back?" she asked.

"Don't."

The mid-day news was all about Hurricane Julius. The Air Force's Hurricane Hunter reported that Julius had moved west overnight without altering course. It was now less than three hundred miles east of us. The various models had also been updated and the prediction cones forecast landfall between Jacksonville and Savannah. Serenity lay directly in the red zone of multiple cones.

NOAA predicted Julius would weaken into Category 4 status before it hit us but that our area could expect the worst of it within thirty-six hours. Life-threatening storm surge and rainfall would affect a much wider stretch of coast. The governors of Florida and Georgia requested federal disaster assistance. I thought of the long, skinny dock *Figaro* was tied to and realized the entire marina could go flying in a serious blow. *Figaro* would be just another piece of old plastic at the bottom of the river.

Late evacuees, most of the folks who'd claimed they would wait the hurricane out, drove their cars north on I-95 and State Route 99 hoping to reach Savannah and then turn inland to Macon or Atlanta. Due to the counter-clockwise rotation of a hurricane, however, the wind and the rain north of Serenity were much more severe. Emergency crews remained busy keeping traffic moving.

58

I woke up at five a.m. on Tuesday morning in a sweat, worried about the hurricane. I flipped on the lights in the conference room, logged onto my PC, and navigated onto the NOAA website. Their morning report indicated that Julius had weakened and swung north and was now headed straight for Serenity. Good news for *Figaro*; bad news for Serenity.

Emergency declarations for southern Georgia were issued as the outer rain bands arrived. More citizens evacuated in earnest. Al even brought it up during breakfast.

"We okay here in Jacksonville?" he asked between bites.

"It's a tilt-up building," said Mac. "Walls of steel-reinforced concrete designed to withstand a direct hit. We'll be okay."

"What about our plans in Serenity?" I asked.

"There's nothing like driving *into* a hurricane to sharpen the senses," said Al.

We finished breakfast and worked on the plan's details.

The network news reported at noon that the Georgia State Patrol had closed both I-95 and Route 99 to southbound traffic fifteen miles north of Serenity. Troops from the Georgia National Guard arrived to back up the staties. But there wasn't much traffic to turn away. Everybody was heading north.

Except for seven vans and a few black SUVs.

Three of the vans were "live eye" news vans from Savannah-based affiliates of major television networks. The rest of the vehicles were from the FBI. All were told by a sergeant with a jaw of chiseled granite that the roads were closed to southbound traffic as the bridge wasn't safe in the high winds. No exceptions.

The news vans got footage of the highway closure, the blowing rain, the trees bending in the wind, and Sergeant Chisel-Jaw's dire warning. The convoy turned west and drove inland to wait out the hurricane. Most of the news teams decided to hole up at a hotel that was still open.

The FBI vehicles, however, turned south at the next state highway. One of the news teams, sensing a story in the making, followed them. They found more state troopers at a bridge crossing the Altamaha River. An eighteen-wheeler lay on its side blocking all traffic. This did not deter the feds. They continued inland and made their way east and south in a large winding semi-circle. The news van followed. Eventually, they found an unguarded dirt road leading toward Serenity.

The FBI personnel separated into two teams and simultaneously descended on Serenity's city hall and police station. They took immediate control of both buildings. The Serenity power structure and its corruption were about to end.

By four in the afternoon, forty-knot winds drove stinging rain into Serenity. Limbs came off trees and rivers swelled with the runoff. Julius had stalled off the Georgia coastline and weakened into a Category 3 hurricane. NOAA warned of dire outcomes when it came ashore.

While others fretted over the hurricane, we loaded the equipment we needed into the Chevy and drove north.

59

REVEREND Sharpe didn't have to think twice when I asked her if I could borrow the church's bus that night.

"Absolutely not," she said. "But I'll drive it wherever you want. And you will fill the tank when we're done."

"This could be dangerous."

She waved her hand in dismissal.

"Just living in this town is getting to be dangerous."

I got in with her and she drove toward *Sidoni*. The wind had increased markedly and old trees bent over from the pressure. I guessed the gusts to be at least fifty knots. It was nearly eleven at night and the folks who hadn't already traveled inland to avoid the storm cowered in their homes. We drove down wet, empty roads.

We passed *Sidoni*, continued another block, and parked in front of an auto repair shop. A green Subaru sat parked across the street. Grace Kinney got out and ran to the door of the bus.

"Why are you so sure the girls are just going to walk out of there?" She had to yell over the sound of the wind and trees.

"They'll be getting some encouragement," I said.

Mac pulled up in the Chevy van. Al sat in the passenger side. I turned to Grace and the Reverend.

"Stay here in the bus," I yelled. "My friends and I will be back in an hour or so and, with any luck, we'll have the girls with us."

I hopped in the van and Mac drove off.

Our approach to entering the building was less subtle this time. Al and I grabbed our weapons and Mac drove onto the lawn. Al shot the two security cameras covering the entrance and I attached one end of a heavy chain to the metal grates built into the big front door. The other end was already shackled to the van's trailer hitch. Al stood at an angle to the door and blasted the door's locks and hinges with his shotgun while Mac hit the gas pedal. The chain stretched taut and we were rewarded with the sound of cracking wood. The entire procedure took less than thirty seconds. Mac traded his shotgun for a Blackout and we ran in.

"I'm heading upstairs to the dorms," said Al over the radio. "You check the Great Room and offices."

"Got it."

"And don't be shy, Bravo. Shoot anything in a maroon robe."

"Roger that," I said.

Al ran upstairs and I headed down the main hallway. The Great Room and the offices were empty. I saw no priests, no "worshippers," and no HKs.

"Nothing down here, Alpha."

"Upstairs is vacant, too," said Al. "No sign of any girls."

We met at the main staircase and opened the door to the basement. The sound of chanting came from below. We walked down as quietly as possible. The stairs opened into a large dark subterranean room with a high ceiling. Massive posts and stout beams held the old courthouse aloft. The flicker of firelight danced on the walls.

Duncan McCord stood in the middle of the room before a group of seated figures. He wore his dark green robe and a necklace of large green stones set in gold. The seated figures wore white gowns. A fire burned in a large open bowl set under a crude chimney. The High Master spoke to them in a loud voice.

"Holy Priestesses of Astarte, the Queen comes tonight to reclaim her servants and make them whole with purifying fire."

I looked at the girls. Twenty-three of them sat on mats laid over the concrete floor. Tied at the wrists to a long white rope that snaked between them, they sat silently. Al and I entered the room.

"How dare you defile the sanctuary of the Rahm Sahn Sidoni?" said Duncan.

"Can that fake religious garbage, you asshat," said Al.

Duncan reached under his robe and pulled out the curved knife he'd held to my neck a week earlier. He pulled the girl closest to him to her feet, spun her around, and pressed the knife against her throat.

"Another step and I'll kill her," he said.

I stepped to my right and walked toward the fire in the bowl.

"This is a bad move, Duncan. Queen Astarte loves her priestesses. She doesn't want them injured."

Duncan turned to his left as I walked keeping the girl between him and me.

"You know *nothing* about Queen Astarte!"

"I know she's loving and peaceful," I said. "I read all about her in that pamphlet you keep upstairs."

I reached the fire barrel and turned to face him a dozen feet away.

"Put the knife down, Duncan. We don't want to hurt you."

Al's Blackout barked and Duncan's head exploded in a thick mist of blood and bone. The young women screamed.

"Problem solved," said Al.

He walked over to where Duncan lay and bent down to examine a wooden crate.

"Willardson said one a.m., right?" he asked.

"Roger."

"He lied, Bravo. There's a timer here that says we've got twenty-six minutes. And there's enough Semtex in this box to dig a decent-sized crater. Time to scoot."

"Come on, ladies," I said. "Let's all stand up and get out of here."

None of them moved. They sat there, faces blank. I raised my voice.

"You need to all stand up immediately and get out of this building or you will all die."

I looked over at Al and he started unscrewing the suppressor off his weapon. I grabbed the girl closest to the stairway, still tethered to the white rope, and pulled her to her feet. Al fired his Blackout into the ceiling of the basement. The sound echoed off the concrete and stone walls and bits of plaster fell from the ceiling. The girls jumped in surprise. Some rose to their feet. Al replaced his spent magazine and fired again. The noise was brutal.

Still tied to the rope, we got them running toward the stairs. One of them tripped and fell. Al picked her up with one arm and up the stairs we went.

I let my weapon hang from its sling as I opened the door into the main hallway. A maroon-robed figure turned toward me with an MP5 but I was too close for him to use it. I grabbed the barrel with my left hand, pushed it toward the hallway, and threw a solid right uppercut to the priest's jaw. His knees buckled.

Two more maroon-robed figures ran down the hall toward us. An MP5 barked at me, its bullets hitting the priest I'd just knocked out. I swung the dead priest's gun down the hall and pressed its trigger, cutting down both attackers. I waited to see if either of them moved. They didn't and I heard no more footsteps in the hallway.

"Anybody hurt back there, Alpha?"

"We're good. Still on the stairs," said Al. "No friendlies down."

I grabbed the first girl on the rope again and dragged her down the hallway.

"Delta," said Al over the radio. "Get to a spot where you can cover the back door. We've got the girls with us and may need suppressive fire."

"Roger," said Mac.

We continued down a smaller hallway to the door overlooking the river. I threw it open and pulled the first girl behind me as I exited. We ran toward the van. Some of the girls cried from the pain in their wrists but they kept moving. Halfway across the lawn, I heard Mac's Blackout fire a burst and looked back to see another maroon-robed figure slump against the church's wall near the back door.

Tree branches and other detritus littered the lawn and slowed the girls' progress. Rain fell in sheets and soaked the girls to the skin. The van stood parked on the sidewalk. Mac stood nearby with a beach towel draped across his arms, concealing his Blackout.

We passed the van and continued along the sidewalk toward the church bus. Grace and Reverend Sharpe, each holding a stack of blankets, stepped out of the bus door. I pulled my knife and cut the zip ties that bound the girls' wrists to the nylon rope. Grace found her daughter and broke into tears. Reverend Sharpe wrapped a blanket around each girl as she entered the bus. I'd examined the faces of the girls as I freed them from the rope hoping I would see Dorothea. She wasn't there.

The girls were all in the bus, now, each sitting on a bench seat, wrapped in a blanket, and shivering from the cold and the rain. I started with the nearest one.

"Where is Dorothea?" I asked.

She shook her head and I moved on to the next girl. None of them knew her.

"Shaysan Ri," I yelled. "They called her 'Shaysan Ri.'"

Some of the girls looked up when I mentioned the name. I approached the closest one.

"What happened to her?" I asked.

A violent explosion lit the night and shook the bus. I looked down the street to see a ball of flame engulf the old courthouse and a minor mushroom cloud climb a thousand feet into the dark sky.

"Where is Shaysan Ri?" I asked again.

The girl I was yelling at cowered in fright. I grabbed her upper arms and shook her.

"She left yesterday with Master Clint," she said.

"She's alive?"

"Master took her as a sacrifice to Astarte."

"Where?" I asked. "Where did he take her?"

She shook her head. Sirens from multiple emergency vehicles

screamed in the distance.

"You'd better get this bus out of here, Reverend."

"I'll take them to the chapel and we'll start calling their parents," she said.

"No. Get them out of town." I handed her a slip of paper with my burner phone's number on it. "If any of them have any information about Dorothea or Shaysan Ri or where Clint might have taken her, please call me immediately."

She nodded. I stepped off the bus and got in the van with Al and Mac.

60

BY two in the morning, Hurricane Julius had weakened into Category 2 and swerved north to take its ninety mile-per-hour winds toward Charleston. Serenity was spared the full force of Julius's wrath. Still, NOAA predicted catastrophic freshwater flooding over portions of Georgia and South Carolina.

The local news station was wrong in their initial morning reports regarding the *Sidoni* fire but I couldn't tell if that was because they were paid off or because initial reports are almost always wrong. The local fire chief stated that their preliminary investigation pointed to a burst gas line caused by either hurricane damage or the shifting of the building on its foundations. He said leaking gas could have been ignited by a spark from an old light switch.

Quelle surprise.

All thirty-one occupants of the building were presumed dead including the church's leader, Duncan McCord; his brother Clint; five priests; and twenty-four priestesses. Recovery of the victims was expected to take several days given the unstable nature of the rubble left at the courthouse site.

"It'll be interesting to see them back-pedaling when they come up short by two dozen bodies," said Al.

"That won't be for days," said Mac. "Clint will be gone by then and it'll be old news."

"The girls will have miraculously escaped," I said. "Clint may even get credit as the hero who saved them."

My phone rang and I recognized the number.

"How'd it go, Grace?" I asked. "How are the girls doing?"

"Pretty well. Reverend Sharpe drove all morning while I examined the girls." Her piercing voice cut right through the phone's speaker and I held the phone away from my ear. "They're doing okay, I think. But they've been through a lot and will need some serious counseling."

"Where are you?"

"We're in Florida, now. Tabitha has a friend who is a pastor in Tallahassee and he's arranged to have a dozen families put us up. We're getting the girls new clothes today and calling their parents."

Mac and Al smiled.

"The police may want to talk to them later. It would be great if we weren't mentioned."

"I can arrange that," said Grace. "But the police weren't all that interested when the girls were held as prisoners. I don't think they'll work too hard to talk to them now."

"Their parents will press for it."

"Good point. There's one more thing, though."

"What's that?" I asked.

"We think we may know where Clint took the girl you are looking for."

"To sacrifice her?"

"No," said Grace. "To keep her."

"Go on."

"One of the girls told me while we were on the road that Dorothea was Clint's favorite. Several of the others confirmed this. It seems they were jealous of his attentions. Clint told Duncan she was going to be sacrificed and the girls overheard that. After the courthouse blew up, though, they realized that Clint took her with him to save her."

"So where is she?" I asked.

"None of them know but one of Reverend Sharpe's parishioners saw Clint, an older man, and one of the girls leave the boat dock behind the church at sunset. And the rumor is the McCords have a house on an island near the river mouth."

"Which island?"

"I have no idea," said Grace.

Al and Mac grabbed some charts and spread them out on the table.

"Thanks. You should probably forget you told me any of this."

"You're one of those guys who requires a lot of forgetting, aren't you?"

She hung up.

"How about some satellite shots of the river mouth," said Al.

Mac went over to his keyboard and opened up the Google Earth app. He zoomed into the river mouth downstream of Serenity.

"Sometimes, I find it hard to believe this stuff is free and that just anybody can access it," he said.

Al took the Intracoastal Waterway chart over to Mac's workstation.

"This is weird," said Al. "The chart shows four islands near the river mouth but the satellite photo shows only three. The one immediately south of St. Paul Island is missing."

Mac moved his mouse around a little and zoomed in.

"Somebody cleaned it off."

"What do you mean 'cleaned it off?'" said Al.

"They obscure geography the government doesn't want seen," said Mac. "Submarine bases, missile silos, Area 51. You get the idea." He pointed at a spot on the screen. "When you zoom in right here, you can see the area is blurred and colored like the ocean. There is something there, we just don't get to see it."

Al turned back to the chart. He pointed to a small shape located at the edge of the Intracoastal Waterway south of the big river that flowed through Serenity. A half-mile of seawater separated it from St. Paul Island to the north.

"So they're on Longman Island?" I said.

"Only one way to know for sure," said Al.

61

WE packed the van with what we needed and were on the road by noon. Mac drove to a couple of places we thought might have good views of Longman Island. From what we could see, the island had rocks, sand, and lots of trees bending toward the west. About an hour before dark, Mac drove us through Serenity and turned east onto the bridge leading to St. Paul Island.

The town there had a half-dozen restaurants, a few small art galleries, some places that sold fudge and pralines, and a golf course. It screamed "tourist trap." But at a time when the late tourism season should be ramping up, the town was vacant and traffic nil. Fear of the hurricane had driven everybody inland.

A state park with an attached marina dominated the southern coast of the island. Its parking lot was almost empty and Mac parked the van as close to the shore as possible. Still, we had to walk through fifty yards of tall grass before we got to the beach. Longman Island lay nearly a half-mile to the south. We pulled out our field glasses.

"There's a dock with a speedboat," said Al. "Security fence beyond the dock. Large stand of trees beyond that. I think I see a roof beyond the trees."

"I've seen that speedboat before," I said.

I studied the fence and the live oak trees beyond it. Like all the others, they grew at an angle bending away from the prevailing wind direction. Their limbs dripped with Spanish moss.

Mac quietly took pictures with a telephoto-lensed digital camera and made notes in a small black journal while Al studied the maps we'd brought.

"I could swim that but a boat would sure be nice," said Al.

"I'm on it," I said.

Al and Mac continued their planning while I ran to the marina. The place was nearly empty with only a few boat owners checking their vessels for hurricane damage. Somebody had propped a garbage can against the gate to keep it open and that was fine with me.

I walked up and down the docks until I found what I wanted, a tired diesel sportfishing boat. Not the pristine kind you see in the boat magazines with gleaming wood and a fancy fighting chair aimed astern. This one had been used a lot, maintained as needed, and cleaned every decade or so. The kind where the wife never comes aboard and the owner leaves the ignition keys inside the cabin.

The cabin door was old wood and the lock and hinges holding it closed let go with one good kick. I stepped below and found the keys in the top drawer next to the galley. I turned the battery switch to "both", checked the fuel level, started the twin diesels, and pulled out my phone.

"I'm on E-dock. Two-thirds the way down."

"You've got something?" asked Al.

"An old Bertram but it runs."

The sun was going down but they had no trouble finding me.

"What a tub," said Al. "But I guess the price was right."

I grabbed two duffels from Al while he climbed aboard and took the helm. Mac untied the mooring lines and threw them to me before walking back up the dock toward the van. Al goosed the twin throttles and piloted the boat out of the marina and into the channel.

"Take the wheel. I need to get ready."

I took the helm while Al unzipped a duffel and changed into a dark long-sleeved shirt and black pants.

"Go past the island on the west side," he said. "Once we're a quarter-mile off, kill the lights and move in. The moon doesn't rise for two hours so we've got some darkness on our side."

Al pulled a mask, snorkel, and fins out of the duffel and put them on. Then he took one of the Blackouts from the other bag and slung it around his shoulder. The last thing he grabbed was his combat knife—his "trusty rusty"—and he fixed it to his belt.

I clicked off the nav lights, slowed down to a few knots, and turned toward the southwestern shore of Longman Island. Al waited until we got closer to shore and then rolled off the port side of the boat. I continued around to the north side of the island moving toward the dock behind the speedboat. A half-dozen security lights came on as I approached the dock. I tied up the old Bertram in their orange glow.

A wire mesh fence stretched between wooden posts separated the dock from the rest of the island. A card-key gate in the fence was the only way in. Beyond the fence, the island lay dark and covered in trees. A security camera and a metal speaker hung on the fence next to the gate.

"You are on private property," said a metallic voice through the speaker. "You are not allowed to access this dock."

I walked up to the security camera, gave it the finger, and fished a small American flag into the top of the wire fence. The fabric waved lightly in the breeze.

"I hereby claim this island for the United States of America," I said. "The rest of you assholes aren't welcome."

"You must leave immediately," said the voice.

"Why don't you come down here and make me?"

I covered the security camera's lens with peanut butter, walked over to Clint's speedboat, and stepped into the cockpit.

Minutes later, I heard steps approaching the security fence. Two men opened the gate. One was a blond fellow, shorter than me and a little more heavily muscled. The other was Clint McCord. Both carried M4 carbines and wore military-grade Kevlar vests with extra magazines. They stepped out onto the dock and pointed their rifles at me. From ten yards away, I was an easy shot.

I took a woman's gold locket and chain out of my pants pocket and held it over the side of the boat.

"Recognize this?" I asked. "It's Loretta's locket. It says 'Forever yours, Clint' right here on the front. Shoot me and the locket goes overboard. And I won't be able to tell you what happened to your dear wife. Or your unborn son."

Clint took his finger off the trigger.

"Don't shoot him, Simon."

"Is that him? The guy who brought it all down?"

"I think so."

"I don't deserve *all* the credit," I said. "I had some help. Right now, I just want to talk about getting Dorothea Millet back to her family."

"You think you're going to walk away with Dorothea?"

"I took this locket from the guy who knows where Loretta and your son are. Seems like an even trade, the locket and some info about your family for Dorothea and free passage out of Serenity. As a bonus, I'll tell my team to leave you guys alone."

"We can talk about that," said Clint. "But I want a piece of you, first. Get out of my boat."

"You're going to fight me while your friend holds a rifle at my back? Hardly seems fair. All I have is a locket and a story to tell."

Clint put his rifle against the fence and motioned for Simon to do the same. I put the locket back in my pocket, got out of the boat, and met Clint halfway. Simon pulled a pistol, pointed it at me, and smiled.

"You seem awful calm for a fellow who is about to be gutted," he said.

A piece of fencepost a foot away from Simon cracked, broke off, and fell to the ground. Three seconds later, the back of his head exploded. His body bent at the knees and waist like a marionette with its strings cut. Clint froze for a moment. I grabbed his right wrist and spun him around. I threw two punches at his kidneys but they glanced off the back of his vest and didn't connect well so I put a hard left into the side of his neck. He spun to his right and tried to grab me but his vest was a mixed blessing; it slowed him down and I ducked back out of range.

Remembering Al's earlier assessment of Clint's MMA skills, I figured my jab would have to be my main weapon. If I could land enough of them, the damage would accumulate. He put his fists up and circled to my right. I tested the waters by throwing a few jabs; he responded with a kick to my right side. It didn't connect but it kept me from closing the distance between us. He crouched as if he were about to take me down but I backed up and stayed low. If he got me on the ground, my height and reach advantage would disappear and I'd be done.

Clint threw another roundhouse kick to my right side and the pain of my cracked ribs returned. He tried for another takedown but I kicked my legs back, dropped my hips, and sprawled on him. I threw a strong right that connected on his ear as I got away. He was slower getting up; the Kevlar vest becoming a major hindrance.

I moved in and landed two nice jabs before he could step away. He paused a moment, moved back into range, feinted to my left, then moved in and threw another round-house kick to my right side. I stepped into it, caught his leg at the knee with my right arm, and threw two quick jabs to his face. He tried to grab me behind the neck and I landed a left hook on his right eye. I felt his orbital bone break beneath my fist.

He stayed on his feet and backed away. I followed. My ribs ached and I knew another kick could re-break them. I had to set up another attack and finish him quickly. I moved in to his right side and faked another jab. He dodged his head to the left to slip the punch but didn't expect my right cross. It connected hard on the nose and sent him down on both knees. He reached into his vest and pulled out a small pistol. I wrenched it from his hand, kneed him in the face, and shot him in the left knee. He screamed and rolled over onto the ground.

I frisked him to see if he had any other surprises and found some zip-tie restraints in his vest. I trussed him up with his hands behind his back.

"That wasn't her locket, was it?" said Clint. "You were lying."

I fished it out of my pocket and showed it to him. The inscription reflected in the gold-colored security light. Recognition showed in his eyes. I pulled a small voice recorder out of my other pocket and pressed the play button.

> "*Loretta had to be killed,*" said Chief Willardson. "*She'd contacted the FBI and was going to turn us in.*"

"You recognize the voice, don't you?" I said. "That's your own pet police chief telling us why your wife and son had to die. Care to guess who ordered it?"

His eyes were red with hate. I pressed the play button again.

> "*Ewing said she had to go. Trevor and I grabbed her one night as she was leaving the mall. We took her out on the boat. Trevor slit her throat and tossed her to the 'gators. I didn't want to do it but Ewing gave the order. I kept her locket, though. For insurance.*"

"It was your dear old sweet daddy, Clint. He told Hickey and Willardson to kill your wife and unborn child. He ordered it."

He swore at me and I kicked him behind the ear. I pulled a small radio out of my shirt pocket.

"Nice work, Delta. I'm going to find Dorothea."

"Sorry about that first shot, Bravo. I misread the windage on that flag. But it still wasn't bad at over nine hundred yards in strong wind. You hear anything from Alpha?"

"Nothing, yet."

"I can't cover you beyond the fence, Bravo. It's too dark behind the lights. You're on your own."

"Then just watch my friend on the ground for me," I said. "Take care of the problem if you need to."

I searched Clint again and found his plastic card-key for the gate. I grabbed one of the M4s, removed the magazine, and stuck it into my pocket. I threw the empty rifle and both pistols into the sea. I picked up the other M4, opened the gate with the card-key and walked out of the light into the trees and the darkness.

A gravel trail from the dock led up a slight incline past some live oaks. The halo-like glare of security lights near another building glowed above the trees. Not knowing what lay ahead, I walked as quietly as possible keeping the rifle butt on my shoulder and the barrel just below my sight line. I treated every bend in the trail as if it hid an ambush.

I stepped around an ancient live oak tree to find an old man with a girl next to him standing in the pathway ten yards in front of me. Golden light from the security lamps reflected off a pistol he held to her head. I kept my rifle trained on him.

"Another step closer and she dies."

"Fine," I said. "I'll just stand right here, then."

"You will drop that rifle."

"I don't think so."

"I have two more armed men who will be here shortly," he said. "They will shoot you on sight if they see that rifle raised against me."

Something moved in the shadows behind him and a knife appeared at his throat. The old man stiffened as the steel pressed against his neck.

"Nobody is coming to help you," said Al. "All your troops are gone, Horvat."

Al reached up and took the pistol away from Ewing McCord. He checked the weapon and sheathed his knife. Dorothea stood quietly. We walked them both along the path toward the dock.

"Where have you been?" I asked.

"I had some trouble in the waves and lost my weapon and radio.

So it took me a bit longer to take out his other two men." He patted the sheathed knife. "Nice and quiet, though."

We approached the fence.

"By the time I finished, Ewing was already on his way down here with Dorothea."

"Anything else?"

"No sign of Hickey."

We returned to the dock and Dorothea spotted Clint. She ran to him and knelt down. I walked over to pick her up and she rose to slap my face. Al grabbed her and pushed her toward the old fishing boat.

"I told your son how you had his wife killed, Ewing."

"You said she left me," said Clint. "She was six months pregnant. Our first child."

The old man shrugged.

"It had to be done."

"You had your only grandson killed."

"She put the entire operation at risk," said Ewing. He turned his head to me as if I were a dispassionate onlooker.

"I have money up at the house," he said. "Six million dollars in cash. In a safe. And only I know the combination."

Al smiled at the thought.

"It could be yours," said Ewing. "Take it and the girl and leave us alone."

"I've got the last of the Horvats or McCords or whatever you call yourselves sitting here in the dirt. I could wipe out the entire line with two bullets and do the world a favor. But I won't. And I won't take your money, either. I'm going to tell the feds about you—the ones that still give a damn—and give them copies of Willardson's confession, the other recordings, and all of the evidence we've collected against you. They can prosecute you for what you are. You can both rot in a federal prison."

"I'm bleeding," said Clint. "I need a doctor. Take us back to town."

"Your wounds aren't that bad and the feds will be here by sunrise. Your dear old daddy can tie a rag around that knee and if he gets you to a doctor anytime this week you'll heal up well enough to limp around the prison yard. Maybe the state will pay somebody to fix your face."

Ewing's eyes nearly glowed with hate.

"I will track you down," he said. "I will have you gutted like an animal."

"I get it. Prison doesn't sound so good and you're begging me to shoot you. It's tempting but that's not how I roll. But I will keep this gun on you until my friend, this young lady, and I are out of here. And if either of you move, I'll shoot you in both knees and grin about it all the way home."

He said a few unpleasant things as we stepped over to the old Bertram. I kept the rifle pointed at them as Al started the engines and cast off the dock lines. I kept an eye on the two McCords as we pulled away from Longman Island.

Once we were out of range, Ewing cut Clint free of his zip-tie bonds. I watched as he helped his son into the speedboat. Ewing stepped to the helm and a giant fireball engulfed the boat and shredded the dock. From two hundred yards away, the sound was jarring.

"Don't you just love the sound of Emulex?"

"Nice," said Al. "Very nice."

"Payback's a bitch, McCord."

Moments later, a larger fireball, well beyond the line of trees, shot flames hundreds of feet into the air. We felt the concussion from a mile away.

"More Emulex," said Al. "Placed under a large propane tank anchored near what used to be a beautiful island home."

"Nice touch."

"Wish I'd known about that safe, though."

62

WE didn't think it would be smart to go back to the marina from which we'd stolen the boat so Al called Mac and told him we were headed upriver. Despite the moon, it was still dark and I was worried about hitting an unseen log or other flotsam created by the hurricane. I slowed down to four knots. Dorothea lay on the floor of the boat curled up in the fetal position. We motored past the crocodile refuge and I thought about Loretta and all the other people Trevor Hickey had murdered and dumped there.

"You killed Master Clint," said Dorothea.

"We saved you," I said.

"We'll get you back to your parents in a few weeks," said Al. "It'll all be good."

We found a small marina four miles upriver and motored along until we found a vacant slip. I grabbed a mooring line as Al turned to back the boat in.

"Look out," Al yelled.

Dorothea had found a knife somewhere on the boat and she plunged it into my thigh. Al rushed over from the wheel and punched her on the jaw. She collapsed to the deck.

"Don't pull it out," said Al. "And lie down right now. I don't want this getting worse."

I lay down on my side with the knife sticking up. I could see blood trickling out from under the blade's hand guard. Waves of intense pain rolled over me and shock set in as I watched Al wrap Dorothea's wrists, then ankles, together with duct tape.

"Dammit," said Al. "We should have seen that coming. Stay down while I get this boat tied up."

The boat jostled as Al moved around and made the mooring lines fast. Then I heard Mac's voice and he was on the boat with his medical kit. He cut away my jeans and examined the wound. He grabbed my wrist with one hand and put two fingers of his other hand against my neck next to my windpipe. He glanced at his watch.

"Pretty rapid heartbeat," he said. "You must be excited to see me."

"A little cold," I said.

"You've lost some blood. I've treated nine-year-old kids with worse injuries."

He dug in his kit, opened a small brown bottle, and fished out a long narrow strip of gauze. He grabbed the knife and pulled it out. The pain was excruciating and I said something about Mac's parentage.

"Did you just cut off my leg?"

"No, it only feels like it."

"I thought you were supposed to leave the knife in," said Al. "Something about not wanting to make the injury worse."

"It's an oyster knife," said Mac. "Dull and painful but a short blade with a wide hand guard. It wasn't close to any arteries. You're lucky she didn't grab a filleting knife."

"Have you got anything to kill the pain?"

"You're young and you're tough and I can't carry you. Plus, I love it when a patient is well enough to insult me. It means they're alive. So you get to stay awake."

Dorothea started to stir and Mac gave her a smaller dose of B-52. She went limp. Al picked her up like a sack of flour and carried her to the van. Mac packed my wound with gauze and wrapped it in a dressing.

"It'll leave a scar but you'll live."

Al returned for the duffels.

"Sun'll be up in an hour," he said. "We need to roll."

They stood me up and helped me off the boat. I couldn't put a lot of weight on the leg so they walked me up the dock like an injured linebacker going off the field. They laid me in the back of the van next to Dorothea, threw a blanket over us, and tossed in the duffels.

"Let's get these two back to the COP," said Mac. "I've had way too much fun for one day."

"Day hasn't even started," said Al. "Can we get some breakfast? I'm starving."

—————

We lay low in the COP working out our exit strategy. Al and Mac did their best to track down Trevor Hickey, but the internet—Surface, Dark, Deep, or whatever—has its limitations. They did track *Sidoni's* jet to Newfoundland and, then, to Milan.

My phone rang a few days later.

"Sim?"

I didn't recognize the voice right away.

"So, you found those runaway lovebirds, eh?"

"I don't know what you're talking about, Frank."

"You say that a lot. Like you really mean it."

"It's just another lovely day here in the sunny Caribbean."

"Except you're not in the Caribbean. And I'm not calling on behalf of Homeland Security."

"I'm guessing our mutual friend, Spencer, is listening in on this conversation. How's his shoulder?"

There was a pause followed by a barely audible click on the line.

"I'm fine," said Spencer. "I suppose I have you to thank for that."

Frank excused himself off the call and let Spencer take over.

"Should I be hanging up right now and calling an attorney?" I asked.

"Is there anybody still alive around there to press charges?"

I said nothing.

"Is there some reason you feel you can't trust me?" he said.

"Funny you should say that. You know, it seems like it's only been a couple of weeks since you and your boss nearly got me killed. How time flies."

"Now, don't be that way. All I want from you is information. Facts, documents, names, places. That sort of thing."

"I'll need to talk to my attorney," I said.

"Have him call me."

He gave me a number and hung up. I called David. I told him what I'd been up to—attorney-client privilege being what it is—and he chewed me out for a solid five minutes. I gave him Spencer's number. Then he put on his lawyer hat, told me to keep my mouth shut, and hung up the phone.

He called back an hour later and I put the phone on speaker so Mac and Al could hear.

"They want every computer file, video recording, and audio file you've got. They want signed non-disclosure agreements with all eight of you."

Al roared in laughter.

"There's only three of us," I said. "What do we get in return?"

"Full and complete immunity from prosecution for any state and/or federal charges that could be brought against you and your little band of brothers. And that is one massive festering pile of immunity, my friend. You should jump on it with both feet."

We wrangled back and forth a bit on the details. He was almost able to convince me of Spencer's sincerity in wanting to do the right thing. I gave in and agreed to put it all together for them. All except the identities of the people who helped us.

I let another day roll by before I called Orson Flake. He didn't waste a lot of time on pleasantries.

"I understand that church blew up," he said. "That's not what I paid you to do."

"That's okay, Mr. Flake. We didn't do it. So, there's no extra charge. How's your family, by the way?"

"We're fine. We were halfway to Canada when our cabin caught fire."

"The men from *Sidoni* did that. The men I warned you about."

"The authorities said it was a gas leak. The insurance company agrees so I have no reason to think differently."

"Do you think your exploding propane tank was some sort of coincidence?"

"I don't know what to think," he said. "But I am not pleased with how this turned out. I wanted the parties responsible for my niece's death to be arrested and brought to justice."

"The FBI arrested Mitch Danforth. He was one of the men who planted the bomb in my truck."

"One of the men?"

"The others got away," I lied. "Sorry about that."

"They got away?" His voice rose in pitch. "How does that even happen?"

"Chaos is the law of nature, Mr. Flake. Order is the dream of man."

"What the h…"

"Henry Adams said that. And it comports with my empirical observations."

"This is very poor performance, Greene. And I am not pleased. Not pleased at all."

"Then I quit."

63

THE bright lights of Jacksonville reflected off a thin overcast cloud layer to the west as *Figaro* rounded the Mayport Naval Station and sailed out the mouth of the St. Johns River. I had watched the weather and waited until a weak low started marching across the country toward the east coast. The wind was out of the west blowing eight to ten knots. Light, but, at least it came from the right direction. The ocean was nearly flat. Marie stepped up into the cockpit bearing coffee as we passed the outer channel marker into the Atlantic.

"How's our little stowaway?"

"Sleeping," said Marie. "She's still having a hard time processing all this."

"It's been only three weeks."

"She's been through a lot. She'll need a lot of time and more counseling."

It hadn't been easy for Dorothea. Since being rescued from Clint McCord and the evil that had masqueraded as a church, Al and Mac had kept her under watch at the COP. Anybody not knowing her history would have thought we'd kidnapped her. Technically, we had.

I'd called Marie after the old courthouse had gone up in flames and asked if she could come down. She was justifiably upset at the months of unexplained "radio silence" I'd imposed on our relationship but she warmed rapidly when I explained the situation and told her our efforts had resulted in the rescue of Constable

Millet's daughter. It helped that she'd already seen news reports—none of which, thankfully, mentioned either Al or me—of the twenty-three other girls who had been rescued that night. She agreed to come down and help.

Dr. Jen came, too. She met with Dorothea and helped her begin the long process of recovery, unwinding the brainwashing she'd endured during the months at *Sidoni*. It took three solid weeks before she was well enough to travel. I spent that time getting *Figaro* ready for the trip. And waiting for the right weather pattern.

Constable Millet wanted to fly up immediately, collect Dorothea, and bring her home. What father wouldn't? But he soon realized that doing so would open up several cans of nasty worms. First, Dorothea had witnessed the goings-on at *Sidoni* and several governments could get interested if they discovered the scope of her involvement. Second, there was this nagging issue regarding a passport for the fictional Stewart Glasgow and the international boundaries violated with it. How would the constable explain his involvement without attracting unwanted scrutiny? Ultimately, Millet agreed to my plan for getting his daughter back home.

Al, of course, had no problems traveling on his own passport. Mac and he would spend a few days cleaning up the COP, wiping computer drives, and disposing of any incriminating items and illegal equipment. Then they'd shuffle off back to their prior lives unimpeded by nasty details.

We'd spent most of Flake's money. But once we added in the cash we'd taken from Harley and the van drivers, we realized we had over three hundred thousand dollars. It was easy to split three ways. Mac shoved his in the lining of his gun case. Al and I wrapped ours in plastic bags and duct tape and hid them under the chain in *Figaro's* anchor locker. That tactic had worked before.

Figaro did not need much to be ready for the trip. She'd been moored in the semi-fresh water of the St. Johns River so her bottom didn't need a lot of scrubbing. I checked her standing and running rigging, verified the seaworthiness of her various systems, filled her water and fuel tanks (including four Jerry cans of diesel), and provisioned her larder.

Given the prevailing winds for November, I figured the trip would take two weeks. Being on the safe side, I planned for a month. Marie's Costco membership allowed me to stock up at prices that were half what I'd pay in the BVI so I crammed every cubbyhole, locker, and compartment with cases of non-perishable goods. The local chandlery in Jacksonville had the same price advantage over Caribbean suppliers so I stocked up on oil, filters, and various boat spares. On a whim, I bought a nice trolling rod and reel to replace my handline. By the time I was done, *Figaro's* waterline rode an inch or two lower than usual.

I knew the route we'd be taking. The Great Circle route back to the BVI is only eleven hundred miles but that course would force us to beat directly into the prevailing east-southeast trade winds. Boat and crew would be pounded mercilessly. To avoid that, we'd take advantage of the temporary west wind at Jacksonville's latitude and sail seven hundred miles due east. Then we'd motor in relatively calm winds another couple hundred miles to the southeast. From that point, the trade winds would be friend instead of foe and we'd have a steady beam reach five hundred miles south all the way to Jost Van Dyke. That was the plan.

Hurricane season was officially over. Julius had been nature's last gasp of nastiness for the year. Three weeks later, NOAA forecast two days of light west and northwest winds followed by a moderate cold front from the north. That was my cue to get *Figaro* moving out of the St. Johns River and into the Atlantic.

Marie's coffee was delicious.

"Dorothea *does* say you saved her life."

"Al and his friend did most of the real work," I said.

"You're allowed to take some credit once in a while."

"Okay." I drank some more coffee. "Hey, this is really good. Much better than when I make it."

"If you're going to change the subject, then I'll just get some sleep. What time do you need me?"

"All the time."

"I mean what time do you need me on watch?" she said.

"This mug will hold me a while. You want to come up at three or so?"

"Okay, Mr. Humble." She kissed me and went below. "See you at three."

We sailed straight east for a day and a half crossing the Gulf Stream and covering nearly a third of the distance to our intended turning point. Long ocean swells rose and fell like undulating sheets of thin blue steel. A strong north wind blew in and we sailed along at hull speed on a beam reach. Several hours later, the wind began to veer behind us. I could see what was coming so I put two reefs in the main and furled half the jib. The front blew in cold from the northwest complete with clouds and rain squalls. We put a lot of sea miles in our wake before the sky cleared and the wind dropped.

Having Marie aboard was a pure pleasure. Despite the obvious advantages she held over my other friends, her experience sailing small boats as a young girl and, later, bigger boats like *D'Artagnan* was invaluable. Marie knew more about sailing and tactics than just about any other person I knew.

Dorothea was useless the first couple of days but by the time the norther showed up and we began sailing in earnest, she was in good enough shape to stand a three-hour watch alone. Now each of us could spend three hours on and six hours off. Those six-hour blocks of sleep were the finest of luxuries.

I knew Dorothea was feeling better when the trolling rig sang out one morning and she jumped up to grab the rod. I disconnected Kyle and turned the boat into the wind to slow us down. She struggled with the rod at first but soon started to bring in some line.

"Did you hook a log or something?" I asked.

"I don't think so," she said. "Whatever is on the other end is fighting back. And it's big."

She tightened the drag on the reel and, fifteen minutes later, brought a sizable yellowfin tuna to the boat. I gaffed it, pulled it into the cockpit, and killed it with a splash of rum. Marie took Dorothea's picture with the fish, her smile broad and healthy. We had sashimi for lunch and poké over rice for dinner.

The wind died shortly after we made our turn to the southeast. *Figaro*'s little diesel engine—the "iron jib"—made up the difference and we continued on. After seven days at sea, we reached the 65th meridian and were, more or less, five hundred miles directly north of the Virgin Islands. We turned south and picked up the easterly trade winds. It felt good to kill the diesel and feel the sails pull again in earnest. *Figaro* took the bit between her teeth and galloped home like a barn-sour race horse.

Dorothea was off-watch and sleeping when Marie came up the companionway one morning to relieve me. The sun hadn't yet begun to peek above the horizon but the eastern sky grew lighter each minute.

"I always forget how beautiful it is at sea," she said. "No matter how many times I have seen a sunrise on watch, it always amazes me."

"You should do it more often."

She thought for a minute.

"I think I know where you're steering this conversation," she said. "But I'm still not ready for that."

"The offer is open."

She snuggled into the lee of my arm.

"Dorothea's in love with you," she said.

"Getting jealous are we?"

"Of a girl half my age? I'm not too worried."

She glanced up at the telltales on the main, stood up, and adjusted the traveller without a word. It's what sailors do when they relieve somebody on watch. Always thinking they can improve on the prior watch's skills and coax some extra speed from the boat.

"There, look at that." She pointed at the knot meter. "One-tenth of a knot faster."

"What's that? Half a football field farther every hour?"

"There's no excuse for sailing slower than you must."

She sat back down and snuggled in again.

"She opened up to me quite a bit yesterday when you relieved her off watch," said Marie. "She told me the whole story. All about Clint and *Sidoni* and all the men she had to 'administer' to over the last five months."

"She's going to need a lot of help and support when she gets home."

"Can she get any counseling on the island?"

I shrugged.

"She's afraid of how her parents will react," she said.

"They love her more than she will ever know."

Marie was quiet for a minute. I sensed she was thinking about how to ask the next question.

"What did you and Al do in Georgia?" she asked.

"Things that eventually brought down *Sidoni* and freed a couple dozen girls from pure evil."

"What things? How did you do it?"

"I don't want to get into any philosophical 'ends justify the means' discussion with you. Al and his friend and I did things we'd been trained to do. Unpleasant, illegal, nasty things. *Sidoni* is gone for good, some very bad people were stopped, and some innocent girls were rescued. So, this time, the good guys won. I'd like to think so, anyway."

She knew pressing for more wouldn't help.

"The big issue is Dorothea," I said. "She was in grave danger and now she is safe. But she is far from whole. If I talked her folks into letting her go with you back to Stamford, could you find her the help she needs?"

"Absolutely."

"Okay, I'll give it a shot."

She took her watch and I went below to get some sack time.

Jost Van Dyke appeared an hour after sunrise on a beautiful

November day. I called Detective Constable Millet as soon as I had cell service. His Royal Virgin Islands Police launch was there waiting for us when we sailed into Great Harbor. Millet jumped aboard *Figaro* the moment we dropped anchor and took his daughter in his arms.

"I cannot thank you enough, Sim."

"You're welcome," I said. "And it never happened."

He looked puzzled for a moment before it sank in.

"Yes, you are right," he said. "It never happened."

They moved back onto the launch and sped off toward Road Town.

Marie and I cleared in with customs and immigration. Just the two of us. I used my real passport.

"We had a fellow here named 'Sim Greene' who was killed a while back," said the Customs officer. The corners of his mouth turned up as if he'd been told a funny story. "Very bad thing. Very bad."

"He must have been a great man for all of you to miss him so much."

"Indeed." He smiled broadly. "Indeed. Welcome *back* to the BVI, Mistah Greene."

Marie and I walked down the beach toward Foxy's.

"May I buy you a drink, Mistah Greene?" she asked. "I think you deserve it."

64

AL walked into the office six months later with a serious look on his face.

"I need some time off," he said.

"I'm not your boss, Al. We're partners."

"I've got some personal business I need to take care of."

"Going to Australia to bring Liv back? You two work things out?"

Al shook his head.

"I still have hopes but that's not it."

"So, what's up?"

His eyes hardened a touch more than usual.

"Like I said, it's *personal* business."

I have done some stupid things in the past—who hasn't?—but I would never be stupid enough to press Al about something he didn't want to talk about.

"Well, the big rush in the tourist season is over and I can get Sonny Berge to help me out with any salvage jobs that come up. When do you need to leave?"

"My flight leaves in two hours."

"Seems rather sudden."

He nodded.

"So, when will you be back?"

"Three or four weeks. Maybe longer."

"Where are you headed?" I asked.

"Out."

He'd grown a full beard since our trip to Georgia and I couldn't really see much of his face. What I could see told me stop asking questions.

"Well, keep in touch."

"No," he said. "I won't be doing that."

I walked him out to his car and saw he had a small backpack on the passenger seat of the Isuzu. He shook my hand, got in the car, and drove off down the Blackburn Highway.

Sonny was a skilled diver and we raised a sunken charter cat together. He also helped with a couple of tourist dives. Still, I missed Al and it ticked me off that he'd left me without much explanation. Liv called me from Australia once to ask if I had heard anything from him. I hadn't. I asked her the same question.

"All he said was that he'd be 'gone walkabout,'" she said.

"He's not Australian, Liv."

"Yeah, but he speaks my lingo."

He walked into the office a month later. He was clean shaven, wearing a nice suit, and dragging one of those carry-on roller bags you see at the airport. He looked like a regular tourist.

"How was your trip?" I asked.

"Good."

"Where'd you go?"

"Italy, Sweden, Spain, Scotland."

He opened his bag and pulled out a shipping tube. He popped off one of the end caps, extracted a rolled-up poster, and spread it out on his desk. I went over to look at it.

The top of the poster read "Plaza de Toros de Las Ventas, MADRID" and below that "Extraordinaria Corrida." A black bull with curved white horns stood in the center. Three brightly-colored banderillas protruded out of the top of the bull's back near its neck. A thin man in white pants and a gold-trimmed jacket stood next to the bull holding a red cape low to the ground. The bull, focused on the cape, circled the man. Spanish names were listed below the bull.

"You've taken up an interest in bullfighting?" I asked.

"Not at all. It's cruel and disgusting. It appeals to the basest and most evil desires of man."

"Then why the…"

"Never mind," he said.

He tacked the poster on the wall above his desk.

"What were you doing in Europe? Visiting an old friend?"

He smiled slightly but didn't answer.

"You should have taken Liv with you," I said. "She would have loved a vacation."

"It wasn't a vacation."

"What then? Business?"

"Personal business."

"Well, I'm glad to have you back."

He emptied a few more things out of his carry-on.

"We had more work than I could handle alone," I said. "Would have been good to have you around."

"Sorry about that."

"Was the trip worth it? Was it successful?"

He reached into a zippered pocket of his carry-on and pulled out a small clear plastic bag. He opened the bag and dumped something out onto his desk. It was a silver earring in the shape of a dagger wreathed in flames.

"Yes," he said. "**Very.**"

<<<<>>>>

You can find out more about the Sim Greene mystery series at **www.robavery.com**.

- **Afloat** (March 2018)

  In this prequel to *Close-Hauled*, Sim Greene is tasked with providing additional security for a scheduled visit from the Secretary of the Navy to the US Navy's "mothball" fleet. Threats are received, a body is found, violent activists are dealt with, and.....Sim discovers a boat. This novella can be found downloadable and free of charge at https://robavery.com.

- **Close-Hauled** (December 2016)

  "Remember Travis McGee, the hard-boiled liveaboard protagonist who prevailed through 21 John D. McDonald crime/mystery/detective books? Sadly he's frozen in time, but readers hungry for more now have a new protagonist: Sim Greene, a modern-day liveaboard sailor in Southern California. In this first installment of a series I'm eager to consume, Sim Greene finds a murder victim outside Ventura Harbor. Right away, the discovery shoves him down the twisting unknowable path that pits his intelligence and intuition against those determined to take not just his life, but also the lives of those close to him." — *Cruising World* (September 2017).

- **Broad Reach** (November 2017)

  "Book two in this series doesn't disappoint. Sim is back on a perilous trail, this time on a tropical island, getting to the bottom of a mystery that tangles bad characters with good and pits loyalty against love." – Michael Robertson, Editor, *Good Old Boat*.

- **Dead Downwind** (July 2025)

  Summer is hurricane season in the Caribbean. It's hot and humid and nice people can turn nasty. A young woman disappears under mysterious circumstances and a second is brutally murdered. The first is the daughter of a Detective Constable; the second was Sim Greene's employee. Sim and his friend, Al Higgins, investigate the crimes, track down the culprits, and take on an evil organization powerful enough to operate in broad daylight. Sim and Al will either destroy this sinister group or die trying.

ACKNOWLEDGEMENTS

There are many people who helped me during this project; too many to properly acknowledge. But I'll list a few anyway (in no particular order): Wes and Cari Clark, Gordon and Frances Smith, Dean and Deanna Sonnenberg, Brett and Jen Boulton, Michael B. McDaniel, Trevor Hickey, Salvatore Palilla, and Jay Allen. I could not have finished this book without their encouragement and advice. Special thanks, of course, to my family: Emily, Cameron, Allison, Jay, Frances, Henry and Teagan who have heard about this book for years and patiently waited for its release.

ABOUT THE AUTHOR

Rob Avery was born and raised in Burbank, California, but spent as much time as he could at the beach or in the Pacific Ocean. He is a criminal defense lawyer by profession and has a passion for sailing. His writing combines the two. Rob also hates referring to himself in the third person but can do so when pressed.